The air pressure in the cave surged backward, its waters spilling over the banks and flooding treasures on the shore. The dog barked a frantic warning, but it came far too late.

In our panicked motions, our bodies occluded our lights. Fragmented shadows leaped upon the walls: a hand, a partial profile, a staff or handle, a writhing flag, a crooked arm and running leg. The drake cried in terror.

A dark mass rose out of the river. Water rushed down a wall of scales, each the size of a target shield. Along with the river spray, I felt a wave of terror radiating from the creature—the dragon. The magical compulsion chilled my veins and set my hands to trembling, but soon it washed over me and I stood fast. Among the screams of the weaker beings, I alone stood calm beneath the wyrm's eye.

In the shifting light, the dragon appeared black and dark blue, yet I saw a glimmer of bronze upon its scales. Holding the *Gluttonous Tome* under one arm, I retrieved the Shadowless Sword. Its magic revealed no illusion. A bronze dragon stood before us.

It turned its incandescent gaze upon me, and I knew only diplomacy would serve. Sheathing my sword, I said, "Forgive our necessary trespass, great wyrm."

"And shall I forgive your unnecessary theft?" The force of the dragon's voice bruised my eyes.

I raised the recombined *Gluttonous Tome* above my head. "I have simply retrieved the missing portion of my book."

"Your book?" said the dragon. "You fool! You have no idea what you've done . . ."

The Pathfinder Tales Library

Lord of Runes

Dave Gross

A TOM DOHERTY ASSOCIATES BOOK
New York

This is a work of fiction. All of the characters, organizations, and events portrayed in this novel are either products of the author's imagination or are used fictitiously.

PATHFINDER TALES: LORD OF RUNES

Paizo, Inc., the Paizo golem logo, Pathfinder, the Pathfinder logo, and Pathfinder Society are registered trademarks of Paizo Inc.; Pathfinder Accessories, Pathfinder Adventure Card Game, Pathfinder Adventure Path, Pathfinder Campaign Setting, Pathfinder Cards, Pathfinder Flip-Mat, Pathfinder Map Pack, Pathfinder Module, Pathfinder Pawns, Pathfinder Player Companion, Pathfinder Roleplaying Game, Pathfinder Tales, and Iron Gods are trademarks of Paizo Inc.

Maps by Crystal Frasier.

A Tor Book
Published by Tom Doherty Associates, LLC
175 Fifth Avenue
New York, NY 10010

www.tor-forge.com

Tor® is a registered trademark of Tom Doherty Associates, LLC.

ISBN 978-0-7653-7451-6 (trade paperback)
ISBN 978-1-4668-4263-2 (e-book)

The Library of Congress Cataloging-in-Publication Data is available upon request.

Tor books may be purchased for educational, business, or promotional use. For information on bulk purchases, please contact the Macmillan Corporate and Premium Sales Department at 1-800-221-7945, extension 5442, or write to specialmarkets@macmillan.com.

First Edition: June 2015

Printed in the United States of America

0 9 8 7 6 5 4 3 2 1

For Jen Laface, first reader, ringleader, and friend.

Inner Sea Region

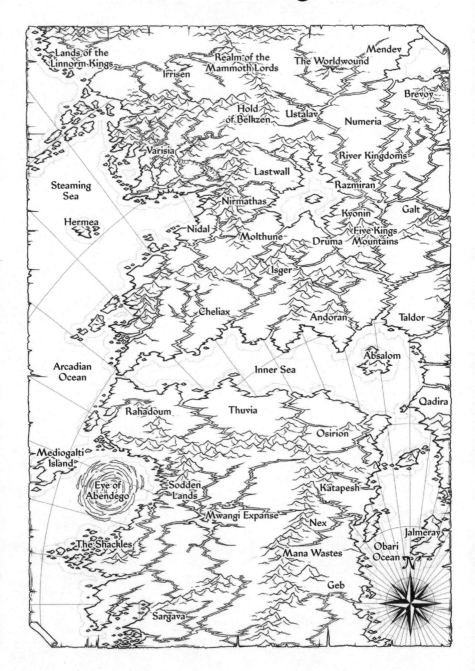

Story Locations

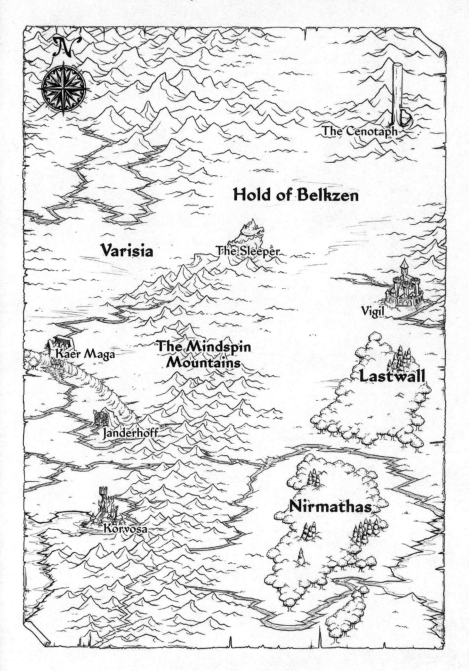

1
The Acadamae
Varian

Radovan had placed seven pebbles on the sundial between the shadow and the next hour. As darkness covered the next tiny stone, he flicked it away. It skittered across the plaza, narrowly missing the toes of a woman hurrying east. By her well-made dress of common cloth, the basket trailing a few errant threads, and the distinctive callus on her finger, I took her for a seamstress. She frowned at Radovan. He offered her a wink and the smirk he refers to as "the little smile." She turned away an instant too late to conceal her own smile.

"A servant will bring me the keys at any moment," I said. "Go."

Radovan stretched, pointing his wicked elbow spurs at the sky. His red leather jacket hung loose on his broad shoulders. The tongue of his belt lolled out from the tighter cinch. In the months it had taken us to reach Korvosa, I estimated he had lost seventeen pounds. He nodded toward the gate. "I don't like the way those guys are looking at you."

I turned to see a trio of students emerging from the Acadamae, the girls laughing at the boy's quip. I could only presume that Radovan referred to the hellspawn guarding the gate. The devil-blooded sentries were notorious throughout Korvosa for abusing students and visitors alike.

One of the guards snarled as the students emerged. "What's so damned funny?"

Unlike Radovan, who boasted he could pass in dim light so long as he avoided the "big smile," these hellspawn would never be mistaken for human. One had vestigial gills and an eel's snout; the other could barely see out from beneath a pair of coiling horns.

The students lowered their heads and hastened past. The horned hellspawn whistled after them. The other turned toward me. His piscine eyes lingered on the sword on my hip and the Ustalavic wolfhound at my heel. He weighed the danger and looked away.

Suppressing a smug smile, I turned to Radovan. "As you can see, 'those guys' know better than to menace a count of Cheliax."

"Not those guys," said Radovan. He plucked another pebble from the sundial and made a catapult of his thumb and middle finger. He aimed at the top of the gate. "*Those* guys."

A spotted raven, a chimera cat, and a potbellied imp peered down at us.

"Radovan, it would be prudent not to—"

Radovan flicked the stone. The half-black, half-orange cat shrieked and fled along the wall. The raven flew into the safety of the Acadamae grounds, but the devil flew toward us, cursing in the guttural tongue of Hell. It demonstrated an impressive vocabulary and a flair for simile.

"That cat might have been a professor's familiar," I said. I drew the Shadowless Sword and plucked a riffle scroll from my pocket. "Or, worse, a master's."

Radovan shrugged, but I saw by his posture he was prepared to produce a razor-sharp throwing dart or star from one of the many secret pockets in his jacket sleeves. "I was aiming for the imp."

Hovering just beyond reach of my blade, the devil hissed, revealing a mouth full of needle-sharp fangs. Radovan hissed back through his big smile, revealing a jumble of teeth a Mendevian general once compared to a demon's armory.

The imp peeped and flew after its cohorts.

Radovan popped his jaw back into joint. He turned to see where the seamstress had gone.

"Go."

"You don't mind if I take the night?"

"Look for me at Upslope House tomorrow. I will return there after I finish cataloging Ygresta's library."

"You got too many books already."

"One can never have too many books. Still, I doubt I shall find any worth keeping. Just strive to remain inconspicuous. Stay out of Thief Camp and Old Korvosa."

"Old Korvosa, huh?"

I should have known better than to present Radovan with a forbiddance. By naming the two districts I most wished him to avoid, I practically ensured he would visit them. "The important thing is to avoid Chelish attention. The moment I receive the queen's summons, I am duty-bound to return home."

Thanks to warnings from military friends in Sarkoris, I had thus far avoided the heralds of Her Infernal Majestrix. I knew what message they must carry: Queen Abrogail would demand to know why I sent her a copy of the *Lexicon of Paradox* rather than the original. I had prepared several excuses, but none would withstand a rigorous interrogation by the inquisitors of Asmodeus. How could I admit that I trusted the crusader queen of Mendev to use the book for the good of all Avistan? How could I conceal my fervent belief that the queen of Cheliax would use it only to further her own power? One sharp question was all it would take to condemn me to impalement upon the tines.

Self-preservation was not my only motive for remaining abroad. What began as a self-imposed exile to escape scandal had become an adventure. Radovan and I had faced many horrors, and wonders too. Some came not from the fabled lands we visited but from within ourselves. One of the wonders—or horrors—within myself remained an unsolved mystery.

And I hoped to find the answer to that mystery soon, here at the Acadamae in Korvosa. Yet as Queen Abrogail's impatience grew, it was only a matter of time before she instructed one of her sorcerers to contact me with a spell. There were ways to avoid such communication, but none I could safely explain to her inquisitors. When I received the summons, by writ or dream, I would answer.

"You'd think she'd cut you some slack now the war's over," Radovan said.

Despite the sun warming my shoulders, I felt a gloom. "The war is never over."

"Come on, boss, lighten up. Take a picnic over to Jeggare Island. Go for a stroll around Jeggare Square. There's a Jeggare Museum, isn't there? You like museums. You like stuff named after you."

"How many times must I tell you—?"

"Yeah, I know. They named those places for your uncle Monte."

"*Montlarion* Jeggare the explorer, one of the esteemed founders of Korvosa, my accomplished great-great—"

Arnisant pricked up his ears at the sound of irritation in my voice. I patted his shoulder. A sly smile grew at the corner of Radovan's mouth. He was trying to be amusing. As usual, he succeeded more at being trying than at being amusing.

"I just wish you could relax is all," he said. "Ever since we hit town, you've been tense."

"Tense" was too small a word for the vexation I felt since meeting with Toff Ornelos. What I sought from the headmaster was an explanation of why the Acadamae had failed to detect my magical bloodline, which I had discovered only recently. For reasons of their own, the proctors allowed me to engage in a futile struggle to master the science of wizardry when they should have turned me away to develop my innate talents under the tutelage of a sorcerer.

Instead of answers, what the headmaster gave me was news that one of my oldest friends had died having named me executor of his meager estate. Headmaster Ornelos would hear none of my complaints until I had dispensed with what he deemed the more urgent matter.

Yet none of that was Radovan's fault. I looked him in the eye and said, "There is a park."

"Huh?"

"Jeggare Green. It is a modest size, but Queen Domina dedicated it to me, not my ancestor."

"'Jeggare Green,'" Radovan mused. "I'll look for it. If you're all right, then I'm going to—" He jerked a thumb over his shoulder in the direction of the vanished seamstress.

"Go!"

Radovan departed at a jog.

I turned back to the hellspawn gatekeepers. They glowered but kept their tongues still. I wondered whether their caution had more to do with my sword or my hound. The Shadowless Sword was swift and Arnisant fearless, but the guards had more to fear from my spells—both those inscribed on the riffle scrolls concealed throughout my coat and those I could summon by force of will, now that I understood that I was a sorcerer rather than a wizard.

The guards turned at the approach of another student from inside the Acadamae grounds. Rather than taunt the woman, they bowed as she passed.

The hem of her skirt swirled about her ankles as she strode toward me with swift grace. Upon each hand she wore a jeweled ring, and around her throat a cameo on a black ribbon. Across her hips hung a plaited belt holding a pair of holstered wands and a tooled-leather pouch, to which she had pinned the silver Acadamae badge that granted her access to the campus. To my surprise, I could not estimate her age more precisely than mid-twenties to mid-thirties. Ordinarily I could make a guess accurate to within two years.

On impulse, I uttered a brief cantrip. The spell indicated powerful magic on the woman's cameo, rings, pouch, and wands, but none on the woman herself.

"Count Varian Jeggare." Her eyes registered surprise as she drew near. "Why, you look entirely rejuvenated, if a bit underfed. You must come to my father's house and let us give you supper."

Unable to recall her name, I bowed and fell back on a banal courtesy: "You are as lovely as ever, my lady."

Her lips quirked—with pleasure or amusement, I could not tell. My inability to read her expression irked me.

My gaze slipped from the woman's deep purple eyes to the cameo at her throat. Carved into the stone was an exquisite death's head moth, its wings dappled in tawny shades fading to ivory.

"Did I see you cast a spell as I approached?" she said.

It was bad form to cast a spell on a fellow noble. "A minor divination, lady, nothing to violate your person. Forgive me. I must strive to shed my wartime habits."

"No apology necessary. We are all grateful to those who held back the Worldwound demons. Besides, no one can cross the campus without being subjected to a few divinations, if not a transmutation when the upperclassmen feel prankish. I just didn't think you could do that."

"Do what?"

"Cast a spell."

"Ah." My disability was not a well-kept secret, but few were bold enough to mention it to my face.

With a gesture for me to follow, the woman led me through the gates. As we strolled along the gravel path, Arnisant snuffled at her shadow and growled.

"Arnisant, heel!" The hound returned to my side, his gaze locked on the lady's feet. "I beg your pardon. He is usually better behaved. Perhaps he too must shake off the rude habits of war."

The woman lifted her skirt a few inches and examined the soles of her boots. They were of a fashion popular decades earlier, one that I found uncommonly fetching. "Perhaps I stepped in something as I passed the conjurers." She appraised Arnisant, who remained calm. "May I pet him?"

She showed no fear, so I nodded.

The hound remained still as a statue as she stroked the curly gray fur on his head. "What a handsome fellow. And what a fine name for him."

Since I was in Ustalav when I found Arnisant, I named him for the famous general who martyred himself to defeat the Whispering Tyrant. "My grandfather always said, 'Give a dog a good name.'"

"Because others will think you a brute if you call him 'Fang'?"

"For that reason too, but also as a practical blessing. When you give a dog a brutal name, your tone grooms him to become a brutal animal each time you call to him. But a dog hears respect as well as scorn. Call him by a hero's name, and he may become a hero himself."

"In that case, Arnisant must be ready to give his life for you."

That notion troubled me more than it ought, for I had grown fonder of Arnisant than of any other dog I had raised.

We continued our walk across campus. Plots of ornamental foliage provided a Chelish order to the grassy swards between the academic buildings. The spring flowers perfumed the grounds. A bell from the Hall of Summoning tolled the hour. Moments later, students spilled out to enjoy a few minutes outside before their next classes began.

"They look so young, don't they?" said the woman beside me. Her smile should have seemed familiar, yet it did not. Still I could not place a name with her face.

In my memory library, the mental construct I have nurtured for nearly a century, I perused the gallery of every Korvosan aristocrat I had ever met. The woman's black hair and purple eyes suggested she shared my mother's Azlanti heritage, the rarest of bloodlines. She bore none of the other Jeggare features, which my father's elven blood muted in me.

I nodded agreement and smiled before looking away, pretending to take in the scenery while wracking my memory for her identity. As we passed the statue of Acadamae founder Volshyenek Ornelos, I found a clue in his countenance.

I last met unfamiliar members of House Ornelos at the funeral of Fedele Ornelos, one of the finest men I ever had the privilege to call friend. After the memorials, I remained in Korvosa to attend to business. In the evenings I renewed old acquaintances and established new ones. Among the new were young scions of the noble families, including House Ornelos. Children seldom leave an impression on me, but I record their names and ages in my memory library nevertheless.

My escort was surely one of Fedele's nieces, making her the grandniece of Toff Ornelos and thus accounting for the deference the hellspawn guards showed her. No doubt the headmaster had sent his grandniece to keep me and my hundred questions out of his office.

Arnisant woofed as a raven swooped near. Once more I drew the Shadowless Sword from its scabbard, but not to strike. In addition to its swiftness, the blade revealed the truth beneath any illusion. It revealed the raven's true form as that of another imp.

"Don't let them frighten you," said the woman. "The familiars are worse bullies than the guards. Professor Ygresta had the right idea. Each term he would destroy one as an example to the others. They never harried him as they do some of the timid professors."

The Shadowless Sword revealed no illusion on the woman. I put away my blade. "Was he not concerned he would kill a colleague's familiar?"

"Oh, no," she said. "He always summoned the imp himself."

Her anecdote brought a nostalgic smile to my lips.

"So it's true he learned that custom from you?" she said.

"Not the idea of a warning demonstration, but I might have provided the inspiration." Even before the rise of House Thrune, summoning a devil was a mandatory exercise at the Acadamae. There was no requirement to keep the fiend as a familiar, however, nor to let it free to torment the citizens of Korvosa, as so many reckless students do. Though the convulsions I suffered while casting the spell were agonizing, I gladly suffered them again to destroy the fiend after the proctors recorded my success. One less devil in Korvosa. One less inch of the world surrendered to Asmodeus.

As we passed the Hall of Whispers, a stench of boiling urine from the necromantic laboratories wet my eyes. I plucked a scented handkerchief from my sleeve and offered it to the lady.

She waved it away. "After four years among the cauldrons, I became quite immune to the stench."

"Ah." The significance of the moth on her cameo struck me. "You specialized in necromancy."

"Your favorite subject." Her tone indicated that she knew of my disdain for her specialty.

"Ah."

"*Ah.*" She softened her mimicry with a smile. "Uncle Toff warned me that you despise necromancers, but I know that can't be universally true. After all, Professor Ygresta was your friend."

Despite our social disparity, Benigno Ygresta had been a friend of a sort. In fact, he had been perhaps my oldest living friend, although I had seldom seen him in the seven decades since we left the Acadamae. I decided not to mention that we first met when I hired the lowborn Ygresta as my bottle-washer, a menial job he gladly accepted to supplement his paltry income.

"You studied with Ygresta?" I asked.

"He was the one who persuaded me to join the Hall of Whispers. I'd always thought only ghouls and grave robbers would study the art, but he caught my attention by demonstrating the best spell I had ever seen. Eventually, his lectures on the ethical applications of necromancy won me over. His life-matter theory alone should have earned him distinction, if only he could have won over the masters."

I nodded sadly, remembering one of Benigno Ygresta's many shortcomings: he had little talent for the subtle politics of wizards, especially the more conservative masters of the Acadamae. "Ygresta always struggled to express his fancies as proofs the traditional necromancers could embrace."

"I'm more than half certain they were more than fancies," she said. "But you're right: He could never satisfy the masters that they were more than eccentric ideas. Everyone always thought it was another part of his hopeless quest to improve the Acadamae's reputation."

I was familiar with Ygresta's arguments that necromancy was not inherently evil. His points were cogent enough, sometimes even compelling. Yet even if I could overcome my disdain for the ghouls and grave robbers, as my enigmatic companion described her colleagues, I would never break a promise to my mother.

"The professor once told me that you could have been one of the best necromancers at the Acadamae, if only you'd chosen to pursue our specialty."

"Arcane theory was my best subject." It was in practice that I had failed, not in principle. Even through the long decades when I barely dared to cast a meager cantrip, my knowledge of the arcane served me well.

"Let me guess: you studied evocation."

"Did the headmaster tell you that?"

"No one told me anything."

"Why do you guess evocation?"

"Am I wrong?"

"No," I admitted. Not only had I failed to read her expressions, but she seemed singularly capable of reading me. "But I still want to know why you guessed it."

"You strike me as the fire-and-lightning type."

Much as I despise being categorized, I held my tongue. One does not wish to seem defensive.

She continued leading the way to Ygresta's rooms. I continued to worry at the knot of her identity.

Realizing she was Toff Ornelos's grandniece narrowed the possibilities. When I had met them, the girls had ranged from ages six to fifteen. This woman was surely not Nicoletta, who married an ambassador to Sargava and likely resided there still. I did not think she was Letizia, whose constant yawning was her singular attribute. Of the others I remembered only names and relative ages. The youngest was Ambra, and her sisters were Filomena, whom Shelyn had blessed with exceptional beauty, and Illyria, whom the goddess had overlooked.

With that thought, I knew the answer.

By virtue of my half-elven longevity, I had seen generations of human children grow to adulthood. Lady Illyria was not the first ugly duckling to become a swan, but hers was the most pronounced transformation I had witnessed. The nose that seemed thin in childhood had grown regal, the fey cheekbones elegant. As a girl, she had barely spoken to me, yet I could now envision her watching the adults in silence while her sisters chattered among themselves.

Past the Hall of Whispers, we came to a row of faculty cottages. At the farthest, she climbed three steps up onto the landing and unlocked the door. Turning with a flourish, she offered me the key.

Also with a flourish, I held the door for her. "After you, Lady Illyria."

"Ah!" she said, still mimicking me. She straightened a pin holding her hair in a display of purple-frosted roses. "I knew my name would come to you eventually."

I recalled that Illyria's mother lived in Westcrown while her father—Fedele's sickly brother, nephew to Headmaster Toff Ornelos—kept a home in Korvosa. "How is your father's health?"

"I am making sure he eats properly before I sail to Riddleport next month."

"To Riddleport?" The city was more popular with pirates than with gentlewomen.

"Some friends are throwing an eclipse party beneath the Cyphergate."

I resisted the impulse to correct her use of the term. The phenomenon is more accurately an occultation of the sun, not an eclipse. Yet one does not wish to seem pedantic.

Inside, the cottage appeared largely undisturbed since Ygresta's death. Someone had stripped the sheets from the sagging mattress in the bedroom. We shooed flies from unwashed dishes in the kitchen but were relieved to discover the pantry had been cleared. A film of dust had accumulated on the furniture.

The sitting room featured a pair of overstuffed chairs beside the hearth. A deep depression in one seat indicated Ygresta's favorite. On the wall behind it hung a portrait of the man. His tall figure was much as I remembered, if withered. It had been decades since we last met, so I had never seen Ygresta's thinning gray hair, his round spectacles, or his sunken cheeks. Recognizing the portrait as the work of a painter who had died twenty years ago, I wondered how much more time had ravaged Ygresta before death. Considering he was the same age as I, and wholly human, he had enjoyed an exceptional life span.

"They say he slipped away in his sleep," Lady Illyria said. Sorrow tinged her voice.

"Then the Tender of Dreams kissed his face." I sketched the wings of Desna over my heart.

Illyria drew the spiral of Pharasma over hers. How strange, I thought, for a necromancer to invoke the Lady of Graves, whose priests abhor the undead. No stranger to the paradoxes of character, I found this anomaly deepened my curiosity about the woman.

After a moment, we broke our separate reveries.

"The library?" I asked.

"Between the dungeon and the torture chamber," she said, her voice sinister yet whimsical.

We descended a spiraling iron staircase. Magical flames sprang up in glass fixtures, casting our shadows behind the bars of the railings. Arnisant followed us down to the wooden floor and sniffed the corners of the room. Again he growled.

"Arnisant!" He came to heel.

Lady Illyria sniffed. "I can't blame him. This place is full of weird stinks."

That was so. The library smelled more like an alchemist's laboratory. Shelves lined the walls, except where they parted for a fireplace and two doors. One door stood open, revealing a cluttered storeroom. Judging from the odor, the closed door concealed a privy.

Librams, chapbooks, scrolls, folios, and loose manuscripts crammed the shelves. The collection was smaller than expected. At a glance, I estimated I could complete the inventory within a day. The sooner the cottage became available for another tenant, the better pleased the headmaster would be. Pleased enough to answer my inquiries, I hoped.

Knickknacks interrupted the ranks of books. Apart from a devil's skull and a brass candelabrum resembling a hand of glory, I spied few tokens of necromancy. Between the shelves stood a pair of tables. One lay empty, one stacked with crates overflowing with packing straw. A ledger, brush, and paste-pot lay beside a stack of blank labels, as the custodians had promised.

Ygresta's desk stood across from the tables, before the little fireplace. Beside it hung a birdcage, empty but for a dry water dish and a carpet of hardened fecal matter. At my approach, a brass lamp flared to life, spilling light on the desktop.

There in the center of the desk, upon a discolored paper blotter, rested a teak box beneath a calling card inscribed with my name.

Without disturbing the card, I scanned the box for magic. Detecting none, I scanned the room. The lamp above the desk and the lights on the stair radiated steady magic. On a few of the shelved books I discerned traces of metamorphosis spells. The latter were likely the residue of simple preservative spells, but their presence suggested more valuable tomes. Those I set aside for further study.

"The professor left his entire library to you?" said Illyria.

"His will names me his executor but indicates no beneficiaries, so in effect he did. After gathering the collection into lots, I will circulate an inventory to the Acadamae librarians and entertain their requests."

"You won't keep it for yourself? I thought you liked books."

"Perhaps one or two volumes." My library surely already contained any interesting volumes I might find here, but I did not say so. One does not wish to boast.

"In that case, may I be the first to lodge a request?"

"On behalf of the Hall of Whispers?"

"On behalf of myself."

So, I thought, Illyria was not merely smoothing over her uncle's sour greeting. She had her own agenda as well. "Name it."

She indicated a shelf of chapbooks. "Professor Ygresta's collection of the *Pathfinder Chronicles*."

My own collection was the most comprehensive I had ever seen. It included volumes dating from the very founding of the Pathfinder Society, with many annotated duplicates. In the unlikely event I should find one I lacked on Ygresta's meager shelf, I would claim it. But I saw no harm in giving Illyria the rest. "Is that all?"

She averted her eyes. "If you aren't taking them, perhaps also your letters?"

"My letters?"

"Please."

Her blush appeared genuine, but a sincere appearance is the goal of every ruse. "My letters to Professor Ygresta?"

"Exactly." She withdrew a pasteboard box from a shelf and lay it before me. I opened the drawer and saw it was full of letters, all addressed to Professor Benigno Ygresta in my handwriting.

Out of a sense of collegial obligation, I had always responded to his letters about current affairs at the Acadamae with some account of my latest excursion. The letters contained nothing not also reported to the Society. Naturally, I never mentioned military, political, or personal matters to someone beneath the aristocracy. I could not fathom what interest they might hold for Lady Illyria.

The foremost letter was my most recent message, a request for Ygresta to speak on my behalf to Headmaster Toff Ornelos, for whom I had so many questions about my admission and education at the Acadamae.

"I'm sorry." Lady Illyria winced. "I knew it was too much to ask."

For a moment I considered whether she was flirting with me. Long before I reached the age of maturity, my mother armored me against the attentions of women attracted more to my wealth than to myself. Yet Illyria did not strike me as the type. An Acadamae graduate would be far too intelligent to expect me to succumb to such manipulation.

Whatever her agenda, I could think of no harm that could come from giving her the letters. Moreover, a favor to her was a favor to the headmaster. I still required answers to my questions.

"You will understand that I must review the letters before deciding."

She brightened. "Naturally."

"Then let us revisit the matter after I have finished cataloging the library."

She rubbed her palms together. "In that case, let me help."

Before I could protest, she drew a wooden disk from her pouch. She wound a string around a slot in its circumference and flicked the disk away. As she uttered the spell, the whirling disk reached the end of the string and vanished. In its place, a whirlwind stirred the loose pages on the nearest shelves.

"Start in there." She directed her invisible servant toward the storeroom. "Dust every surface, but move nothing."

While I appreciated her careful instructions, I preferred to discharge my duty in solitude. "Lady Illyria, I assure you I require no assistance."

"You'll choke to death on these cobwebs before we can have you to dinner." She fanned away the cloud already emerging from the storeroom. "There must be a window in one of these rooms."

She cast a light on the palm of her hand and entered the storeroom.

With a resigned sigh, I sat before Ygresta's desk. The chair felt too large, but so did my coat. Radovan was not the only one who had lost weight during our journey. Arnisant sat at my foot, sniffing to confirm I had no food to share. I admonished him with a look, and he laid his head on his crossed paws, the guilty beggar. During the worst of our privations on our journey from the Worldwound, I had succumbed to pity and secretly fed the hound a portion of my ration. He learned to linger whenever I ate. Now I had to be strict with him lest he learn to beg whenever I sat before a table.

The box on Ygresta's desk appeared to be of recent construction, no more than a year or so old. The golden teak was of a type commonly imported to Varisia from eastern Garund, but in the carving I spied the iconography of ancient Thassilon.

I lifted the card bearing my name. Engraved on the box's lid was the sihedron, a star with each of its seven points notched like one of Radovan's throwing blades. I had seen the symbol etched on artifacts recovered from the demesnes of the long-lost runelords and their predecessor, the great King Xin, Emperor of Thassilon.

Illyria emerged from the storeroom with a bottle of wine. "Was 4690 a good year?" She presented the bottle like a sommelier.

The label had begun curling at the edges. The bottle was from one of my best vineyards, but an early frost had bruised the grapes that year. "That vintage has not aged as well as others."

"There's plenty more where that came from. What's a good year?"

"Is there any '84?"

"I see bottles dated back to the Age of Enthronement. You could open a shop with all of these."

Since I left Korvosa upon my graduation from the Acadamae, it had become my custom to send a gift of each year's wine to friends and associates in the city. Benigno received only one bottle annually, so I was surprised so much remained. "Did Ygresta stop drinking wine?"

"We didn't exactly run in the same social circles."

"No, of course not." Despite his academic accomplishments, modest though they were, Benigno Ygresta remained a vintner's son.

"What have you found there, a sihedron?" Illyria sat on the corner of the desk and peered at the box. "You see all sorts of adventurers with those lately."

"Do you?"

She nodded. "Fortune-hunters have been dredging up Thassilonian artifacts all across Varisia. So many Pathfinders have been exploring the region that they opened a new lodge in Magnimar. Oh, but of course as a venture-captain you already knew that."

In fact, I did not know of a new lodge, but I had no desire to discuss my estrangement from the Society and its ten anonymous leaders whose motives I no longer trusted.

I opened the box. Inside I found a thick stack of unmarked parchment. The pages fit perfectly inside the box's velvet lining, suggesting the container had been made to size. I retrieved a magnifying glass and a pair of clean white gloves from the satchel. A cursory inspection offered no clue as to the parchment's age or origin. Even with the aid of my glass, I could not identify what animal's skin constituted the material. Removing the parchment, I felt its substantial weight. Its outermost pages, only slightly thicker than the rest, formed its only binding.

"It's a book," said Illyria. "A codex, to be precise."

The study of ancient manuscripts remained one of my abiding interests, so I appreciated her specificity. "You must have earned full marks in Paleography."

"One of my best subjects." She made no attempt to disguise her pride.

I flipped through the pages. The interior was as blank as the covers.

"A gift of stationery?" said Illyria. "The professor often said how much he enjoyed reading accounts of your travels. Maybe he intended you to use it as your next journal."

"Perhaps. But if it was a gift, why not send it to me?"

"Maybe he wanted to give it to you in person."

"Then why leave a calling card with my name upon it? Except for a recent message I sent him, we had not corresponded in several years. He never told me I was to execute his will. He left me no instructions."

She picked up the calling card I had set aside. "Perhaps he had just begun making arrangements."

That was as reasonable a suggestion as any, but it hardly satisfied the questions of the carved box and the blank pages. Setting aside the box, I began to lay down the codex but paused when I noticed the stains on the blotter. Among the usual ink spots and food stains lay a dark spatter surrounding a rectangular void.

"Let me tear that away for you." Lady Illyria reached for the blotter page.

"No, leave it." I laid the codex in the blank space within the spatter. Its corners fit one side of the blank. I opened the pages to lie flat, and it fit perfectly within the unblemished space.

"He must have spilled wine," said Lady Illyria. "Later he cleaned the pages with a spell."

That was possible, but I did not like the color. I rubbed a gloved finger across the stain. Faint granular residue remained on the white cloth. "Not wine. Blood."

"How interesting."

I raised an eyebrow.

She wrinkled her nose. "I mean, how gruesome."

The stain was beyond interesting. Ygresta had left me far more than a codex of blank pages. He had left me that which I love best: a mystery.

2
Old Korvosa
Radovan

There were way too many witnesses, so I moved along.

Weaving through the late afternoon crowd, I headed west down the street. Whenever a horse or donkey got too close, I slid into the nearest alley to avoid a commotion. I wasn't looking for trouble. All I wanted was an intersection without so many people around.

By the time I'd made it halfway across Endrin Island, I was ready to give up. For the crime I had in mind, the streets of Old Korvosa were just too busy—especially this one. I'd have to wait until after sunset to snag myself a sign that read JEGGARE STREET.

Down the street, a gang of dwarves led pony-drawn carts out of a noisy ironworks. With the sun sinking behind them, I couldn't get a good look at the pinched little faces under their beards. Probably they were locals, nothing to do with the lords of Janderhoff. Still, better safe than stabbed, I always say. Besides, those ponies didn't want me anywhere near them.

On my right rose a high hill dotted with old manor houses and watchtowers. A crumbling wall encircled all that was left of the fort that started the city of Korvosa. There was nothing I wanted up there, so I cut left, back toward the narrows.

Across from the foundry, brick tenements huddled in groups. Shacks and lean-tos made another ragged city on the rooftops, complete with a highway of planks connecting them.

Up on the third floor, women pulled in their clotheslines. Old men leaned out of windows to smoke their pipes. They traded gossip from window to window. I couldn't make out the words over the clang of the ironworks.

A pair of drakes swooped down between the buildings, their long tails whipping out at each other. For a second it looked like they were scrapping. It turned out the little green one was just trying to get a grip on his orange sweetheart. Their tails linked, and he clung to her as she kept flying. One of the old geezers leaning out his window used the bit of his pipe to draw the wings of Desna over his heart. I did the same with my thumb and kissed my fingertips as the drakes flew into the sunset. Lady Luck smiles on those randy little reptiles. I figured that for a good omen on my night off, even if I had lost the seamstress before crossing the bridge onto Endrin Isle. There were plenty of fish in the sea, plenty of drakes in the sky, and plenty of—

Three dwarves came barreling up the lane.

"Desna weeps!" I barely stopped myself from pulling the big knife. Instead I jumped out of the way and watched the burly little guys run past. Behind me, up on Jeggare Street, one of the ponies had slipped his harness. The teamsters scrambled to keep the cart upright until their reinforcements arrived.

I cut through a tenement alley to get away from the dwarves. They soured my good mood so much that my gums started throbbing again.

The barber had wanted four times the going rate to scrape my teeth. They always raise their price once they get a look at my choppers. Since I'd already spent too much on a disappointing bath—the elves spoiled me for what should happen during a bath—I tried talking him down. I pointed out how much worse my teeth would've been if I hadn't been brushing. When he asked what I meant by that, I produced the toothbrush from one of my jacket's secret pockets.

The man's eyes went wide. He jabbered something about the devil's spoon stealing soup from his bowl. In the end, he demanded six times his price and made me break my toothbrush in front of him. I did it because I had four more stashed in the Red Carriage.

Any other time, I wouldn't have minded the money. Despite all we'd been through since leaving home, the boss and I raked in plenty of loot. The trouble was, the boss is what you call "prudent." All the treasures he'd had shipped back home under heavy guard. The cash he'd had locked in the vaults of Abadar, where the banker-priests would smite would-be thieves—with interest. So our riches were secure, but on account of we were keeping a low profile, the boss didn't want to go to the bank. Instead, he'd sent messages to a couple friends on the down low. We'd be flush again in a day or two.

Until then, I had just enough jingle to get started. I shook off the shudder the dwarves had given me and let the breeze blow me back toward the narrows. I'd heard about these five ships lashed together, each selling a different sin. I wasn't interested in the shiver den, but there was a gambling hall. If Desna smiled, in a few hours I'd be spending their gold in the boat of frisky women.

Past the tenements, I stepped into a beggars' alley. After the stink of cheap wine, the second thing I noticed was that all the beggars were missing bits—a hand here, a nose there. They wore the rags of their old uniforms, and every one had a Worldwound badge or two.

Somebody tugged on my jacket. It took an effort not to jump back when I saw it was a dwarf, but he didn't look the assassinating type. His peg leg looked like it'd been broken off a barstool. Fire had puckered the better part of his face, leaving a silky rope of beard hanging off one cheek. "Spare a silver, Sarge? Couple pennies?"

Nobody'd called me "Sarge" for months. I'd almost forgot what the demon on my shoulder was supposed to mean. I'd only kept the insignia because it looked wicked. Back in Sarkoris, it said that my job was to keep soldiers like these alive and fighting. I didn't always do a good job of that.

I reached for my purse, and the other beggars moved in. Their eyes glittered with hunger. I poured the coins into my hand and did the arithmetic. I plucked a few more from the secret pockets in my jacket until all I had left was my lucky penny from Ustalav. Nobody was getting that one.

I divvied up the wealth as equal as I could and put a share in each beggar's hand.

"Iomedae bless you," said a woman with half a red skull.

The dwarf touched the toe of my boot. "Torag give you strength."

"Desna smile on you," said a skinny young man. His dark eyes marked him as Varisian. The fox tattoo on his neck marked him as Sczarni. During the Worldwound crusade, plenty of thieves got sent to war instead of prison.

"Know a good fishing hole?" I said. At my waist, I made the Sczarni hand sign for picking pockets.

He squinted at me. It's hard to see past my devilish good looks, but my human blood is pure Varisian. He saw it and nodded. "Dancers like the Traveling Man, Waydon Street side. Plenty of out-of-town guests. If it's slow, there's Jeggy's Jug."

Some of the cant was universal. The local lingo was easy enough to suss out. A dancer had to be a pickpocket. But one thing I didn't get. "Jeggy's Jug?"

"Jeggare's Jug, oldest tavern in the city, named after Montlarion the explorer. What's so funny?"

"Fancy joint, is it?"

"The opposite."

I laughed louder. "Desna smiles."

The Sczarni shook his head. He didn't get my private joke, and I couldn't explain without mentioning the boss. Still chuckling,

I left the beggars and sauntered down Waydon Street. It'd been a while since I practiced my saunter. It felt good.

I warmed up along the way. The first mark looked so easy I hesitated, figuring it for a trap. Instead I reminded myself how dumb the average guy is, which means half are dumber. Half is a lot of dummies. As the guy fumbled with his shoe buckle, I snipped his purse without breaking stride.

Over the next few blocks I caught some more goldfish. I passed on jewelry because I didn't know any local fences, but I pulled a fat purse along with some papers out of a courier's bag. I stuffed the papers in an ash can and kept moving. A few seconds later, the courier started shouting, but I was already gone.

By the time I made it to Jeggy's Jug, my purse was heavy enough to sap an ogre. That was fine for my night out, but I decided it wouldn't trouble me to bring a little dosh back to the veterans. I went inside.

The Jug was a little joint, but the Sczarni boy had steered me right. More than half the customers were overdressed. The rest looked like hayseeds blown into in the big city. I spotted two other pickpockets—dancers—before I reached the taps. I took a seat under a framed landscape. The picture was made of torn strips of overlapping colored paper. Pretty as it was, looking at it made me feel cold and kind of sad

"What do we drink here?" I asked the barman.

He drew a pint of brown ale and poured me two fingers of Chelish pepper whisky.

"That's what old Jeggy always had," he said. "Afterward, he'd buy a bottle to pass around. For good luck."

"I'm already pretty lucky."

"You can never have too much luck."

"I'll think about it." I set my elbow spurs on the edge of the bar and watched the people. Pretty soon I spotted a third pickpocket. Three in one place was a lot of competition.

The first was a big brown fellow with mixed Varisian and Shoanti features. He followed a drunk out the door, steadied the man on the steps, and walked off in the opposite direction—with the man's purse. Couple minutes later, he came back in through a side door, exchanged a nod with the barman, and paid for a pint he didn't get.

The second dancer was the barmaid. She poured herself over the shoulder of a merchant who'd had enough pepper whisky to turn his face red. Every time she pressed against him, she peeled one or two coins out of his pocket. He'd pay for drinks the rest of the night without realizing how much he'd really spent.

The third was a soot-faced slip chatting with somebody in a blue hood. I imagined the halfling's story. He probably cased houses as a chimneysweep, tipped off his burglar pals, and built a public alibi while they did the work. He pinched his chin to let me know he saw me. I did the same to say I saw him back. He tugged open an eyelid to show me the stink-eye.

That kind of stuff just encourages me. I started thinking of ways to lift the goods from all three pickpockets on my way out. It wouldn't be easy, but if they caught wise, I'd show them how we did things back on Eel Street in Egorian.

Remembering how the boss wanted to keep a low profile, I reconsidered. Time was I'd shrug off that kind of warning. He didn't own me. Nobody owned me, not anymore. I was even rid of the devils that used to take turns riding me around.

Over the past few years, something had changed between the boss and me. Sometimes he called me his friend instead of his bodyguard, even in front of other people. He even said I could call him Varian. You'd think I could use his first name, but I never could. Force of habit, I guess. We'd been together almost fifteen years. The boss knew things about me nobody else did. I knew all his secrets, too. A bunch of them, anyway. I didn't figure anybody knew them all, maybe not even him.

But I knew plenty. For instance, I knew he was scared to go back home. He didn't show it, but when you know a guy long enough, even one who puts on a cool face, you know when he's scared.

As a count of Cheliax, the boss had just one boss of his own: Queen Abrogail. With a big-shot devil as her general and a legion more to command, she didn't ask for favors. She told her lords and ladies what she wanted, and she expected it done. Ordinarily, the boss was one who got things done, so she was happy with him, and that was good. Only lately the queen wasn't so happy, and that was bad. Real bad.

So it wasn't that I was afraid of a little trouble in Korvosa, especially not from some two-penny slip pickpocket. I just didn't want to make things worse for the boss.

I knocked back the shot and started to push off. Still, I couldn't make myself walk away after the slip gave me the stink-eye. I didn't like the idea of letting him think he'd run me off, so I took my pint to a table near the side door and put my back against the wall. I'd finish my pint, and I'd take my time. To give my hands something to do, I took out my harrow deck.

It had held up pretty good the past few years, ever since I stole it. It was a good way to break the ice with new soldiers, teaching them to play towers and letting them win. Other times, I just liked the feel of the cards. I liked looking at the pictures on their faces. They reminded me of people I'd known, places I'd been, things that'd happened.

I shuffled and dealt three cards: The Eclipse, The Crows, and The Brass Dwarf. The last one gave me a shudder. I was no harrower, but sometimes I can't shake the feeling the cards are warning me. It didn't help it was getting dark outside, and the tavern lamps threw shadows all around. I looked around to make sure no dwarf was creeping up on me.

Mucking the cards I'd dealt, I did a Sczarni shuffle to stack them back in the deck: top, bottom, and center. Then it was time for a little riffle stacking. Putting the cards right on the top or bottom is no great trick. Putting them second, third, or fourth from the top is hard. If you could put the one you want right in the middle—and find it again—well, that's the next best thing to being a wizard.

Like I was starting a game of towers, I dealt four hands, half from the bottom of the deck. I turned the cards I'd dealt myself. There between The Sickness and The Snakebite were The Eclipse and The Brass Dwarf. So far, so good. I rubbed my thumb and middle finger together for luck.

Before I could make the cut, a slender hand slapped down on the deck. The hand belonged to a Varisian woman, slim as a boy and a good hand shorter than me. She held a staff wrapped in golden-yellow cloth with some sort of pattern in blue. After a second I realized it was a flag wound around a steel pole. A loop of cloth held it in place with a metal snap.

With her hand still on the harrow deck, the woman eased herself onto the seat across from me. She kept her pretty dark eyes on my fiendish yellow eyes. I shrugged to make sure she got a good look at the spurs on my elbows. She didn't seem impressed. That was all right. I could always break out the big smile if I wanted to give her a scare.

"No one should trifle with harrow cards," she said. She cut the deck and showed me The Crows—the card I'd been ready to wizard out of the middle.

That was a tricky cut even if you were the one that put the card there. Maybe she'd used some actual magic. Anyway, I didn't want her thinking I was impressed. "That don't mean nothing."

"No?" She shuffled the cards and set them in front of me. "I am Zora. Let me show you a true mystery. Touch the deck that the cards may feel your soul."

No way was she a true harrower, I thought. On the other hand, I'd thought that before and been wrong. I drummed my fingers across the top of the deck.

Zora took back the cards and dealt a crescent. The one time I'd seen that pattern before, there'd been some spooky business going on. "Hey, now."

"What?"

"Where'd you learn to throw a crescent?"

"An old Varisian woman." She leaned in to whisper. Her hand disappeared under the table. "Who else?"

I set my purse on the table. "Nice try, sweetheart."

She shrugged like I hadn't just caught her fishing. She put her own pouch on the table and took out a couple of cheap crystals, like that's all she'd meant to do.

She went into her harrower patter. She said I'd traveled far but was closer to home than I realized. I might think I'd lost something, but I'd find it on the road ahead. The usual stuff.

Before Zora could turn over the first card, the tavern door opened. An armored woman stepped inside.

I'd seen enough of the city to know her armor wasn't from the Korvosan Guard or the Sable Company. The gray helm was painted in black angles forming a lion's face. A red plume spilled down like a mane onto a tattered half-cape.

Realizing I'd been distracted, I looked back to see where this harrower's hands had gone. With one she was tugging at her scarf, which I noticed covered a blue hood. I'd seen that hood a minute earlier—from behind.

She was the one who'd been sitting with the slip pickpocket.

I glanced at the halfling's table, but he wasn't there. He was running past us, little legs churning.

"Scram, Zora. It's Janneke!" He dashed out the side door.

The armored woman pointed a gigantic crossbow at us. "Don't move!"

I raised my empty hands.

"I said don't—!"

My body moved before my brain realized she'd pulled the trigger. I lunged toward Zora, meaning to pull her out of the way, but she was gone. A mule kicked me under the armpit, and the table exploded in my face.

That's how it felt, anyway. I rolled away but got tangled up in a mess of rope and thin wooden slats. I felt my side, but there was nothing sticking out of me. The armored woman shot me with some kind of net, but it hadn't opened all the way.

Shrugging off the tangle, I stood up in time to get knocked down again. The big woman—this Janneke—ran right over me and straight out the door.

"Sorry, little guy!" Her voice echoed inside her big helmet. "Get out of the way next time."

"'Little guy'?!" That tore it. I got up and slapped the sawdust off my hands. After getting shot and knocked down, I was ready to get in her way plenty. By the time I caught up with her, I'd—

The boss wanted us to lie low. I wouldn't screw that up just on account of a few bruised ribs. It was time I found that gambling ship and made some real cash. This Janneke could chase this Zora all the way across Old Korvosa for all I cared.

I looked for my purse among the net and slats on floor. It wasn't there.

Maybe Zora snagged it when I got hit, or maybe the slip was a better pickpocket than I figured. So I'd lost an hour's pay. That I didn't mind so much. I could fish on my way to the gambling den. The problem was, I didn't see any harrow cards, either.

That I minded plenty.

I ran out into the twilight streets. Three bystanders were just getting back up off the ground. Dodging the first two and jumping over the third, I caught a glimpse of Janneke's red plume. She was running full out, long legs eating up yards even despite her armor and a backpack. She must have weighed a ton. No wonder she'd knocked me down so easy.

Still running, I tugged a riffle scroll from my sleeve and gave it a snap. The pages ripped over my thumb. Magic tingled in my feet. Seconds later, I caught up to Janneke.

She looked surprised to see me. "I told you to stay out of the way. This is my bounty."

"Too bad." I poured on the speed and ran past her. "Your bounty's got my harrow cards."

As I rounded the corner, a quarter ton of horse reared up, screaming at me. Zora ducked into an alley across the street as I screamed right back.

Horses have hated me ever since I was little. Some run away. The rest try to stamp me into a puddle.

This horse was one of the second kind.

The rider lost the reins while the big animal bucked. I dodged left, and it turned to trample me.

Still fleet-footed from the scroll, I ran a few steps up the nearest wall and flipped backward over horse and rider both. I landed neat as a Sarini tumbler, but everybody was so busy getting away from the panicked horse that nobody cheered.

Sometimes I wish I could see myself in action. I must look pretty great.

Janneke came around the corner. Dropping her crossbow, she grabbed the horse's reins like it was easy. "Steady, girl."

The horse settled down, whinnying instead of screaming, stamping instead of bucking. It was going to be a very touching scene, I could tell. I didn't need to see how it ended. I tipped Janneke a wink and ran after Zora.

She made it easy on me by stopping halfway down the alley. My eyes adjusted to the gloom. All the colors died, but on account of my devil blood I could see every detail in the shadows. Zora's hand came away from her mouth. She gulped like she'd just swallowed something nasty.

"Just a second, sister." I figured were past "sweetheart" at this point.

Giving me a sly smile, she climbed straight up the tenement wall, fingers and toes sticking to the bricks like a spider's legs.

"So you *do* have a little magic," I muttered. "All right, then." With the right riffle scroll, I could do that trick too. Only I didn't have the right one. I tugged a different scroll out of my sleeve and thumbed the edge. As I felt the magic coiling like steel springs in my thighs, a clank of armor came up from behind.

I jumped. My first leap took me to the top of a ground-floor window. Kicking off, I bounced across the alley to a second-floor window. My foot left a muddy print on the sill.

"Get away, moth!" A woman swung an iron skillet, missing my toes but sending a shower of sausage and peppers down on Janneke.

The bounty hunter cursed, shook the food off her cape, and aimed her crossbow at me. Before she could pull the trigger, I was over the top, landing right beside a chimney.

Zora was already halfway across the roof, popping back up after ducking a clothesline. Either she also had great night vision or else she just knew the territory that well.

She turned at the sound of my landing. Her eyes went wide.

"That's right, lightfingers," I yelled. "You don't get away that easy. Give me back my cards."

Behind me, I heard a heavy *thunk* of metal stabbing stone. A steel spike sank into the chimney. A whining sound grew higher and higher until Janneke's plumed helm popped up over the edge. She unclipped a device on her belt to free herself from the line.

I ran after Zora, ducking the clothesline.

"Hey!" Janneke followed me. "Don't make me take you both dow— *Gughn!*"

The line caught her in throat. She went down hard. For a second she lay so still that I worried she'd broke her neck. Then I heard a moan inside that lion-faced helm. It'd saved her from cracking her skull, but those little eye slits were why she didn't see the line.

"Take a minute, get your wind back," I said. "I don't care about your bounty. I just want my cards."

I didn't wait for an answer. Zora had already vaulted to the next roof and was running for the third. The shacks and lean-tos grew thick over there, forming their own fourth floor. Zora ran up a twisting ramp between a water tower and a shack overflowing with the sounds of talk and laughter.

I jumped the gap, dashed across the roof, and jumped again. At Zora's call, a crowd spilled out of the makeshift tavern. A potbellied man in a stained undershirt nodded at Zora and got in my way.

"Go back, hellspawn," he said, hefting a tankard big enough to crack my skull. "No passage for strangers on the Shingles."

I kept moving. He moved to block me. I slipped to the other side, folded him with a kick behind the leg, and grabbed his shoulder to keep him from spilling his beer as he went down to one knee.

"Drink your drink, pal." I pushed off his shoulder and rejoined the chase.

Just past the water tower, the ramp ended in a short platform with a couple chairs and an ash can that smelled of pipe tobacco. Ahead was a street too wide to jump, even with a pole like Zora's to vault it. I didn't see the thief, but a cable ran from an alley across the street to a spot over my head.

Something fluttered over the edge of the water tower. I jumped halfway up the ladder and grabbed a rung. It came off in my hand. I fell, hollering and flailing. My hand caught another rung, and that one held. Hot pain shot through my shoulder as I hit the side of the tower hard enough to hear the water slosh.

"Tricky little . . ." Despite the pain, I was starting to admire this Zora, purely on a professional level. I was also getting an idea how dangerous it was to run through her territory. Either she laid traps herself or she knew where others put 'em. The beer bully was right about one thing. I was a stranger to the Shingles. I needed to watch my step.

I climbed up, avoiding another tricky rung before rolling onto the roof. As my weight settled, I heard the fluttering again. The thief stood on the other side of the tower, her flag unfurled to expose the steel pole underneath. She held the staff across the cable and looked back at me.

"Better luck next time, *sweetheart*." She blew me a kiss and slid across the street. The cable sang against the steel pole. The flag fluttered behind her, making the blue swallowtail butterflies look like they were flying beside her.

"Desna likes you, girl," I muttered as I followed her. "But I'm gonna get my cards back."

My third step went straight through the water tower roof. A swarm of wings exploded out of the hole I'd made.

That fluttering I'd heard before wasn't her flag after all. My first thought was birds, but the little freaks each had four wings and stiletto-shaped beaks.

I hate bloodbugs. The damned things make vampire bats look cuddly.

One stabbed right through my jacket and between my ribs. I smacked it, but it stuck fast. I could feel it sucking my blood through its nozzle.

"Guh!" The dance you learn the first time you walk into a spider web took control of me. I crushed one of the hateful things under my arm and felt a warm gush of blood—mine and the bug's together. As they squealed and flapped around me, I swatted and kicked. My foot caught one hard enough to send it over the roof's edge. The rest flapped away. I wasted another couple seconds pulling the bug's nasty sipper out of my side. It hurt like hell.

Zora had already made it across the street. At the mouth of the alley, she waved her flag. There was a different pattern on either side. Each time it turned, the butterflies shrank into four yellow spots: the sun and the moon with a couple of big stars above them. After a few shakes of the flag, she laughed and thrust her thumb between two fingers.

"Shoot me the fig, will you?" I tore off my bloody jacket and slung it over the cable. "Desna's smiling on you, but before the night is through, I aim to make her laugh."

I pushed off of the tower and zipped across the street, hanging onto my jacket sleeves. Only then did I realize all Zora had to do was cut the line to dump me. Instead, she fled into the alley. I slid all the way across and tumbled onto the spot where she'd been taunting me. Rolling up to my feet, I saw why she hadn't cut the line.

Four tough-looking Sczarni stood shoulder to shoulder to bar my way. There were more behind them, and behind *them* Zora was already climbing a rope ladder to the roof.

The tallest of the toughs stood a foot higher than me. He had a snarling cougar tattooed on one side of his bald head, a giant gecko on the other. He spat at my feet and said, "Dead end for you, Chel."

That word doesn't bother me the way it does most Chelaxians who travel outside the homeland. To catch my breath, I shrugged on my jacket, making sure to show off the way my spurs fit through the slits at the elbows. The weight of the big knife at the base of my spine was reassuring. It might look like an imp's tail, but it leaves a lot worse than a sting. "Patter me Sczarni."

Tough guy sneered at me. "I don't care if know our words, hell-spawn. You're no Sczarni."

Technically that was true, but at least one Sczarni clan thought I was pretty great. Too bad for me they were a thousand miles away. "I just want my cards. Zora can keep my coins."

"What'll we keep, then?" he said. "That jacket's seen better days, but I like the demon head."

Whether or not it was time to replace the jacket, nobody was getting my Worldwound badge who hadn't paid blood for it. "I got a better idea," I said, offering a suggestion for another way the Sczarni could amuse themselves.

They showed me their knives. I tensed to pull my tail. With any luck, I could scare these thugs off. If I had to kill one, the boss was going to be pretty hot.

Footsteps came up behind me. I glanced over my shoulder: five more Sczarni cut off my escape, grinning like I was easy prey. At nine to one, they had cause to think so.

I grinned right back because I saw something they didn't.

"You guys are real cute," I said. "You think nine to one's good odds."

They heard the hiss of steel on rope a second too late. Holding her crossbow over the line, Janneke flew into the alley, knocking thugs down like candlepins. She released one side of her crossbow at just the right moment, tumbled forward, and came up in a kneeling stance with a bead on the Sczarni leader.

She should have seen herself. She looked pretty great.

She pulled the trigger. A long cylinder shot out, thin planks scattering to release the surprise inside. Instead of a net, a bunch of wooden balls spread out, cracking Sczarni ribs and skulls. The tough guys fell back, but they didn't run. The ones Janneke flattened were getting back up.

She dropped her crossbow and pulled a pair of straight clubs out of the top of her backpack. She stepped past me. "I'll take this side."

That's all she had to say. I faced the ones behind us. Since she'd pulled sticks instead of blades, I left my tail alone. Fists and kickers would do the job.

Behind me, Janneke's club rapped a skull. My guys hesitated, so I feinted a punch at one and grabbed the next one by the arm. He got a knee in the gut before I broke his wrist. He went down to one knee, wailing.

When his buddy tried to perforate me, I swept his legs. He went down as well, twisting to avoid falling on his own blade. I moved to kick the knife away.

"Stay close," yelled Janneke.

I backed up to cover her.

"You know how to switch?" she said.

"Sure."

She reached back, and we hooked elbows. For a second we couldn't decide who'd lead, but then she swung me around. I raised my feet. One heel smashed baldy's nose flat. The other foot caught the guy beside him in the throat.

Dropping flat on my back surprised the Sczarni the way it's meant to do. The other two guys hesitated while I kicked back up to my feet. It was a good move, and I could see it in their faces. Janneke's entrance was a lot better, though. Maybe I could top it. The fight was young.

"What's this riot?" yelled a man back on the street. A clatter of hooves announced the city guard. They came from both sides of the alley, lanterns scattering the shadows.

The Sczarni leader whistled. His boys ran for it, some limping, some dragging their pals. A couple spooked the guard's horses by running under their bellies. Others climbed the rope ladder Zora had used and pulled it up behind them. Faster than you could say "Desna weeps," me and Janneke were the only ones left in the alley.

Janneke unfurled a parchment and held it up to the lantern light. "I was pursuing a legal bounty. These Sczarni got in the way."

The guard captain ignored the wanted poster and squinted at her. "You know I don't like you wearing that helmet."

Janneke pulled off her helm. Red-gold braids spilled out. Freckles crossed her cheeks and nose. She jutted a defiant chin. "Your commander says it's all right, as long as I keep it painted."

"I know what the commander said. People don't like to be reminded of the Gray Maidens."

They had a little staring match. After a few seconds, Janneke lowered her gaze just enough to give the captain face in front of his men. I'd seen that look before. I'd *given* that look before. It's one of the things you learn when you cross the guard as a regular thing.

"Is that all?" she said.

He squinted at me. "Who's the 'spawn?"

Before I could speak, Janneke said, "My apprentice."

I wanted to object, but she was giving me cover. I kept my yap shut.

The captain shook his head. He heard the lie in her voice. He just didn't care enough to push back. "Take it easy, Jan. Keep the property damage to a minimum. And watch where you point that crossbow while you're wearing that damned helmet. You'll spend all of your next bounty replacing broken windows."

He turned his horse to leave. Janneke shot him a fig. I laughed. One of the guards gave me a dirty look. I put my devil fingers around my throat and showed him the tines. He snarled, but he walked away.

"Apprentice?" I said to Janneke. "You're no older than me."

"You're not tall enough to be my partner."

She was taller than the boss, so I didn't argue. I just grumbled, "I'm bigger than I look."

"You'd have to be, wouldn't you?" She fetched the spent cylinder from her crossbow, and I tried to figure out exactly what she meant by that. It didn't matter.

"We were a pretty good pair there, you and me." I picked up some of the wooden balls.

"Leave them," she said. "They're cheap. Too much bother to collect."

"I was just thinking, if you're done for the night, we could maybe get a drink, exchange a few professional tips, see what—"

She grabbed the front of my jacket and pulled me in. I tensed for a head-butt, but instead of breaking my nose she took a long look at my face. My chin's a little pointy, and there are some ridges there and along the eyebrows that regular guys don't have. Maybe my ears are a little pointy—but just a little. I kept my smile small so as not to scare her. She ended up looking into my pretty yellow eyes. I looked back into hers, blue as deep river ice and just as cold. I didn't know what she was thinking then.

Before I could ask, she shrugged and pulled me up into a warm, wet kiss. Usually I'm the one that does the pulling, but I didn't mind. Before I could really make an effort, she set me back down and sucked in her lip, like she was considering.

"I got a room over in the Heights," I said.

"Too fancy. Too far." She shrugged again, like that was that. She put the crossbow on her shoulder and jogged down the alley.

I thought about the drakes I'd seen earlier. So much for good omens.

At the mouth of the alley, Janneke called back to me. "My flat is on Wave Street. Try to keep up."

I put a kiss on my fingers and blew it to the sky. "Desna smiles."

3
The Fencing Academy
Varian

Ringing steel and the whisper of leather shoes on a wooden floor spilled out of the open windows above. On the oaken door before me, a pair of carved knockers depicted an imp and drake locked in mortal combat. Diametrically opposed in almost every regard, the venom-laced stingers at the ends of their agile tails formed a visual rhyme to the hissing rapiers, equal but for the skill and determination of their wielders. To me, the image also symbolized the city of Korvosa, the first bastion of Chelish civilization on the Varisian frontier. In many ways the drakes resembled the free-spirited Varisian people, in other ways the dour but independent Shoanti. The cruel imps, I regretted to admit, characterized the draconian regime that had ruled Cheliax for most of my life. I framed a silent prayer to Desna that the drakes would fare better against the imps than the natives had against my homeland.

Rounding the corner of the building, a young man in homespun clothing set aside a broom and hastened toward me. To continue sweeping the porch so long after sunset, he must have been desperate to impress the fencing master. With a glance at my bearing and attire, the young man recognized my station. He bowed and opened the door for me.

Arnisant's ears perked up as he saw the fencers inside. He looked to me for instruction. I gave him the sign to remain by my side. His ears remained up, alert to any danger that might threaten me.

Inside the grand hall, four pairs of young students fenced. Slightly older students judged each bout, all under the watchful eye of Master Dengaro. He glanced up, clearly surprised to see me after so long an absence. If he despised me still, he hid it behind a veil of courtesy. He clicked his heels and bowed with a Korvosan flourish. He raised his eyes, indicating the one I sought was on the balcony, before returning his attention to the fencers.

As we went to the stair, I appraised the students. Black mesh masks obscured their faces, and they were garbed head to toe in white canvas uniforms. Their slender bodies moved with both natural grace and practiced skill.

Two stood out among their peers, a boy and a girl. Almost simultaneously, both won final touches, bowed to their opponents, and doffed their masks. The girl looked up to the balcony for approval. The boy looked to the girl for the same. After a moment's search, both sighed with disappointment.

Some things never change. With a sad smile, I ascended the stairs.

Balconies overlooked the great hall on all sides. Two rows of chairs gave the east and west wings the appearance of a playhouse. That resemblance was not far from reality, as the Orisini Fencing Academy hosted exhibitions throughout the year to ensure a steady stream of applicants. Those from wealthy houses paid outrageous fees, allowing the impoverished to win entrance with a demonstration of devotion involving menial tasks and proof of exceptional talent. The boy outside was undoubtedly one of the latter.

On the northern balcony, a lone figure sat at a table. Before him lay his supper: a loaf of bread, a bottle of cheap wine, a crock of butter, and a plate of fruit and cheese. Beside him rested a rapier in a plain leather scabbard. Behind him stood a pair of iron candelabras with only two of its candles lighted. The spring breeze tickled the flames.

At my approach, the man stood. He noted the blade at my hip. On the table, his sword remained well within what I knew to be his draw range. He clicked his heels and offered me a curt nod. "Count Jeggare."

I returned the gesture. "Master Orisini."

"I heard you'd been eaten by werewolves."

"I heard you had been hanged for treason."

"Later, a visiting Pathfinder mentioned you'd been chopped to pieces by Tian brigands."

"But then I asked myself, 'How could Orisini be hanged if he had already been trampled in the Blood Veil Riots?'"

"Some say a Kyonin dragon made you its slave. Its *intimate* slave."

"Some say that, do they?" Orisini's eyes twinkled as he saw he had scored a touch. I made a note to track down the source of that rumor for a later reckoning. "One might as soon credit the tales that you'd grown too old to teach swordplay."

"No sooner than one might believe you'd joined the Mendevian Crusade. Count Varian Jeggare, crusader of Iomedae? Ha!"

"Or that you once donned the helm of a Gray Maiden and performed the dance of Shelyn's seven feathers for the Sable Guard."

At that he lunged toward me, his reaction confirming that the rumored details of his escape from the Sable Guard had substance. He enveloped me in bone-squeaking embrace. Arnisant growled, but I gave him the sign that all was well.

"I *hadn't* heard you won the bid on the sun orchid elixir, you old bastard."

"Have a care, Orisini. Men have suffered for lesser insults."

"Lesser men, perhaps." He slapped my back a little harder than friendship allows. "I'm saying you look twenty years younger than the last time I saw you, and I don't mean elf years. You never learned to take a compliment like a man."

He knew perfectly well it was his reference to my parentage that vexed me—not his notice of my revived youth, which had nothing to do with the fabled age-reversing elixir of Thuvia. I held him at arm's length for a better look.

The years had been crueler to Vencarlo Orisini, whose blood was entirely human, than they had been to me, whose human blood mingled with elven. Vencarlo's hair had grown more white than gray and more gray than black, although he still wore it tied back in the classic swordsman's queue. He had gained a few more lines on his face and a few more inches around his waist. The glove on his right hand had not escaped my notice, nor did the fact that two of its fingers never moved. And yet in his storm-green eyes stirred the same violent righteousness for which the man had become famous—or infamous.

Vencarlo leaned out of the balcony. "Matteo! Make yourself useful and bring our guest a plate and goblet." He offered me a seat. "I hope you will pardon the wine. I finished the last of yours last winter."

"I recall your imbibing little."

"I like drinking wine more than I used to." In his sigh I heard the echo of my own regrets, all the more poignant since he had been little older than a boy when we first met, and now he looked older than I appeared. "Anyway, I drink more."

"I shall instruct my factor to increase your shipment." I produced a bottle from my satchel. "In the meantime, we have this."

"The '84?" He lowered his voice in mock awe as he accepted the bottle, yet I heard some sincerity beneath the scorn. He set to work on the cork.

"Here is a little more to replenish your cellar," I said, removing the other bottles I had taken from Ygresta's store room. The enchantments on my satchel made its interior the equivalent of a bookshelf—or, for tonight, a wine cellar. "An old friend recently passed on to Pharasma's Spire, leaving behind seventy years' of stock. If only he had told me he had given up drink, I would have sent some other token of remembrance."

"Then we must toast the old teetotaler and beg Cayden Cailean for forgiveness on his behalf."

"The god of drunkards never punishes the abstemious," I said. "He pities them."

"As must we all."

Matteo came pelting up the stairs, pausing only to walk a wide path around Arnisant, who clearly outweighed him. Regaining his composure, the young man lay a pewter plate and goblet on the table. Over one arm he bore a basket containing more bread, fruit, and cheese, which he set before us. At the smell of food, Arnisant gave Matteo a firm poke with his nose.

"Arnisant!"

The hound froze as still as a Tian guardian statue. Seldom did he require a verbal admonishment, but he was quickly becoming a disgraceful beggar. It was time to reinforce his training.

"Is there anything else I can do to serve you, Master?"

"No." Vencarlo's stern expression betrayed not a shred of approval.

The boy's shoulders slumped. He bowed and turned away. I raised an eyebrow at Vencarlo. He struggled to conceal a smile. Before Matteo reached the stairs, Vencarlo called out, "There is one more thing."

Matteo turned, his face glum.

"Tell Dengaro your lessons begin in the morning."

"Yes, Master!" The boy's face brightened like the dawn. He bowed, nearly throwing himself to the floor in his excitement. "Thank you, Master!"

"Now leave us."

Matteo practically floated down the stairs. A moment later, Dengaro's voice boomed over the sound of the fencers. "What?!"

Matteo said, "I swear, Master Dengaro, I have only repeated the master's words."

"Is he so drunk already?"

Vencarlo chuckled. His voice had grown richer over the years, lairing deep within his chest.

"Dengaro will think you have gone soft."

"Perhaps a trifle sentimental." He filled my goblet, dashed out the contents of his, and refilled it from the fresh bottle. "To absent friends."

We drank.

"On my way from the Acadamae, I heard a commotion on the Shingles," I said. "At first I thought it might be the villain Blackjack, but the laugh sounded more like a woman's."

"If you mean the hero Blackjack, who liberates the wealth stolen from the poor . . . Well, I agree the laugh could use some work." He thought for a moment. "*Was* it a woman's voice?"

The implication surprised me. If he was unsure whether the new Blackjack I had heard was a man or a woman, he must have had more than one successor. "You are expanding the franchise?"

"Forget I said anything." He shrugged. "I should be more circumspect when talking with a count of Cheliax. After all, we have not always been on the same side."

"Indeed." I left unspoken what we both understood: it remained possible we would be set against each other again one day. "I still say yours was the best laugh."

"Did you know that Fedele once confided in me, during a lesson, that he wished he had come up with that laugh first? He had no idea he was complimenting his nemesis. He always wished he were more of a swashbuckler. It galled him that Blackjack had more panache than the captain of the Sable Company."

"He always admired you."

"As Vencarlo Orisini, the fencing master."

"He admired both of you."

After a moment's reflection, we raised our cups again.

"To Fedele Ornelos."

We drank.

We refilled our cups and sat. Vencarlo filled his plate. I wanted only a few olives and a bit of bread. My appetite, so long denied, returned reluctantly.

"Do you mind?" I held a lump of cheese over Arnisant's head. In an instant, the hound was drooling.

"Not at all."

Setting the morsel on Arnisant's nose, I replenished the wine in my cup and relaxed in my chair. Vencarlo watched the hound, his eyes gradually widening as he observed Arnisant's discipline. At last, I gave Arnisant the sign. His gray jaws blurred, pink tongue licking out once. The cheese vanished.

"That is a good dog."

My old fencing master and I exchanged stories of the past decade while listening to Dengaro correct his students. When they finished a few hours later, Dengaro called up to say he was locking the building. Vencarlo and I continued reminiscing as the night birds sang outside the balcony. Across Garrison Hill, carriages returned nobles from their visits, and night watchmen called out the hour. Vencarlo opened the third bottle.

The tales I shared of my recent journey were mere sketches of what had proven some of the most eventful years of my life. As I recounted my travels through Ustalav, Tian Xia, Kyonin, and Sarkoris, Vencarlo reacted with skepticism.

"Just how many dragons do you encounter in a year? On average."

Undeterred, Vencarlo told me his own stories, each more improbable than the last, and one with a dragon of his own. Despite my respect for the swordsman, I suspected his competitive pride caused him to embellish the truth.

The stories he told of the person—or persons—who had taken on the mantle of Blackjack seemed tame by comparison. One such anecdote involved recent murders near the Acadamae, which Blackjack or Blackjacks had investigated to no avail.

"The victims were all found drained of life. After a lull, most believed the killings were the work of a vampire that sated its hunger and moved on."

"You say 'most believed.'"

Vencarlo nodded. "Over a year ago, there was a string of disappearances, also around the Acadamae."

"Do you think this killer became careless in disposing of the bodies?"

"Maybe, but the descriptions of the missing differ from the recent dead. The ones who disappeared were almost all big men. One was a half-orc, strong as an ox. They were laborers, street criminals, brawlers, mercenaries—what the Sczarni call 'hard men.'"

"And the recent victims?"

"All sorts, but generally night workers: lamplighters, street sweepers, watchmen, harlots, and the occasional Acadamae student who went out drinking. They don't fit the profile."

"A deduction worthy of the celebrated Count Jeggare."

Vencarlo choked on his wine. He eyed me over his cup. "I can't decide whether that's a compliment, and you're just that conceited, or it's an insult, and you're just that foolish."

"Perhaps a bit of both."

As he drank his wine, his eyebrows rose at a new thought. "You don't think this friend of yours was a victim of the killer, do you?"

"It seems unlikely. My understanding is that he died of natural causes, found in his own bed after he failed to appear in class."

"So there was no investigation."

"The death of a man nearly one hundred years old raises no suspicions."

Vencarlo began nodding but stopped and looked at me. "Nearly one hundred? You and he weren't by any chance . . . ?"

"The same age? In fact we were cohorts, born in the same year."

"No wonder you came so far for his funeral."

"Actually, the news of his death—and that he had named me executor to his will—came as a surprise."

"What was his name?"

"Benigno Ygresta."

"To your friend, Benigno Ygresta."

We raised our cups and drank. I considered Ygresta's passion for what he deemed the misunderstood art of necromancy. He believed that one day necromancers might mend the sick as an alternative to clerics, who usually tended only their faithful or those who paid high prices for their services. He researched spells intended to restore lost limbs or increase longevity, always with an eye toward making such miracles available to the common people.

It occurred to me that he and Orisini had that in common. While one sought to serve the common people with arcane healing, the other "recovered" their taxes by robbing the wealthy.

"Did you know him?" I asked. "Ygresta, I mean."

Vencarlo shook his head. "I never met the fellow, but I did hear something about his funeral. The Acadamae necromancers raised four undead ogres to carry his coffin."

"As some sort of honor?" Students and faculty of the Hall of Whispers were perverse even by Acadamae standards.

"Not as far as I know," said Vencarlo. "The way I heard it, none of the usual pallbearers could lift the weight."

Benigno had looked out of place among our fellow students, most of whom fell into one of two categories: the sickly or the obese. Benigno had been tall and muscular, but not unduly heavy. He had been raised a laborer, picking grapes for his family's land-lord, and his labors were reflected in his physique. He would have looked more at home among the Sable Company than at the Acadamae.

Noting my surprise, Vencarlo patted his belly. "Age presents us all with a choice: we swell or we wither."

For a while we pondered our mortality in silence, and we drank.

"Benigno did leave one mystery," I said. "Perhaps two." I told Vencarlo of Illyria and my surprising bequest.

"A blank book," said Vencarlo. "And no explanation?"

"None, although his choice of the box might be some clue. It was covered in Thassilonian runes."

Vencarlo frowned. "Even a swordsman like me knows that rune magic is dangerous."

"I have some experience with perilous texts."

Vencarlo chuckled.

"You do not believe me?"

"I've had enough wine believe in your dragons, the unicorn, or the dangerous books. Pick one."

"Even the keenest blade is no match for the power contained in an arcane tome." When he smiled his doubt, I said, "Very well." From my satchel I retrieved the original text of the *Lacuna Codex*, my copy of the *Lexicon of Paradox*, and the blank codex Ygresta had left me.

"All right, the books it is. It's too late to quarrel about the rest." He held his gloved hand over his heart. "I, Vencarlo Orisini, believe that these books are dangerous weapons . . . for those who can master their secrets."

"As I have."

"How many times have you told me that you understand magic but can't use it?"

"There has been a development."

He shot me a skeptical look. I took a riffle scroll from my coat and offered it to him.

He examined the tiny book, a rectangle little more than three inches long and barely more than an inch wide. At one end, a brass brad held the several dozen pages tightly together. He fanned the pages, revealing the fractional runes inscribed on each. For several years, riffle scrolls had been my crutch, the only means by which I could cast a spell without becoming physically ill.

"What language is this?" he asked.

"What you see is the alphabet of the arcane, or rather divided fractions of individual letters. On a traditional scroll, those letters would form a contiguous sequence of words that, when uttered in the presence of any required material catalysts and while the trained speaker visualizes—"

He yawned and tossed the riffle scroll back to me. "Is that a spell to put me to sleep?"

I caught the scroll, turned it in my hand, and pressed my thumb against the open edge. As the pages burped free, one of the unlit candles behind him flared to life.

"All right, so the little books let you cast spells."

"Not exactly. I cast the spell when I inscribe the riffle scrolls. The riffle scrolls allow me release the magic without becoming sick."

"I see."

"But that did not reveal why I had difficulty casting spells in the first place. The answer to that mystery I discovered only recently." With a snap of my fingers, I pointed to another of the candles, lighting it as I had the first.

"So you need the scrolls, or you don't need the scrolls?"

"Yes."

"What?"

"I need the scrolls to cast a spell *as a wizard*. But what I have learned is that I am not a wizard. I am a sorcerer."

"I'd blame the wine, but I'm fairly certain you're the one giving me this headache."

"Sorcerers are born. Wizards are trained. The Acadamae accepts only prospective wizards, and so they screen applicants for any trace of a sorcerous bloodline. When I discovered in Sarkoris that I have a sorcerous bloodline—"

"—you came to the Acadamae to learn why you'd slipped past this screening."

"Exactly."

Vencarlo nodded. "What a mess. You could avoid the whole issue by concentrating on the masculine art of swordplay instead of this effeminate gibberish."

"It is as dangerous to insult a sorcerer as it is a wizard," I said. "Do not forget that the arcane quill is more powerful than the most practiced sword. Now that I have embraced my heritage, I need no riffle scroll to do this."

Before Vencarlo could move, a mass of rainbow-colored veils fell upon him. They were flimsy things, and their material would soon evaporate, but the reminder of his unfortunate disguise in the Dockside brothel was worth the expense of magic. "For your next performance before the Sable Guard."

Vencarlo brushed aside the veils with a snarl, but he could not suppress an amused smile. "I forgive this slight only because you brought a bottle of good wine."

"More than a bottle," I reminded him. "I hope it is enough for both forgiveness and a favor."

He smiled as if he had been expecting me to ask for something all along.

"I just wish to know what you have heard of Illyria Ornelos."

"Ah, of course. You don't believe she's intruding herself on your business just for your letters to her professor?"

"The idea is flattering, but no."

"Maybe she likes the sound of 'Countess Jeggare.'"

"Too flattering still."

"You may be an old man, but you don't look like one."

"Well . . ."

"And you are the richest count in Cheliax, aren't you?"

"A gentleman does not address such matters."

"You mean it hurts your vanity to think she wants your gold rather than your person."

He went too far. "When was the last time a young woman showed interest in you?"

Vencarlo's smile dimmed. He remained silent for a moment while rubbing his gloved hand.

I was the one who had gone too far.

"My apologies."

"What is it the dwarves say? 'There's no fool like an old fool.'"

I raised my cup. "To old fools."

"And the beautiful young women who make us foolish."

We drank. Veils of nostalgia descended upon both of us, casting the candlelight in gauzy blurs.

"She is beautiful, isn't she?" Vencarlo's tone was rhetorical.

"You know her?"

"All of the Ornelos girls studied fencing here, although not with me. A few advanced beyond the basics. Illyria was not one of them. She made an effort, but her gifts were more intellectual than athletic."

"Yet you remember her."

"Her family is well known, even though her parents hold separate households here and in Cheliax. Her mother lives in Westcrown, I think. When the girls came out in Korvosa, Illyria had her share of suitors, at least for a while."

"Why only for a while?"

"She was known for a sharp wit and sharper tongue. None of her suitors was clever enough to keep up."

Few things appealed to me more than a quick-witted woman, although I could do without the sharp tongue. Illyria had not seemed especially shrewish, but that could be because she wanted something from me.

"Later, it was the necromancy that put them off," Vencarlo said. "One of Dengaro's best students was smitten with the girl, and he was quick enough to keep up. Once he learned she'd joined the Hall of Whispers, though . . ." Vencarlo blew imaginary feathers from his fingers. "Poof!"

"Young hearts are fickle."

He raised his goblet. "To faithful hearts!"

"Now you are making any excuse for a toast."

"To excuses! To toasts!"

We drank.

Vencarlo's gaze fell upon the Shadowless Sword. I had seen him peek at it several times over the past hours, perhaps waiting for me to show it to him. He could wait no longer. "May I?"

I nodded.

He unsheathed the blade, murmuring at its fine craftsmanship. "I can't say I approve of the style," he said. "You should have kept to the rapier. If nothing else, think of the stunts with which we entertained the ladies."

"Do you still do the candle trick?"

"What do you think?"

"Show me."

He handed me the Shadowless Sword and drew his rapier. Within the span of a second, he lashed several strokes at the nearer candelabra. Each of the flames vanished, their wicks cut from the candles.

"Not bad."

"I'd like to see you do the same with that cleaver."

I lifted the Shadowless Sword.

"It won't work with such a wide blade. The weight alone—"

With a sharp ki shout, I lashed out and sheathed the sword in what appeared even to my eyes a single swift motion.

Vencarlo clucked his tongue. "You see? That was very theatrical, and doubtless authentic to the Eastern style, but—"

I stamped the floor and four candles wobbled and fell, each cut in two places with an elegant curve.

He stared at the candles. He stared at me. He stared at the sword.

"May I try it?"

I passed him the blade. He assumed a classical stance, reconsidered, and stood tall. With a snap of his wrist, he lashed the candles twice. Four tumbled, each cut twice.

"This is quite a sword." He put his eye to the guard and peered down its blade, first at one of the remaining candles, then out into the moonlit street, and finally at me.

Whatever he saw in my face gave him a start.

"What is it?" I asked.

He hesitated. "A trick of the light."

"The Shadowless Sword reveals illusions. Did you detect one on me?"

"I don't know," he said. "It just appeared that a shadow crossed your face."

Outside, a cloud drifted off the face of the moon.

"Ah," I said. "Perhaps it was just a trick of the light."

"What else does this sword do?"

"The crown princess of Quain gave it to me as a token of gratitude for service to the throne, and you ask what more it does?" His question annoyed me both because he belittled the significance of my prize and for the reminder that I had never conducted a thorough exploration of the weapon's powers.

"It's a fine weapon," he said, sounding as contrite as I had ever heard him. Perhaps I had been too defensive. He returned the sword over his forearm. "Fine, that is, for a foreign machete."

"Would you care to test your rapier on this foreign machete?"

"Now you're talking like a man," said Vencarlo. An instant later, his blade was in his hand. We kicked away the chairs. He assumed an old-fashioned Chelish guard stance. I did the same, but in the Tian style.

"Do not forget who won our first duel," I said.

"Better that you recall who won our last."

He made a good point, but I had learned much in my recent travels. Besides, there was no blade swifter than the Shadowless Sword.

He beat my weapon and feinted an advance, but I refused to be gulled. With a smile, he attacked again, beating twice and cutting under the Shadowless Sword. I surprised him by doubling under and beating his slender blade out of line. He retreated half a step and lunged.

I parried and followed through with a riposte. Rather than retreat or defend, he turned the point of his rapier into the blood groove of my sword. The sharp point slid down my blade, hopped over the shallow crosspiece, and stabbed my hand between finger and thumb. I hissed at the pain.

Arnisant advanced with a warning woof.

I gave him the sign to sit. He obeyed, but his gaze locked on Vencarlo.

Vencarlo stepped back and performed a smart salute. Apart from a sheen on his eyes, he betrayed little evidence that the wine had impaired his skill. "You want a basket on that hilt."

He made his point, but he need not have made it with such force. Sheathing my sword, I pinched the wound. It was deep and bled profusely. As I reached for a napkin on the table, several fat drops of blood spilled on the blank pages of the codex.

"Your book!" said Vencarlo. He reached for another napkin with which to sop the blood.

"No, wait."

The blood beaded and rolled across the parchment surface. For an instant I thought the pages were impervious to moisture. Then a fine network of red lines appeared in the wake of the dribbling blood.

"What is that?" said Vencarlo.

I wiped the beaded blood across the page. Where it wet the parchment, it revealed more hidden script. I recognized two different languages, one arcane, the other as ancient as the runelords themselves. "Thassilonian."

As the blood trickled across the parchment, I thought of the stain on Ygresta's desk blotter. He must have discovered the book's secret before his death.

I removed the napkin and pinched the flesh beside my wound to produce more blood. Smearing it across the page, I revealed more and more text.

I squeezed my hand again. Vencarlo touched my arm. "You'll bleed yourself dry before you cover another page."

"You are right, of course." My mind reeled with possibilities. Thassilonian history enthralled me, as it did most members of the Pathfinder Society, but I had never devoted the time to mastering the subject.

"It's late," said Vencarlo. "Tomorrow, you can buy a few chickens from the market."

"Perhaps I can find a night market. I want to know what mysteries this book contains."

"It's late," he said. "Let it wait until tomorrow."

"But what will I do until then?"

He filled our goblets. "A toast!"

"To what?"

"Give me a moment," he said. "I'll think of something."

4
The Laboratory
Radovan

Sunlight stabbed me in the eyes. I rolled away from it and fell out of bed onto a carpet of dirty clothes. Last night I'd been too distracted to notice, but Janneke's place was a pigsty.

The bounty hunter stretched out over the sliver of bed she hadn't already claimed. I liked the way the morning light picked out the tiny hairs on her skin. Light brown freckles dotted her back and arms. Her braids had come undone, spilling red gold across her muscled shoulders. She was stronger than she looked. I had the bruises to prove it.

Searching for my clothes, I found Janneke's double crossbow under a rumpled quilt. I picked it up to feel the heft. It was heavier than I'd guessed, with an iron cap on the butt and steel reinforcements on the sides. Instead of a string, the mechanism on top had a metal cup on four springs. The bottom looked like a regular crossbow except with a fat cylinder feeding quarrels into the groove: gnome craftsmanship, real smooth. If I found out where she had it made, I'd ask the boss to buy me one.

I put down the bow and stepped in a spill of cold noodles. I'd known some slobs in my days, but Janneke was in the running for the worst one.

I picked up a few more things off the floor until I found my pants and one of my kickers. I pulled them on and stood on the boot foot to avoid another nasty surprise.

More clothes spilled out of a doorless wardrobe. A pitcher and basin sat on a little table by the window. Against the inner wall stood a bigger table with a couple chairs. Janneke's mismatched armor settled on one. Her backpack sat on the other. Its openings were all on the top. Along with her two billy clubs, the ends of a dozen different crossbow cylinders stuck out. The butts were painted in different colors with different patterns molded onto the caps. I guessed that let her choose the right ammo by touch.

The table was the only tidy spot in the flat. A neat row of open cylinders lay beside the surprises Janneke packed inside them. I recognized the nets, coiled line, wooden balls, and brick spikes. She also had a box of caltrops, jars of powder, and different colors of glass vials. The jars and vials smelled pretty bad, and I knew I wouldn't want to get hit with one of those cylinders. Whatever was in them, Janneke looked ready for anything.

I opened the windows for some fresh air. At the squeak, Janneke moaned and covered her head with a pillow. Seconds later, she went back to snoring.

Wanted posters covered the walls. Except for a few gnomes, hellspawn, or half-orcs, the faces were human. I pegged the artist as a Chelaxian because all the Varisians looked sly and all the Shoanti savage. The hellspawn looked ugly as sin. Most do. Desna smiled on me that way.

Most of the posters read KORVOSA, but others read MAGNIMAR, RIDDLEPORT, KAER MAGA, or JANDERHOFF. I memorized the faces on the last one. For all their talk of daughters' honor, I wouldn't put it past the dwarf lords to hire an assassin.

That thought made me want my knife. My other kicker turned up first, but then I found my jacket pushed up under the bed. Careful not to wake Janneke, I made sure the blade was still in the built-in sheath.

"Whazzatonnerbah?"

Janneke arched her back as she stretched, proving she was a couple inches longer than her bed. She swallowed and cleared her throat. "I said, what's that on your back? A tattoo?"

"What? No, I don't got any."

"Oh. I just figured you Sczarni boys usually go for tattoos."

"You think I'm Sczarni?"

"Well, you sound like a Chel, but you look Varisian. Aren't you?"

"By blood, yeah." I looked over my shoulder but couldn't see whatever she saw. Maybe she bruised me worse than I figured.

"Turn around." She sat up and turned me herself. Whatever she saw made her let out a big, beer-hall guffaw.

"What? What?" I tried to see but found myself turning around like Arni chasing his own tail. "You got a mirror under all this garbage?"

"No," she said, still laughing. "But look."

She pointed at a wanted poster beside the bed. Last night she'd caught me up in some northern wrestling move and pinned me there for a nice little while.

The ink was smudged from where it'd come off on my skin, but I could still make out the words:

8,000 ALIVE, 2,000 DEAD

ZORAN

Human Male Varisian

Wanted for Great Theft

May Possess DEADLY Arcane Artifacts

Known associates: Sczarni, Chimneysweeps, Cerulean Society

Report to Citadel Volshyenek

KORVOSA

The image was smeared, but the freckled nose and pointed chin looked familiar. "This guy related to the thief who robbed me?"

"What?" Janneke blinked and scowled at the bright eastern window. "No, it was him I was chasing. Zoran."

"That was a woman."

"Zoran is a master of disguise." A few strands of hair fell across her face. She gathered them up and started weaving them back into braids. "The city guard thinks he disguises himself as a servant to get inside the houses he burgles."

"I know the difference between a man and a woman."

She shrugged. "If you see him again, tip me off. I'll cut you in."

"I don't know how long we'll be in town. Depends on how long it takes the boss to settle his business." Digging around for my belt, I came up with her helmet. The black paint made for a pretty good cougar face, but I could see it used to be gray steel. "That guard captain didn't like your hat. How come?"

"You've never heard of the Gray Maidens?"

I shrugged.

"We were a special unit answerable only to the queen. When that went bad, we split up. My commander formed a new outfit. We went north and hired ourselves out as guards, bounty hunters, whatever we could find. When *that* went bad, I came back here to freelance. What kind of work do you do?"

"I'm a . . ." I had to think about it. Over the years, my arrangement with the boss had changed. He'd called me his friend, but that goes only so far when one of you's a lord of Cheliax and the other's whatever the hell I am. Whenever the question came up, we always ended up where we started. "Bodyguard."

Janneke nodded. "And your boss? What's he?"

"He's what you call incognito."

"You mean he's traveling incognito."

"No, we're traveling in a carriage. He's incognito."

It took her a second to decide whether I was just that adorable. She hit me with the pillow. "I don't understand even stupid jokes before my first cup of coffee. Let's get some. There's a gnome with this wild steam machine down by the Traveling Man."

"That sounds great, but I'd better . . ." I jerked my thumb over my shoulder. "Business and pleasure, you know. On the job. Professionalism." Once I heard myself, I realized I was babbling.

"Yeah, sure." She didn't like it, but she heard what I was really saying. "I could use some more shuteye."

"If I see your gal, I'll let you know."

"Guy. But sounds good."

There was a little more of that before I got out the door. Not my cleanest getaway, but I'd had worse. Sometimes much worse.

I cut north to Jeggare Street, hoping to snag one of those street signs, but the place was already lousy with people. If I was going to steal one, it'd have to be late at night or not at all. I headed back toward the bridge and got a surprise.

The boss strolled down Fort Korvosa Boulevard with Arni at his side. By his delicate posture, I knew he'd had a night of many cups.

Sleepy-eyed, he didn't notice me, but Arni did. The dog gave me the upward nod but didn't give me away as I slipped up behind the boss. He wouldn't let anybody else do that, but we were pals.

In a frail voice, I said, "Spare a few coins for a war vet, milord?"

The boss turned real slow, raising an eyebrow as if I was the one caught stinking of wine in Old Korvosa.

"Radovan." He spoke all careful. "I have discovered the most extraordinary thing."

"Me, too." I pointed at a JEGGARE STREET sign.

He blinked. He turned to look at the sign. He turned back and blinked again. "Very amusing. What are you doing here?"

"I'm being discreet. What are you doing? It looks like you drained all the taps at Jeggy's Jug."

His eyes got big, his face turning red. "Never refer to that establishment by that odious name." He winced at the volume of his own voice. "As for my nocturnal activity, I was visiting an old friend. We spent the night reminiscing."

He had a bandage on his hand. "You got hurt?"

"That is precisely what I was trying to tell you. Quite by accident, I have discovered the secret of the mysterious book."

Not another mysterious book, I thought. But I knew better than to say it. If the boss had a specialty—in a way he had hundreds, but if he had only one—it'd be books. Mysterious books, cursed books, books in foreign languages, books on scrolls and tablets and wood carvings, evil books, forbidden books, even sometimes naughty books with pictures, which I liked to peruse while I was waiting for him to come back to his library. Anyway, the boss liked books, all kinds. "Maybe you better catch me up."

The boss started talking, only he went in loops instead of his usual straight line. He started with something about a girl, then he told me about his old classmate's library. He mentioned something about the girl's sculpted hair, and he said his school chum had left him a blank book. He said he wanted to find out more about the girl, so that's why he visited his old fencing master.

I narrowed in on the important point. "So you like this girl."

"You will refer to her as Lady Illyria."

"She's a looker?"

"That is quite irrelevant."

"So she's a hag?"

"How dare you?"

"So she's a looker?"

"I would eschew your crude lingo for a more fitting term like 'beauteous' or 'exquisite,' or perhaps— That is quite beside the point. What matters is that I do not trust her. I am not even sure I like her very much. She is impertinent."

"I'm impertinent."

"My point exactly."

If we kept on that way, I was going to irritate him. It was better he woke up all the way before I tested his patience. "How about we eat a bun and drink some coffee?"

He covered his mouth to hold in a burp, or worse. "A splendid suggestion."

The boss looked impressed at the gnome's crazy steam gizmo. It seemed like a lot of trouble to make such a little cup of coffee, but it was damned fine coffee, and hot. I bought sweet rolls from a street vendor, palming one to feed Arni under the table while the boss admired the coffee machine. He sent me back for more while he ordered more coffee.

Four cups and six buns later, we strolled back across the bridge to the mainland. The boss looked better, but I still didn't crack wise when we crossed Jeggare Circle. If I wasn't careful, one day he was going to poke me with that sword. Instead, I got him to tell me his story again. This time it made more sense.

"While I finish my inventory of his books, I want you to examine Ygresta's rooms."

"Got it."

The boss saw things I couldn't, especially when he used a spell or held his Shadowless Sword. But sometimes I could spot things he'd missed. He said that was on account of "triangulation," him looking down from his tower and me looking up from the gutter. I say it's because I grew up on robbery and hiding from the city guard.

"Will Lady Illyria be there?" I said all innocent-like.

The boss squinted at the horizon and then at the sun. He had a knack for estimating the time by the height of the sun and knowing what day it was, which I never really understood. "She will meet us by the gates in approximately twelve minutes. We need her to escort us into the campus, but we can leave on our own. There is no reason for her to stay while we conduct our investigation."

"You sure you can't think of a reason?"

He let his hand rest on the pommel of his sword, but he didn't say nothing. He didn't have to.

When we made it back to the Acadamae gates, I spotted this Illyria. It couldn't be anybody else with her hair frosted purple to match her clothes—and her eyes, too, I noticed. They were like the boss's, a deep violet, only a little brighter than his.

Illyria sat on the edge of the sundial where I'd waited yesterday. She was reading a little book, holding the pages open with her thumb. She wore snug woolen trousers and a leather jerkin and boots, both dyed deep purple. They matched the frames of her spectacles and the cute little hat pinned in her hair.

She stood up as we got near, fumbling to hide her specs and the book at the same time.

The boss made his special occasions bow. "Lady Illyria, may I present my man Radovan."

"Charmed." I tried saying it all smooth, like a gentleman. With me, it always comes out a different kind of smooth.

Illyria slipped her book into a little pouch, turning the cover so the boss couldn't see the title, but I got a peek: *The Red Rose and the Black*. She gave me the up and down. "How rugged."

The boss has his knacks. I got mine. Not that I was horning in on his action. That'd be a hell of a way to end the partnership.

Inside the Acadamae walls, we walked past students sitting on the lawn. Like street gangs, different groups tended to wear the same colors or kinds of clothes. The necromancers were easy to make, all in dark robes, most of them pale as mushrooms. The diabolists wore lots of red and black to match their imps, the colors of the Thrice-Damned House of Thrune and Abrogail II, our fearsome queen. The others I couldn't figure what magic they did, only that they liked the same hats or familiars.

An imp flew up from behind. Arni woofed and I slapped my sleeve to put three darts between my fingers. Before I could perforate the little devil, the imp pointed at the boss and whispered, "You know, he's going to drop that sword."

The boss was stepping lively, focused on Lady Illyria. Yeah, the way that sword was bouncing around, he was going to lose it any second.

"You'd better grab it for him," said the imp.

That's a good idea, I thought. I skipped forward to grab it before the boss tripped and fell.

Arni woofed again, this time at me.

"What are you doing?" The boss stepped away, grabbing the grip of his sword before I could touch it.

"It was just . . . You were about to . . ."

All hell broke loose.

Imps came down from all directions. One sank its stinger into Arni's flank. The hound yelped and damned near folded himself in half to bite the imp, but it disappeared. Arni nipped at his wound.

Another one flew right into my face. I felt its stinger hit me in the chest, but the little prick didn't get through the leather.

The boss swatted one with the flat of his blade. He put the lady behind him and sketched a spell with his free hand.

Illyria didn't wait to be rescued. One hand went to her pouch, which spat out a bone needle strung with red gut. With her other hand she made a clamping gesture at an ember-colored imp.

The little creep pointed at her and yelled, "You should just lie on the ground and— *Umph!*"

Wormy red tendrils grew out of the imp's lips, stitching its mouth shut.

Illyria tilted her head at the boss and said, "*That* is the spell that made me choose necromancy."

"How frivolous."

"You'd understand if you grew up with four sisters."

Another couple of devils came in low and fast. I threw my darts. Only one clipped an imp. I dodged that one, but the other jabbed me in the leg. The sting was hot and cold as hell. I broke out my colorful language.

"Avoid killing them," said the boss. He ducked another imp and stopped himself from zapping it with a spell.

"Do we really care about that now?"

"We do," said Illyria. She shot a nasty look at a circling imp and cursed. Not the regular kind of curse but the magic kind—the kind that leaves a mark. Her voice went all spooky. "But perhaps Radovan can tear that one to pieces as an example to the others."

The imp hovered, staring at her, then at me, all horrified. It fiddled its fingers, unsure what to do. "Maybe this wasn't such a hot idea."

"Boo!" I said.

The imp flew off, but a bolt of green fell from the sky and clobbered it. The imp and drake hit the ground together, each trying to scramble away from the other's lashing tail and the poisoned barb at its tip.

The green drake wasn't alone. All at once the air was full of wings and claws. Red and black imps scrapped with drakes of all different colors.

The students backed off, nobody lifting a hand to help us out with a spell. A crowd formed around one of the diabolists. She was taking bets. I yelled one of the regular kind of curses, hoping to hurt her feelings if nothing else.

The boss threw a magic shield around Illyria and swatted another imp out of the way with the flat of his sword. Arni jumped up to bite at imps, but they'd already figured out he was playing for eats and kept out of reach.

A little drake hit the ground beside me. Blood and venom oozed from between its purple-red scales. Three imps hopped toward her, tails raised like scorpions as they closed in for the kill.

Arni bounded over the fallen drake. He snagged an imp by the head and shook once, breaking its neck. The second imp hesitated for half a second, which was all the time I needed to kick his little red ass. He flew a good ten yards before his flapping turned into flying. He jabbered some hellish curse but didn't waste any time looking back. He was done with this fight.

The third imp hovered, fingers twitching, getting ready to throw a whammy on Arni. Before it could finish its spell, a big blue drake crashed into the little devil. The imp clawed and squirmed, but somehow the drake had managed to get the imp's whole head into its mouth. A wet crunch later, the imp's body fell away. The drake choked and spit out the mangled head. Even Arni looked impressed.

"It's Skywing!" shrieked a splotchy black-and-white imp. "Every imp for himself!"

The blue drake flared his wings and trumpeted. To me the sound was kind of cute, but the imps scattered like they'd heard a cavalry horn.

The other drakes chased after the imps. The little purple one rolled on the grass, mewing in pain. Arni moved over and nosed the drake, smelling it.

"Arni, don't!" I thought he might eat the critter. The blue had the same idea. He flapped over, hissing until he saw the hound was only licking the little one's wounds.

The boss fumbled in his satchel. "I have no more healing elixir."

"I have something." Illyria put her hand to the mouth of her bag, and a little jar appeared in her hand. She unscrewed the lid and dabbed a bit of goop on the drake's wounds. When she was done, she let Arni lick her fingers. The wounds on his flanks evaporated.

The blue drake strutted over, sniffed the ointment, and touched noses with the purple drake. Purple mewed back at him.

"She'll be fine," said Illyria.

"How can you tell she's a she?" I said. "I thought the lady drakes were bigger."

"This one is still a youngster," she said. "Look at her talons. When she grows into them, she'll be bigger than her sire."

Like he understood what Illyria said, big blue nodded and curled his neck around the little one. After a squeeze, he hopped away, looking back for her to follow.

Instead, purple hopped over to Arnisant and stretched up to touch noses.

"Aw," said Illyria.

I kept my mouth shut to maintain a manly demeanor. Desna smiled on me, because the drakes flew off before I could embarrass myself.

"The imps usually aren't so aggressive," said Illyria.

The boss gave me a sidelong look. "I am afraid they were antagonized."

Illyria gave me another up and down. "Good for you. The little wretches could use a lesson now and then. I'm sure Count Jeggare agrees."

"Radovan, if you would bring the carcasses," said the boss.

I snagged a couple dead imps, and we hurried over to his dead pal's cottage before there was any more trouble.

At the house, we went straight downstairs. First thing I noticed was the basement was smaller than upstairs. That doesn't always mean anything, but sometimes it does. I dropped the dead imps on a table. The boss scooped them up and took a stack of parchment out of his satchel. While he did his thing, I poked my head into the other rooms. I found a couple narrow windows high on the walls. They'd be at ground level outside.

"I'll be right back."

The boss nodded, but he was focused on smearing the imps' blood on his book. I'd seen him do weirder stuff.

Arni followed me outside. He sniffed a few spots around the foundation. I pushed back the weeds and found what I was looking for six times.

Six is four more than two. You can't fool me.

Back downstairs, the boss had tied the imps' ankles to a birdcage. Their blood trickled over the book. Where it touched the parchment, the blood soaked into the pages to form words and diagrams.

"What have you found?" said the boss. Illyria watched over his shoulder as he smeared blood across each page before turning to the next.

"Wait a sec." I pulled books off a shelf and felt around for a latch. Nothing on that one, so I did it again a shelf lower.

Click. The middle part of the bookshelf swung out, followed by a stink of vinegar, mold, rot, and other bad smells. Some of them were really bad, like so-long-breakfast bad. I tried breathing through my mouth, but that only made it worse. The taste!

"How did you know there was a room back there?" Illyria asked.

"I got a knack." I tipped her a wink. She smiled back. The boss frowned at me, so I added, "There's six vents outside, only two in here."

"What's in there?" Illyria pushed past me.

"Wait for me," said the boss. He squeezed an imp's body, trying to get every last drop of its blood on his book.

Illyria didn't wait. The boss waved me after her while he flipped pages and smeared blood.

Just as my eyes adjusted, Illyria cast a light on the palm of her hand. For a second all I could see were green stars and a forest of shadows. Then I saw we'd found a lab.

The space behind the bookcase was twice as big as the rest of the basement. An empty brass vat shaped like a giant toad crouched on one side of the room. Workbenches sat on the other, both full of flasks and instruments. Between them stood a big oak-and-iron slab on a rotating iron frame. Hooks and lenses and other creepy stuff hung from ceiling chains. Jars and cabinets and all kinds of junk filled the shelves and the dark corners of the room.

"You didn't know about this place?" I asked.

Illyria shook her head. Every time she turned, shadows stretched away from her open hand. She looked as curious as I felt.

The boss came in, wiping blood from his fingers with one of his hankies.

"Can I get some more light on the floor?" I said.

The boss twisted his diamond ring and shined the magic light on the floor. Illyria followed his lead. Footprints stood out in the dust and mold. They were small prints—not slip small, but lady little. Someone had squeezed through one of the little windows, walked along the shelves, and gone back the same way. It was harder to tell since we'd come in, but it didn't look like anybody had come through the secret door in a long time.

"What do you make of this laboratory, Lady Illyria?" said the boss.

"He was building a golem."

"I concur," said the boss. Still, he looked surprised that she'd said it. He let out a sorrowful sigh. "That may explain the missing 'hard men,' if not those whose bodies were left in the streets."

"What are you talking about?" said Illyria.

"The more urgent question is, 'Where is the creature now?'"

Illyria did a double-take on the boss. She didn't miss the fact that he hadn't answered her question. "Perhaps he never completed it."

"Or perhaps he did, and the monster murdered him."

Illyria looked surprised. "But they say he died in his sleep. Surely there would have been signs of violence."

"Did you know of Ygresta's efforts to construct a golem?"

"No," said Illyria. She matched his stare. "I *didn't*. I certainly can't imagine him killing people for material. I *do* know he was always looking for ways to impress the masters, especially Uncle Toff. A successful animation on this scale might have done that."

"Touch nothing. Let us see what we can learn from the remaining materials."

While they poked through the lab equipment, avoiding each other's eyes, I made a circuit of the room. Arni followed, whining now and then when he found a new smell. We found a stink of acid and some gray gunk in the frog vat. Somebody had sketched charcoal runes in one corner. Nearby stood a stool with a half-melted red candle dribbling over its seat.

I followed the boss as he inspected the shelves. He turned to me and said, "What do you see?"

"There's stuff missing."

He nodded. It'd been a while since he quizzed me on that sort of thing, but he liked hearing that someone else noticed what he did. Or maybe he was just theatrical. Sometimes I think he wished he could have been an actor but couldn't on account of "count."

Illyria went right away to the empty spots we'd noticed. The boss raised a hand like he was going to stop her. When he saw that she wasn't touching anything, he stopped himself.

Illyria turned her light on each of the spots: a circle here, a rectangle there, a set of three spots where there'd been a tripod, and things like that.

"Do you recognize any of the missing items?" said the boss.

Illyria took a long look at the empty spaces. "Here there were books, obviously. I can't tell you what the other things were. Until today, I didn't even know Professor Ygresta had his own laboratory."

The boss knelt to inspect another of the empty places. He turned his face away from Illyria, but I could see in his eyes that he was deciding whether he could believe her. From what little I'd seen, I couldn't decide either.

I knelt beside him and touched one of the spots where something had been taken. While the rest of the place was covered in a carpet of dust, there was a lot less where the missing stuff had been.

"What do you think, boss?" I whispered, even though Illyria was all the way across the room. She was looking at the shelves through a round lens attached to a black ribbon. "Three, four days?"

He pulled a hankie from his sleeve and wiped a blank spot. Peering at the dust that came off, he nodded.

"So it's not like she stole anything while you were here yesterday, or after you left."

"No, but she is the one who gave me the key."

"Look here." Illyria waved us over. "Everything that is missing was magical."

The boss shook his head as we went over to her. "How can you discern that?"

She handed over her lens. On its ribbon, it looked more like a monocle. The boss peered through it. His eyebrow rose. He used it to look at his rings and then he unsheathed his magic sword and waved it before him. "Fascinating. The lens reveals not only the source of the magic but also the residue in its passing."

"A graduation present." Illyria plucked the lens out of the boss's fingers and put it to her eye. "Much stronger than the cantrip we all learn the first week of study, but not without its limits. It will show a mark around your finger for minutes after you take off that ring, for instance. Your sword could leave trails in the air for days."

The boss looked at the Shadowless Sword like he was seeing it for the first time. It was sharp as hell—I'd seen it cut through steel spears—but except for letting him see through illusions, he hadn't uncovered any other magic in it. He put the sword back in its sheath.

"Can we assume the items in question were powerful and that they were removed within the past few days?"

Illyria looked back at the empty spaces and nodded. "Depending on just how powerful they were, yes."

"Who had access to this cottage?"

"Uncle Toff gave me the key just before I found you at the gates. I imagine the custodial staff had it before he did. But they wouldn't have been able to get in if Professor Ygresta had warded his home, as the faculty tend to do. The Master of the Hall of Whispers must have been present when they found the professor's body."

"Wards seem likely, especially for those hiding golem laboratories. But why should he keep it secret? Surely Ygresta had access to all the resources of the Hall of Whispers."

"Well, Professor Ygresta did not have many friends among the faculty," said Illyria. "He might have needed equipment that required favors."

"I recall him as a gregarious fellow."

"Oh, he was very sociable, for one of his class. I meant he wasn't popular in the Hall of Whispers. While the headmaster appreciated his ability to appeal to those who find necromancy distasteful, most of the faculty and students felt he looked down on them."

"Because of his lectures on the ethics of necromancy?"

"Exactly."

"Perhaps a resentful colleague saw an opportunity in Ygresta's death and looted his laboratory."

"That's possible," said Illyria. "But wouldn't they have looted the library, too?"

"Not if they knew of Ygresta's bequest to me and wished to avoid drawing my attention."

"Yes, no one would risk attracting the eye of Count Varian Jeggare, scourge of kleptomaniacs everywhere."

The boss got all rigid. "Do you mock me, lady?"

"I haven't decided yet. Ask me again in a little while."

I was warming to Lady Illyria. I said, "It didn't have to be an inside job. It could have been a burglar."

"One would have to be bold indeed to break into a college of wizards," said the boss.

"There's a thief in town who specializes in this kind of break-in."

"The count said you didn't know Korvosa." Illyria managed to look down her nose, even though she was a good four inches shorter than me.

"Yesterday I went to the barber. Now I'm pals with a bunch of war veterans, three or four pickpockets, a bounty hunter, some Sczarni cutthroats, and half the city guard."

Illyria laughed like she didn't believe me, but when she looked at the boss, he nodded. He gives me a hard time, but he backs me up. "Radovan has a knack." He looked at me. "Do you think this bounty hunter might suggest suspects for these thefts?"

"She might, but I can tell you who did it. She's wanted by the Korvosan guard."

"You've spent one night on the town and you expect us to believe you know this burglar by name?" said Illyria. "That's preposterous."

"I know, pretty great, huh?"

"That is not what 'preposterous' means."

I knew what it meant. "You want to see her picture?"

"You have her picture?" said the boss.

"Sort of," I hiked up my jacket.

"Radovan! There is a lady present."

"Sorry."

"I don't mind," said Illyria. "Let me see how rugged he is under that ragged jacket."

"Ragged?" Maybe it was a little scuffed, but I'd kept it longer than any of my other jackets.

"Go on," said the boss.

I shucked off my jacket and shirt to let them have an eyeful.

"Why is it upside down?" said Illyria.

"This bounty hunter and me, we went back to her flat for some—"

"Radovan," said the boss.

"I guess you had to be there."

The boss pulled me over to the slab. It'd been made for somebody two feet taller than me, but I leaned onto the heavy oak. The boss released a lever, and the slab tilted until I was flat on my belly.

The boss and Lady Illyria moved around for a better view. He read the text of the wanted poster out loud. He thought for a second and asked, "What is this bounty hunter's name?"

"Janneke."

"Do you think she can tell us where to find this Zoran?"

"Maybe. We almost had her last night, until her Sczarni pals got involved."

"'Her'?" said Illyria. "The poster says—"

"The poster's wrong. I know the difference between a man and a woman."

"You couldn't tell the difference between a male and female drake."

"That doesn't mean nothing."

"I want you to find this Janneke," said the boss.

"All right," I said. "And then what?"

"I want you to hire her for me."

5
Upslope House
Varian

The declining sun cast a glare on the windows, forcing me to shade my eyes. It blinded me at the same time each day. I had begun taking it as a sign that I should retire from my studies, if only long enough for a light repast.

Before descending to the dining room, I went again to the mirror. My cheeks had filled out after another week of proper eating and the occasional snack to fill in the corners. After adjusting to our return to civilization, I realized how much I had missed dining for pleasure rather simply for sustenance.

I drew the Shadowless Sword and gazed into the mirror, searching for the shadow Vencarlo said he saw on my face. Perhaps it had been simply a trick of the light, or of the wine he had drunk before I joined him, but it troubled me. I wondered whether it was possible that, for all its power, the sword had a blind spot. Could it reveal the true nature of its wielder or only of others?

A knock at the door interrupted my thought. I sheathed the sword and set it aside.

"Come."

The innkeeper entered. "Your Excellency, I beg your pardon, but the lady asked . . ."

"Insisted." Illyria swept past holding a waxed-paper box tied with a satin bow. She paused to find a surface not covered with opened books. Setting the box on the divan, she surveyed the suite. "There's a nice room buried under this library, isn't there?"

The innkeeper winced. It pained the man that I did not allow his servants to disturb my careful arrangement of reference material. "If you wish me to send up a chambermaid, Your Excellency—"

"Not at all. Everything is arrayed as I wish it."

Illyria summoned a coin from her pouch and pressed it into the innkeeper's hand, dismissing him.

Illyria surveyed the books. "They're reproducing faster than drakes in springtime. Where do you find them all?"

"A few are mine. I kept one or two from Ygresta's collection. Some I borrowed from the University of Korvosa."

"They can hardly refuse a Jeggare after your family built them a library."

"Indeed. Most of these volumes came from the Theumanexus."

"That won't please Uncle Toff, your going to the rival college of wizardry."

"He should have considered that likelihood when he declined to assist me."

"He can't bear the thought of an outsider interfering in Acadamae matters."

"That much I understand." After we presented Headmaster Ornelos with our findings, he confiscated my key and rescinded my welcome. Illyria promised to entreat him to reconsider, but each day she visited with news that he remained intractable. "Have you been able to soften your uncle's position?"

"Today he wouldn't even see me, the brute."

"My thanks for the attempt."

"I didn't come away completely empty-handed. I visited the Hall of Seers. Their diviners confirm that Professor Ygresta was not murdered."

"Yes, but—"

"They also confirmed that he died."

So much for my latest hypotheses. "If only they had permitted me to direct the phrasing . . ."

"Don't tell me you've abandoned your principles." She saw that I did not understand her inference. "I read your essay on the dangers of relying on divination."

"Ah." Beyond the essential cantrips to reveal magic, poison, or otherworldly intrusions, I eschewed divinatory magic. Excessive reliance on them dulled the mind's greatest tool, deductive logic. However, there were limits to how far even I would present myself with a handicap to hone the intellect.

"Uncle Toff's secretary told me Professor Ygresta put on a hog's weight these past few years. And I have discovered the cause." She tugged open the ribbon and opened the box she had brought. Inside lay a circle of cream tarts crowned with glazed berries.

I picked one out and took a bite. "Delicious."

"Apparently the professor was fond of this shop. I've never seen such sincere grief as on the confectioner's face. She says the professor bought so much that he had to conjure a second servant to carry it all home."

"I can understand why." My hand flew to my mouth. I had spoken with my mouth full.

Illyria laughed and mashed a tart between her teeth. My gaze strayed to the next tart in the box. Illyria said, "I brought enough for your bodyguards, but the spoils go to those who claim them first."

Hungrier than I realized, I took another tart. "Radovan went to meet his bounty hunter, and Arnisant needed a walk."

Illyria went to the desk and peered at the blood-scribed codex. "Have you discovered anything new?"

"Not in the text." Illyria already knew what the blood of eight chickens had revealed. The eighth folio offered instructions for constructing an amalgamation of corpses—a golem. The preceding seven contained necromantic spells, from simple rays to mighty symbols. After browsing the book, Illyria assured me it contained nearly every necromantic spell she had ever seen.

Necromantic spells were like an unpracticed language to me, yet I began to view them in a new light. Their formulae stirred my imagination rather than my intellect. I saw them no longer as problems but as poetry.

Wizardry and sorcery are but two of many arcane traditions, yet they are by far the best known and most widely practiced. Together, they represent the extreme ends of a spectrum.

To a wizard, spells are logical constructs. The practitioner sets their formulae in the mind like traps awaiting a trigger of incantation, gesture, and sacrifice to release their power. To a sorcerer, those same spells magnify emotions—fear, desire, hope, or fury—and unleash their power by force of will.

"What is it?" asked Illyria.

Her words shook me from an almost transcendental reverie. I realized my lips had been moving, reciting the verbal components of a spell I had sworn never to utter. With a chill, I realized I hungered—not for food, but to complete casting the spell.

"Do you feel any strange compulsion associated with the codex?" I asked her.

Lady Illyria furrowed her brow and slipped the monocle from a pocket in her vest. "Let me look at you."

Standing still, I endured her scrutiny.

"Nothing but your usual enchantments," she concluded. She turned the monocle on the codex. "Still nothing."

"That is more troubling than reassuring."

She nodded, understanding as well as I that only the most potent of arcane artifacts radiated no magic. She said, "What is it that you feel when reading the spells?"

"Naturally, I understand the theory. That much is universal across all schools of—"

"That's not what I asked. What do you *feel*?"

When I revealed my sorcerous bloodline to Illyria, I had braced myself for scorn, or at least her usual badinage. Instead, she had reacted with acceptance, curiosity, and even concern. Yet even to so sympathetic an ear, I hesitated to admit the truth. "I feel a certain affinity for these spells, detestable as they are."

"Don't forget what the professor would say," she said. "Few spells are truly evil. They're tools. How we use them is what matters."

"I remember Ygresta's arguments."

"But did you truly hear them? He may not have been the most brilliant wizard at the Acadamae, but he had a big heart."

"Perhaps because it was full of these delicious tarts." I eyed another. "Do you mind?"

"Not at all, but be careful. You'll have a big heart soon, too."

Illyria jested, but she did not know my secret. Since Radovan informed me that the lady enjoyed romantic novels, I knew my tale of escaping death through the healing power of a celestial dragon's heart would impress her. I was tempted to tell it.

Yet one does not wish to seem vainglorious.

"I have been wondering why a burglar would loot Ygresta's laboratory yet leave the library untouched."

"I thought you decided it was because your name was on it, and no thief dares cross the celebrated Count Varian Jeggare."

"Would you recognize Professor Ygresta's handwriting?"

"It has been a few years since he last marked one of my essays. But yes, probably."

From the settee I fetched the card I found atop the box containing the codex. "Is this his hand?"

Illyria inspected the card. She appeared ready to nod, but then she seemed to change her mind. "It could be."

"My reaction exactly. It appears to be his handwriting, but it is not quite right. Here, compare it with this." I showed her a copy of Cevil Charms's *Eidolon*, which Ygresta had annotated in pencil. His elegant script appeared exactly as I remembered from our correspondence.

Illyria studied the two samples. "Someone forged the card."

We raised another pair of cream tarts in celebration of our conclusions.

"The question is . . ." I began.

Illyria licked a cream mustache from her lip. I quite forgot what I was saying. She finished my thought: "'Why?'"

"Exactly. It would appear that someone wished me to believe that Ygresta left the codex for me."

"But again, why?"

"That depends on whether the culprit knew the book's secret. If so, then it was to draw my attention *to* the codex. If not, then it might have been a gambit to draw my attention *away* from the secret laboratory."

"It has to be the first one."

"Why?"

"Because it would be too great a coincidence for a schemer to mistake the codex for a blank book and then use it as a distraction."

Our eyes locked for a moment. In unison we said, "And there are no coincidences."

"So it follows that Ygresta's death was not coincidental to my arrival."

"But the seers said he wasn't murdered."

"Then we cannot trust their report. They may have intentionally deceived you, knowing you would share their report with me."

"So perhaps the professor *was* murdered—well, not for the codex, which they didn't take—but maybe for whatever was stolen from the lab?"

"That seems more likely."

"Do you suspect someone from the Acadamae murdered him?"

Keenly aware that Lady Illyria could be reporting to her uncle as much as to me, I kept my response vague. "Most murderers are known to the victim."

Illyria frowned. "But if the thief was adept enough to break into his laboratory, why kill the professor? And why not take the stolen items then instead of waiting until a few days before your arrival?"

"Perhaps the motive relates to Ygresta's creation of a golem."

"Which we haven't found."

"And which he might never have completed."

"Do you think he might have hidden this codex because he knew someone was after the golem manual?"

"An attractive hypothesis, but what evidence do we have to support it?

She hesitated before answering. "It makes more sense if he had written the note himself."

"But he did not."

"That means he didn't put it on the box, either."

"Ah!" I retrieved the teak box in which I had first found the codex.

"Ah!" she mimicked me.

I frowned, but in truth I was beginning to enjoy her teasing. I showed her the trade stamp under the velvet lining of the box. "What do you make of this?"

"Kaer Maga," she said, recognizing the symbol. "The professor was getting fat. What do fat wizards and Kaer Maga make you think of?"

"Bloatmages." I shuddered to think of the blood-gorged practitioners of hemotheurgy.

Illyria shivered in agreement.

"It seems unlikely Ygresta had turned to blood magic. The weight gain among hemotheurges is a symptom of their organs' generating surplus blood to fuel their spells. Besides, one of Ygresta's colleagues would surely have noticed a ruddy appearance, the burst veins, and of course the leeches."

She gazed at me with an uncomfortable intensity.

"What?" I said.

"We're in the middle of one of your stories, aren't we?"

"Pardon me?"

"The stories you told when you visited after Uncle Fedele's funeral. Most of them started with you not knowing the answer to a problem. That's where we are now. You're just starting to solve a mystery, and I'm helping you." She spoke with such open delight that I dared not trust its sincerity. Better to change the subject.

"Ah." I took another tart and held it up as evidence. "As for the bloatmage theory, your confectioner's testimony suggests a more quotidian explanation for Ygresta's obesity."

"And for yours, too, if you keep inhaling those like snuff."

I would have protested, but it is rude to speak with one's mouth full.

"Perhaps the codex holds the answer. Professor Ygresta must have known you'd discover its secret. What did he want you to do with it?"

"If he suspected a threat to his life, perhaps he meant me to solve his murder." The words had barely escaped my lips before I dismissed the theory. A man does not plan for another to revenge his death when there is time to prevent it. "Never mind that. It is preposterous."

She tapped her chin as she thought. "You know, I recall a guest lecture about famous spell collections. 'Obscure Necromantic Texts,' or something like that."

That lecture had not been part of my Acadamae curriculum. "The speaker was not memorable, I take it?"

"Dry as dust, but I remember bits of the talk. Most of the texts covered were caught halfway between legend and history. Could Professor Ygresta have found such a book?"

I touched the teak box. "It stands to reason that the sihedron is another intentional clue, either from Ygresta or from whoever placed the codex in the box. The sihedron suggests King Xin,

Thassilon, and the runelords. Do you recall the names of the last runelords?"

"Alaznist, Belimarius, Karzoug, Krune, Sorshen, Xanderghul, and Zutha." She curtsied like a child presented to her parents' friends—which was precisely how we had first met.

I chided her. "Rote memorization is the least of the academic virtues."

"Shall I recite their associated sins, Professor?"

Illyria clearly knew the foundations of rune magic as well as any Acadamae student. The original runelords aligned their magic specialties with the ideals of just rule. Sadly, the later runelords perverted these ideals into the seven sins. It was a perfect allegory for the way each school of magic had its positive and negative sides—even, I had to admit, necromancy.

My imagination careened at this suggestion that Ygresta's codex had a connection to the runelords of Thassilon. Yet it was Illyria who arrested my attention. Her girlish demeanor put me on my back foot. Accustomed if not immune to the designs of women drawn to my wealth and title, I found myself quite unable to determine Illyria Ornelos's motives. Was she attempting to manipulate me? Or were her flirtations as genuine as they were obvious? As though caught in some transgressive act, I cleared my throat. "There is no need—"

"Wrath, envy, greed, sloth, lust, pride, and gluttony."

As she pronounced the final word, I found myself with another tart in my mouth. A sudden intuition caused me to choke. Setting aside the uneaten portion of the pastry, I scanned the library books for a particular volume.

"What are you looking for?" said Illyria.

"Gluttony is the sin of necromancy."

"That never made sense to me," she said. "Most undead don't eat anything."

"But the exceptions are striking. Vampires crave blood, for instance. And ghouls crave rotting flesh."

"Zombies eat brains."

"That is a myth perpetuated by penny dreadfuls. How could you credit such a ridicu—?"

She was laughing again. "For such a clever man, you are rather easily gulled."

"Only by—" I stopped myself before concluding, "alluring young women." Instead, I tossed aside a copy of an old volume of the *Pathfinder Chronicles* and found what I had been seeking: Anders's *The Fall of Thassilon*. "Only when distracted."

"Distracted by what, pray tell?"

She could fish for compliments all she wished, but I would not bite. "By the thought that the runelords were all wizards, and all wizards collect their spells in grimoires."

"You don't think honestly believe the professor left you a runelord's spellbook, do you?"

"I recall a reference to a *Gluttonous Tome* in which Runelord Zutha collected all of the spells known to the necromancers of Thassilon."

"That sounds familiar. I think it was one of the lost texts in the lecture."

"What do you remember about it?"

"Not much, I'm afraid."

I found the relevant chapter in *The Fall of Thassilon* and summarized for her. "The runelords foresaw Earthfall, the terrible meteorite strike that destroyed their empire and ushered in a thousand years of darkness. They devised various means to survive the event, or to instruct their followers how to return them to life. Karzoug was one. And here, Zutha was another. He compiled the *Gluttonous Tome*, an enormous volume of leathered human flesh bound in bone and inscribed with the blood of a thousand slaves."

"Charming."

"There is little here to describe its contents, except that it contained 'both his knowledge and a portion of his power, that it might never be stolen from his person.'"

"It doesn't seem likely that a wizard as powerful as a runelord would worry about burglars."

"Must I remind you that one of the most fearful aspects of necromancy is the power to steal one's life essence?"

"Oh, don't worry. I hardly ever use that sort of thing. Not unless a boy tries to get fresh." She went to the desk and leafed through the codex.

I found no further reference to this *Gluttonous Tome* in *The Fall of Thassilon*. I set the book aside and envisioned my memory library. From the imagined shelves of my past readings I drew a slim volume. History retains little of the cataclysm known as Earthfall, when the Starstone fell to Golarion, its impact leaving the crater that became the Inner Sea. The collision destroyed two great empires: Azlant, which sank into the sea, and Thassilon, much of which remains buried beneath mountains and steeped in swamps across northwestern Avistan, where we now stood.

Much of the information in my imaginary library involved the survivors of Earthfall, most of them descending into barbarism after the deaths of their great wizards. Their priests and scholars dissolved into sects. New warlords arose, their conquests muddying with dogma and propaganda what could be reliably understood about their cultures.

Searching for references to the magic of the runelords, I found far more romance than chronicle. Too many historians embellish and amalgamate their meager facts.

That thought reminded me of Ygresta's golem and the mystery of its absence. Like the study of history, my investigations depended on balancing fact with hypothesis. The latter could suggest a direction for exploration, but only on fact could one lay a foundation for the truth.

Between my borrowed books and my memory library, I had too few facts on which to build a more substantial theory. I needed more information, and I had an idea where to find it.

"I must go to Kaer Maga," I said.

"How wonderful. I have always wanted to see the City of Strangers."

"But you have an eclipse party in Riddleport."

"Oh, that tedious thing. I'd much rather have a ride in your famous Red Carriage than another sea voyage."

"But your friends are expecting you."

"Do you always do what your friends expect?"

"They invited you."

She understood what I had left unstated, but she did not accept it as an answer. "They will certainly understand that I couldn't refuse your invitation. You should probably offer me one now, so I won't have to lie when they ask me."

Her manner had gone far beyond impertinent. My initial suspicious arose again. She wanted something more than she had revealed. Worse, she had abandoned all pretense of flirtation in favor of absolute bullying. "Lady Illyria, what exactly do you want from me?"

She fixed her gaze on me. "Everything you promised."

"Pardon me?"

"The stories you told my parents and all their friends. I heard all of them."

"After you had been sent to bed? I hardly think so."

"Please. I was one of five sisters. I learned to escape the nanny before I could walk. Whenever she put us away, I just crept back out and listened from the top of the stair. To this day, I remember every detail of your Pathfinder stories."

"Surely not. No doubt your imagination has exaggerated my little stories."

"Your guide on the expedition to complete your *Bestiary of Garund* was a boy named Amadi. He was a talented artist, and he helped you catalog your discoveries."

"Much of that information appeared in the *Pathfinder Chronicles*, which you told me you read."

"You fell off the first time you rode a flying carpet in Qadira, but the satrap's concubine saved you with a spell that made you light as a feather. You were so grateful that you cheated the bandits out of thirty-four camels and gave them to her new husband as a dowry."

"It was less cheating than leveraged negotiation." I was impressed that she remembered the precise number of camels.

"But you never reported that in the *Pathfinder Chronicles*, did you?"

"No." In fact, it might have been indiscreet of me to share the story of my duel with the Keleshite prince. Fortunately, he was long dead at the hand of another, whose torments they say lasted thirty-seven days before the djinn ended his agony along with his life. I had been sometimes reckless in my younger years.

"A noble lady of Ustalav seduced you in Caliphas. You fell so desperately in love with her that you arrived six weeks late to Lepidstadt University. You never revealed her name, however, so I suppose you are still a gentleman even after telling that story."

I winced at the thought of a child's overhearing such an intimate story. "That sort of anecdote is exactly why parents send their children to bed before cordials."

Her lips formed a wicked angle. "I didn't just hear your stories. Sometimes I stayed up even after the adults had gone to bed. I spied you canoodling with my mother's friend Sestina."

"Ah." That was even more indiscreet than my tale of Caliphas.

"'Ah' was definitely one of the sounds I overheard."

My face burned. "Is it your intention to embarrass me? Is that what you want?"

An exasperated sigh escaped her. "What I want is everything you described in your stories. I want mystery, adventure, far lands and dangerous people. I want what you have. I want it for myself."

"Then why not join the Society?" Nobles were not unknown among the Pathfinder Society. Some hesitated to join because of the menial tasks demanded of applicants—a requirement easily avoided by placing a purse of platinum coins in the right hand—yet some of my most cherished Pathfinder colleagues, as well as one of my most persistent nemeses, were noble men and women. With her intelligence and knowledge, Illyria would soon distinguish herself among the famous company of adventurers, geographers, archaeologists, and secret-seekers of all stripes. Neither station nor nationality offered impediment to membership.

"How many of your stories took place during Pathfinder expeditions?" she said.

"Most of them. Well, many of them. Quite a few, anyway."

"You see? I don't want to be a Pathfinder. I want to be like you, free to travel the world without waiting for some functionary to send me instructions."

Overlooking the fact that as a venture-captain I had been the very functionary she disdained, I pointed out the obvious. "Your family has more than sufficient means. What prevents you from mounting your own expedition anywhere you like?"

"I don't want to go alone."

"Of course not. That is why one hires guards and bearers and guides."

"That isn't what I meant. I didn't spend my teenage nights dreaming of going on an adventure with hirelings." She stepped close and caught my coat by a button hole. "I dreamed of going with you."

Her overture took me by surprise. Wonder rendered me mute and paralytic as our faces drew close. A scent of violet in her lip rouge. The flutter of her eyelash upon my cheek. I could not tell which of us was moving toward the other.

"Boss! Boss!" Radovan's voice accompanied a tumult of footsteps.

I retreated a discreet step away from Illyria, who turned and pretended to examine the nearest book as Radovan burst through the door. I felt equal measures of relief and frustration at the interruption.

Arnisant pushed past Radovan to sniff my feet and Illyria's. His initial wariness of her had dissolved after we left Ygresta's chambers, reinforcing my belief—or was it a hope?—that what the hound found objectionable lay within the Acadamae, not in her person.

An armored woman followed Radovan into the room.

She was tall even for one of the Ulfen, the hardy warrior tribes found primarily north of us in the Lands of the Linnorm Kings and wintry Irrisen. Her attire needed more tending than she gave it, but her easy bearing gave me hope that she was as much a professional as Radovan estimated.

"Boss, Lady Illyria, let me present Janneke Firepelt."

Janneke made a greeting gesture of the eastern clans, plucking the air above her heart, her lips, and her brow before nodding to me. I returned the gesture and replied in Skald, the tongue of her people: "May there be no lies in our hearts, on our tongues, or upon our thoughts."

She blinked in surprise that a Chelaxian should know Ulfen customs. Her eyelashes were the same red-gold as her hair. "Excellency. Lady."

"Janneke's got a line on Zora."

"Zoran," insisted the bounty hunter. "And I have several leads, but one is stronger than the others. You'll be more interested to hear what I squeezed out of the fence."

"Indeed I might." I cleared some books and offered her the largest of the chairs. Taking the hint, Radovan cleared the divan for Illyria and me. As he finished, I caught his eye. "Drinks?"

With a nod, Radovan went to the sideboard, where the wine I had kept from Ygresta's store room had remained largely untouched since my visit to the Orisini Academy.

"Nothing for me," said Janneke. "Not while on the job."

"The boss don't mind," said Radovan.

"I'll have a drink when the job is done."

While Radovan poured a glass for me and another for Illyria, I gestured for the bounty hunter to share her news.

"Zoran's been wanted all over Varisia for nearly six years. For most of that time, he was known for burglaries of noble houses. Silver and gold, jewels and art. Never anything from a vault."

"Purely a second-story gal, eh?" Radovan settled into his own chair. Arnisant sat on the floor beside him, looking up once in hope of a treat before settling his head on his enormous paws.

"A couple years ago, this fence says Zoran stopped visiting so often. He assumed it was just a dry spell, but Zoran would leave town, sometimes for months. When the fence pried, Zoran said he'd been working for a special collector. The fence warned that the Cerulean Society wouldn't like that if they weren't getting their cut."

"What's this Cerulean Society?" said Radovan.

"Thieves' guild," the rest of us said in unison.

"Fancy name."

"It didn't matter to Zoran," said Janneke. "He told the fence he couldn't move the sort of things he'd been stealing."

"Arcane objects?" said Illyria.

Janneke tapped the side of her nose. "Powerful ones. Things this fence could never afford."

"That must have meant much more danger for this Zoran."

"Right, and not just from the Cerulean Society," said Janneke. "The fence could tell Zoran was more scared of whoever he was stealing for, and that scared the fence enough to stop pushing."

"This information conforms to our current hypothesis," I said. "But it does not tell us where to find this Zoran."

"That's the good part," said Radovan. "Go on, tell him what else you found out."

Janneke shot him a look that said she did not need his help. "Zoran visited the fence two nights ago. He wanted to move some decorative plaques on the quick, and he couldn't wait for a good price. Zoran also had a bag full of loot, but he wouldn't show it. He said it was too hot to sell in Korvosa. He'd have to take it north."

"To Janderhoff?" I said.

"It's possible." Janneke sounded dubious. "The fence said he got the impression Zoran meant somewhere farther north, like Kaer Maga."

Illyria and I exchanged a nod.

"That's just where I would go to sell stolen magic," said Illyria. "Especially if I had stolen it from the Acadamae grounds."

"The bloatmages of Kaer Maga seem less daunting when the alternative is to remain and face the wrath of an entire university of wizards," I said. "Do you know whether Zoran has already left the city?"

"I don't," said Janneke. "But in the past I've heard he travels with Varisian caravans. I asked around in Thief Camp. None have gone north in the past three days, but one is leaving tomorrow morning. That's as much as I found out before a Sczarni cutthroat marked me as a bounty hunter, and the rest of the Varisians clammed up."

"Excellent! Can you drive a carriage?"

"Sure."

"Are you free to accompany us to Thief Camp and, if necessary, on to Kaer Maga?"

"Kaer Maga, huh? That's a long ride to a bad town."

I named a figure. Janneke hesitated before saying, "For the whole trip?"

"That is a daily wage."

She pursed her lips but stopped herself before whistling in appreciation. "And I collect the bounty when we catch Zoran?"

"The bounty is all yours. I wish only to question the thief, and you may have him."

"After I get my cards back," said Radovan. "From *her*."

"All right," said Janneke. "But I want a contract and a guaranteed two weeks' pay minimum if we go a day away from Korvosa."

My estimation of the bounty hunter's professionalism increased. She knew how to barter, and she understood the value of a contract. "You shall have them both. Can you be ready to depart within the hour?"

"I can go right now."

"Excellent. Radovan, see that the carriage and team are prepared."

"Way ahead of you, boss. I did that before we came up."

"Well done."

"Just one thing. You don't want to hire more guys? I mean, what's this Thief Camp?"

"It's where all the moths and horsers go to avoid the city watch," said Illyria. Radovan blinked at the terms. She explained, "Varisians and Shoanti."

"So it's a rough place?"

"Not for a rugged fellow like you."

"While Thief Camp has a deserved reputation for lawlessness," I said, "it is also a staging area for Varisian caravans. We may even bolster our supplies and hire additional guards there, if all goes well."

Illyria turned to Radovan. "When was the last time all went well?"

"That never happens."

"Radovan," I said.

"Right, right." He gathered my belongings and placed them inside my satchel. I knew from experience that collecting his belongings from the adjoining room would take something less than a minute.

"Lady Illyria, I must take my leave of you now. If you have not left for Riddleport by my return, may I call on you at your father's house?"

"You may not," she said.

"But why? Have I done something to offend—?"

"Don't be preposterous, my dear count. You can't call on me at my father's house because I am coming with you."

"But, no. That is not what I meant to suggest." Ignoring me, she helped Radovan gather books for my satchel. When she started taking them from him to put them in order by topic, he retreated to stand beside me.

"So she's coming?"

"No," I said quietly.

"Then how come you're whispering?" He picked up the confectioner's box and reached for the remaining tart. "Hey, you gonna eat this?"

Before he could touch it, I snatched it up and popped in it my mouth. It provided small comfort.

6
Thief Camp
Radovan

On the street outside Upslope House, I climbed up the back of the Red Carriage. On the other side, Janneke checked the harnesses on the team before nodding to the hostler who'd brought them around. The big bays looked fit and well rested. They hated me, but I couldn't hate them back. They'd saved our lives too many times for me to hold a grudge.

I double-checked the supplies we'd secured along the edges of the roof. We kept most in the boot to balance the weight, but I left some on top to keep the surprise a surprise.

The boss stepped out of the guest house, Arni following at his heels. The boss was filling out at last. We'd both got mighty thin on the way over from Sarkoris, but he was going to need a visit to the tailor if he didn't cut back on the pastries. He looked left and right before calling up to me. "Any sign of Lady Illyria?"

"She's gonna be mad we didn't wait."

"Are you saying that you trust her to accompany us?"

He looked serious. It wasn't one of those rhetorical questions. He really wanted an answer. "I like her all right. I don't know I trust her. You know, on account of 'necromancer.' But that don't seem to bother you so much."

"I am more concerned that she may be presenting us with a façade." He paused. "A façade is a false front."

"I know what a façade is."

"Before you interrupted us, she made a sudden overture of affection."

"So you don't trust her on account of she likes you."

"Appears to like me."

"Maybe she does. No accounting for taste. You like her?"

"She is . . ." He furrowed his brow, and I figured the word got away from him.

"Oh, you got it bad, boss."

With one last glare at me, he got inside and slammed the door.

"All secure back there?" Janneke had set the pack with all her fancy ammo on the seat beside her, her plumed helmet on top of that. It made her look like she was riding beside a dwarf. I looked around just to make sure none were creeping up on us.

"Yeah, I'm good. Let's go."

She cracked the reins and got the horses moving. Right away I could tell she was good with them.

Janneke drove us around the Heights and up toward North Point. Much as I enjoyed the scenery, I gave the scorpion another once-over.

About halfway through our stint in Sarkoris, the boss got tired of being the only one who could bring down a flying demon. It didn't matter I could perforate 'em with a crossbow. He needed me to drag them all the way down, where me and the big knife could do our thing while he frosted the rest with his sorcery and riffle scrolls.

To do that, he called in a favor with an old military buddy. That guy got his siege engineer to rig something special for the carriage. He put it on a folding steel base, so we could travel with it low to the roof and pop it back up as needed. Mostly we kept it down, because when it was up it threw off the balance. Still, you wanted it to pop up when you needed it.

They call it a scorpion, but it's really a giant crossbow that fires steel bolts that look more like whale harpoons. Some were rigged so the razor-sharp heads snapped open like backward bear traps, making the hole ten times bigger. Demons can shrug off a lot—lightning, fire, poison, all kinds of stuff—but no matter whether you're from Cheliax, Hell, or the Abyss, big holes in the chest cavity pose a problem.

So we put 'em in them.

"What've you got back there?" Janneke strained to look back at me. The carriage started drifting over to a cart of roasted hens.

"Keep your eye on the street."

"Is that what I think it is?"

"It is if you think it's a scorpion."

"I want to see."

"Maybe later."

"Why don't you drive while I look it over? I'm good with crossbows."

"Sweetheart, you do *not* want me in that driver's seat. More important, the horses don't want me there."

"I don't want you calling me that while we're on the job."

"What, 'sweetheart'?"

"That's right. Knock it off."

I muttered something that maybe ended in "sweetheart."

"What was that?"

"I said 'all right'! All right?"

The boss knocked on the roof. Well, the ceiling. His ceiling, my roof. I leaned over the side and saw he'd opened the window.

"Fetch a pair of those roast guinea hens." He pointed at the cart Janneke was trying to pass.

"Don't you want three?" I figured Janneke deserved a snack.

"Yes, make it three."

I hopped down, snagged three birds, leaving a bit more than their price, and ran back to the carriage. Each came with its own bit of waxed butcher's paper to keep from burning your fingers. With three, I had to juggle a bit.

Back up on the ladder, I passed one through the little window. The boss reached out and grabbed the second one.

"Aren't these for me and Janneke?"

"You should have said you wanted one. You can run back if you like."

By the time I passed him the third, he was already sucking the flesh off a leg bone.

Janneke drove past the statue of Montlarion Jeggare standing tall and portly in the middle of the circle. I didn't see much family resemblance, but I muttered down at the boss. "You'll look like him one day, you're not careful what you eat."

"What?" said Janneke.

"Nothing."

We rode along Northgate Avenue toward a big bridge. While I kept my eyes peeled for trouble, including Lady Illyria, I couldn't help but admire the scenery. We passed a couple of big buildings sitting side by side. The first, with its scales of Abadar and spirals of Pharasma carved onto its façade—I know what façade means—looked like a prison. The word LONGACRE was chiseled into its face. Next to it was Korvosa's City Hall, full of clerks in stupid-looking hats winding their way through white columns.

I liked that the city buildings were still white, or near enough. Ever since House Thrune made their deal with Hell to take over the empire, they got their smudge on everything. In Korvosa, thieves and forgers didn't get the rope. Here they hanged murderers, not pickpockets.

I could get used to a place like that.

We were just about to reach the bridge when an indigo-colored horse dashed out from St. Alika Way and blocked our path.

"That lady sure likes purple," I said.

Lady Illyria sat high in the saddle. Even at a distance I could see the heat in her eyes. I liked her jacket and her leather pants, each a different shade of purple. Her black boots laced all the way up to disappear under her jerkin's skirt.

I rapped the warning knock on the carriage roof. The window opened, and I said, "Hey, boss."

"I know." I could hear he was talking with his mouth full. For a second it sounded like he was tidying up, and then the window slammed shut again.

As we came close to Illyria and the bridge, I figured it was time for a diversion. I cupped my hand to my mouth and shouted, "I like your phony pony!"

She tried to keep on her mad face, but she couldn't help cracking a smile. "It's a horse!"

"I know," I shouted back. "But horse doesn't rhyme with 'phony.'"

She rode up alongside the carriage. The way she peered down her nose at the carriage window, I guessed the boss had drawn the curtains. I'd seen that man take down half a dozen demons while crusaders healed themselves to get back into the fray, but his courage didn't always extend to the ladies.

"I take it you've seen Count Jeggare conjure a magical steed?" Illyria said.

"Plenty of times. I can do it myself."

"You?" If she sounded any more surprised, I was gonna get my feelings hurt.

"Sure." I plucked a riffle scroll out of a sleeve pocket and showed it to her. "You play your cards right, I'll show you sometime."

"You play your cards right, I might let you."

"Why don't you try calling *her* 'sweetheart'?" Janneke called back to me, not quite loud enough for Illyria to hear. "That'd be interesting."

Looking around for something to throw, I found an oilskin rain cape tucked between a couple of the boss's bags. I don't know why we'd held onto it. It smelled of bear fat, and I didn't like remembering what happened to the big Kellid who used to wear it. Anyway, it kept off the rain, and it gave me an idea. I threw it at Janneke. "Put that on."

"It's not cold."

"Yeah, but you're not exactly inconspicuous in that getup. You said the Sczarni ran you off last time you visited this Thief Camp?"

"Yeah. All right. I get the idea." She sniffed the cape, winced, and put it on anyway. With her helm off, she didn't stand out so much.

Down below, the carriage window opened again. The boss said, "What a swift transformation from your previous attire."

"Swifter than you'd like, was it?"

"I simply meant you had plenty of time. There was no need to rush."

"You promised to meet me at Jeggare Square!"

"Did I? I thought you wanted to meet at Thief Camp."

"You know perfectly well what I said."

"It is possible that in the excitement of Janneke's report I misheard you."

I'd heard this conversation a thousand times before, just not from the boss. Something told me it wasn't going to end well for him. I wanted to climb up front to join Janneke, but I'd just spook the horses.

Instead, I lowered the scorpion and locked it down. The top of the bow barely peeked over the luggage we'd stored around the roof's edges. I settled down on a footlocker and enjoyed the evening sun sparkling on the Jeggare River for a while. Eventually, the carriage door opened again. I peeked over the side and didn't see Illyria's phantom mount, so she must have gone inside.

On the other side of the bridge, a couple little villages hugged the river just outside the gates. They had their own docks and plenty of nets to keep up appearances, but I'd bet there was more smuggling than fishing going on. In the one closer to the city walls, a caravan had started forming. Some of the wagons were still empty, and none were hitched to horses. Looked like Janneke's information was good, and they weren't leaving anytime soon. Besides, the sun was sinking into the ocean on the other side of the city. We didn't have much light left.

I rolled off the roof to hang onto the back ladder. The boss opened up the little window. On the other side of his map table, Illyria looked at him over a wine goblet. Judging from her narrow eyes, he had some more apologizing to do.

I said, "So I'm hiring guards for a trip to . . . ? Where's a good place to go in Varisia?"

"Janderhoff."

I gave him a dirtier look than Illyria to see if he was yanking my chain. He was. "Very funny."

"Say we travel to Baslwief to look at horses."

"Got it."

"Come back as soon as you find a lead on this Zoran. If he is here, give me a sign. Do not try to take him on your own."

"Don't worry."

So I hopped off the carriage and sauntered into this place they called Thief Camp. The smell of stewed mushrooms with garlic was the first thing to hit me. I got a taste for that stuff in Ustalav, so I followed my nose.

"Sweet mead!" A man waved a wooden tankard at me and started filling it from a little keg on his table.

I waved him off. "I don't like the sweet stuff."

He started filling the same tankard from the other keg. "Dry mead!"

"No thanks."

I passed a couple of bare-chested Shoanti squaring off in a ring of wooden spikes. The Varisian bookmaker waved me over, but I shook my head. Everyone else watching the match looked local, and I wasn't here to be an easy mark.

The waterfront tavern smelled more of fish than beer. I peeked inside but didn't see our gal. Or guy. Janneke had me second-guessing myself. I'd seen this Zora or Zoran use magic. I guess a spell could have fooled me, but I didn't like to admit it.

Next door was a shop full of woven blankets and rugs. I made a show of looking them over while scanning the local traffic, especially anyone who looked in a hurry. Most of the people outside the city were Varisian or Shoanti. Some looked tough or shady, but most looked to be shopping or doing more or less legitimate business. I bought a couple blankets and moved along.

An old woman with a face like a dried apple ladled me up a bowl of mushrooms from an iron cauldron. I ate while her fossilized husband caught me up on local events. Someone's boy had been sent up to Longacre. A local girl got married the day before, but only after her groom managed to beat his rival unconscious. I said I was looking to hire guards. The woman told me to avoid the Shoanti wrestlers, who were both drunks. I asked who was worth hiring. The man and woman both shrugged. I wiped the bowl clean with a hunk of bread, which I munched while walking away.

A hunched woman carried a couple of bags on a stick across her shoulder. I couldn't see her face under her big scarf, so I pretended to find a coin in the dirt and peeked up to see her lumpy face. If it was a disguise, it fooled me. She was headed toward the boss, anyway, so if she was under an illusion, the boss would spot her with his sword.

Thunk! A gang of Varisian teenagers took turns standing against a couple of thick boards. The game was to throw a knife as close as possible to the other guy, who wasn't supposed to flinch. Then you took the knife and threw it back. There were a lot of ways to lose.

Beside them was a fortune-teller's wagon. The stars and butter-flies painted on the side stirred up memories of Ustalav.

They also gave me an idea. There was nobody outside, so I went to knock on the round door. Before I could touch wood, it opened. Out stepped a man skinny enough to crawl through a keyhole. On the tattooed top of his head, the sun cradled a crescent moon. Trinkets rattled in his white hair and tobacco-stained beard.

"Welcome, seeker. May Desna smile on you."

"What do you know? I feel lucky already."

"Shall I cast a harrowing for your journey?"

"Not that lucky." I peered into his wagon. It was a market stall in there, the curved walls filled with gimcracks and gewgaws. "I'm looking for my own deck."

He brightened and turned toward the wagon. "I have three different styles."

"I mean a particular deck. Maybe somebody sold you one a little while ago."

He scrunched his nose like he smelled a fart. "I never buy used decks."

"Not even a special one? Old-fashioned backs, Ustalavic?"

"Never. Once a harrower touches a deck, it becomes infused with his spirit. The lingering essence can skew a reading. That is in the best case."

"And in the worst?"

"Haunting, curse, the evil eye. The perils are endless."

It was bad business to annoy fortune-tellers, even the fake ones, and I needed some goodwill. "All right, let's see 'em."

He showed me his decks. One caught my eye.

On the cards' backs were blue swallowtails with Lady Luck's eyes on their wings. The faces were a little different from what I was used to seeing. The Rabbit Prince looked more like a badger, the Queen Mother some kind of whale with tentacles and three eyes. The Dance showed a hellspawn and an angel strangling each other.

"How much?"

He named a price. I had the cash, but I didn't want to insult him. I let my jaw drop and handed back the cards. "What? Do I look like the Rabbit Prince?"

"Surely you are a prince among your people." He took a look at my jacket and reconsidered. "But perhaps you have fallen on hard times."

We haggled for a minute, but my heart wasn't in it. As I counted the coins into his palm, he looked disappointed in me.

"My old friend Zora said to say hello if I was ever in the area."

"I know of none by that name." His gaze slipped over my shoulder, where I heard a heavy *thunk* as the boys threw another knife. "Someone at the tavern might know."

"Thanks." I headed back to the tavern, but I glanced at the knife-throwing boys. There was no way short of magic any of them was Zora, but they saw me looking. They sneered back at me, chins out, nostrils flaring. I tipped them a wink to show I wasn't scared. One wearing a vest over his bare chest raised a knife, making like to throw it at me. I stood still and didn't flinch, making him look stupid. He squeeze off a fig at me. I shot him the tines. He threw the knife.

If he'd thrown at my feet, I might have let it go. He threw for my head. I dipped low, caught his knife, and threw it back too fast for him to dodge. The point stuck in the board behind him, quivering an inch from his ear. He flinched, but his buddies didn't laugh at him. Their eyes stuck to me as they showed me their knives.

I pulled my "tail" and showed the boys the big knife. It was an ugly thing, scarred and blackened by demon ichor.

"Think twice, boys." Sometimes a look at the big knife could run 'em off.

This wasn't one of those times.

The knife boys moved in, grinning. I had a feeling how come. The Shoanti wrestlers and some hard-faced Sczarni men drifted toward us. The fortune-teller tipped off the boys, I figured, but I missed the signal passing through the rest of Thief Camp. Waving the big knife to keep their attention, I slipped a riffle scroll into my hand and snapped it off. By the time the magic tickled my feet, I'd put the dead scroll in my pocket and was pulling out another.

Four bobbing lights went up on the other side of camp. They bobbed through the air, following a fat bearded gent riding a dark horse. As I watched, the illusion melted away. The rider was the woman who'd robbed me.

"Radovan," the boss whispered in my ear, even though he was still far away. I looked over at the carriage to see him standing on the roof, his sword pointed at the rider while he pointed a finger to send his magic message to me. "We spotted her!"

"Her! I knew it was 'her'!"

"Hurry back."

"I'm trying."

The knife boys spread out between me and the carriage. None of them looked too keen to get close, but a Shoanti bruiser ran at me, a couple of Sczarni covering each side. I snapped off the second riffle scroll. Bright magic flared in their faces, dazzling their eyes.

I went for the knife boys. Two raised their blades, but one shied away. I feinted at one and tumbled through the gap. Rolling, I came up to my feet a good ten yards past them, fleet as a fox. With the magic in my feet, I'd win any footrace. I hightailed it toward the carriage, but they were already in trouble.

A hatchet-faced man cracked a horsewhip to spook the team. Janneke stood on the driver's perch, struggling to control them.

Whipper wasn't alone. Men and women from Thief Camp ran up to shout and throw whatever was close to hand. A potato struck the lead horse on the face. He reared up, screaming mad.

Through a carriage window, Illyria waved a white feather at the attackers and cast a spell. The men and women on that side of the carriage screamed and ran. So did a nearby donkey, thrashing until it pulled out its tether and ran straight into the gang running after me.

"Thanks," I muttered. A donkey never did me a favor before.

Up top, the boss cast spells, some by hand, others by riffle scroll. Lucky for the people attacking, he held off on the fire and lightning. Sometimes the magic you don't see is the most powerful.

Arni ran off the man scaring the horses, chasing him until he dropped his whip and kept running. The hound came bounding back, barking at anybody close to the horses.

I flattened a man throwing tankards from the mead table. I shoved aside a woman banging a pot and jumped onto the carriage ladder. As I climbed onto the roof, I heard the snap of a crossbow. A bolt caught the boss in the belly.

"No!" shouted Janneke. She let go of the reins to grab her own bow.

"Control the team," the boss snapped at her. He brushed away the bolt. It had put a hole in his coat but couldn't pierce his warded skin.

Illyria leaned out the other window and scared off another half-dozen folk from Thief Camp. I was glad we were taking it easy on them. They might be a bunch of robbers, cheats, and cutthroats, but they looked after their own. I couldn't hardly blame them for covering Zora's escape. Still, I wanted my cards back. And I guess I wanted the boss to figure out his thing, too.

Janneke got the lead horse back under control. She turned the carriage toward the opening Illyria's spell made. It was the right idea, but the people of Thief Camp were ready for it. A drover was leading his oxen into the path Zora took.

"Get out of the way," Janneke yelled.

The drover pretended not to hear her, but it was obvious he was blocking her on purpose. He wasn't alone, either. People were streaming out of the tavern and other buildings, even leaving their market stalls to block our way wherever we turned.

Half the camp looked to be in on it, covering for the thief's escape.

"Time for a demonstration," said the boss.

"You bet." While he made his arcane gestures, I kicked open the latch on the scorpion. It popped up and clicked into firing position. I slapped a bolt into place and swung it around to menace the crowd. They had sense enough to scatter.

The boss's lightning bolt came down in front of the oxen. The big animals bolted, lowing in panic.

I aimed and pulled the trigger. The mead table exploded. The big bolt obliterated the keg of sweet mead and sent tankards flying in all directions.

The people of Thief Camp ran everywhere except toward us. For a second, it looked like we'd won. Then the mead vendor stood up, drenched from head to toe and covered in the splinters of his tankards.

"Kill them!"

I held my breath, hoping the others would see that was a bad idea. Instead, another flurry of crossbow bolts rained down. A couple bounced off the boss. One perforated my jacket but didn't catch me.

"Boss, I don't think we can hold back anymore. We got to take out a loudmouth or two."

He made a grim frown and nodded.

I grabbed another bolt and started cranking the scorpion. He pointed the Shadowless Sword at our target, a Shoanti aiming his short bow at our horses. Just as I drew a bead on the guy, I heard a flapping of leather wings. The boss's sword arm dipped as a drake landed on the flat of his blade.

Not just any drake, but the purple we'd seen at the Acadamae.

"Not now!" The boss tried to shake the reptile from his sword. She slid down the flat of the blade and hopped onto his wrist, where her claws clung tight enough to make him wince.

"Stop!" cried a familiar voice. The skinny harrower came forward, the crowd parting for him. "Everyone, stop fighting. It is an omen!"

The boss raised his free arm, and the drake hopped onto his wrist like a falcon. She opened her wings and let out a little cry, not at him but at the harrower.

I watched his face. He frowned like he was listening to the drake, but I didn't think so. I figured he was weighing the cost of letting us go against the damage we were sure to cause if they kept trying to keep us there.

"Let them pass," he said. "Desna smiles on these travelers."

"What about my mead?" wailed the wet guy.

The boss gave me the nod. I fished out a purse and tossed it at the whiner, not too gentle.

"Go now," said the harrower. "And do not return."

I gave him a salute with the bolt in my hand. When I started to put it in the scorpion, the purple drake hopped off the boss's arm and right onto the groove.

"You're a clever little lizard," I said.

She spread her wings to look all big and fierce. It would have worked better if she weren't so cute.

The boss climbed down and got back into the carriage, holding the door open until Arni jumped in.

Janneke cracked the reins. Once the team got going, she looked back at me. "What just happened?"

"I don't know," I said, wishing I had a bit of meat to give the drake. "Maybe the boss finally got himself a familiar."

7
The Dawn Shadow Path
Varian

With sigh I had come to find disconcertingly agreeable, Illyria closed Hendall's *Razing of the Pale Tower*. "Nothing."

"Are you certain?" I asked.

"I might not have your perfect recall, but I'm sure there's nothing here that mentions your codex."

"It is hardly perfect."

"You said you had an eidetic memory."

"That is so, but it is far from perfect. The last time I tested myself, my reading retention proved approximately ninety-three point seven percent accurate."

"'Approximately'?" She snorted.

Three days out of Korvosa, I could at last reliably determine when Illyria was mocking me: the conclusive evidence was that her lips were moving. "One does not wish to appear imprecise."

She chuckled. "One must be very proud."

"It is a gift, not a learned skill. You have doubtless heard of idiot savants, incapable of rational discourse but flawless in executing complex mathematical problems or in memorizing long sequences." Speaking those words made me consider that memory and intellect mirrored the relationship between sorcery and wizardry. One was an inherited talent, the other a skill cultivated over years of study. But to the matter at hand, I added, "The average reader retains less than thirty-four percent."

"How do you even know that figure?"

"An Arcanamirium colleague conducted a study in which I participated. Since then I have refined his methods. I test myself every few years."

"You attended the Arcanamirium?"

"Only for a term."

"How many schools did they kick you out of?"

Despite the knowledge that she provoked me intentionally, I could not suppress a defensive impulse. "None."

She smiled to see her barb had stung me. "Well, how many schools have you attended?"

"Formally? Only nine, most only for a few series of lectures. I have visited many others to consult their libraries or scholars."

"I thought the whole point of graduating from the Acadamae was so you could go out and experience the world, not to keep coming back to roam the stacks."

"Sometimes I experience the world through archaeological digs or frontier expeditions." I shrugged. "Sometimes, I experience it through libraries. A million ghosts of love and conquest haunt the pages of history."

"You make them sound very nearly romantic."

I raised an eyebrow. A remark like that, under different circumstances, would surely be an invitation to make an overture. Instead, I said, "What would you like to read next?"

She regarded me through half-lidded eyes. I could not tell whether she was disappointed or perplexed. Before I could study her expression further, something outside drew her attention.

Radovan charged past on his phantom mount. He whooped and thrust a fist to the sky. Ten yards behind, Arnisant replied with a hearty woof.

Perhaps because natural equines reacted to him with such violence, Radovan seldom missed an opportunity to run the conjured steed at a breakneck pace. It brought him such joy that I hardly resented the need to reinscribe the riffle scrolls he wasted. Besides, it was good practice for him to use the scrolls regularly. Over the past two years, his knack for triggering them had improved. In time, I thought, he might be able to cast truly powerful spells with little danger of electrocuting himself.

Whether he or I summoned it for him, Radovan's horse always had a distinctly infernal appearance. When I asked him whether he visualized a particular beast when casting the spell, he replied that he never gave it much thought. One day we would need to pursue a more rigorous examination of his knack for triggering scrolls and its relationship—if any—to his unique infernal bloodline.

The carriage lurched. I heard the distinctive sound of the scorpion unlocking above us. An instant later, it launched a bolt.

Seeing nothing amiss on the southwest side of the carriage, I looked to the northeast. The Mindspin Mountains loomed in the distance, the rising sun casting their shadows toward us. Between the foothills and the road lay a sea of green grass broken only by the occasional stand of trees or a lonely hillock.

"What the hell are you doing?" Radovan yelled. Craning my neck, I saw him recovering from a sharp turn on his conjured mount. He pulled on the reins to turn it before stretching down to retrieve a scorpion bolt. He failed to notice the enormous hare still bounding away from the site of its near-death.

Janneke shouted from the carriage roof. "Sorry! I wanted that rabbit."

"You can't hit anything with that damned bucket on your head!" he snarled. "You nearly perforated me."

Irritated, I opened the carriage door and climbed up to the roof. Janneke appeared surprised to see me clamber up so easily, but I had years of practice. "I do not want you firing that weapon while the carriage is in motion. Not unless absolutely necessary."

She removed her helm. "But I— Yes, Your Excellency."

"You understand the reason."

"Yes." Guilt deepened the blush on her cheeks. "It puts the carriage off balance."

I glanced at the driver's seat, where Illyria's phantom driver held the reins. While the conjuration resembled a gaunt man in a stovepipe hat—a superfluous but amusing touch—it was no more sentient than the spell with which Illyria had dusted Ygresta's rooms. Perhaps Illyria had the right idea. I mused on the advantages of an entirely conjured staff, one that did not fire the siege engine against my wishes.

"I don't mind your leaving the reins to Lady Illyria's creature, but I need you or Radovan alert at all times for any sign of our quarry or danger on the trail."

She folded the weapon's mount and locked it down. "You're right, Excellency. I'm sorry. It won't happen again."

Her regret seemed sincere, so I withheld further rebuke. I nodded to indicate the matter was settled if not forgotten.

"Any sign of the drake?" I asked.

"None." Janneke shielded her eyes from the sun and peered into the clear western skies where the drake had flown off an hour earlier. Part of me hoped she would find her way back to her brood in Korvosa, but I could not help feeling her appearance held some greater meaning. Surely she was not sent as a sign from Desna, as the villains of Thief Camp believed. In any event, her presence would make a similarly good impression on any other Varisians we might encounter. I hoped for her return.

The drake flew off several times a day, presumably to hunt. I had spoken to the creature in Draconic, but she did not reply. Some of her kind could communicate telepathically. Some even became familiars to wizards or sorcerers they deemed worthy. Illyria fed the drake scraps of her meals in an effort to win its favor. A house drake was unlikely to choose a necromancer as her mistress—nor a lord of Cheliax as her master—so I made no such overtures. Besides, I preferred to clean my plate.

Even that thought caused a pang of hunger. My yearning appetite had to be some trick of my imagination. We had eaten a full breakfast, but our supplies had dwindled sooner than anticipated, in part because of Illyria's unexpected presence. We might have resupplied at Janderhoff, but I refused to expose Radovan to the dwarf lords' vengeance. Instead, we cloaked the carriage in an illusion of a well-guarded trade wagon and continued toward the Storval Plateau.

Inside the carriage, I found Lady Illyria deep in study. She no longer tried to hide her spectacles from me, either because she no longer cared whether she attracted my eye or—more likely—because she realized how fetching I found them. Every aspect of her appearance, from her tinted black hair to the ribbon at her throat, the monocle from her lapel to her tooled leather boots, evoked fond memories of past decades. Had such things suddenly returned to fashion during my recent journeys? I suspected not. Illyria must be one of those rare ladies who eschew modern style for that of a previous age.

I approved.

We spent the morning in relative tranquility, occasionally showing each other some interesting passage from the borrowed books. We learned that Runelord Zutha divided his *Gluttonous Tome* into three sections, which his minions had secreted in distant locations. The portion Ygresta left me was known as the *Kardosian Codex*. Another section including the cover and spine was called the *Bone Grimoire*. Of the final third we learned only a title: *The Black Book*.

We passed two caravans and a trio of riders, pausing only to exchange news of the road. Shortly after noon we drove the team into a shallow stream. The horses drank as Janneke wiped them down. When Radovan and I traveled alone, I had become accustomed to tending to them since he could not. Tending to six horses was too much for one person, so I joined her. She appeared only briefly surprised as I peeled off my jacket, rolled up my sleeves, and set to work with a curry brush.

As we worked, Lady Illyria brought the feedbags from the carriage boot. Beside her, a half-filled sack of oats hovered in the grasp of her invisible servant.

"Don't look so surprised," she said as she handed two to me. "I spent many happy summers at my mother's country estate, and I was no stranger to the stables."

As we watered and fed the horses, Radovan erected a table so Lady Illyria and I might enjoy a break from the carriage. We dined on preserved fruit, flatbread, and peppercorn salami.

As I reached for a second piece of bread, Illyria pulled away the plate and handed it to her invisible servant. "Put that back in the boot."

"I beg your pardon," I said. "I was not finished."

"Yes, you were. I can see my father isn't the only one whose diet I must manage."

As the servant passed Arnisant, who dozed near the rear wheel, the hound rose up like a breaching whale and snatched the remains.

I opened my mouth to protest, but the little drake chirped from her perch atop the carriage. I was glad to see she had returned safely.

"See?" said Illyria. "Even Amaranthine thinks you're getting fat."

"'Amaranthine'?"

She glanced up at the drake. "I named her."

"Amaranthine is the shade of your handbag."

"It's closer to the color of this amethyst, although I might call that heliotrope." She showed off the gem on her left hand.

"How many synonyms do you know for 'purple'?"

"All of them."

The affectation might have seemed childish in another woman, but it was a refreshing change from the black and gray necromancers with their skulls and cobweb lace. Besides, Illyria had the excuse of her purple Azlanti eyes and exceptional taste. I had come to anticipate her emerging from her conjured shelter each morning in a different ensemble.

She pointed at me. "You've lost a button on your waistcoat."

As I felt for the missing button, I realized just how tight my clothes felt. I *had* already eaten as much as my custom. It was just that the salami and pear relish tasted so good together. Nevertheless, the evidence was undeniable: I was growing plump. "Perhaps I have overcompensated for the weight I lost traveling to Korvosa."

"Don't you worry it's more than that? This book you seek must be called the *Gluttonous Tome* for a reason."

"Gluttony is the sin of necromancy." While we had raised the issue before, neither of us knew a satisfactory reason why each of the seven sins was associated with a school of magic. I had long assumed it was simply a personal reflection of the runelords, each of whom had mastered one type of magic. Perhaps the runelord of necromancy was a notorious glutton. "Could it be because the desire to extend one's life through the dark arts is a sort of gluttony? A desire for more life than we deserve?"

"That's as good a reason as I've read," said Illyria. "Speaking of which, I have been casting an epiphany spell each morning, hoping to catch some fragment from a library you haven't visited."

Despite the imprecision of her spell and my personal disdain for divination, I envied Illyria's ability to cast her thoughts by magic across the pages of distant books. The very idea made my memory library feel small. "And?"

"What do you know about Zutha's fight with Tar-Baphon?"

"Runelord Zutha fought the Whispering Tyrant?" She could not have surprised me more if she had struck me in the face. Everyone knew Tar-Baphon as the most dreadful necromancer in history. As a Pathfinder, of course, I knew a great deal more. Yet I knew nothing of any connection between him and Zutha.

In life, the wizard-king Tar-Baphon ruled central Avistan nearly four centuries earlier. Only the now-dead god Aroden was able to end his reign—the first time. Two millennia later, Tar-Baphon returned as a lich—a powerful undead spellcaster—and proceeded to rule the country of Ustalav for centuries more. Only the supreme sacrifice of General Arnisant allowed the Shining Crusade to imprison the corpse-king beneath his fortress of Gallowspire.

The idea that Tar-Baphon had fought a runelord would forever alter history's perception of Avistan's greatest villains. It also strained credulity. "Please pardon me for saying so, my lady, but that's a rather bold theory. The runelords died or disappeared millennia before Tar-Baphon was ever born. Where did you encounter records of such a clash?"

"As part of my necromantic history research. Because of my uncle's position, I had privileged access to rare books from the Hall of Whispers."

"What was the title of the book?"

She shook her head. "Sorry. I don't remember much about it. I was looking for something else entirely."

"Please," I said. "Tell me as much as you remember."

"Until the spell jogged my memory, I remembered practically nothing. Like the other runelords, Zutha prepared himself to survive Earthfall. His method was to preserve his secrets in a tome, which he divided into three parts, as we've learned. He entrusted the tome to his most loyal minions, to return it to his tomb after the devastation. Some of these minions or their descendants fell to agents of Tar-Baphon, who tortured them into revealing the location of Zutha's crypt. The Tyrant went there, woke Zutha, and stole a portion of his power."

"Stole his power? There must be some mistake. A clash between two of the mightiest liches in history would surely appear in every major text."

"Not if they didn't wish it to. Perhaps the link was intentionally obscured."

That news was almost enough to make me regret renouncing necromancy. "Do all necromancers know this secret?"

"No," said Illyria. "As I said, the only mention I found was in the masters' most secret collection. To be honest, I probably wouldn't even have remembered it without the divination. It was a brief reference in a rather broad history of liches."

We relocated our discussion to the carriage while Janneke and Radovan resumed our journey. Throughout the afternoon, we consulted our books and compared our memories to consolidate what we knew and suspected about this *Gluttonous Tome*. We suspected more than we knew, unfortunately, and uncertainty breeds fear. Illyria was the first to give voice to my growing dread.

"You're cursed."

I could only nod agreement. "Ygresta must have suffered the same curse from reading the book. That may be what killed him."

"If Professor Ygresta knew he had been cursed, could he have hired the thief himself?"

"To find a cure?"

"Perhaps," she said. "Or perhaps to find the other two books."

Either possibility seemed plausible. Surely the scrupulously ethical and moral Ygresta would have wanted to escape the effects of the *Codex*. Another possibility occurred to me. "The curse could be a device to compel its bearer to complete the *Gluttonous Tome* in an attempt to escape its effects."

"To what end?"

"To restore Zutha's power?" Even as I said it, I shuddered with a premonition.

"Is that even possible if Tar-Baphon destroyed him?"

"Did you read that Zutha was destroyed?" I said. "You said only that they fought, and that Tar-Baphon stole his power."

"True." Illyria's brow furrowed. "I can cast the spell again tomorrow. Perhaps it will help me remember more detail. But I'm afraid there might not be much more."

"Many sages reside in Kaer Maga. We may find one who can tell us the whole story."

We read a while in silence. I became increasingly conscious of my tight waistcoat. Vencarlo had heard that Ygresta grew so obese that the necromancers animated ogres to bear his coffin. How long before I suffered a similar indignity?

"You'll find a way to lift the curse," said Illyria. Her concerned expression told me she had read my face, not my thoughts. "Professor Ygresta must have read the book months or even a couple of years ago. That's plenty of time for Count Varian Jeggare to solve the problem."

I offered her a smile of thanks, but I did not share her optimism. Our conversation ebbed as we returned to reading with a renewed urgency.

We stopped to make camp shortly before dusk. Amaranthine hissed when I hovered near the cook pot. I wondered how much the drake understood of my conversations with Illyria. The creatures were notoriously intelligent, even those who did not communicate with people. Was it possible she had already bonded to Illyria? I suspected nothing would please the lady more than to adopt a familiar whose purple scales matched her dress.

It took every ounce of willpower to resist gorging myself at supper. She said nothing to the others, but Illyria fixed her gaze on me the moment I finished my plate. She watched until Radovan and Janneke finished the remainder. I accepted defeat, consoled in the knowledge that it would prove temporary.

When Illyria went to conjure her private shelter, I walked around the carriage and opened the boot. I cut myself a generous portion of the pepper sausage and put it in my pocket for a snack later.

Janneke picketed the horses while Radovan lay down a bedroll beside the fire. In their exchange of glances I imagined some secret communication. If they planned some late-night assignation, I did not mind, so long as it was during my turn at watch and did not frighten the horses.

As had become her habit, Lady Illyria stood beside the door to her cottage as Radovan delivered her firewood. As had become my habit, I waited for Radovan to emerge before bidding her goodnight.

"You know you don't have to sleep in the carriage," said Illyria.

My surprise at her suggestion must have been obvious. She barely constrained herself from laughing.

"I meant I would be happy to show you the spell so you can summon your own cottage."

"I understood that." That sounded weak even to me, so I added, "One of the drawbacks of sorcery is that I must focus my energies on fewer spells. So many that I learned as a wizard are beyond my ability to cast by will alone."

"That must be frustrating."

"You have no idea."

My transition from the intellectual science to the emotional art was far from complete. Without the original copy of the *Lexicon of Paradox*, which added its chaotic powers to my will, I could no longer wield the more powerful magic I had mastered as a wizard. As I grew stronger in sorcery, I remained able to cast lesser spells as a wizard. Doing so still made me ill, so I confined that activity to an hour each morning to replenish riffle scrolls for Radovan and myself.

"Well, Your Excellency," said Illyria. "Good night." She made no move to withdraw, but neither did she move toward me.

She had chosen necromancy, but she was unlike any necromancer I had known. I could not trust her as a wizard, but as a woman I could hardly resist her. I took her hand. "Illyria, I—"

Above us, the Amaranthine shrieked a warning. She dove to land at our feet, hopping and beating her wings against our ankles.

Illyria withdrew her hand. "Our chaperon objects."

"No." Turning, I drew the Shadowless Sword.

Radovan had already leaped onto the carriage ladder and rolled onto the roof. Shielding his eyes from the light of the campfire, he turned to scan all directions. Janneke joined him a moment later. I drew Illyria to the carriage and opened the door. She pulled away.

"Don't be ridiculous." She drew a wand from the holster built into her high boots. "If there's trouble, you'll need me out here."

Firelight appeared all around us, less than fifty yards away. The smell of oil and smoke followed, and then screeching voices rose in a chant:

> Chop the horse and gut the hound,
> Smash the longshanks to the ground!

"Is that goblin-tongue?" said Illyria.

"Yes." I declined to translate the words for fear they would cause the others to underestimate the threat. I had seen veteran warriors chuckle at the childlike lyrics of a goblin war band, only to die under their dogslicers.

I helped Illyria climb and followed her onto the carriage roof.

> Break the wagon, burn the hut,
> Goblins kill, and goblins cut!

Visualizing the effect I desired, I sketched the cryptic sigils and spoke the esoteric words. My heart swelled with the thrill of release as I pointed at the largest mass of torches and shot a bead of fire at the darkness-hidden goblins. The bead grew larger as it flew, exploding in a huge sphere. The sound of its eruption smothered the goblin screams and cast their spindly bodies into silhouette.

A dozen goblins died in the explosion, but the orange light revealed dozens more approaching on either side of the blast. Most rode atop enormous, hairless rodents. All wore dog-hide armor, the heads forming hoods on the goblins' own melon-shaped craniums. Most clutched spears or the misshapen blades known as dogslicers. Others shook flaming torches above their heads, while their warchanters cracked whips in time with their horrid doggerel.

> *Tear the innards all apart,*
> *Break the bones and eat the heart!*

Teams of the biggest goblins ran forward carrying long poles. Oil-drenched captives—also goblins, presumably of another tribe—wriggled on the crosspieces, howling for their lives. Cackling, the attackers ignited their prisoners. Raising the living brands, they rushed Illyria's cottage and the Red Carriage.

Janneke swiveled the scorpion and shot a bolt with perfect aim. The missile impaled three goblins, pinning the third to the ground while the first two fell with fist-sized holes in their chests. Their immolated captive fell to the ground, writhing for a few agonizing moments before withering in the flames.

Janneke reached for another bolt, but I caught her shoulder.

"Go with Arnisant. Guard the horses."

"But—" She balked only for an instant. "I'm on it." She hopped off the carriage roof and hit the ground running toward the horses.

"Arnisant, go!" The hound chased after Janneke.

Radovan lingered on the carriage. Usually he plunged into the fray without awaiting orders. Instead, he braced his feet and raised his arms toward a descending flame. He caught the immolated goblin bare-handed and shoved it aside, hurling the burning captive away from the carriage. He slapped out the flames flickering across his hands and winced. Resistant as he was, naked flame often proved too hot even for him.

Illyria scattered a handful of teeth onto the ground while intoning a spell. I followed her example, visualizing the gleaming scales of a silver dragon as I made the sign and drew in a sibilant breath. I blew it out in a cone of brilliant ice crystals, extinguishing the flames on another sacrificial goblin and freezing another nine attackers to the ground.

> Burn the flesh as black as toast,
> That's what goblins like the most.

Where Illyria had sown her teeth sprouted an awful crop. Hairless bodies rose from the ground, gray with corruption. Long black tongues wiggled like eels from distended mouths. The creatures hissed, crouching as they looked around for a meal.

"The goblins," Illyria shouted down to them. "Devour them all, and nothing else."

The leader coughed out some unintelligible command, and the ghouls lurched into the fray. I reeled from their stench. Even more, my mind reeled that this elegant lady would conjure such abominable minions.

Below us, the goblins made another rush toward the carriage. I felled several with arcane missiles. Illyria did the same with black bolts from her wand. The flames from my spell and the goblins' torches had spread to surround us.

Against the bright wall of flame, Arnisant ran back and forth before the frightened horses. A big goblin charged toward the hound on the back of his ugly steed. Arnisant rushed forward to meet them. I heard the impact over the screams of the goblin warchanters. The goblin's mount ran on, riderless, while Arnisant savaged the throat of its fallen rider. The "goblin dog" turned, running back to attack Arnisant from behind. Janneke's crossbow snapped twice, and the grotesque creature fell.

I could not see Radovan at first, but then I spied his silhouette dashing from goblin to goblin. With a slash of the big knife, he felled one. Turning, he thrust an elbow spur into the eye of another and ran on. Behind him lay a long arc of murdered goblins.

Illyria slipped. Grabbing her arm, I fell as well. The carriage roof had become slick with some foul substance. The cackling laughter of the warchanters told me the cause. I pointed at them. "There."

Illyria nodded. With her wand, she knocked two of the wretches to the ground. An instant later, I hurled a thunderbolt. The impact tossed the goblin casters into the air. They fell back limp and black, their flesh sizzling.

We climbed down from the carriage. Illyria's ghouls had cut furrows through the goblin lines, leaving only a few nearby. I dispatched two with the Shadowless Sword. Illyria shriveled another with a black ray.

"Arni, look out!" Radovan shouted.

An enormous shape bounded across the field toward the wolfhound. Unlike the hairless goblin dogs, the black hound bristled with fur. Despite the surrounding firelight, I could distinguish no eyes or teeth in its inky silhouette. It fell upon Arnisant with a savage roar. The dogs tumbled across burning patches in the grass, snarling, biting, and crying out.

Radovan would never reach him in time. I shot another volley of arcane missiles. They sank unerring into the black hound. Illyria did the same, yet still the foe tore at Arnisant, who struggled to rise. I ran toward them, but Amaranthine was faster. The tiny drake swooped into the frenzy, her agile tail flicking again and again.

"Don't!" cried Illyria. I shared her concern that the fragile drake would not survive.

A sharp whistle pierced the clamor. The black hound scrambled away. Arnisant began to chase but returned to where the drake hopped on the ground, standing protectively beside her. The dark hound ran toward its master, who stood in stark contrast against the flames.

The shadow appeared as an attenuated figure, almost but not quite human, its arms and legs too long, too thin. As the hound came near, the figure collapsed like a paper cutout of a man, vanishing. The hound leaped over the dwindling flames and vanished into the dark.

For an instant, almost as an afterimage, I saw another figure standing beyond the fire. Like the first, it was tall, but where the first appeared thin this one was hulking. It hunched over a pair of canes, as if it could not stand under its own bulk. As with the hound and its master, I could make out no details of the figure, but I felt its gaze upon me like a cold shadow on a warm day.

I raised a hand to cast a spell. It raised a hand as well, at first I thought to fling some spell back at me. Instead, it waved, one cane dangling from its thumb. The big shadow stepped back and vanished into the night.

Janneke fired her bow and Radovan threw his blades after a few retreating goblins, but the rest were dead or fled. The horses had all survived unharmed, although one was red to the fetlocks with the gore of the goblins who lay dead nearby. Goblins may hate us "longshanks," but they hate dogs more, and horses more than dogs. Before me lay the reason.

Only Arnisant had suffered serious injury, which Illyria's salve soon mended. While she tended to him, I drew the attention of her remaining ghouls and incinerated them with dragon's breath.

"We must move on," I said to the surprise of no one. Janneke and I calmed the horses before hitching them to the carriage. Illyria dispelled the burning remains of her cottage, while Radovan and Janneke stalked the field to finish the wounded goblins. By the time we were done, Arnisant whined at the carriage step until I called him inside to sit at my feet. Illyria took her place across from me. Her eyes searched my face, but I could not meet her gaze after seeing her summon the ghouls.

From the moment she admitted she was a necromancer, I knew Illyria must be capable of raising undead minions. Somehow I had hoped never to see it, and if I had to see it, I hoped she would create something simple, like skeletal automatons. Yet the sight—and especially the smell—of these ravenous cannibals, these foul devourers of flesh living or rotten . . . It was too abominable to imagine as the act of an otherwise admirable and beauteous lady.

The carriage lurched into motion. I cast a glance across the compartment to see Illyria looking back at me, a question in her eyes. I could not hold her gaze nor mask my disgust. She turned away.

Arnisant whined and nosed my leg for the sausage hidden in my coat pocket. I patted his head in sympathy and gave him a piece. "I know, my boy. Fighting goblins is hungry work."

Feeling Illyria's critical gaze upon me, I refused to meet her eyes. After the spell I had seen her cast, I would suffer none of her judgment on my diet. I bit off a hunk of sausage and chewed. It no longer tasted delicious, but it gave me some comfort.

8
Kaer Maga
Radovan

The boss told me some of the city's nicknames, since nobody remembers what "Kaer Maga" means. "The City on the Cliff" is what you call self-explanatory. So is "The Hex," on account of its six sides. Those are boring names since they mean just one thing.

"The Asylum Stone" is better because it has two meanings. You can say the big rock was where people go for sanctuary, but it's also a kind of madhouse. Me, I'm partial to "City of Strangers," on account of Kaer Maga gets plenty of visitors and each one is stranger than the last.

We started at the bottom of a cliff separating green Varisia from brown Varisia. That is, the grassy lowlands from the rocky plateau, home to the Shoanti, giants, orcs—all kinds of bad company. A thousand feet above, a little strip of wall with a few towers peeking over was all we could see of the city. The Yondabakari River poured past huge stone heads near the top of the cliff. Most of the water turned into mist along the way, raining all around us, but the main stream hit the nearby river with a roar.

Through the carriage window, the boss showed me a hand sign and tossed me a fat purse. Keeping well shy of the horses, I ran to the head of a long line of travelers. Most of them included porters carrying heavy packs or animals pulling wagons full of trade goods. They gave me nasty looks and shouted a few choice words for budging. I shot them the tines and let them see my teeth. They piped down.

At the head of the line I found the Duskwardens, tough characters who guide visitors through tunnels up to the city. They took my bribe as an insult, but they took it. I ran back to let Janneke know she could drive past the cheap folk.

The Duskwardens loaned us charms and led us through a cavern to a road winding in and out of caverns all the way up to the city. The wardens called it the Halflight Path and warned us to be quiet or else tunnel worms and other nasty critters would come eat us. Some of the tunnels were kind of worm-shaped, if they made worms as big as dragons. Maybe the Duskwardens were jerking our chains, but I didn't want to see one that big.

After a couple hours in the dark, we came out up top. All around us was a shantytown built in a gap in the city wall. The place reminded me of Korvosa's Shingles. A dozen kids ran up to the Red Carriage, offering to be our city guides. Janneke shooed them away. "Warren rats," she said. "We don't need them."

A few of the rats didn't give up until Janneke lifted her crossbow and yelled, "Rat skewers!" They scattered, but only to swarm the next group coming out of the Halflight Path.

We passed scaffolds forming like scabs over the ruins, spilling past the original line of the wall. Here and there a wall had been rebuilt, but most of the scaffolds looked as old as the ruins. Maybe somebody was trying to heal the wound to the city, but it was slow going.

We drove into a market district. "Downmarket," said Janneke, her voice muffled through the helm.

"What?"

"This area," she shouted. "It's called Downmarket."

I cupped my ear and leaned in. Janneke twisted around and socked me on the arm, a little harder than you like. She said she kept her helm on to stay ready for action. I said nobody could hear her through the faceplate. Really, I just liked watching the sun on her red-gold braids. I wasn't going to win that battle today, so I watched the people we passed in the street.

There were all different colors and kinds. I showed off the languages I'd learned by greeting people in Tian, Varisian, and Elven, except on the last one I spit by accident, and then I ran out of languages. The boss could have gone on all day. I can't remember a time when he couldn't greet some foreigner in his native tongue.

It wasn't just humans in the market. A goblin juggled hedgehogs as people threw coins at his feet. A troll dressed up like people cut itself to read auguries in its own guts, while everybody walked past all nonchalant-like. I spotted gnomes, elves, and even orcs. Not half-breeds but big-as-Shoanti green-skin howlers. One stood beside what looked to be his son on an auction block. A couple of bidders decided to split the lot. The orc's eyes welled up as he realized he and his boy were going to different masters. I had an idea how he must have felt.

I had a better idea how his kid felt.

As we rode through eastern Downmarket, high towers rose to the south, and I realized I'd seen them from below.

"Highside Stacks," said Janneke. She pointed north across a small lake to another fancy neighborhood. "Widdershins."

On our side of the lake, a huge Shoanti totem marked a gathering spot. More city guides called out to visitors, and other folk loitered, maybe waiting to meet somebody. A scar-faced Chelish woman stared at me. I stared back. She wore a long scarlet cloak and leaned against a tall silver-gray shield.

It occurred to me that the woman wasn't staring at me but at Janneke. "Somebody you know?"

Janneke shook her head. Again I wished I could see her face under that helm.

A shadow crossed over us. A boy hanging onto a giant kite soared overhead, heading toward the lake. The corner of his kite clipped the edge of an amphitheater dome, and he crashed into the water. His friends ran after him, shouting as they pushed through the crowd. He popped up a few seconds later. "I'm all right! I'm all right!" He didn't notice the water rippling behind him. I wanted to see what happened next, but the totem got between us.

There was plenty of other weird stuff to see. We passed a woman with her mouth sewn shut. A pink-haired gnome chattered nonstop at her side. A tattooed sorcerer rode by on a steel horse, a mechanical drake on his shoulder. Amaranthine chirped, and the little metal dragon puffed smoke from its nostrils.

Past the lake we entered another neighborhood.

"Hospice," said Janneke. Before I could crack wise about not hearing, she showed me a fist. I rubbed my arm and kept my trap shut.

The boss called out directions to an inn. Janneke nodded like she knew the place. Six or seven streets later, we saw it.

The place was built up around a ring of seven squat towers. There was an ancient rune carved onto the face of each tower. I knew they were Thassilonian, but I couldn't read what they meant.

"The Seven Sins," said Janneke.

"Sounds like a brothel. I'm surprised the boss picked it."

"You'd think so, but it's just a fancy inn. A wizard built the towers long ago. His heirs sold them off. They changed hands a few times before somebody got the idea of building wings of rooms between the towers and turning the whole place into an inn. Only the rich can afford to stay in the towers."

Arnisant stayed with the boss and Lady Illyria as the porters lugged the bags up to a tower. As Janneke and I pulled away on the carriage, Amaranthine flew off to perch on the boss's shoulder. The boss looked surprised, then pleased with himself. He made a bit of cheese appear in his fingers and fed it to the drake. Lady Illyria looked all jealous.

I nudged Janneke. She'd seen the look but didn't find it so amusing. I said, "You know a good stable?"

"If you don't mind paying tall stacks."

"We got them."

We'd driven the horses hard since the goblin attack. They needed more than a rest. They needed the royal treatment, and I knew the boss wouldn't mind paying top coin.

On the way to the stables, we passed the fattest wizard I ever saw. She couldn't even walk. She just floated along like some kid's escaped balloon. Instead of a nice round shape, her flesh sagged out of rips in a robe that looked more like a torn fishing net. The worst part was the leeches clinging to her flabby arms and legs.

"Bloatmage," said Janneke. Her voice was spooky inside that helm. I didn't blame the warren rats from running from her. "They use blood to fuel their magic."

"You think the boss's pal was becoming one of them?"

Since he had Lady Illyria to talk magic with, the boss hadn't been keeping me informed. Usually, he told me all about stuff even if he knew I wouldn't understand it. Sometimes I surprised him and understood it anyway. Anyway, I'd gotten used to being the one to hear it. I didn't like feeling left out.

Janneke shrugged. "I don't listen much to the magic talk."

"How come?"

"A little knowledge is more dangerous than none."

I didn't think that was true. You get a little knowledge, it's not so hard to get a little more. Still, I understood her point, and I didn't mind if we stayed out of the wizards' way for a while. "Say, once we finish with the horses, we're not really on duty anymore."

"I'm on duty until I collect my bounty."

"That could be a while. The horses aren't the only ones who deserve a little rest and relaxation."

"What you're talking about isn't rest."

"A little exercise, then. We've been sitting up here all day."

"I told you, I'm on duty."

"All right, all right." She was still mad about my cutting out on her back in Korvosa. I could tell because I'm sensitive that way.

The livery was a huge building with eight stables with separate entrances. I understood why when I saw a stable boy lead an axe-beaked riding bird out of one. In Kaer Maga, even the ponies were strange.

The hostlers named their price for looking after the team and carriage. I paid up front and promised a big tip to pamper the horses and polish the carriage.

As we walked away from the stables, we passed a skinny hellspawn with blood-red skin and a scorpion's tail. A drunken harlot hung on his arm. When he saw me, he cocked his head and squinted his yellow eyes.

I walked on.

"Do you know that fiend?" said Janneke.

"Never saw him."

"He seems to know you."

"Ignore him." I could think of half a dozen reasons why the hellspawn might recognize me, but none of them made me want to talk with him.

It'd been a long time since my devils spilled through me and into the world. They were free of me, and I was free of them.

Sometimes I wondered what mischief they were perpetrating, but mostly I tried not to think about it. I liked the idea I was a real boy, not just a pony for my devils to ride around the world—and definitely not a gate to Hell and the other place.

"There's something you aren't telling me."

She wasn't wrong about that. "You're the one who wants to keep things professional. Hell, you won't even take off that helmet. Talking to you is like talking to an iron golem."

She sighed and pulled off the helm. Beads of sweat rolled down her face. She looked left and right, then behind her. It finally hit me. She wasn't wearing the helm because she expected an ambush. It was her disguise.

"Someone's looking for you?"

"No."

I gave her my I-don't-buy-it face.

"It's nothing to worry about."

"That woman at the meeting post. You knew her."

She sighed again. "Former colleague."

"She got friends?"

Janneke nodded.

"Friends that look like that?" I pointed.

Walking toward us were two women, a red-headed Varisian and the Chelaxian we'd seen earlier. They wore swords at their hips, and both had the same kind of shield on their arms. Like Janneke, they wore mismatched armor, but I was starting to see that some pieces each of the three wore came from the same set.

Janneke turned around. "Dammit."

Three more women approached from the other side, long red cloaks flaring behind them. Two wore mismatched armor, but the tall one in the middle had the whole silver-gray suit—including an unpainted version of Janneke's helm. I bet that was how the Gray Maidens looked before they disbanded.

The tall woman took off her helm. Her short hair was thick and black, with a white streak on either side. She'd broken her nose more than once. She handed her helm and shield to the women at her sides and walked toward us alone.

"What's going on?" I asked.

Janneke shoved her crossbow and helm into my arms and stepped forward.

The two women circled each other like prize fighters, hands loose at their sides. Janneke had a good four inches on the other woman, but somehow she didn't seem any bigger.

"Kaid," said Janneke.

"Some of the girls have been hoping to see you again," said Kaid. "I told them you weren't stupid enough to show your face in Kaer Maga."

"That shows how smart you are."

"Are you back to turn in your armor?"

"Did you finally hire someone big enough to take it from me?"

"You always were a conceited, insubordinate—" Kaid grabbed Janneke around the waist and lifted her off the ground. I dropped Janneke's gear and braced for a fight, but Kaid spun her around and set her down again. "—goat-lover! I'm surprised you haven't traded it in for Hellknight armor."

"There's no need to be insulting." Janneke pounded Kaid on the back. It looked friendly, but the sound echoed off the nearby houses, and those didn't look like tears of joy in Kaid's eyes.

The other women relaxed a little, but the one holding Kaid's helmet gave Janneke the stink-eye.

Kaid nodded at me. "Who's the shaved dwarf?"

"Hey, now." If that's the way Kaid talked to her friends, I could understand why her nose was broke so much.

"This is Radovan. He's touchy about his height."

"I'm plenty taller than a dwarf."

"I'm working for Radovan's boss. Radovan, this is Faceless Kaid Brandt, my commanding officer during the queen's reign."

Kaid spat. "That Dis whore's daughter."

Janneke spat to show she agreed with that sentiment. I spat so as not to get left out.

"I see a couple of new faces," said Janneke.

"You know Cosima, Belle, and Stiletto," said Kaid. She took her helm back to the Chelaxian, Stiletto. I liked that name. Kaid nodded at the Garundi. "This here's Danai. She joined us after a raid in the Bottoms."

The Chelaxians and the Varisian looked as us like we were three-day-old trout. The Garundi bowed and touched a blue dot painted on her forehead. I tipped her a wink, but it didn't take. She looked right through me.

I picked up Janneke's stuff and gave it back to her. She scoffed at me for dropping it. Kaid led us a few streets away to a tavern. We sat down to three porter ales while Kaid's women stood guard. Janneke and Kaid said things like "long time" and "not the same" and other harmless stuff. It was enough to make me relax for a minute.

Kaid raised her mug. "Steel and gold!"

"Steel and gold!" we agreed.

"Tell me you aren't still hunting Shoanti for five gold a head," said Janneke.

"Not when something better comes along. We had a good run through the Undercity last winter. You wouldn't believe the things that live down there."

"Tunnel worms?" I asked.

"And worse things," said Kaid. "Much worse things."

"I prefer hunting two-legged prey," said Janneke. She looked over at Danai, who stood guard like a seasoned veteran. "And I don't mean capturing escaped slaves."

I didn't like the sound of that, and my expression told Kaid as much. She just shrugged. "We take the work that pays. And you came to Kaer Maga for a reason. You're on the hunt, aren't you?"

Janneke nodded. "If you and the girls aren't busy, maybe we could cut you in for, say, twenty percent."

"One-fifth? I've got more than thirty women in the company."

"Your cut would be sixteen hundred," said Janneke. "That's a lot of Shoanti heads, and all you need to do is locate our target. You find him, we'll capture him."

"Her," I said. "The boss saw through the disguise."

Janneke rolled her eyes. "All right, 'her.'"

"What's to stop me from collecting this bounty myself?" said Kaid.

"Apart from the fact that I haven't told you who he—*she*—is, I can think of three reasons. One, it pays in Korvosa."

"I hate that city."

"It's different now. Better, for the most part. Still, I don't think they'd welcome you except to a dungeon cell."

"I like it fine right here in Kaer Maga. What's the second reason?"

"You don't want to cross the man who's paying me. He's a powerful wizard."

"Sorcerer," I said.

"Whatever. He's not the kind of employer you want to disappoint, and he's got another sorcerer traveling with him."

"Wizard," I said. "That one's a wizard."

"Drink your drink," said Janneke.

"What's the third reason?" said Kaid.

"The bounty pays well only for a live capture. Not exactly your specialty."

"You make a good point. Tell you what, make our cut one-quarter. You need to check with your employer first?"

"No, the bounty's mine. He just wants to question him—*her*—first. One-quarter it is."

They punched each other over the heart and clasped hands. "Deal."

"The subject's name is Zoran, or Zora. She uses disguises to break into the homes of wizards and steal enchanted objects. We think she's looking for a buyer in Kaer Maga."

"That's a good bet," said Kaid. "But it doesn't narrow things down too much. I can think of a dozen places in Downmarket and the Promenade where someone might unload that sort of thing—and dozens more throughout the city."

"I know it won't be easy. But with more than thirty women in the band, you can cover a lot of territory. Don't try to take her—and definitely don't kill her—just let me know when you've spotted her."

"In that case, you'd better take this back." From her belt pouch she dug out a silver whistle on a chain and passed it over.

Janneke showed it to me. "This is why we want Kaid's Band for this job." Without explaining further, she hung it around her neck.

Kaid and Janneke drained their beers and ordered another round while I nursed mine and listened to their conversation. I concentrated on remembering the names of merchants and fences they knew and the places they figured on staking out. Pretty soon it was like I wasn't even at the table. Kaid and Janneke were talking like partners who'd worked together for years.

The boss and I had moments like that away from home and the nobility. Once another aristocrat showed up, though, it was back outside the tent for me and Arni. The boss called both of us his bodyguards. Mostly I didn't mind, and I knew he didn't mean it in a bad way, but it was a reminder that in Chelish society I ranked farther below a count than I did above a dog.

With Lady Illyria the boss had someone who could talk both magic and high society. Maybe I should have been happy for him, even if the two of them weren't exactly cozy since the boss called her out on conjuring ghouls. Maybe I was just jealous.

Maybe I needed to spend more time with Arni. He still looked up to me.

9
The Therassic Spire
Varian

For days I haunted the labyrinthine avenues of the Therassic Spire, a towering repository of lore nestled in the Highside Stacks of Kaer Maga. The library housed countless ancient texts, including one of the greatest collections of Thassilonian lore in existence. It was one of the best possible places to seek knowledge of the runelords.

Much of the time I spent browsing, pausing now and then to ponder the logic of a system that placed bawdy tavern songs beside chronicles of the saints. Previous visits had taught me that a subtle method lay beneath the seeming chaos, but I had yet to comprehend it. Now was not the time to spend unraveling that particular mystery.

Fortunately, the venerable librarians could guide visitors unerringly to shelves devoted to any subject, from the reports of Varisian naturalists to the poetry of ancient Vudrani philosophers. They had already led me to a trove of chronicles about the runelords, including some of the oldest records I had ever perused.

My heart pounded when I first saw an unfamiliar language etched on bronze plates. The tarnished sheets had worn thin over the ages. Because my sorcerous spells inclined more toward war than divination, to decipher the script I depended on my dwindling wizard spells. Thus, I spent a morning alternately inscribing riffle scrolls and retching into a bucket in my room at the Seven Sins before returning to the library. There I released a scroll allowing me to apprehend the meaning of any language. Unfortunately, sifting through records of crop production, road expansion, births, deaths, and tax collection did little to expand my existing knowledge, but perusing them allowed me to organize what I had already learned of Zutha and his domain.

The runelord reigned over Gastash, a region now held by the orcs. In ancient days, Gastash served as the breadbasket of Thassilon, exporting food to all the other regions. Selling to both sides in times of conflict, Zutha profited from every war between his fellow runelords, none of whom dared threaten his territory for fear of starving their own troops.

On a few points I might have admired this lord of a bountiful land. Ancient scholars speculated that Zutha was the original subject of one of my favorite aphorisms: that the quill is more powerful than the blade. Among the rulers of Thassilon, Zutha was known for scholarship, diplomacy, and exquisite penmanship. If his was the hand that composed the *Kardosian Codex*, I could attest to the latter virtue. The scythe was his sigil, although with his many rings and magical Azlanti stones he could raze villages with a gesture or render armies to dust with a glance.

In defiance of natural mortality, Zutha performed the rituals necessary to become a lich, but not the emaciated mummy popular in Avistani art. A massively corpulent man in life, he retained his obese stature in death, continuing to feast and stuff a body that no longer needed to eat. Reveling in his gluttony, Zutha never dined on the same meal twice. As the last of his humanity evaporated, he turned his appetite to "meal-slaves," indulging his cannibalism with victims from every tribe of Golarion.

I noted certain parallels between Zutha's chronicle and my own life, although most were common to the noble class. The gluttonous curse from the *Kardosian Codex* was troubling. The circumstances of my own extended life troubled me even more. I had lived as long as Benigno Ygresta, yet rather than succumb to old age I felt more vigorous—if perhaps not as fit—than I had in thirty years. The divine source of my rejuvenation—the heart of a celestial dragon, given freely as a reward for valor—bore no resemblance to the occult art of necromancy, but I could not help wondering whether I would resort to the same methods Zutha had employed if the alternative was death.

Since I had paid the exorbitant entrance fee, the venerable librarians guided me through the twisting avenues of six great floors of tomes, compendiums, dictionaries, codices, and books of all varieties. The history of the runelords had been a popular subject in recent years, especially among Pathfinders and other explorers. They cautioned me that previous visitors might have mislaid some of the volumes for which I searched.

This news encouraged me. I dared to hope that I was not alone in seeking the missing portions of Zutha's *Gluttonous Tome*. When I noticed upon my third day of research that someone had disturbed the volumes I had set aside for further study, I realized I had a rival for the information. There are no coincidences.

Thus, whenever I heard another approach, I concealed myself and spied upon him. Usually the intruder turned out to be one of the librarians escorting a guest to the desired materials. Others wandered the stacks in an effort to comprehend the repository's organization. The library's holdings were vast and varied, but not always selective. One might as soon happen upon a fawning biography of a living merchant as a chronicle of Azlant. The librarians were known to shelve the great Chelish operas beside cheap romances of the sort Lady Illyria concealed behind her fan.

At the sound of another person on the stair, I left open the book I was studying and stepped behind a shelf. Peering around the corner, I drew the Shadowless Sword an inch from its scabbard and watched.

I recognized the man immediately. Sheathing my sword, I saw that it had revealed no illusion or disguise. He was as he appeared, a human of perhaps thirty-five years. Since I had last seen him, a scar had cut across his right cheek and brow but spared his eye. He still kept a beard neatly trimmed along his jaw, and a thin braid dangled behind one ear. The most significant change was his skin, which had faded to a ghastly pallor.

Noticing the lamp I had left burning, he went directly to the spot I had vacated. When he saw which book I had left open, his head snapped up, scanning the aisles. I stepped out to reveal myself.

"Eando Kline," I said. "It has been too long."

He tensed but kept his hand from his sword. "Not long enough if the Ten sent you, *Venture-Captain*."

"I assure you they have not. In fact, I no longer serve in that capacity."

"In that case, well met." He cast a skeptical look at me. "Did you quit, too?"

"My standing with the Society has become ambiguous." That was as much as I cared to share until I resolved my misgivings about the Decemvirate, the secretive inner circle of the Pathfinder Society. Their enchanted masks concealed their identities as effectively as their private councils cloaked their motives. "I am here to conduct an investigation of my own. Is it possible you are researching the same matter?"

"You're researching runelords."

"One runelord in particular."

"Which one could that be, I wonder?"

I wanted to know more about what he knew before I shared details, so I changed the subject. "You look pale."

"You look younger than I remember," he said. "A bit fatter, too."

I tried not to bristle at that remark. "I suppose you have found the *Bone Grimoire*. Or is it the *Black Book*?"

He smiled without mirth. "The *Grimoire*. You must have read the *Kardosian Codex*."

He knew more than I dared hope. "We have much to discuss."

"Yeah, but not here. The librarians . . ."

I nodded. "I have a tower at the Seven Sins. My associates should return—"

"Until I know more about what you're really after, I'd rather this stay between just you and me."

Despite my respect for his work, I considered how much I knew about Eando Kline. That he had left the Society after a dispute with the Decemvirate was a mark in his favor, in my revised opinion of the Pathfinder inner circle. Yet I could not forget that Kline also appeared to suffer the effects of a curse. In that regard, at least, we were both compromised. The situation called for some measure of trust. "Very well. Where shall we go?"

"I know a place. You leave first. I'll join you in a few minutes."

Wary that he meant to abandon me, I considered my options. Eando Kline had always appeared to embrace the values of the Pathfinder Society: explore, report, and cooperate. Obviously we both continued to explore. For our individual reasons, it appeared neither of us obeyed the second duty. I hoped we would both embrace the third.

Arnisant awaited me outside the Therassic Spire. While the librarians accepted my word that I would not smuggle out any of their books in my satchel, they remained adamant that no non-familiar animals were permitted inside. I wondered how Lady Illyria fared in her attempts to entice Amaranthine to become her familiar. She could hardly conceal her jealousy that the drake had perched on my shoulder when we arrived. When I left the Seven Sins, Illyria declared that "we girls" were going shopping while "you boys" went to the library. I did not voice my opinion that Amaranthine would soon be immobile if Illyria did not stop bribing her with cheese and butter, much as I wished to point out she should devote more energy to minding the drake's diet and less to bothering with mine.

Illyria had been my sole source of intelligence from the Acadamae since my expulsion, leading me to wonder whether she had ulterior motives for helping me. Did she act independently or as someone's accomplice? Had Benigno Ygresta entrusted her with some task after his death? Was she, in fact, his murderer?

My disgust at her sowing ghouls' teeth tainted my opinion. In many ways, Illyria seemed *too* ideal, presenting herself as the sort of woman I find most appealing. Yet if she designed herself for me, why did she not conceal her affinity for necromancy, which so many knew I found repellent? The longer our association, the deeper her mystery.

Kline appeared as he had promised, dispelling my suspicion that he meant to slip away. With a glance over his shoulder, he led the way out of the Highside Stacks and into the Ring districts, where the streets and shops were hollowed directly out of the city's massively thick walls, and often completely enclosed. Arnisant followed at my heel.

We cut across Cavalcade, an industrial district where the sun slanted through gaps broken through the ceiling. A metallic percussion from the ironworks accompanied a drone of water-wheels, grain wheels, timber mills, and forge bellows. Coal smoke stung my nostrils before the breeze swept it away with the steam. At our feet, all the streams of Kaer Maga congregated to form a miniature archipelago before falling from the cliff to plunge into the lower Yondabakari River.

We stepped aside to make way for a pair of kiln-fired golems bearing loads of bolts and gears. We followed them into the district of Bis, its cavernous space lit by thousands of lamps hanging from the ceiling far above. While the floor where we walked was crowded, the grandest homes and businesses rose up the district walls on shelf-like balconies, some hanging directly overtop others. In Bis,

I knew, the height of one's dwelling generally correlated to one's social status.

The Kiln was a prominent exception. Inside the noisy fortress, the Ardoc Brotherhood oversaw construction of their arcane-mechanical creations, from winged spy-eyes to massive steeds and war-golems. As we passed the entrance, Kline nodded at a pair of men wearing chisels as a badge of office. The men smiled back at Kline and eyed me with suspicion. I received the message: Eando Kline had friends in Bis.

He led me to a narrow wine house across the street from the Duskwardens' Guildhouse. I directed Arnisant to stay beside the door. He sat facing the street, poised like a Tian guardian statue.

The moment we crossed the threshold, the smell of roasting meat started my mouth watering. I swallowed so hard that Kline laughed. "Hungry?"

"Ravenous."

His smile faded. "That's not a good sign, you realize."

"I am aware. Still, if I do not eat soon . . ."

"Say no more." He showed the barkeep two fingers. We went directly to the back of the establishment. There we settled into a private booth and drew the curtains.

I spoke first, recounting the tale of my unexpected bequest, the revelation of the *Codex*'s hidden text, and our pursuit of the thief Zora. The proprietor arrived with the wine, and we paused to let him pour our first goblets.

After he departed, Kline asked a few keen questions as I resumed my story, reminding me of why I held him in high regard among Pathfinders.

As my story finished, our host presented a pair of sizzling aurochs steaks with grilled tomato and herbed rice. He opened another bottle of wine and left us to enjoy our meal.

"About a year ago, I came to Kaer Maga looking for the books," said Kline. "I'd heard stories that a taiga giant had gathered all three somewhere in the Hold of Belkzen. Using the secrets of the book, he made himself a lich, raised an undead army, and declared himself Zutha reincarnated—but that boast seems unlikely to have been true."

"Why?"

"Because a band of fortune-seekers destroyed him."

"And a true runelord could destroy armies with a wave of his hand."

Kline nodded. "About fourteen months ago, some of those fortune-hunters came to Kaer Maga to sell a pair of ancient tomes. I followed them. No one in Downmarket or the Promenade could pay their price. They were starting to make appointments with wizards from Widdershins and the Stacks when one day they started asking after a thief—someone had stolen one of their books. With only one left, they went into the Undercity to negotiate with some faction of creatures dwelling in the depths. With no clue where to start tracking this thief, I followed the fortune-hunters instead."

"Into the Undercity?"

He nodded.

"Alone?"

"I didn't think of myself as alone as much as an uninvited member of their company."

I raised my goblet to his courage.

"The hard part was staying close enough while remaining hidden. A few times they got ahead of me. Once or twice I had my own troubles and had to catch up. The last time I lost them, they had just fought off a mob of undead. The last time I *found* them, there was little left of their bodies, but their belongings were more or less intact."

"You would have helped them if you could."

"Would I?" said Kline. "I wonder, myself. They were happy to sell the *Bone Grimoire* to the highest bidder, even one of the monstrous dwellers beneath the city. I doubt they even warned potential buyers of the curse. Look at me. I scare myself every time I look in the mirror."

"It could be worse," I said, patting my growing belly.

"We need to find a way to break both our curses."

"But how?" I took another bite of hot, juicy steak.

"By destroying the books," he said.

I choked on the meat. "Destroy them, you say?"

"Yes, but there's a problem." Kline took a long sip of wine before elaborating. "I haven't been able to harm the book—not with tools, fire, or acid. My research suggests that the three parts of the *Tome* are completely indestructible until recombined into the original whole. Even then, the methods for destroying it range from unlikely to ridiculous."

"For example?"

"One source suggests that the only way to destroy the tome is 'to burn it as fuel for a fire used to feed a king who has fasted from new moon to full.'"

"Is that one you deem unlikely or ridiculous?"

With a rueful smile, Kline tipped his goblet to me and drank. I finished the steak and mopped its juices with a crust of bread.

"Almost all the sources I've read seem more fabulous than factual. It's impossible to divide the history from the legend."

"No doubt Zutha's followers intentionally muddied the issue," I suggested. "After all, they were devoted to their master's return, not to the destruction of his *Tome*."

"Exactly."

"You said these fortune-hunters came to the city with two books. Where is the third?"

"I was wondering whether you'd noticed that detail. As near as I can figure, there never *was* a third book. Or rather, this giant lich didn't have it. What he had was a forgery. Perhaps it was destroyed in the battle that finished him."

"And so his killers had only two to sell. That seems likely enough."

"Before you arrived, I sent a few messages to friends in Riddleport, Magnimar, and Korvosa in case the *Codex* turned up. But now you tell me that you have it."

I nodded. "And you have the *Bone Grimoire*?"

"I'll show you mine if you show me yours."

"Agreed. But first, let's summon the proprietor. That steak was delicious, but I need to fill in the corners. Let have the same again."

He stared at me. "I'm stuffed to the eyes. You'll make yourself sick."

I began to protest, but of course Kline was right. Although I was ashamed to admit it, in the past week I had twice eaten to the point of regurgitation. At the time I blamed the incidents on my inscription of riffle scrolls, but I had to acknowledge that I had become a slave to my appetite. It was foolish to order more food. And yet . . .

"Shall we at least order dessert?"

As we passed through Downmarket, I paused to buy a skewer of fried cinnamon bread. Kline pulled me away before I could receive the order for which I had already paid. Arnisant woofed at him, resentful that I had no treat to share with him—not that I was in a sharing mood.

"We had no dessert!" Even to me the complaint sounded feeble.

"You'll thank me later," he said. "Or maybe this Lady Illyria will thank me."

"Leave her out of this," I snapped. In a cooler tone, I grumbled, "She watches my plate like a hawk."

"Sounds like a keeper."

"Did I mention she is a necromancer?"

"You said she was a benign sort of necromancer."

"Her mentor was, surely. But she sowed ghoul teeth in our battle against the goblins."

Kline hurried me along as I slowed to savor the aroma of roasting pheasants in honey. "Did the ghouls turn on you?"

"No, but they were ghouls. Cannibals! Eaters of flesh, living or rotten." I shuddered. "Abominations."

"I never took you for a Pharasmin."

"One need not devote oneself to the Lady of Graves to abhor the undead. Or do you approve of raising cadavers as servants?"

"It's not my first choice, but it gets the job done. Don't tell me you've never used distasteful methods. No one becomes a venture-captain without getting his fingers dirty. Hell, Jeggare, you're a count of Cheliax and an Acadamae wizard—or sorcerer, I suppose. You must have summoned devils."

"When necessary."

"Well."

"Well?"

"Well. That's all I'm saying."

We made a shortcut through the Warrens to reach Oriat. The western breeze lifted colorful pennants from the taverns and play-houses of the city's libertine district.

Kline's defense of Illyria's ghoul spell pricked at my unspoken fear: The more I read of the *Kardosian Codex*, the more its contents intrigued me. How long would it be before I succumbed to temptation and summoned ghouls of my own? Repugnant as that thought was, I had to admit I wanted to know whether I could cast the spells inside the *Codex*. Their formulae had less to do with the dross of flesh and bone than with pure life and death energy. For the first time, I appreciated the strange beauty in their seemingly asymmetrical logic. I could understand more clearly than ever how Benigno Ygresta had been drawn to such spells.

Kline had had the last word with me, and that troubled me as much as my misgivings about necromancy. I said, "I do not make a habit of summoning devils."

He chuckled. "Does your lady make a habit of summoning ghouls?"

I should have anticipated that reply, but we passed a woman eating a peach. I entertained a brief fantasy of snatching it out of her hand until I had to turn away from the sight. "I acknowledge your point. Still, I cannot dismiss the fact that necromancy is an inherently despicable practice."

"Many think so, but I don't know that it's a 'fact.'"

"They think so because it's true."

"And many think the same of diabolism."

"Which I also do not embrace!"

Kline stopped and looked me in the eye. "Listen, Venture-Captain—Count Jeggare, Your Excellency, Varian, all of you—I'm not saying you're wrong. I'm just saying that people like you and me—Pathfinders or whatever we are now that we've quit the Society—we've seen things most people never imagine, met people we never knew existed. I've encountered a few necromancers who weren't trying to rule the world with skeleton armies. You have, too, considering what you've said about your friend Ygresta. Now I don't know what happened to you—maybe a necromancer kicked your dog when you were a child—and I don't think it's a terrible flaw in your character that you don't like necromancy. I'm just saying that things aren't always what they seem. Keep your eyes and mind open. I don't know why I'm telling you this. You already know it all."

"Are you quite finished?"

"That was a bit of a lecture, wasn't it?"

"You went on so long that I find myself hungry again."

"Come on. My flat is just up the street. Try not to faint of hunger before we get there."

Kline's tone struck me as more collegial than impertinent. I said, "You remind me a bit of Radovan."

Kline was a decade older and, as far as I knew, fully human, but both men were similarly inquisitive and argumentative.

"Who's he?"

"My faithful companion. He warns me when he thinks I am mistaken."

"Is one man enough for that job?" he laughed. "What about the others you've brought from Korvosa?"

"The mercenary seems professional, if lacking experience in this sort of venture. Lady Illyria . . . Well, I am susceptible to her charms, so my opinion is compromised. The one I trust is Radovan."

"Is this Radovan the hellspawn who was your bodyguard in Egorian?"

"The same."

"I heard some peculiar stories about him. Something about his transforming into a devil?"

"He is no longer troubled by such occurrences."

"Still, if he's connected to Hell, I'd be worried. You're sure you can trust him?"

"With my life."

"Everyone should have such a friend," he said with a wistful note.

I patted Arnisant's head. "You need a hound."

Just in sight of the Lyceum, Kaer Maga's college of the arts, Kline led us up a narrow staircase to a flat above a bakery. The smell of fresh bread was maddening, but I stopped myself before suggesting we buy a loaf. Kline turned three different keys in three different locks. He motioned for me to wait as he dispelled a magic ward. We entered.

There were only two rooms in the flat, a bedchamber and a small sitting room. Two chairs stood across from an empty table.

A washbasin and pitcher sat beneath a window, along with a lone cabinet bearing visible wards in addition to its sturdy lock. On the floor between the cabinet and wash table lay orderly stacks of books, letters, and a few curious-looking artifacts, each with a tag attached by a piece of string.

"I see your departure from the Society has not curbed your curiosity," I said. "Or are all of these related to the *Bone Grimoire*?"

"Only a few." He set to work unlocking the cabinet and disarming its wards. "The rest are interesting things I've come across while continuing my research. I'll investigate them further once I've rid myself of this curse."

Arnisant sniffed the corners of the room and came to sit at my foot.

Kline opened the cabinet and retrieved a large rectangular parcel. He carried it to the table and removed its burlap wrapping to reveal the *Bone Grimoire* with its binding of twisted rib bones and one leathery cover I recognized as tanned human flesh.

"May I?"

"I must warn you: My pale skin isn't the only effect of the curse. Ever since I read this book, magic no longer heals me. After a scuffle with a cutpurse last week, I thought my healing salve didn't work because it had gone stale, so I went to the temple of Abadar. The clerics were so perplexed when their spells failed to cure me that they actually refunded my money."

"But the curse did not take hold until after you had read the book, yes?"

"That's right."

"Then a cursory examination should cause no harm." Despite my bravado, I suddenly feared my gluttonous impulse was only a symptom of a more complex malady. What other effects might the *Codex* have had on me? Regardless, these two volumes of the *Gluttonous Tome* were our best sources of information on the third. After a moment's hesitation, I opened the book and scanned is pages.

Despite its name, the *Bone Grimoire* contained no spells, only theorems and diagrams, philosophies and hypotheses, all concerning necromancy. I recognized the graceful handwriting as belonging to the author of the *Kardosian Codex*: Runelord Zutha himself.

Even at first glance, I found the book's conjectures dizzying with possibility. The author had an almost primal understanding of necromancy, describing the channels between the realm of negation and the material world in breathtaking simplicity. The proofs were so elegant that I no longer saw the results of necromantic spells in terms of withered flesh and yellowed bone. Instead, I had my first glimpse into a universe of binary clarity, positive and negative energy pulses competing and collaborating in the eternal conflict resulting in life force. I skimmed twenty or so pages before forcing myself to skip toward the back, where I found an appendix identical to the one in the *Kardosian Codex*.

"Each of these books contains instructions for building a golem."

"Interesting," said Kline. "You know the Ardoc Brotherhood specializes in golem construction. Could they have been prospective buyers?"

"The Brotherhood does not work in flesh, do they?"

"Good point."

"Nothing here would prove useful for their arcano-mechanical creations. Still, you raise an interesting question. Perhaps the possessors of the books came to Kaer Maga for a reason. Do necromancers still rule the district of Ankar-Te?"

Kline shuddered. "Along with the high priestess of the child-goddess, yes."

"Such individuals might well crave this sort of knowledge."

Kline nodded, his brow furrowed in contemplation as I skimmed the rest of the *Grimoire*. He masked his impatience, but I sensed his restless energy. I closed the *Grimoire* and passed it back to him. "My turn."

As I drew the *Codex* from my satchel, it lurched like a magnet held beside its polar twin. An invisible force thrust the book away from me.

Across the table, Kline struggled to keep both hands on the *Grimoire*. The books were not repelling us; they were drawn toward each other.

"Get back!" said Kline. He knocked over his chair as he wrestled with the force pulling the *Grimoire* away.

I dropped the satchel and turned my body, placing myself between the occult books. Their attractive force trembled in my chest like a fishing line through water. I could not breathe. A terrible strength wrenched me around. For an instant I saw my panic mirrored on Kline's pale face. Neither of us was willing to relinquish his book to the other.

Arnisant barked, turning in confusion as he sought a way to defend me.

Kline grimaced, locking his arms around the rebellious *Grimoire*. I did the same with the *Codex*, a terror of loss rising in my heart as I felt the pages slip through my arms. I cried out as the book leaped from my grasp.

A sickly green flash blinded me. Vertigo spun me against the wall. I tumbled to the floor on hands and knees.

My luncheon rose from my gorge. My body heaved with sickness as I emptied my stomach onto the floor and befouled my sleeves. My hand slipped in a steaming puddle of vomit. Still blinded by the flash, I heard Kline suffering a similar fate from across the room. I wretched until the last strength left my body and I flopped helpless onto my back. An instant later, a weight hit my chest.

As my vision returned, I peered at the thing squirming inches from my face. There the *Bone Grimoire* and *Kardosian Codex* coupled like fiends, gripping, biting, and penetrating each other. The twisted bones of the *Grimoire*'s spine pierced the *Codex*, blood trailing from the wounds. The pages fluttered like the wings of insects trying to escape a spider's web. After a brief and futile struggle, they lay still in submission.

The horror that had paralyzed me gave way to terror. I meant to push the combined book away, only to find myself hugging it in a possessive embrace.

"What did you do?" groaned Kline. He wiped the vomit from his mouth and glared at me, but his expression immediately changed. "Oh, Jeggare. You poor bastard."

The color had returned to his face, and I could almost feel that it had drained from mine. Standing, I felt the weight of the book in my arms mirrored as a weight upon my soul. I knew then that the combined *Grimoire* and *Codex* were now mine alone. And so were their curses.

10
Tarheel Promenade
Radovan

When the boss first told me about the passages inside the city walls, I thought of the ant kingdom in his greenhouse. Living between the walls seemed like being trapped between a couple panes of glass. But when Janneke took me into the Ring Districts, it wasn't anything like that. Sure, there were little nooks and tunnels all around the edges, but the middle opened up big enough for whole neighborhoods. Daylight seeped in through windows here and there, but the place wasn't much brighter than a starry night except along the streets lined with lamps, torches, and magic lights.

We strolled through a neighborhood called Tarheel Promenade on account of this weird black road running through the center. It was like Downmarket, but instead of all the tents and carts there were permanent shops. Every third one had a magic eye over the door, or the sign of a god and an advertisement for cures.

Tarheel was also sort of a temple district. The priests of Abadar and Asmodeus planted big temples there. The Judge of the Gods and the Prince of Law got along fine where there was money to collect and contracts to enforce.

Janneke led me down the Street of Little Gods, with dozens of little shrines and idols. The statues ranged from a six-winged snake-woman with a star for a head to four mammoths holding a globe on their backs. One I had seen before was a Tian dragon perched on a packing crate littered with rotten fruit and little yellow envelopes full of prayers. A Keleshite mystic balanced on the point of his spear. A couple of pale twins held hands and asked if we'd like to hear about the purple bower. We didn't.

"There," Janneke pointed. "The Wheel Unbroken is one of Kaer Maga's most exclusive magic shops."

The round building stood apart from its neighbors, which slumped against each other like drunks on the way home. Inside, the Wheel was cleaner and better lit than any place I'd visited lately. Cleaner and better lit than joints that usually let me in, anyway.

While Janneke wandered the shelves, I let a young guy try to sell me on a new set of leathers. All subtle-like, I worked in a few questions about whether he'd bought anything from a stranger lately. Quick on the uptake, he realized I wasn't buying and wandered off to find a better quality of customer.

I noticed a few folks going upstairs, which sounded more like a tavern than a stockroom. When I tried to head up there, a tattoo-faced elf stopped me. "Are you a wizard?"

"That depends. Some would say I'm a wizard in the sack." I winked at Janneke. She closed her eyes and shook her head. "Nah, not exactly."

He sighed. "Members of the Arcanists' Circle and guests only. You're welcome to browse down here."

The boss could check out this one later.

"I know a friendlier place," said Janneke.

She led me down a few streets to a shack painted brighter than a fortune-teller's wagon. Its name was painted in big letters: The Flame That Binds. It was another magic shop, only with less light and a lot more clutter. One wall was filled with tiny drawers with labels like "hag's tooth," "lark's tongue," and "powdered unicorn hoof." There were sections devoted to various furs, sinews, eyes, and dungs.

This joint didn't look or smell half as nice as the Wheel, but it also didn't seem half as snooty. The customers weren't just browsing the goods. A Garundi woman with a set of gold-and-ruby teeth sat down with a beady-eyed gnome to smoke a pipe and compare illusion techniques. Across the cluttered room, a gnome and a half-orc haggled over a mewling box. A fat bald fellow leaned over a counter to listen in. I didn't see any leeches, but his sweaty skin and the pink stains around his collar made me suspect he was another bloatmage.

"That's Carthagos," said Janneke. "Owner."

"You know the guy?"

"Not really. I came here to look around once or twice. Carthagos is the main seller of arcane reagents in the city. Pretty much every caster comes by eventually. As you can see, he doesn't mind a little trading between customers as long as he gets a cut."

"The guy's a fence, only right out in the open. How come we didn't come here straight away?"

"We did," she said. "Kaid did, anyway. I figured it wouldn't hurt to check in again."

"Good idea." It might look like the former Gray Maidens were getting along, but Janneke went freelance for a reason. I wasn't going to trust Kaid and her girls to play straight with us until I knew that reason. Still, they were the only local backup we had. "Keep that whistle handy."

Janneke touched the silver whistle hanging around her neck. Every member of Kaid's Band had one just like it. It was like a dog whistle. Nobody could hear it unless they were wearing one as well. Then—no matter how far away they were—they knew exactly where you were.

Over at the counter, the hagglers agreed on a price. The half-orc counted out coins. Carthagos kept a few and pushed the rest to the gnome, who slid over the box. The half-orc opened the lid and licked his lips before closing it and walking away.

"Welcome!" Carthagos had a big voice and an accent I couldn't place. "It is always good to see a new member of Kaid's Band."

"An old one," said Janneke. She cleared her throat, seemed embarrassed. "Former member."

The big fellow eyed the helm she held at her hip. "You have been in here before. Shopping for crossbows, I think."

"That's right."

"I have two new cases of bane quarrels," he said. "And if you're looking for something special, I have several new slayers."

"No, I can't afford—"

"You know, I might be interested, and I *can* afford 'em," I said. Janneke squinted down at me. "The boss likes everybody to have what they need in case we get into a bad situation."

"Excellent!" Carthagos rubbed his chubby palms together. "Are you hunting wyverns? Orcs? The undead beneath the city, perhaps?"

"Let me think on that. Got any enchanted darts?"

"I have some Tian throwing stars. Will those do?"

"Perfect. And how about some healing ointment?"

"A batch fresh from the Temple of Calistria!"

"I'm going to need all of it."

"All?" He started to look dubious.

I showed him one of my heavy purses. He didn't look impressed until I spilled out the coins: platinum, each with a sapphire chip in the middle. He cast a little spell to make sure they were real, and *then* he looked impressed.

"Right away, sir."

"There's just one other thing," I said. It'd be easier now that he liked the taste of the hook in his mouth. "I've been looking to buy a few particular items that came on the market not too long ago. The seller arrived just a week or so back, but I don't think she's found anybody who could meet her price."

"I know just who you mean," said Carthagos. Before I could blink twice, he'd fetched the bolts, the throwing stars, and the healing ointment and was humming as he tallied the cost with a grease pencil. He held up the paper to show me the total. Even for all this stuff, it looked high. He smiled at me.

"You know just who I mean?"

"Most assuredly."

"And?"

"No doubt the details will come to me the moment my mind is no longer occupied with this transaction."

"I get you." I knew better than to lean on a wizard, so I counted out the coins until my purse looked puny. Even if Carthagos's information was no good, we needed the stuff. The moment I paid, Janneke began loading the magic bolts into a cylinder.

"There was a Varisian man here yesterday," he said. "Small, affecting a hoarse voice. He did not give his name, but he had a Korvosan way of speaking."

"How do you mean?"

He called the Shoanti 'horsers' and referred to gold coins as 'sails,' for example."

I nodded.

"He showed me a conjuring brazier, an enchanted figurine, and a scrying orb. They were excellent pieces, but I was disinclined to meet his price. I offered to line up a buyer in return for a commission. He acted as though he suspected a trap. He left at once, and I have not seen him since."

"This figurine, did it have a base about this big?" He nodded at the rectangle I made with my thumbs and fingers. "And did this brazier have three round legs?"

"Just so."

"I don't suppose you know where he would have gone next."

"I have a very good idea," said Carthagos. "He asked where he might find Gadka Burtannon, and I replied that one may invariably find his cart of frauds and overpriced cantrips at the corner of Fever Street and Half-a-Chicken Walk."

"You know the place?" I asked Janneke.

She nodded. I noticed she'd finished loading her ammunition cylinders and had them back in her pack.

I pocketed the throwing stars and ointment. "Nice doing business with you, Carthagos."

"Come again," he said. "And happy hunting."

We hustled down Tarheel Promenade, cut over to Fever Street, and kept our eyes peeled for anything that looked like half a chicken. We spotted the wagon first. I took Janneke's arm and guided her into an alley across the street.

"What's the idea?" she said.

"Is that Gadka?" I nodded toward the fellow peeling the tarp off of the wagon.

"Could be."

The burly guy kept his brown beard nice and short, but he wore one of those tall pointy hats that actors playing wizards wear. Just above the wide brim, a ring of eyes ran around the cone. They moved, watching the people passing by. Something about him put me off, and it wasn't the hat. "He's a dwarf."

"What have you got against dwarves?"

"It's the other way around. They're mad at me."

"What did you do?"

"It wasn't my fault. Anyway, they're overreacting."

"I want to hear the rest of this story, but we're on the job."

"Don't you ever relax?"

"Relaxing is how you lose your quarry." She pointed down Fever Street. "Look."

A cloaked and hooded figure strolled in the general direction of Gadka and his wagon. It was too warm for a cloak and too dry for a hood. I couldn't see much of the face behind a bushy beard and a fat red nose, but "he" stood the right height for Zora. The clincher was the staff he carried. Even with a sack wound over the top, there was no mistaking Zora's flag.

"Gotcha, sweetheart."

Janneke cranked the launcher on her crossbow. Just as I was about to say it made too much noise, Zora looked right at us. Her eyes went wide. The beard slipped. She turned and ran.

I plucked a riffle scroll from my sleeve and snapped it off. Janneke stuck the whistle in her mouth and ran, blowing on it. Her cheeks puffed out, but I didn't hear a sound. Once the running magic filled my feet, I sprinted past her.

Zora must have remembered my fleet-foot spell from last time. She gestured and said a word, and then she was a blue-gray weaving through pedestrians. She jumped onto a moving wagon, ran across the back of the giant lizard pulling it, and darted down an alley toward the central districts.

I paused to put some jump in my legs with another riffle scroll. Janneke caught up. I pointed her in Zora's direction and ran up the nearest tenement staircase, taking the steps six at a time until I reached the roof. Since it never rained inside the Ring, the roofs here were mostly nice and flat. There weren't any shanties, but there were some support pillars, and here and there a stairway or ramp went all the way up through the ceiling. Still, there was less in my way than there was back on the Shingles in Old Korvosa. This would be easier.

I sprinted across to look down at the Tarheel Promenade. To the northeast, a couple of leather-strapped boys were picking themselves off the ground, cursing at someone who'd just turned the corner.

"This way!" I couldn't see Janneke, but I hoped she could hear me. I was starting to think I should have got myself one of those whistles.

I jumped the gaps between the buildings like they were potholes. Between the fleet feet and the grasshopper legs, I felt ambitious. At a wide street, I jumped in a high arc all the way across to a Tian-style roof. I landed hard. Tiles crumbled beneath my weight. I slid down but managed to keep upright. Looking around,

I caught another glimpse of Zora's blue cloak. She'd doubled back on us and was heading into the next Ring district.

"Back this way!" I ran out of roof and braced myself for the drop.

"Sell me your dead!" cried a man pulling a cart below me. "Or bring home a fresh one, no questions asked!"

I landed on his cart, barely avoiding the gray-green carcasses. "These don't look so fresh." I jumped away before the stink made me puke.

Zora had disappeared again. I knew she hadn't got past me, and I didn't see her to the south. I ran north.

Up ahead, a flat-topped pyramid rose almost to the ceiling of the ring. A parade of worshipers marched past, trampling a blue cloak and what looked like a false beard.

Zora had ditched her disguise.

She wouldn't drop her flag, I bet. Looking for anything like a spear or a pole, I ran to the next intersection. Zora was nowhere in sight. Just as I was winding up a good string of curses, Janneke shouted from the next street inward. "Over here!"

The bounty hunter had already busted through a group of Vudrani women in bright silks. With that helmet on, she probably didn't even see them. I ran the gauntlet of Vudrani curses and shaking fists to join Janneke.

Halfway up the next street, a woman wearing Gray Maiden greaves waved us on and yelled, "She's heading into Oriat!"

We ran through a street full of people who whistled and clicked through lips sewed shut. I couldn't understand what they were saying, but somebody had just ruffled their feathers.

We followed the trail of agitated whistlers to a wider street. There we spotted Zora sprinting through the crowd. She'd held onto her flag, like I'd guessed.

Zora crashed into a street fiddler, interrupting his song. That didn't make much difference, since music and laughter spilled

LORD OF RUNES 171

down from all Oriat rooftops, along with enough rush light to make the streets bright as early dusk. Now that we'd spotted her, Zora would have a hell of a time disappearing again.

She ran toward a shop painted with colorful designs—lightning bolts, magic sigils, animals, religious signs, all kinds of stuff. Without breaking stride, Zora yelled, "Blanks coming your way, Bull, looking for trouble!"

Janneke cursed and swapped out the load on her crossbow. I ran faster, my feet still fleet, but tattooed men and women spilled out of the ink shop to cut me off. Half underfed arty types, half street toughs, they all had tattoos, piercings, brands, or more painful-looking changes to their bodies.

A couple hard men moved toward me. Behind them, a shirtless half-orc pointed at me. "Leave my kids alone, 'spawn."

With a silent prayer to Lady Luck, I poured on the speed and jumped. The magic sent me sailing ten feet above their heads. I gave them a little wave as I flew past.

I would have made it if it wasn't for that one damned kid.

He wore a pair of bright green thigh-high boots with magic of their own. He leaped straight up and caught me by the ankle. We fell down together. Before we hit the street, I kicked the grin off his face. He lolled on the ground moaning about a missing "toof" while I snapped back onto my feet.

The other kids closed in, but I swept the legs out from under the first two and cracked the third one's jaw. That made the others hesitate long enough for me to run again. Without green-boots to stop me, they could only eat my dust.

Behind me, I heard the snap of Janneke's crossbow and the clatter of wooden balls pelting the kids. I glanced back long enough to see her scattering them.

"Go!" she yelled. "Get her!"

The tip of Zora's flag disappeared around another corner. I zipped around the corner in time to see where she'd make her next turn. She looked back, face scrunched with worry. Sweat pasted a few strands of black hair to her cheek. She was panting, but she wasn't running so fast anymore. Her spells were wearing off. Mine were going strong. She must have barely been a wizard.

Zora ran northwest, toward the Ring's outer wall. A fresh breeze lifted the streamers and pennants hanging from the corners of every building. She hesitated before a fire-blackened monastery surrounded by a low wall. She looked afraid of the place, which I had to admit looked pretty scary. She looked back at me, made a decision, and vaulted over the wall.

"I'm not going to hurt you, girl," I yelled. "I just want my cards!"

Zora made it halfway through a crumbling courtyard before three blurred figures intercepted her. Three men in brown robes and black leathers stood in fighting stances, half crouched. I didn't recognize their style, but they were definitely monks.

I ran up and grabbed Zora by the arm. She flinched like she expected me to hit her, but I pulled her back and put myself between her and the monks. I sank into the stance my evil old master taught me back in Quain. The fact was, all of my best moves died with the devil body I was wearing back then, but these guys didn't know that.

"You will never reach the seal," said one of the monks. He peered at me, all judgmental, from under a blue-and-black headband. "We were warned of your attack, Scions."

"Who're the Scions? We were just—"

I caught more movement out of the corners of my eyes. More brown-robed monks appeared, fading into view as they stepped out of the shadows of the ruins. They formed a loose circle around the five of us. I noticed two things then, both at about the same time, both too late to stop what happened next.

First, the newcomers had yellow headbands instead of blue ones.

Second, one of the new arrivals—a scar-faced redhead—appeared like magic right behind the monk I was talking to. He was already drawing back a knife, leaving a bright red smile under the blue monk's chin.

"Eámon!" yelled another blue monk. "Traitor! Murderer! Wretch—"

A yellow monk caught him in a chokehold. A couple more closed in on the other blue monk, who turned to keep them at bay.

"Aldair will do," said Red. He flipped his dagger like a dandy and caught it like an assassin. "What about you, hellspawn? Or do you want to know what's behind the seal?"

"What are you talking about?" said Zora.

"Ah!" said Aldair. He spun his dagger again, the point on the tip of his finger, which told me he had great balance, a flair for the dramatic, and a knife that needed sharpening. "For hundreds of years, the Brothers of the Seal obeyed our elders' orders without question, defending an ancient seal that lies deep below our monastery. Eventually some of us began to question what was behind it—what was so important as to require our constant devotion and protection. And when we did, our elders said, 'Do not ask why. You are sworn to obey, not to ask questions.' Tell me, what would you do in our place?"

"Listen," I said. "We've got nothing to do with this . . . this whatever-it-is. If it's all the same to you, we'll just be on our way—"

"Ah, but it's not the same, is it?" said Aldair. "One does not come between the traditionalists and the Scions without making a choice. Even the Duskwardens know better. So now you need to choose."

"What?" said Zora.

Aldair offered me his knife. I got the picture. His buddies dragged the blue monk over, pulling his head back to give me a good shot at his throat.

"No!" shouted the blue monk's last pal. He'd kept the Scions from grabbing him, but he couldn't reach his buddy.

Aldair watched me looking down at his knife. The tip might have been dull, but the edge did a neat job on the man he'd just killed.

"You can't be serious," said Zora. "It's murder."

"You don't have to tell me, sweetheart. I grew up on Eel Street, where it took two murders to pay rent. If you were *real* lucky." I drew the wings of Desna over my heart, hoping she'd get the message.

She recoiled from me, but her eyes flicked down. Maybe she got it. Maybe she didn't. With or without her, I was going to need that luck.

Aldair smiled and shoved his knife at me. I waved it off, and his smile vanished. Before he could get riled, I tugged the big knife out of its sheath.

"This is what we call a knife back in Egorian," I said.

Aldair smiled at that. I smiled back at him. Then I smiled bigger, and he yelped.

Zora pulled lose the strap holding her flag closed. She whipped out the staff and caught one of the Scions holding the blue monk. At the same time, I flipped a throwing blade at the other one. His head snapped back, blood spouting from his eye. Blue monk gave them both an elbow to the gut and broke free.

"Thank you!" he shouted. "My name is Balthus."

"I'm Ordun," shouted the other one. He took advantage of the surprise to kick out the knee of one of the Scions after him. "We will not—"

A Scion cracked him on the back of the skull with a round-house kick. He didn't finish what he was saying. The way his head hit the stones, I didn't figure he ever would.

I was ready for Aldair to move on me, but he slipped away instead. One of his mooks came for me. I caught his hand and bent his wrist. One kick to kneel him, one to take his breath, and one to knock him out. So far, so good.

Somebody I didn't see coming kicked me in the breadbasket. Another one planted a knife in my thigh—nowhere near an artery. I kissed the air to thank Lady Luck.

Turning, I tried to kick the one who stabbed me, but Zora hit him first quicker. She whirled her flag around. The cloth snapped out like a living thing, wrapping around the Scion's ankle. By herself she was too little to move him, but the momentum of the flagstaff was enough to pull his leg right out from under him.

In the same motion, Zora whipped the flag up and over to my other side between me and another Scion. The four eyes of Desna—sun, moon, and two stars—looked back at me.

The Scion's fists punched into the banner but only made shallow dents, like he was punching into a curtain made of chainmail. There was some big magic going on there.

"Hit him, Radovan!" said Zora. "Through the flag!"

I didn't think about whether to trust her. I just did it.

I punched through the fabric. Instead of a hard curtain, my fists pushed through like there was nothing but thin cotton between us. My first punch broke teeth. The second made a hollow *thunk.* Zora snapped up the flag. On the other side, the Scion lay unconscious on the courtyard.

"Look out!" she said, whirling away to defend herself from a couple more monks.

I turned, hopping to spare my injured leg. Another Scion cartwheeled toward me, which looks great but gives the target lots of time to move. Only I didn't move. Catching his rhythm, I closed in just before he got into kicking range. One hard boot to the kidneys, and he went down.

"Hold it right there!"

Everybody stopped fighting as Janneke leveled her crossbow at one of the Scions. Beside her stood Kaid and three of her mercenaries. Six more were running up from the Warrens.

The Scions ran for it, except for two who couldn't stand. Ordun finished off the fallen with two swift stamps to the neck. After the first one, Zora screamed, "No!" That didn't stop him. Considering what the Scions had done to the his buddies, I wasn't going to judge.

"I said hold it!" yelled Janneke. With her helmet on, her voice sounded scary enough that I'd have obeyed. On the other hand, I'd seen her shoot that crossbow with the helmet on, so I took a couple big steps away from Ordun.

"You have no authority here, Maiden," he said. He put a fist against an open hand and bowed to me. "Thank you for your help, brother. Return to us when you are prepared to defend the Seal."

He ran deeper into the ruins while Kaid's girls grabbed Zora. They took away her flag, a couple of belt pouches, and six concealed blades.

"Gimme those." I took the pouches from the mercenary called Stiletto and found my harrow deck in one. I kept my deck and showed it to Zora. "That's all you had to do. There wouldn't have been all this trouble if you'd just given them back in Korvosa."

Arni woofed from down the street. Behind him came the boss and a man I didn't know. They both looked like they'd been through the wringer, but the boss had it worse. His shirt was wet, and hung open under his coat. When they got closer, I saw that his eyes looked too dark, the irises too big and the whites bloodshot.

"How'd you find us?" I said.

"I followed the sound of riots." His voice was weak, but it was definitely a joke.

At least he still had his sense of humor. But I couldn't see so much as the shadow of a smile on his face, and his eyes stared through me, not at me.

"Eando Kline, this is my man Radovan."

Eando gave me a nod. I gave him one back, wondering whether he'd been fighting the boss or fighting beside him. The boss introduced the mercenaries and then turned to Zora.

"I presume this is the notorious burglar of arcane artifacts."

She kept her chin up, but the little Varisian looked tiny between a pair of Kaid's big Maidens.

"Have you nothing to say for yourself?" said the boss.

"Your hellspawn has his cards back, and all of my money is in that purse. There's nothing more to take."

"What of the items you stole from Professor Ygresta's laboratory?"

She opened her mouth to speak but shut it again. Her teeth clacked so loud I felt my own teeth hurt.

"For whom did you commit these thefts?"

Again with the mouth, open and shut. *Clack!* She winced.

The boss and Eando cast spells at the same time. Not different spells, I could tell by the words and gestures, but exactly the same spell. They squinted at Zora, looking so much alike it would have been comical another time.

The boss said, "She is bound by a geas."

Eando turned to the rest of us and explained. "A geas is a magical compulsion. It prevents her from speaking on certain subjects, or forbids her from performing specific deeds."

"I know what a geas is," I said. It was true!

Eando turned to the boss. "I can't break a geas. Can you?"

The boss shook his head. "Nor can Lady Illyria, I fear. Do you know someone in Kaer Maga who can?"

Eando cocked his head to the side. "As a matter of fact, I might, and it's someone you already want to meet. But we'll have to go without these mercenaries."

"Fine by me," said Kaid. She put a hand out to the boss. "My job is done."

The boss fished a pair of heavy purses from his satchel and handed them to me. I passed them to Kaid. She passed them to Stiletto, who started counting right there in the ruined courtyard of the Brothers of the Seal, which I didn't think was a very good idea. She was fast, anyway, and she nodded at Kaid.

"A pleasure to serve you, Excellency," said Kaid. "If you need anything else, you can always find one of my women at the Meeting Post."

Janneke slapped a pair of manacles on Zora's wrists.

"Not so rough, you hill giant," said Zora.

"Yeah, take it easy," I said.

Janneke gave me the shut-up face and turned back to Zora. "So you can talk after all. Where are the things you stole?"

"I hid them. Let me go, and I'll split the money with you."

"Maybe we'll do that later. Were you working for Ygresta or somebody else?"

She opened her mouth and snapped it shut again.

"There is no point questioning her before we can break the geas," said the boss. "Dare I hope this oracle can break my curse as well?"

"He might. He's very old." Eando peered at the boss. "Not as old as you, of course."

The boss didn't react. A remark like that usually got at least a death stare.

"Was that a crack?" I asked. "That sounded like a crack."

"You're were right about him." Eando patted me on the shoulder. "He's smarter than he looks."

"He'd have to be," said Janneke. "Wouldn't he?"

11
The Bottoms
Varian

My companions' chatter ebbed at the shore of my perception. They did not distract me so much as serve as a reminder that I was not alone, despite my growing fear of solitude in a world I only now began to realize I never understood.

Combined with the *Kardosian Codex*, the *Bone Grimoire* offered me a surprising new perspective on the continuum of life and death. Though I pored over the combined texts, I had still only barely glimpsed the truth. What I had previously perceived in stark terms of darkness and light, I now saw as the nadir and acme of all energies in the universe, extremes between which all truths lay.

Compared with such pure ideas, the exotic sights, smells, and sounds of Kaer Maga were nuisances—even the voices of my companions.

"To the Shoanti, we're all *tshamek*," Kline was saying. As we walked through the noisy avenues of the Bottoms, he prepared the others for our meeting with the oracle. "That means 'outsider,' but not in a good way."

"What's the good way to be an outsider?" said Radovan.

"Shut up," said Janneke. "I'm listening to this."

He winked at her. "You take off your helmet, you hear all kinds of things."

To ensure that none of the residents of the Bottoms would mistake Janneke for one of Kaid's Band, who were known to raid the district for escaped slaves, I insisted she buy a change of clothing. A mercenary's excuse would do little to calm the hatred the residents held for their former owners and those hired to recover their property.

The bounty hunter had left her crossbow and armor behind, carrying only a single club at her hip while wearing tough leathers. The reinforced shoulders of her jacket had been dyed blue, and the craftsman had sewn a tooled patch of a firepelt cougar on the back. The feline image combined with Janneke's towering stature to give the impression of one of Taldor's Ulfen Guard, famous across Avistan for their sole duty: protecting the Grand Prince from his own disgruntled subjects.

"I think she looks beautiful," said Lady Illyria. Amaranthine perched on the shoulder of the lady's own new jacket, which I noted had been reinforced for exactly that purpose. "It was quite a challenge to find becoming clothes for a woman of such . . . heroic proportions."

"It was a nice change of pace," said Janneke. "And you were generous to pay for me, my lady. Thank you."

"Call me Illyria, won't you?"

When I entrusted Illyria with helping Janneke, I had not anticipated the women would spend the better part of a day among the stalls of Downmarket and the shops of Tarheel Promenade. Perhaps the drake's attention was not the only prize Lady Illyria intended to wrest from me. Now I would have to take care that I said nothing in Janneke's presence that I did not wish Lady Illyria to know.

While the women perused the markets, Radovan and Kline acquired the gifts for our introduction to the oracle, leaving me and Arnisant to guard the prisoner. Arnisant's mere presence so intimidated Zora that—apart from an ill-conceived experiment with a letter opener to confirm Kline's warning that the curse I had usurped from him prevented magical healing (it did)—I spent the time engrossed in the theories of the *Bone Grimoire*.

"I think you both look real nice."

"Why, thank you, Radovan." Illyria favored him with a smile. Despite my faith in Radovan's loyalty, I disliked her flirtatious attention to him. She did not realize how susceptible he was to feminine charms. Or so I hoped.

"Aren't you also a tshamek, Eando?" said Radovan.

"I'm the *nalharest* of Tomast from the Sklar-Quah."

"What's a nalharest?" said Radovan. "What's a Tomast? What's a Sklar-Quah?"

"Nalharest is a word more or less equivalent to 'blood brother.' Tomast is a warrior of the Sun Clan, the Sklar-Quah. The oracle we're going to see is an elder of the Skoan-Quah, or Skull Clan."

"Skull Clan?" said Janneke. "That sounds ominous."

"Not the way you might think. The Skoan-Quah are guardians of the Shoanti burial grounds. They commune with their ancestors through animal spirits. They're fierce when defending their people, but they aren't necromancers."

Lady Illyria cleared her throat. It was a practiced sound. Musical. Rather fetching.

"Begging the lady's pardon," said Kline.

"Considering the circumstances, the lady pardons you."

"The Skoan-Quah are destroyers of the undead, so it might be best if you don't mention your specialty."

"But of course," said Illyria. "On first acquaintance, a lady never talks politics, religion, or the dark arts."

The conversation waned as we passed a clamorous smithy. It seemed every second building in the Bottoms housed a cobbler, wainwright, cooper, or other artisan. It was no coincidence that many of the district's residents were escaped slaves who sought refuge among those who called themselves Freemen, defenders of those who escaped the slavery permitted elsewhere in the city.

Kline had already explained the conflict between the slavers and Freemen, but I watched Radovan for a reaction. His mother had sold him into slavery as a child. One of the reasons he had agreed to work for me was that, unlike my peers, I had never owned a person and never would. In Egorian, Radovan tended to treat slaves with a certain wounded scorn. I often wondered whether that disdain was sincere or a cover for rebellious yearnings. His expression offered me no clue.

In its own hideous way, *Gluttonous Tome* was making a slave of me. The thought that I could no longer trust my appetites and desires horrified me. Yet before I could long dwell on that comparison, I realized its fault. A book of arcane secrets enthralled my imagination and compelled me toward gluttony. My captor was the power of a long-dead necromancer, my shackles formed of magic. Fellow humans had claimed ownership over Radovan. I had been trapped by a curse, but he had been betrayed by his own family. No matter how wretched my current predicament, I could not compare it to his.

"What's this oracle's name?" said Radovan.

"I don't know. Many Shoanti don't share their birth names with tshamek. They have names based on their role in the Quah, or from some memorable deed. The oracle's daughter Kazyah, for example, is 'the Night Bear.'"

"Because she's cuddly like a bear cub?"

"Give it a rest." Janneke punched him in the arm. Radovan grinned. Doubtless he had hoped for such a reaction.

"Because when she was a teenage girl, her tribe sent her into a cavern deep in the Mindspin Mountains. They stood vigil for days, refusing to let her emerge until she'd killed an animal and brought back its skull. Most Shoanti braves bring back the skulls of lizards or giant bats, sometimes animals that were already dead. Kazyah brought back the head of a giant cave bear, its blood still dripping from her klar."

Radovan whistled his appreciation. "What's a klar?"

"Would you stop interrupting him?" said Janneke.

"A klar is a Shoanti weapon. You'll see one at the yurt."

"What's a yur—? Ow! Not so hard!"

"Go on, Kline," said Janneke.

"The oracle is very important, both among his people and in the Bottoms, where he helps the locals. Does everybody have the gifts I gave you?"

Everyone else nodded.

"What about me?" said Zora. She carried her cloak over her wrists to hide the manacles Janneke had placed on her. The bounty hunter remained close by her side.

"You don't need a gift. Until the oracle removes your geas, you're *skentok*."

"What does that mean?"

"Literally, it's a child who's been kicked in the head by a goat. Still functional, just not very useful."

"Typical horsers," spat Zora.

"And none of your Korvosan slurs. We have to be polite. The good news is, polite for the Shoanti mostly means keeping your mouth shut. Don't stare at Kazyah's tattoos. Don't look her in the eyes. And whatever you do, Radovan, don't mention you're from Cheliax. Apart from your spurs and those teeth, you look more Varisian, so you've got that going for you. Just don't mention where you were raised."

"Not a problem," he said. "But what about the boss?"

"I'm hoping we can smooth that over." He turned to me. "How's your Shoanti?"

"Good, but I speak a Lyrune-Quah dialect."

"That's fine. The oracle's father was from the Moon Clan, and the cave bear is one of their totems. Some mistake Kazyah for Lyrune-Quah because of her bearskin cloak and helm."

"Another helmet fancier." Radovan nudged Janneke. "You two ought to get along."

Janneke pointed to a dome-shaped yurt. "Is that it?"

"That's it," said Kline.

A fence surrounded the aurochs-hide tent on three sides, creating a yard containing a cook fire, a water barrel, and a pair of tethered goats. Just outside the fence stood a man and a young girl, anxiously watching the closed yurt flap. Inside the fence, an enormous woman sat on a log beside the fire.

Nearly my height, she appeared twice my weight, all of it muscle. She wore dark buckskins over a homespun tunic, both sleeveless. Her biceps would have shamed a stevedore. Behind her lay a bearskin cloak with a preserved head for a helmet. One of the massive mauls the Shoanti call earth breakers lay on its head beside her. From the butt of its handle hung a bladed buckler crafted from the head of a horned spirestalker gecko.

"*That* is a klar," I told Radovan.

"I want one." He was gazing at the woman, not the klar.

"Don't stare."

I could hardly stop myself from doing the same. Every inch of the woman's exposed skin had been tattooed. Black ink made a death's head of her face. Along her arms, Shoanti warriors and shamans battled armies of the undead. Great spirits of stone rose up to fight beside them as they summoned storms and earthquakes to devour their foes.

We walked toward the yurt, careful to stop outside the unmarked fourth border of the fence.

"I greet you, Kazyah, Night Bear." Kline slapped his chest as he addressed her in Shoanti.

"Be welcome, my cousin." The woman rose from the log. Her long black hair spilled down to her waist. Her facial tattoos made it difficult to judge her age, but I estimated she had lived closer to fifty than forty years.

"This is my friend, Varian Jeggare, a Pathfinder like me."

"Wielder of claw and thunder," I spoke in her native tongue and proffered the pouch Kline had purchased. "I greet you with a gift of salt."

Kazyah regarded me. Her eyes lingered on my satchel, not my sword. She looked at Arnisant, who sat at my heel. With a barely perceptible nod, she accepted the parcel and said, "Be received, stranger."

Kline named the others, except for Zora. In turn, each offered a gift of corn, leather, and smoke. Kazyah showed more interest in Amaranthine than in Lady Illyria. She locked eyes with Janneke, but the bounty hunter looked away first, for which I credited her professionalism. At last, Radovan lit the pipe and drew on it before passing it to Kazyah.

Kazyah puffed on the pipe and eyed Radovan before completing the ritual and accepting the pouch he held out, which he had filled with coins rather than tobacco. She felt its weight and said, "I accept your gifts. Sit. The oracle will see you soon."

She sat on the log, leaving enough room for someone to join her. While the rest of us sat on the ground, Radovan looked to me. The Shoanti protocol eluded me, so I replied with a subtle shrug. With a shrug of his own, Radovan sat beside Kazyah. He nodded at her weapons and said, "Nice klar."

Beside me, Eando choked.

Kazyah leaned over, looming over Radovan more by mass than by stature. She peered over his shoulder down the back of his jacket. "Nice tail."

Radovan pulled the big knife from its built-in sheath. He offered it to her grip-first. "Want to hold it?"

I glanced at Kline to see whether Radovan was insulting the oracle's daughter. Kline looked back, equally nonplussed. By the time I had exchanged similar glances with Lady Illyria, Janneke, and even Zora, Radovan was examining Kazyah's klar while she studied the scarred and spell-inscribed surface of his blade.

A pregnant woman emerged from the yurt, bowing thanks to the occupant before rejoining her family at the fence. Kazyah returned Radovan's knife and said, "Wait here."

She went into the yurt and closed the flap. All eyes turned back to Radovan, who appeared puzzled by our attention. "What?"

The rest of us could only shake our heads. We sat in silence until Kazyah opened the tent flap and beckoned us to enter. I bade Arnisant to sit outside the yurt.

Inside, an old man sat across a circle of stones. He looked perhaps seventy, but the lines of his face indicated a weight of hardship as well as years. Beside him, an aromatic steam rose from a simmering pot. On the other lay jars of colored sand and three stacks of books bound in tooled leather.

Within the circle lay a sand painting. Its colored patterns formed the image of a sunset over red hills. At intervals around the circle lay six wolf pelts. Kazyah knelt beside the old man and fanned the steam toward his face. He leaned in to breathe deep as we took our places.

Hide shields and fetishes of dyed string and bone hung from the yurt walls. Above our heads, gourds dangled among glowing glass spheres in nets. The smell of roast meat and soured goat's milk lingered in the yurt, along with a fainter scent of tobacco.

The oracle spoke in a reedy voice.

"I have prepared for this day since first meeting this *skentok*." He nodded toward Zora, who jutted a resentful chin at the term. I had not even considered that the thief would have visited the oracle, but it made sense if she had been sent to find the *Kardosian Codex*.

The oracle waved a leathery brown hand above the sand painting. With a soft hiss, the colors shifted to form an image of a bearded man standing before the yurt, holding out an empty hand. Zora's distinctive scarf betrayed the figure's true identity. "She came to me with a false face. She gave me a false name. She had stolen one part of the terrible book, and she wished to know where to find the others. I warned her of its dangers, but she would not hear me. I sent her away."

He waved his hand. The yurt remained, but the visitor changed into the stylized but unmistakable likeness of Eando Kline.

"Later Eando Kline came to me. He too had found a part of the book and wished to be rid of it. Because he is nalharest to the Sklar-Quah, I tried to help. But the curse of the *azghat* was too strong for me to break."

"What's an azghat?" said Radovan.

"Hush," Illyria whispered in his ear.

I said, "Azghat is the Shoanti name for the runelords."

"They are demons," said Zora. All eyes turned to her. She looked away, appearing to regret drawing our attention.

The oracle gestured above the circle of sand. "When Eando Kline left my yurt, my ancestors kept watch over him." The sands shifted to depict Kline reading books from the Therassic Spire. They shifted again to show him consulting sages in Widdershins. They changed again, this time showing me and Kline as we struggled to hold onto the *Codex* and the *Grimoire*. "When I saw the reunion of two parts of the terrible book, I knew you would come to me."

He waved the sands into an image of a fertile landscape dotted with great cities.

"To understand what I will tell you, you must know the history of our land. Once, all were part of the Empire of Thassilon. It began with the wizard-king Xin."

The sands formed the image of a tall man with the distinctive Azlanti features: purple eyes, a regal nose, and long black hair with a widow's peak.

"Xin led thousands of followers to this land to form his own kingdom. His knowledge was great, but he consulted wise and powerful allies."

The oracle's hand moved, and an image appeared of Xin addressing five dragons with scales of brass, bronze, copper, silver, and gold.

"Xin set before his people the example of the goddess Lissala, who in those days represented the best qualities of just rule." In the sand, a king stood before three kneeling servants. One held a black sword, another a quill, and the third an open hand. Behind the king stood a six-winged woman with the tail of a snake and a sihedron star for a head.

"I've seen that snake-lady on the Street of Little Gods," said Radovan.

Illyria patted his arm to hush him. From her perch on Illyria's shoulder, Amaranthine stretched her neck to nip at Radovan's ear.

"In those days, Lissala's virtues had different names," said the oracle. "In the common tongue, you would call them earned wealth, nurtured fertility, honest pride, shared abundance, eager striving, righteous anger, and deserved rest."

The image transformed into a scene of farmers harvesting crops and warriors defending caravans from giant insects bursting up from the ground. "Xin's people divided themselves into two castes, brave warriors and cunning providers. Working together, they were fruitful and their many accomplishments were great. In time, the empire grew beyond King Xin's ability to rule it. He appointed seven wizards to govern his domain while he turned to arcane studies. These are the azghat, now known as the runelords."

He shifted the sands to show seven figures, each clutching a different polearm. "Each azghat wielded only one sort of magic, unlike King Xin who studied all. The azghat of rich Shalast used magic to fill his vaults with hoarded wealth. The azghat of bounteous Gastash used magic to feast on all manner of flesh. Thus were the virtues of Lissala corrupted into the seven sins.

"As their powers grew, the azghat forged pacts with evil dragons, outsiders, and even the veiled masters of legend. They grew cruel, treating their citizens as chattel." In the sands, the runelords presented slaves to dragons of white, black, green, blue, and red scales.

"One day a pillar of scarlet flames consumed Xin's Crystal Palace, and King Xin vanished. The azghat claimed his lands." The sands formed a map of seven domains, each marked by different colors and different runes.

"King Xin lived only a little more than a century," said Illyria. "Had the runelords discovered the secret to eternal life?"

"No," said the oracle. "The azghat passed down their mantles of authority from master to apprentice."

"What of the tales that one or more runelords survived Earthfall?"

The oracle nodded as though he had expected that question. "It is said that the azghat foresaw the cataclysm and prepared different ways in which to survive. Zutha chose the deathless path. His undead body lies hidden, awaiting the return of his *Tome* to revive him."

"What I want to know is why the hell your 'friend' left you this cursed book." Radovan made no attempt to disguise his anger.

"Perhaps he hoped you would know how to destroy it," said Illyria.

"If so, he would have left a warning . . . unless he did, and someone removed it." I turned to Zora. "Did you?"

Her mouth opened and snapped shut again. Yet again, the geas prevented her from speaking.

I turned back to Illyria. "Did you remove anything from Ygresta's chambers?"

She raised an eyebrow but answered smoothly. "No."

I shivered at a chill in the air. Already the power of the combined books seemed to be affecting me.

Heedless of our conversation, the oracle sifted a handful of sand onto his painting. The images whirled again, reforming into the rough outlines of our continent as it had appeared over eleven millennia earlier. A glowing meteor descended, crashing into the land where the Inner Sea now divided Avistan from

Garund. "Earthfall shattered our world, but the Thassilonian people endured. The warriors are the ancestors of my people. The Varisians descended from the providers. But the descendants of the azghat also survived."

He spilled a handful of purple sand on the painting, and another image of King Xin appeared. "The scions of the azghat are scattered, like these grains of sand, throughout the peoples of Avistan. We know them by their Azlanti eyes and hair." He waved his hand, and the image of King Xin divided into two faces. A half-elven man and a human woman—both faces familiar.

The yurt became silent but for the hiss of the brazier and the bubbling water. The oracle leaned over to breathe in its steam while the rest of us exchanged troubled glances.

"We came to ask a question," Kline said at last. "And to request your help breaking the geas on this woman and the curse on Count Jeggare."

"I cannot break the curse of the terrible book," said the oracle. "The only way to escape its power is to surrender it to a stronger bearer of another section—or to die."

Kline looked at me across the circle. The images now depicted a great shadow holding a smaller figure by the throat. "I don't know whether to apologize or thank you for taking it from me."

I waved off his remark. "You are not to blame."

"The geas I might break," said the oracle. "As for the question you came to ask me, I know the answer."

"What question?" said Radovan.

"You wish to know where to find the third part of the terrible book."

"This guy is good."

"That is part of the curse. The book wants to be completed. Then it will compel you to seek out the Crypt of Zutha, where it will revive its master." The oracle turned to me. "Before I answer your question, you must answer mine. Search your heart before you speak. There can be no lies within this yurt."

"On my honor, I will answer truthfully."

Despite my oath, he chanted a prayer and traced a sign over his eyes. The word of a count of Cheliax meant nothing to him, but his ancestors would reveal any falsehood.

"What will you do with this terrible book when it is whole?"

"I have no intention of reviving Runelord Zutha."

"Yet the book compels you to gluttony, and the curse—or your own nature—compels you to continue reading, even as you know that only strengthens its grip on your mind."

Kline said, "You'll destroy it, of course."

"I have been a Pathfinder since before you were born," I said. "The thought of destroying any knowledge rankles."

"You can't mean to deliver it to the Society."

"I trust the Decemvirate no more than you do, especially after I found the last dread tome I entrusted to them in the hands of an enemy."

"You should entrust it to the masters of the Hall of Whispers," said Illyria.

"Those necromancers most likely to desire Zutha's return?" I said. "I think not."

"You can't keep it for yourself," said Kline. "No matter how highly you think of yourself, you have to admit the curse is affecting your mind."

"You underestimate my willpower, Kline. You are not the one who has plumbed the mysteries of the *Lacuna Codex* and unraveled the conundrums of the *Lexicon of Paradox*. You can hardly imagine—"

"Boss," said Radovan.

His voice was an antidote to my reckless thoughts. I removed the book from my satchel and lay it before me. "These equations of life and death hold a powerful allure, even for one who has renounced the practice of necromancy. Perhaps as a Pathfinder and an arcane scholar, I have been more susceptible to its powers. Yet I know what I must do. When I recover the missing third, I will restore the *Gluttonous Tome*, and then I will find a way to destroy it."

"But you said yourself, there are spells in there you've never seen before, not to mention the theory," Illyria said. "How can you allow such knowledge to be lost forever?"

"My lady, the prospect of destroying any book pains me more than I can express. Yet so long as any part of the *Gluttonous Tome* exists, so does the threat of returning Runelord Zutha to resume his tyrannical rule. In destroying it, we consign him to the grave forever. We have the opportunity to destroy one of the ancient evils of the world. Shall we not take it?"

"When you put it that way . . ."

"Your answer?" said the oracle.

Recalling Kline's skepticism about the methods to destroy the *Tome*, I answered with care. "I swear to seek out a means of destroying the *Tome* or, failing that, to prevent it from reviving its dread master."

Despite my equivocation, the oracle appeared satisfied. "The spirits say that the missing portion of Zutha's terrible book never left the capital city of Xin-Gastash."

"But where is that?" said Illyria. "The cities of Thassilon were all destroyed during Earthfall."

"The ruins of Xin-Gastash lie beneath the Sleeper. Kazyah will show you the way."

"No," the Shoanti woman said. "I must stay with you. You need me."

"Not for much longer. Our ancestors have given me strength to endure this long so that I can help our visitors in their task."

"I won't let you die. I'll use your scrolls to call you back from the River of Souls."

LORD OF RUNES 193

"You may call, but I will not come. It is time for me to take my place among our ancestors. But first, I have strength enough for a few last tasks." He gestured to Zora. "Come here, *skentok*."

"Stop calling me that," said Zora.

"Once I free your mind, you will be as you were before. Come."

I made way for Zora to take my place beside the oracle. She knelt before him, uncharacteristically meek as he lifted his palms to either side of her head. He chanted his prayers, concentrating as sweat beaded on his face. When he was finished, he sank back, breathing heavily. Kazyah wiped his brow.

"The geas was too strong?" said Kline.

"It is broken," said the oracle. "But it was like the skin of an onion. Beneath it are more spells. This may take some time."

"You must rest," said Kazyah.

"I must finish." He sat up and began another chant. "Our work is not done, not until our skulls are gathered."

With a look of pained resignation, Kazyah dropped another handful of herbs in the pot and waved the vapors toward her father. After a long look at his straining face, she shooed us from the yurt. "Go. Wait outside."

I cast a last look upon the oracle. When I was his age, my half-elven blood put me in my prime. Until the gluttonous curse took hold of me, I had felt younger still, thanks to the gift of half a dragon's heart. Looking upon the oracle, I once more began to feel old.

Outside, Radovan fed another log to the fire. We sat around the crackling flames without speaking. From inside the yurt we heard the oracle chant spell after spell. His voice rose again, this time in a Shoanti valediction to the living. Before he finished the song, his voice dwindled to silence. Kazyah's wail rose in its stead. She resumed his funereal song.

Zora emerged from the yurt, face pale, manacled hands clasped in an incongruously pious gesture. Rather than run into the Bottoms, where surely escaped slaves would welcome her, she came to us and knelt beside Illyria.

"I can tell you everything now," she said. "Just please don't ask me yet."

Kazyah's mourning song stirred memories of my own losses, especially the last moments of my mother's life. So many things I wish I had said to her then or long before, but I had only listened and agreed as she extracted promises from me. Since that day, I had kept every promise. I prayed I could continue keeping them.

12
The Cinderlands
Radovan

Two things I'll always remember about Kazyah, who her people named "the Night Bear," and not because she's cuddly.

The first was helping her bury the oracle.

Three days east of Kaer Maga, she told Janneke to stop the carriage. While the others made camp, Kazyah took the oracle's shrouded body in her arms and told me to bring as much water as I could carry.

Her asking me was a surprise. I figured she'd pick Eando. He was an honorary Shoanti, after all. So maybe the Sun and Skull Clans don't mix. Maybe she didn't like Pathfinders. Maybe she didn't like the fact that he'd been cursed before the two books joined up and stuck to the boss. Whatever her reason, she chose me.

She carried the body in her arms, chanting in Shoanti from the first step away from the carriage. After a little while, I caught onto the words. Real quiet-like, I sang along with her. She nodded at me, so I sang a little louder.

The sun beat the hell out of us. It had to be worse for her, since she wore a big furry bear hat and cloak. Even so, she never asked for water. I didn't feel like I should drink unless she did. I kept singing and tried not to think too much about how much my tongue was going to look like a scrap of old leather.

We walked for over an hour through rough red hills. Stone markers lay scattered on the ground everywhere. Most could have just tumbled there for I could tell, but a few had Shoanti runes carved on them. I couldn't understand the signs, but Kazyah knew where she was going. She found the stone she was looking for and lay the old man's body beside it.

Just as I was thinking we should have brought a shovel, Kazyah stuck out her hand and made a chopping motion. A line formed in the dirt, like the mark of a wave on the water. Dust blew up to either side, and the clay growled until it coughed up a grave-sized hole.

Kazyah told me to bring the water as she unwrapped the body. She washed the old man's corpse, singing to him the whole time. The pain in her voice was as sharp as it had been the hour he died.

At last, she got me to climb into the hole. She passed his body to me, and I lay it as gently as I could at the bottom. She pulled me out like I weighed no more than a duck, reminding me she was strong as Janneke—stronger, maybe.

She filled the grave with another chant to the earth.

Afterward, she drank some water and tossed me the skin. I took a swig and passed it back. She cradled it in one arm, her other hand resting on its belly. I couldn't help thinking of a mother and her baby.

She got up, and we walked away. She didn't say anything, but since she wasn't chanting, I figured it was all right to make small talk. I said, "I never knew my old man."

My father was dead before I was old enough to remember his face. To make up for the lost income, my mother sold me to his gang, the Goatherds. For a long time I blamed my father for dying.

I wanted to ask Kazyah what kind of father the oracle had been, or even what his name was, but I was afraid to poke at a fresh wound. She didn't seem like she wanted to talk, so we didn't talk. We didn't sing. We just walked together for a while.

After we left the oracle's yurt back in Kaer Maga, the boss had sent Janneke off with a message for Kaid's Band. I had an idea what that was about. Kazyah stayed with the oracle's body. The rest of us went back to our tower at the Seven Sins. It was time for a chat with Zora.

The boss had a room four times the size of mine, and mine was what you call spacious. His windows faced the inn's courtyard, where sometimes there were plays. He closed them before we got started.

The boss set his satchel and sword on the desk before taking a seat behind it. A peacock carved out of dark wood and bright gems looked over his shoulder as the rest of us pulled up chairs and footstools. Zora got the seat of honor, right in the middle.

"Start from the beginning," said the boss.

"All right," she said. "I'll tell you whatever you want to know. I'll even give you the things I took. They must be worth more than I'm worth to Janneke."

I realized the boss had sent the bounty hunter off for at least two reasons. One was to give Zora hope she could cut a deal. What she didn't understand was that the boss already gave Janneke his word that she could arrest Zora. He wouldn't go back on a bargain.

"Tell us," he said.

"It began two years ago. I was inside a house when I heard a sound from my lookout. He was choking, trying to call out to me. At first, I didn't see anybody with him in the alley. Then I saw the shadows were strangling him."

I've seen some eerie stuff, but that still gave me a shudder. "What did you do?"

"My aunt taught me a few spells. Mostly I use them to help me get in and away, but I know one or two that sting. I hurt one of the shadows enough to make it let him go. I slipped down and we ran, but a black ray shot out from the other end of the alley. It drained all my strength. I could barely stand, much less run. The shadows grabbed us both.

"The spell came from a third shadow, bigger than the other two. The others called the big one 'Master.' It amused him that he'd caught thieves breaking into the house of one of his colleagues.

He asked whether we'd done it before. I was going to lie, but I had a feeling he could hear my thoughts. So I told him we'd been burglars for years.

"That's what saved my life. The Master said all I had to do was keep stealing and he wouldn't turn me over to the city guard. The difference was that from then on, he'd choose what I stole."

"He sent you after the *Gluttonous Tome*," said the boss.

"Not right away. I don't think he even knew about it. He sent me after all sorts of magical things. Most I didn't understand, but sometimes I recognized scrolls or books detailing ways to create a soul vessel, preserve a dead body, that sort of thing."

"This 'Master' was a shadow, but he wished to become a lich?" said Eando.

"He may not have been a shadow," said Illyria. "There is a spell taught in the Hall of Whispers that allows the caster to project his spirit into a shadow body. It could have been anyone, but all you would see is his shadow."

"When did you find the *Kardosian Codex*?" said the boss.

"The blank book?" asked Zora.

He nodded.

"The Master sent me to Kaer Maga to steal anything I could from a local necromancer. His house was too well warded for me to break in, but I spied on him. He was interested in books a group of treasure hunters were trying to sell after fighting in the east."

"Where had they come from?" asked Eando.

"Somewhere in the Hold of Belkzen," she said. "They claimed they'd slain an undead giant and taken the books from him."

Eando and the boss exchanged a look. They knew more about that.

Zora went on. "The problem was, they wanted a king's fortune for each book. That was good, because it meant they hadn't sold them yet. They also didn't trust each other, so two of them each kept one of the books. One was a wizard, but the other was a fighter who worshiped Cayden Cailean the old-fashioned way. There were no wards on his room, so all I had to do was wait until he drank himself into a stupor.

"When they discovered the book was gone, they started tearing Downmarket apart. I knew it was only a matter of time before one of the spellcasters found me, so I ran back to Korvosa. At first, the Master was happy—so happy I didn't want to spoil it by telling him about the other book. As time went on, though, he grew more agitated. When he finally learned the other book had also been in Kaer Maga, he flew into a rage. He said there was no way I could steal the second one before it was too late."

"Before what was too late?" said Illyria.

"Before the gluttonous curse destroyed him," said the boss. He looked around like he expected one of us to say something. "Is it not obvious?"

Everybody else shook their heads. I had an idea what he was going to say, but I didn't want to spoil his moment. He straightened up and looked around like an actor about to read his great line. "Benigno Ygresta is the Master."

We all looked at Zora for confirmation. She kept her mouth shut and didn't move an inch.

The boss said, "You can tell us the truth. The oracle lifted your geases."

"The Master said I would die if I revealed his identity."

"But you have already betrayed him, haven't you?" said the boss. "Despite the Master's spell, you found a way."

A little smile crept across Zora's lips, but a fearful look wiped it away.

"It was you who wrote my name on the calling card, wasn't it?" said the boss. "A fair forgery, but it was not Ygresta's hand. He would have left the book on the shelves to let me find it on my own. And he never ordered you to approach Radovan, did he? That was your attempt to lead us to Kaer Maga."

Zora started to nod. She looked past us into the dark corners of the room.

"Lady Illyria, Eando, if you would be so kind?" The boss pointed at the shuttered windows, and a bright light appeared on the latch. Illyria did the same thing with the latch on the door. Eando threw another one on the beak of the carved peacock. When they were done, there was hardly a scrap of shadow left in the room.

"There is nowhere for Ygresta's shadow spies to hide in this room," said the boss. "I am the only master you need fear now."

The room went quiet. Everybody kept facing Zora, but their gazes slid toward the boss. His face was paler than I'd ever seen it. Despite his paunch, his eyes and cheeks had grown hollow.

Zora answered in a small voice. "Yes. Professor Ygresta is the one who calls himself the Master of Shadows." She winced, but there was nothing coming for her.

"Then the diviners lied about his death," said Lady Illyria. "They lied to me!"

"They did not," said the boss. "Ygresta did not fake his death, only the corpse he left behind."

"How do you fake a corpse?" I said.

"Of course!" said Illyria. "Reshaping dead flesh is one of the first spells we learn in the Hall of Whispers." She gave the boss a long look. "You already deduced that, didn't you?"

He gave her one of those shrugs that means he's pleased someone noticed his cleverness. For a second, he looked a little less scary. "It seemed the most likely prospect, but I was not certain until we spoke to the oracle. Without the missing volumes of the *Gluttonous Tome*, Ygresta realized that death was the only way he could escape the curse of the *Kardosian Codex*."

The Curse of the Kardosian Codex sounded like a good title for one of Illyria's penny romances. Then I got an idea. "Wait a second," I said. "Why did he have to die? You've got Eando's book now, and he's not dead."

"Nothing in the *Codex* describes such a reaction," said the boss. "Ygresta could not have known how the books would behave."

"There's nothing about it in the *Grimoire*, either," said Eando. "And it wasn't like I handed it over. It felt like the books wanted to be together. It was just dumb luck that the count ended up with both."

The boss got that look that meant he didn't agree but wasn't going to say so.

Eando saw it too. "What?"

"The *Grimoire* came to me because it sought to join the more powerful sorcerer."

"And you know this how?"

"I can . . . I hate to use such an ambiguous term, but I can *sense* it." His voice sounded eerie and far away. "Since the books rejoined themselves, I can almost hear . . ." He noticed us staring at him and cleared his throat. "That is not the matter at hand. We were discussing the disposition of the *Codex* before I discovered it. Its text must vanish upon the death of its current 'owner.' But why did Ygresta bequeath it to me in particular?"

"Because he wanted *you* to find the other two parts," said Illyria. "He always said there was no cleverer man than Count Varian Jeggare. He followed your adventures through the *Pathfinder Chronicles*."

The boss struggled with a smug little smile. He knew the answer. He just wanted somebody else to say it.

"You see!" said Eando. "That's exactly what I've been saying. Sometimes sharing our discoveries is the worst thing to do."

"Ygresta must have an accomplice capable of restoring him to life," said the boss. "He killed himself to break the curse, was resurrected, and then shaped a corpse to look like his own and left it in his bed. What concerns me now is how he intends to reclaim the *Tome* once I find the *Black Book*."

"The shadows," I said. "He'll send his shadows to steal it for him."

"They can't carry things," said Illyria. "They're intangible, useful mainly as spies." Her eyes widened. She turned to the boss with a stricken expression. "One of them must have been hiding in my shadow the day we met at the Acadamae! That's why Arnisant barked at me."

The boss gave her a slow nod. I could see by his expression that he was deciding whether she was surprised or just pretending.

She saw it, too. She tried not to pout, and I tried to figure whether that was real or pretend.

"The point is, they can't carry things," she said, turning away from him. "That's why Ygresta needed Zora."

Zora nodded.

"I don't like fighting something I can't get my hands around its throat," I grumbled. "Shadows! Makes you wish we still had the paladin."

"You had a paladin?" said Zora, sounding all dubious.

"Not *had* had, but yeah. Elf maiden. Unicorn and everything."

The boss ignored me. I guess he was getting tired of that joke. He said, "Ygresta also succeeded at creating his golem."

Zora nodded again. "The Master calls him Durante. The Mast— Ygresta constructed him from the bodies of the strongest men in Korvosa. Durante was the only one strong enough to carry him after Ygresta gained so much weight from the curse."

"Carry him where?"

"Somewhere far from Korvosa is all I know."

"We must take what precautions we can," said the boss. "Ygresta will not risk acting before we have obtained the *Black Book*. The question now is how to defend ourselves against a necromancer, his shadows, and a golem."

"The question is how can we can *destroy* the book," said Eando.

"That as well," said the boss. When he saw Eando staring at him, he added, "Very well, that foremost."

From that point, everybody started talking logistics. Eando wanted in, probably to make sure the boss did what he promised.

There was no getting rid of Illyria without the boss taking her home first, like a gentleman.

Janneke would take Zora back to Korvosa to collect her bounty, which was too bad. Even though she was less fun on duty, I was going to miss her.

I was going to miss Zora, too. Stolen cards or not, she'd gotten caught up in something way bigger than her, and she'd tried to beat it anyway. She had moxie. I liked the way she'd fought beside me in the monastery, and I liked that she stayed because she didn't like seeing the blue monks get their throats cut. The fact that she was alive took more than luck. It took a lot of heart. And guts.

One part of Zora's story still bothered me. While the others talked maps and supply wagons, I moved to sit beside her. "Say, whatever happened to your partner?"

"I never saw him again." Zora looked down at her manacles. "For the longest time, I hoped he got away. When I snuck into Ygresta's laboratory, I found his ring on the shelf. That's what I was really after when I broke into his lab. The other stuff was an afterthought. I figured it would fetch enough money to keep me out of Korvosa for a long time."

She held up her thumb to show me. It was a cheap bit of tin and enamel with a picture of a seagull. I touched the Ustalavic copper piece hanging from my neck. Sometimes the cheapest trinkets mean the most.

After a while, Janneke came back to tell the boss that Kaid's Band was in. What was more, Janneke was coming too.

"What about me?" said Zora.

"You aren't leaving my sight until I collect my bounty."

"I said you can have the things I stole. They must be worth at least as much as the bounty."

"There's my reputation to consider."

I looked to the boss, but he was looking over maps with Eando and Illyria. Me, I thought it was a bad idea to bring Zora. All the heart and guts in the world wouldn't keep her from getting killed if we found something else bigger than her.

On the other hand, maybe some time on the road would soften up Janneke. Maybe the bounty hunter appreciated moxie as much as I did. Maybe they'd cut a deal.

I like to be an optimist.

Much later, the boss sent the others away but told me to stick around. I took the opportunity to tell him where I thought we were making some mistakes. Top of the list was Lady Illyria.

"Maybe she knew, maybe she didn't," I said. "Either way, do you really want a necromancer along while you try to find a book and keep it away from another necromancer?"

"That is a stronger argument in favor of keeping her with us." He looked around the room like he'd dropped something. "While the *Gluttonous Tome* is a veritable encyclopedia of necromantic lore, I have no practical experience with the craft."

"So you trust her?"

"We have less reason to distrust her now, but no, of course I do not trust her. We must remain on guard."

"And Zora?"

"If her story is true, then she has every reason to help us against Ygresta." He looked behind me.

"I buy that, but she hasn't exactly volunteered. She's still in manacles."

The boss considered the point. "I shall raise the issue with Janneke. I would hate to lose her services. She has proven herself more than competent." He peeked under the desk.

"What are you looking for?"

"I was certain there were some buns left from dinner."

"Lady Illyria took them away."

"She did what?" A little red came back to his white cheeks.

"Relax, boss. She's just doting on you. We like it when pretty women dote on us. Remember?"

"You have no idea how it feels to be constantly hungry."

After our trip from Sarkoris, he couldn't have been wronger about that. We'd both starved for months. Only Arni came out of it without losing weight, on account of I snuck him a bite of my ration now and then. I poked the boss in the belly. "I got an idea how it *looks* to be constantly eating."

His lips moved for a few seconds before he made any sound. "How . . . dare . . . ?"

I had to admit I surprised myself with the poke, but the boss needed it—and maybe a couple more. "You got room for a tailor in the carriage? The way you're going, you'll need one to let out your pants every couple days."

He started sputtering so bad he got some on my face. That was my cue to change my tune.

"Listen, boss. Illyria, Zora, all the rest, I can see how you'd worry about them. But me? I've seen books do nasty stuff to you before. First there was the *Lacuna Index* in Ustalav. That one made you forget stuff. And in Sarkoris the *Lexicon of Chaos* damned near wrecked you. When I remind you what this curse is doing to you, you know I'm trying to help. Right?"

He clenched his jaw and walked behind his desk. He sat down maybe thinking it covered his potbelly, which it didn't.

"*Lacuna* Codex," he said. "*Lexicon of* Paradox."

"So you remember what they did to you."

"This curse," he sighed. "'These curses,' I should say. I cannot always see how deeply they affect me. This insatiable appetite and the constant chill might be only symptoms of much deeper effects. Sometimes my thoughts . . . I tell you, the secrets in this book . . . I cannot begin to describe how profoundly they alter my perspective. It is possible my judgment is impaired. If so, I must rely on yours. I know I can depend on you to correct me—in private, and without poking me."

"No promises." I got up to go. "I can hear this door open from across the hall. Don't even think about sneaking down to the kitchen."

"Certainly not. I need only pull the bell for service." The boss has a perfect straight face. If only he still played cards, we could make a fortune.

"Keep an eye on him, Arni." I scratched the hound's chin and went back to my room.

The next day we left the city. We had six in the Red Carriage and thirty-four mercenaries on horseback with three more on a supply wagon.

Kaid's Band had already spent the boss's advance on crossbows, weapons, and new pieces of armor. Every one of them had something—a greave, a gauntlet, a breastplate—from the Gray Maiden uniform. Only Faceless Kaid wore the whole outfit. Since her helmet wasn't painted like Janneke's, I could see where she got her nickname with that blank mask. Unlike the bounty hunter, she knew better than to wear it all the time. She looked a little rough around the edges, but she had a good smile. I caught her looking at me a few times.

I wondered whether Kaid shared Janneke's idea of professionalism. And then there was Danai. She acted shy, but maybe that was just her mask. She caught me looking at her a few times, and she took a few seconds to look away.

Anyway, surrounded by so many women, I'd never liked my chances any better.

A few days after burying the oracle, we crossed the river and got back on the Yondabakari trail. The caravans had mostly gone through a month earlier, before wildfire season.

I wanted to ride out to scout, but I was down to my last pony scroll. The boss was busy enough without making more riffle scrolls for me. I knew how much that took out of him, and I knew he didn't want to throw up each morning with Lady Illyria around.

The boss spent the days reading and rereading his creepy book, while Eando and Illyria took turns keeping him from eating all the supplies.

Most of the time, Kazyah sat beside Janneke on the drivers' seat. One day she borrowed a horse from one of Kaid's Band. She was gone so long that the mercenaries started to grumble that she'd stolen it and run off. Just after dusk, Kazyah rode back on a wild stallion she'd tamed, the mercenary's horse following without a tether.

Another day we saw lightning in the distance. Kazyah said those sometimes meant flash floods, sometimes wildfires. As long as we stayed close to the river, we didn't have to worry about the fires. On the other hand, near the river the floods would get us. After a while we didn't have a choice. We ran out of river and kept riding east at the foot of the mountains.

The day after we saw the lightning, Kazyah started each day by whispering into the dirt and putting her ear to the ground. Like the oracle, she had a connection to her ancestors, but it was different. They spoke to her through the earth, she said, because that's where they were buried. After she listened to what they said, she'd tell us what sort of weather to expect, whether we'd see a herd of aurochs or find water, things like that.

She was always right.

Once she told us to stop the carriage because some "burrowing behemoths" were nearby. We waited for the better part of an hour until she said it was safe. A couple miles later, furrows crossed the trail. They reminded me of the giant mole-sharks we saw back in Sarkoris. Even the demons didn't mess with those things. They eat horses whole. I wondered if the bigger ones could eat the carriage in one gulp.

Kazyah and Eando took turns telling me the names of the plants and animals we passed. I recognized some from our trip to Korvosa, but then we'd been too busy staying alive to talk what the boss called "natural history."

It was a cindersnake that bit one of the Maidens' horses. I knew what aurochs were, and that they were tasty, but I didn't know the hyenas were called bush tigers. I half-expected the boss to have Janneke kill one so he could stuff it and give the Katapeshi hyena in his library some company. We saw plenty of scorpions and horned lizards, which Eando said were called spirestalkers for the way they climbed up the hoodoos.

Akyraks were the giant spiders that were hard to tell apart from the galtroot bushes, so I said let's stay the hell away from galtroot bushes. Kazyah rode out to pluck the leaves from one to show me I was chicken. They made for strong medicine, she said, and the young men of the Sun Clan mixed them with other stuff as a drug to make them brave. She offered to make some for me, which everybody else thought was very funny.

Kazyah warned us to stay away from the water-storing purple cactus called a basilisk barrel, on account of its poison would paralyze you and then an akyrak would come and eat you alive.

Arni caught scrub rats and brought them back for praise. The rats didn't look exactly wholesome, but Kazyah said they were all right to eat. Right away I gave Arni the sign, and he gobbled them down. I didn't want the boss to see one and order somebody to roast it for him.

At night, Kaid's Band pitched tents and stood guard, leaving the rest of us to take it easy. After supper and a stretch, Eando and Illyria went back to the carriage to put their heads together with the boss. They had actual maps on the map table, but mostly they talked about what the boss had read that day, even though they agreed he shouldn't oughta be reading it. You can't get a book away from the boss. Not unless you get his sword first.

At bedtime, Illyria conjured her little cottage. She'd offered to make another, but there still wouldn't be room for everyone. Instead, she invited Zora, Janneke, and Kazyah to share it with her. Janneke accepted, which meant Zora had no choice, since she wasn't getting out of her sight, especially now that she was out of the manacles. Kazyah preferred to sleep under the open sky. That left a few bunks for Kaid's Band. They drew straws to see who got to sleep in a bed each night.

When we were on the move, Eando always took a turn scouting. He said it would be better for everybody if the Sun Clan ran into him before the rest of us. Either they were roaming somewhere else in the Cinderlands or they saw us and kept hidden. After Eando's stories of how they put young boys in front of wildfires and made them run for their lives in order to prove themselves, I was fine not meeting those mooks.

Eando didn't go out so much once we passed into orc country. I didn't blame him. Orc throat-cutters made his worst stories about the Sun Clan sound like schoolboy pranks. Kaid started sending her scouts in groups of six instead of two.

I started to feel left out, and finally asked the boss to make me some more pony scrolls. He said he'd think about it, but Illyria took pity on me and made one for me without a scroll. Even though she was the one that made it, it ended up looking the same as mine always do: a big red horse with a smoky mane.

It was good to ride again. I ran a big circle around the carriage. Janneke gave me a jealous look. Illyria conjured up a driver to give her a break sometimes, but the boss insisted that she remain in the driver's seat "in case of mishap." That's the price of being a professional, I wanted to say. I also didn't want a punch in the snoot, so I didn't.

Kazyah's stallion came when she called. She rode bareback, holding onto the wild horse's mane while swinging that big hammer over her head like it was a switch. I decided I'd rather take a punch from Janneke than one from her.

Without a word to anybody, Kazyah rode ahead. I ran after her, in part so she wasn't scouting alone, but mostly to find out whether my phony pony was faster than her wild stallion. When I came up beside her, the stallion screamed.

"Sorry!" I veered away. When I ride the pony, I sometimes forget real horses still hate me.

Kazyah was looking up at the eastern sky. Something glided high above the ground. It was too far for me to make out anything more than a pair of bluish wings and a long tail.

"Dragon?" I tried not to sound as worried as I felt.

"Only a wyvern."

"Well, that's a relief. 'Only a wyvern.'" Looking back, I couldn't see the carriage, but I could tell where it was by the plume of dust rising behind it. I started thinking we should stay closer.

"You have seen a wyvern before?"

"Not, you know, in the flesh." I'd seen a picture in one of the boss's books. Kazyah nodded in a way that made me feel small, so I added, "Mostly we've run into actual dragons."

"Is that so? What sort of dragons?"

Now it was her turn to be impressed. "Well, I couldn't see the first one, on account of I was blind at the time, but I hear it was the biggest. The green one was big as a house."

"You escaped a green dragon?"

"Actually, we got on pretty good. You could say we're friendly."

"You are friends with a green dragon?" Her tone said she didn't think much of that idea. Green dragons don't exactly have the best reputation. I was starting to feel judged.

"Let's just say the enemy of my enemy is a great big green dragon."

Kazyah frowned, but she seemed to be thinking it over. I had a feeling she wasn't going to call me chicken again.

A little while later, she jumped off her horse and put her ear to the ground. After a moment, she nodded at whatever her ancestors told her. She got back on her stallion and led me a few miles off the trail to four hoodoos that looked like old men in wide hats leaning into the wind. Stepping into the shadows between them felt like stepping out of a forge and into a beer cellar.

We found a pool. We drank, and then she let her horse drink. Mine didn't need water, on account of not being real or from our world—something like that.

When the stallion had his fill, Kazyah whispered into his ear. He wandered the base of the wind-carved pillars, tearing out weeds and wildflowers. My pony just stood where I left it, looking ahead at nothing.

The stillness of the place reminded me of the hill where we'd buried the oracle. I'd buried the dead before, but never anyone that close to me. That thought made me think Kazyah was still mourning her old man.

"I guess this trip is harder on you than anyone else," I said. "You wouldn't even be with us if your father hadn't promised your help."

"The oracle was not my father," she said. "He was my son."

I took a minute to work that out in my head. The oracle had to be way over sixty years old, but Kazyah didn't look much over forty. It was hard to tell through all those tattoos.

Considering the things I'd seen, Kazyah's youth was no big deal. Hell, these days the boss looked younger than when I met him. It wasn't seeing old people look like young people that threw me. The thought that rattled in my noggin was Kazyah watching her boy grow older than her—so old he died of it.

"My youngest son," she said, "and the last to die."

We were quiet for a time while I let that thought sink in. I'd seen pain in the eyes of a lot of parents whose kids had suffered or died. I never wanted to feel that way.

A long time ago, I bought a potion to make sure I'd never have a son of my own. It wasn't because my father got killed on account of our evil blood. It wasn't even because my mother sold me after that.

It was because of how everybody looked at me every day of my life. They looked into my yellow eyes and saw something that didn't belong in this world. They hated me or feared me. Even the women who wanted me, what most of them really wanted was the little bit of Hell they smelled on me. There was only one way to be sure nobody looked at a child of mine that way.

That was never to have a kid.

That was my plan, anyway. A few years back, a devil told me the potion was a fake—not that you can trust a devil without a contract. Since then I'd been extra careful.

So I didn't really know how Kazyah felt. Until you get hurt a particular way, you don't know nothing. And you've got no way to take the hurt away from those who do. All you can do is say the thing you're supposed to say.

"I'm sorry."

Kazyah didn't reply. She dropped her bear hat and spread her cloak on the ground. She stripped off her sweaty clothes and stepped into the pool. Even after she knelt, the water barely reached her round hips. She scooped handfuls of water to wet her black hair. In the shadows, her tattooed skin looked as dark as the red rocks surrounding us.

She didn't ask me to leave or turn my back, so I watched her bathe. As she spilled each handful of water after the next, her body changed.

The heavy muscles of her arms and legs grew thinner. The wrinkles at her eyes spread across her face, visible even through all that ink. A couple of her teeth disappeared, and the rest turned brown and yellow. Her fingers thinned, and her knuckles swelled. Her dark hair grayed and whitened. Her heavy breasts sagged and flattened.

She turned to me and said, "This is how I should look without the blessing of the earth."

She poured more water over her shoulders. Her skin smoothed. Her muscles returned, but not as heavy as they'd been before. Her long black hair spilled past her waist. She turned a soft smile on me, her teeth whiter. "I was this age when I emerged from the cave of the Night Bear."

I was going to say something then, but my tongue got tangled. She beckoned to me, and I didn't need another hint. I dropped my kickers and leathers beside her bearskin cloak and joined her in the pool.

Our conversation got what the boss might call "nonverbal." Once we were clean, she drew me over to lie on the bearskin cloak. Her kiss tasted like a penny, sharp and bright. Our bodies moved together, slow for such a long time that I couldn't tell when it got fast.

The first time felt like the echo of thunder on the horizon. I could almost smell the lightning. Her body slipped back into the shape I'd first seen, all muscle and round turns.

The second time felt like falling down a mountain. After, I thought I'd never catch my breath again.

When she came to me in the shape she should have had, I didn't pull away. She looked different, sure, and she didn't feel the same. But she was the same woman she'd been when she stepped out of that bear cave.

The third time felt like the whole earth opened up. Kazyah held me so hard I thought she was dragging me down into a grave. The things she knew and the things I'd seen her do, she was a power in the world. Maybe not as mighty as an ancient green dragon, but closer to that than to me. If she wanted to die, and if she wanted me to die with her, there wasn't a thing I could do to stop her.

But in the end we didn't die. It only felt that way. We came back to life a little at a time. Kazyah went back to looking the way she had when we'd met. We washed ourselves in the pool, put on our clothes, and headed back to meet the carriage.

That afternoon between the hoodoos was the second thing I'll always remember about Kazyah. And after the way things turned out, it's the one thing I wish I could forget.

13
The Sleeper
Varian

Through the rear window, Radovan said, "Boss, you're going to want to see this."

I stepped out onto the running board and swung around to catch the ladder, as I had done a hundred times before. This time I slipped. Radovan grabbed my wrist before I could fall under the wheels. He guided me onto the rear ladder. I clung there for a moment to let the beating of my heart slow before climbing to the roof, where I crouched with one hand on the baggage rail.

Radovan gave me a concerned look rather than remark on the added weight that threw off my balance. A jape would have been preferable to his pity.

Despite my companions' concerted effort to restrict my diet, I managed to pilfer a snack now and then, just to fill in the cracks. It was the only way I could check my ill temper. Between the constant chill and hunger pangs, it was a miracle I had not yet reduced someone to ash with a bolt of lightning.

From the drivers' seat, Janneke pointed toward a distant mountain. Having seen it sketched in Eando Kline's own report to the Pathfinder Society, I recognized the famed Sleeper.

From a distance it appeared much like any of the other great wedges of granite jutting up from the Mindspin Mountains to scrape the clouds, yet this one was no natural formation. Three times around the conical mountain wound a stone dragon clutching its tail in its rear claw. Despite the erosion of millennia, the monument resembled a sinuous eastern wyrm. What I had first taken as a low cloud appeared to be smoke rather than vapor. It streamed from the dragon's open jaws to drift over the foothills.

On either side of the carriage, Eando Kline and Lady Illyria leaned out of the windows. Illyria gazed ahead, but Kline turned his neck to search the skies.

"What are you looking for?" said Radovan.

"Chimeras."

"The lion-goat-dragon things? Aw, they were made up by one of those—what do you call them? The guy that stuffs the dead animals."

"Taxidermists," called Illyria

"That's it. A taxidermist sewed up a goat, a lion, and a snake and sold it for a fortune. The things aren't real."

"No doubt there are hoaxes, but I promise you chimeras are real," said Kline. "I ran into some the last time I passed through this way. Right over there." He pointed toward the Sleeper.

Radovan whistled appreciatively. "Tell me that's not a real dragon."

"That is not a real dragon," said Kazyah. "It is a mountain."

"I was just kidding! I know the difference between a mountain and—" Radovan stopped talking as he saw Janneke nudge the shaman sitting beside her on the driver's perch. Kazyah made an admirable but ultimately imperfect attempt to suppress her smile.

"Do you know the Shoanti don't have a word for 'gullible'?" Kline asked him.

"Nice try, but you can't fool me twice," said Radovan. "Not twice in a row, anyway." He grinned down at Kline. In their faces I saw the thrill of exploration and camaraderie that once propelled me through decades of expeditions for the Pathfinder Society. I longed to share their enthusiasm, but I felt only dread weighting my empty stomach. Hunger, both physical and intellectual. I craved the knowledge concealed in the third and final portion of the *Gluttonous Tome*, yet I harbored an ineffable premonition that finding it would destroy me.

We reached the foot of the mountain a few hours later. Janneke drove until we found a box canyon sheltering a pine wood. There we hid the carriage and our supply wagon out of sight from the caravan trail. The horses would enjoy the shade and fresh water from the stream. Kaid dispatched scouts and set guards while I consulted my expedition.

While he had never accompanied me on a proper dig, Radovan had considerable experience exploring lost crypts and subterranean complexes as my bodyguard. Kline was as seasoned an explorer as I could have desired. While Kazyah's role was that of guardian to her ancestors, she had already demonstrated astonishing powers of geomancy and divination. And, while her expertise was in capturing fugitives, Janneke had proven herself a skilled fighter and an obedient hireling.

My doubts rested on Lady Illyria. There was no denying her arcane talents, and her necromantic expertise would prove useful if the Sleeper were indeed an entrance to the subterranean city of Xin-Gastash. But there were too many coincidental connections to the *Gluttonous Tome*: I had met her when she was a child, her great uncle was the Acadamae headmaster, she studied with Benigno Ygresta, and she shared the same Azlanti heritage that the oracle had claimed traced our bloodlines back to the runelords. Too many coincidences.

And there are, I reminded myself, no coincidences—neither in life nor in death. From the *Codex* and the *Grimoire*, I had come to see life and death energy as an unbreakable continuum. The sins of the past became the sins of the present. Bloodlines were just another form of fate, a disease of predestination. Just as Kazyah called upon the spirits of her elders to guide her, so did my sorcerous bloodline connect me to . . .

That line of thought dizzied me. Or perhaps I grew faint from hunger. I went to the boot of the carriage, only to see that Illyria had already supervised the removal of our remaining foodstuffs.

Instead of snacking, I retrieved the essential gear and stored it in my satchel, replacing the incomplete *Gluttonous Tome* near the top. Having it near to hand felt more comforting. Radovan shrugged on a light backpack, which I knew included our rations. Perhaps I could contrive to adjust it for him.

Once I saw that everyone was appropriately outfitted, Zora presented herself. "Let me come along," she said. "You might need a good lockpick."

"I'm a good lockpick," said Radovan, but he shrugged and turned to me. "Another set of hands can't hurt. It's not like she's running off into Orcland without us."

"I don't want a knife in the back," said Janneke.

"I'm a thief, not a cutthroat," Zora said. "Besides, the Master made me his slave. Even after I stole everything he demanded, he still killed—" She swallowed. "If I can hurt him by helping you, that's as much revenge as I can hope for."

I could not resolve my memories of Benigno Ygresta with the cruel behavior of this shadowy "Master." What had brought him to employ such wicked methods?

"I don't like it," said Janneke. "What if she dies in there? She's worth a lot less to me dead."

"I say give her a chance," said Radovan.

"As do I," said Lady Illyria.

"You do, do you?" I said.

"I know how it feels to be distrusted. All the girl wants is a chance to prove herself." On Illyria's shoulder, the little drake rustled her wings. "See? Amaranthine agrees with me."

"I vote we bring her," said Kline.

"There are no votes," I said. "This is my expedition. The rest of you are—" I sought a diplomatic term that would still support my position.

"The rest of us are helping you," said Illyria.

Exasperated, I turned to Kazyah. "What do you think?"

"We should start climbing before we lose any more daylight."

Seeing no profit in further discussion, I agreed.

Radovan fetched Zora's flag from the carriage roof. Janneke shook her head as she saw him return the thief's unorthodox weapon, but she said nothing else as Zora shouldered her own pack. I noted that the bounty hunter left her helm behind, as Radovan had continually advised. Considering her preference for the crossbow, it seemed wise counsel.

We left Kaid's Band to defend our camp and began our ascent.

We passed two half-hidden cavern mouths as we traversed the dragon's spine. I marked their locations on a hasty map in my journal, but we continued toward the obvious entrance. After Kazyah confirmed that the fumes emanating from the dragon's mouth were not toxic, we covered our faces with damp kerchiefs and entered the smoky maw.

The chamber within resembled the interior of a dragon's mouth. Toward the back, two passages lead deeper into the mountain: one rose in a ramp while the other terminated in a descending spiral stairwell. Smoke blackened the ceiling and much of the walls, but occasional traffic had worn gray trails along the bone-strewn floor. Most of the remains appeared to be those of birds, perhaps devoured by previous inhabitants.

The smoke emanated from a pair of stone braziers on either side of a marble altar. Fist-sized chunks of a coal-like material produced heat and smoke, but precious little light. A cool draft rising from the stairway carried the smoke through a pair of circular apertures forming the dragon's nostrils.

Whatever icon had once rested on the altar had long since been cut away. Only a bronze ring, blue-green with verdigris, remained embedded in the marble. Runes surrounding the altar's lintel had long since worn to unintelligible shapes. I sketched them anyway, along with the altar, crafting the beginnings of a new map.

While I worked, the others examined the room. Radovan found a rusted buckle of indeterminate origin. Arnisant whined at a hole which, judging from the droppings, provided entrance for a family of giant rats.

Since there was little left of the mountain above us, I decided we should clear that portion before going below. We found two chambers above the dragon's mouth entrance.

Along the circular walls of the first, some ancient artisans had carved a panorama of the surrounding mountains. While sketching it into my journal, I noted a discrepancy in the carving. A quick return to the dragon's mouth confirmed my guess: the carving exactly duplicated the view from the mountaintop, except that one mountain in the carving was absent from the real landscape. I noted the anomaly for later investigation but doubted it had any bearing on our mission.

In the lookout above the round chamber, we found the skeletal remains of an orc. Judging from its shattered femur and a long-dried bloodstain on the floor, the brute dragged himself into the shelter to die.

Radovan and Eando searched the room. Zora found an air vent choked with the debris of a long-abandoned bird's nest. She cleared it, and the air sweetened enough that we lowered our damp kerchiefs.

"See how helpful I am?" Zora tried not to look at Janneke, but it was clear whose favor she meant to curry. She and Radovan exchanged a glance. I suspected collusion and hoped they would not be too disappointed when the gambit failed. Janneke did not strike me as the lenient sort.

We dispensed with the upper chambers and descended into the belly of the dragon.

In labyrinthine passages we found all manner of scavengers and predators. Most were little more than beasts, easily dispatched with a spell or a display of force. The provisional nature of their lairs left no doubt that the territory frequently changed owners. Whatever artifacts may once have lain in those chambers had been looted long ago. We went deeper, searching for some passage that others had not yet escaped.

Our first serious ordeal came after Radovan returned from scouting. "Orcs," he said.

I offered him a kerchief and nodded at the spur on his right elbow. "How many?"

"I counted fifteen, not including the two I introduced myself to." He wiped the blood from his spur and pocketed the handkerchief, knowing I would not want it back. "I bet they have a couple sentries down the other two passages."

"Nineteen. Hardly an insurmountable force."

"Their boss has a devil's head mounted on his shoulder. He was talking to it, and it talked back."

"Lovely," said Illyria. "Did the head appear living or undead?"

"It was a head with no body," said Radovan. "I don't know. Living, I guess."

"Pity," said Illyria. In response to my raised eyebrow, "I didn't meant to suggest I wanted a trophy, just that I'll have fewer ways to control it."

I felt it best not to point out that I had meant to claim it as a trophy myself. A passage on reanimating outsiders from the *Grimoire* inspired me to consider an experiment.

We followed Radovan to the point where he had dispatched the orc sentries. They seemed only asleep until the light from my ring revealed the blood pooling beneath them. With hand signs, Radovan signaled we were near. Quiet incantations rendered us invisible, at which point we concealed our lights and followed Radovan hand to shoulder. Arnisant was accustomed to the procedure, which we had practiced during our time in the Worldwound crusade. To my relief, the drake remained silent on Illyria's shoulder.

On entering the orc lair, I appreciated why the orcs had chosen the site. One wing of the cross-shaped chamber had collapsed, a stream trickling down a multicolored wall into a pool of likely potable water. A breeze indicated an air passage that drew out the smoke from a bonfire at the center of their camp.

Half a dozen orcs sat near the fire, sucking the marrow out of small bones, scraping the hair from swatches of hide, sharpening blades, and performing other tasks. More slept on nests of skins and detritus scavenged from the ruins. Several sleepers snored so loudly that I felt assured we approached unheard.

Before a painted hide tent sat three more orcs, two in positions deferential to their leader, whom I recognized from Radovan's description. A yellow-skinned devil's head strapped to his shoulder stood out from the orc's unusually red skin painted in the sigils of Hell.

The diabolic signs gave me hope. One can treat with a devil. Had the orc served a demonic master, we would have had no choice but to fight.

Drawing the Shadowless Sword, I confirmed the only illusions within the room were the spells concealing our party.

I patted Radovan's shoulder, signaling our prearranged entrance. He went off to deal with the sentries while I made a silent count and took a riffle scroll in hand. At the appointed time, I touched Illyria's hand, knowing she would signal Kline, and so on down the line. We took our positions between the fire and the diabolist's tent and awaited Radovan's return. Silently he reappeared in one of the other two passages, offering a slow wave to indicate he had dealt with the other sentries before sinking back into the shadows, where even the magic of my sword could not reveal him.

I cast off my invisibility and waited a moment for the orcs to notice me. When they did not, I spoke in an archaic and formal dialect of their guttural tongue: "Your sentries are dead, but the rest of you may buy your lives with submission."

Behind me, I heard the sound of an orc lunging for his weapon, followed an instant later by a heavy impact and a sickening crunch. I kept my eyes on the spellcaster and his counselors, trusting that Kazyah had revealed herself.

"Death stands beside each of you," I said, "awaiting only another treacherous act to fall upon your head."

The shaman stared at me, eyes wide in apprehension. He commanded his followers, "Still your hands."

"You will tell me what you have found in these passages. When I am satisfied with your answers, you may depart forever."

The leader's hand trembled near a bone wand hanging from his hip. I saw the conflict in his mind reflected on his face. Submission would cost him loyalty from his followers. Seeing only me and Kazyah, he weighed the cost of resistance.

"Coward!" the devil's head shrieked into the shaman's ear. "I bring you the gift of hellfire, and you cringe before this half-breed elf? Burn him! Burn them both to cinders!"

I raised the riffle scroll, ready to thumb its pages and activate the spell. "Defy me and die. No further warning."

The caster glanced at the devil's head, then at his counselors. In the craggy lines of his face, I saw the resolve forming. Before he could turn it to action, I unleashed a volley of arcane bolts at his infernal familiar. The head exploded in shards of bone and chunks of preserved flesh.

Janneke fired a cylinder at a pair of orcs rising from their nests. A glass vial shattered and splashed them with gray fluid. The orcs howled as the acid burned through their hide armor.

Illyria flicked a white feather as the orcs around the fire rose. As she finished pronouncing her spell, they too wailed—not in pain, but in terror. They cowered before the necromancer as Amaranthine flew toward them, lashing her barbed tail at their faces.

Kazyah called out a Shoanti chant, and the ceiling appeared to fall upon another orc. In an instant, the rubble rose in the form of a whirling earth spirit, lumpy limbs pounding the orc to gore.

Radovan, Kline, and I moved forward to attack with our blades. Radovan killed two before Kline and I reached our foes.

"Count!" cried Zora. I turned to see one of the leader's counselor's gripping the empty air, his spell evoking a red blaze.

I began a counterspell, but I could see it would be too slow. Zora whirled her flag, the banner rippling in the air as it crossed between the orc and me. His infernal bolt flared behind the flag but vanished as it struck the cloth. With a flourish, Zora continued the arc of her sweep and snapped the cloth around the orc's ankle, pulling him to the ground. A moment later, Kline and I were upon him, our blades finishing the job.

The rest was a brief succession of clamors and flashes. In the end, we stood over the broken bodies of the orcs, the only sound our panting and the grinding growl of Kazyah's earth spirit. I regretted only a little the lack of intelligence we might have gleaned from a survivor. The fact that they had set camp suggested they had not penetrated much farther into the complex.

Beyond the orcs, we moved cautiously through trapped passages whose mechanisms Zora and Radovan disarmed. When we came to seeming dead ends, Kazyah opened the walls with a chant.

In a catacomb, a pair of wights stalked us until Arnisant barked a warning. Lady Illyria paralyzed them with a spell while Kazyah and Janneke smashed their undead bodies to pulp.

Soon after, Kline threw a handful of glittering dust over a seemingly empty expanse, revealing an invisible stairway. At the bottom, I incinerated a nest of albino arthropods with a spray of flame.

Together, we drove off a pack of hulking brutes with three-fingered claws, doglike legs, and hideous maws. The rumbling of their bellies was audible even over the fight, and ribbons of drool hung from their slavering jaws. Despite their disgusting appearance, I felt a pang of sympathy for their hunger. We stopped to fortify ourselves with a handful of rations. Or two.

Consulting with Kline and Lady Illyria, I identified discrepancies in my map to reveal hidden passages and access to undisturbed chambers. We descended ever deeper.

In time, we came to a series of slanting rooms lined with painted tiles. In the detritus, Radovan discovered a drain on a wall, suggesting that the now-vertical surface had once been the floor. Kazyah traced her fingers across a span of hard-packed earth until she found a softer spot.

She concentrated, listening to voices the rest of us could not hear. She thrust a finger into the rubble. The dirt parted as easily as if it were water.

"Don't try to follow," she said. "Wait for me here."

Humming a deep note, she thrust her entire hand and then her arm into the earth.

"Is she going to—?" Before Radovan could finish, Kazyah disappeared into the wall.

We stared after her, watching as the disturbed dirt settled. As the minutes passed, uncertainty weighed upon us. Our gazes shifted from the wall to each other, yet no one dared speak.

Without warning, a nearby section of wall collapsed. Kazyah stumbled out, gasping for breath. Wet mud caked her lower legs, and dry dirt sifted down from her bear's helm and cloak.

"What did you find?" I asked.

"A river," she said. "I should have brought a light. But it's close enough that I can make a path, if you wish it."

"Do the spirits tell you it leads to a larger area? To Xin-Gastash?"

She nodded.

"Make a path."

She set aside her earth breaker and produced a small steel blade from her belt. From a pouch she removed a crumb of loam, a bit of clay, and a pinch of sand. Mingling them in her palm, she thrust the blade forth and uttered a deep tone. An inhuman harmony joined her, just within the lower range of my hearing. It vibrated in my bones and raised the hairs on the nape of my neck. Pebbles leaped and scattered across our toes.

The floor parted like the trough of a cresting wave, creating a descending passage perhaps seven feet wide. As we watched, the channel penetrated deeper into the earth until a sudden gust of moist air blew dust in our faces.

Radovan moved forward.

"Wait," said Kazyah. "Not yet."

The shaman went ahead, pausing twice to mold a piece of clay. In sympathy with her spell, stones flowed and reformed in the shape of a crude brace to support the channel walls. She did the same at two farther points before beckoning for us to follow.

We emerged from the trench in cold water up to our calves. The opposite bank lay nearly thirty feet away. Downstream, the river gurgled through a rapid decline. Upstream, the passage widened.

"Be careful," said Kazyah. "It is much deeper in the center, and the current is strong."

Radovan and I took the lead, wading near the river's edge with Janneke close behind. Illyria illuminated the head of Kazyah's earth breaker, and the shaman covered the rear.

We followed the shallow river for perhaps seventy yards before the ceiling rose and the passage opened into a large, glittering cavern.

Upon its shore lay a treasure trove.

Gold, silver, and copper coins formed hillocks on the shore. Among them lay goblets, plates, tapestries, wooden carvings, suits of armor, swords, shields, spears with crusader pennants, chests and coffers (some open to spill out their jewels), a wagon-wheel with gold inlaid in its spokes, and even a canopy bed.

Eando Kline and Lady Illyria simultaneously cast divinations. I did the same rather than rely on their reports.

"Is this what I think it is?" said Janneke.

"That depends." Radovan brushed away some coins at the water's edge, revealing the furrow of an enormous claw. "Do you think it's a dragon's lair?"

"We should have brought more wagons," said Zora. "Look at all this treasure!"

"Take nothing," I said. "We are not here to steal."

"Except for your book," said Radovan.

"Except for that." I disliked thinking of acquiring the *Black Book* in terms of theft, but Radovan made a valid point. "We must find it and depart before the, ah, resident returns."

"We shouldn't be here." Janneke cranked her crossbow.

"Look here," said Eando. He stood atop an enormous marble head of a fleshy woman crowned with a ring of Azlanti stones. He pointed. Ten feet above the statue's brow, a half-collapsed stairway rose to a higher chamber.

I looked to Eando and Lady Illyria. "Can either of you levitate someone up there?"

Kline shook his head. Illyria said, "If we rest a while, I can prepare a spell."

"If somebody can find me a spider, I can climb up there," said Zora. "Not too big, though. And not a hairy one."

"What are we doing?" said Radovan. He waved Eando down from the statue's head and took his place. "We don't need magic for every little thing. Boss, can I get the mallet, spikes, and rope ladder?"

I opened the satchel and removed the *Gluttonous Tome* to reach the gear. Just as I set it aside, a mound of treasure shifted.

Coins streamed down its sides, the sound of the disturbance rising to a loud ringing.

Something deep beneath the surface burrowed toward us.

On Illyria's shoulder, Amaranthine spread her wings and hissed. Arnisant jumped in front of me, barking.

The rest of us braced for attack, but only a familiar green radiance seeped out from beneath the coins.

As one, Kline and I said, "Oh no."

A black shape burst out from the treasure, scattering coins in all directions. I writhed in wracking pains. Covers like leathery wings beat against my body as the book's spine, like bony claws, scrabbled to clutch its pages. A distant fraction of my will wished to let it go, but with the panic of a drowning man, I held on as the *Black Book* rejoined its accursed siblings, the *Bone Grimoire* and *Kardosian Codex*.

At last, the book and I fell exhausted to the cavern floor. The Shadowless Sword clattered beside me. I heaved up the contents of my stomach. All around me, the others suffered their own agonies, caught up in the nauseating aura of the books' reunion.

Some indeterminable time later, Radovan and the shaman lifted me by the arms. I snapped at them, clutching the *Tome* to my chest with both hands lest someone take it from me. The combined book fluttered open as though flaunting its final secrets.

The *Black Book* consisted of a scorched back cover and another hundred pages of smoke-darkened parchment. The inscriptions were in the same elegant hand as in the previous volumes. Only when Radovan spoke did I realize I had skimmed the pages before me and turned to read the next.

"You feel all right?"

My hands trembled. "I have it. It is all here before me. It is mine."

"Now we must destroy it," said the Pathfinder.

"By fueling a fire to cook for a fasting king?" I said. "You will forgive me if I first study these new pages for a less preposterous suggestion."

"The more you read, the tighter the curse grips you."

"Then it is a race," I said, rising to the challenge. "I must discover the means to destroy the *Tome* before it can destroy me."

"*We*," said the necromancer woman. "*We* must discover it together."

I turned, irritated to be corrected.

Whatever the woman saw in my face caused her to flinch.

For the briefest instant, I regretted my reaction, but the instant was fleeting. She needed to learn how to treat me with respect. Fear was a comparatively crude rod, but it would serve. Tending to the feelings of my subordinates would only distract me from my true purpose, which I was beginning to understand was also my destiny: to comprehend and master the secrets of the *Tome*. Only then would I destroy it.

Or perhaps I would not.

It belonged to me, after all. The Pathfinder had tried to wrest it from me, and he had failed. If the necromancer intended to take it from me by subtler methods, she would be disappointed.

A premonition tickled my mind. I sensed a nearby presence, strange yet familiar. Beneath these mounds of coins lay something else, something powerful.

Something that belonged to me.

"Search the hoard," I ordered them. "There is something else hidden here, something I require."

"What are you talking about, boss?"

"Do not question me. Just do as I say."

"Count Jeggare," said the necromancer. "Varian, listen to me, you don't—"

"Enough!" I shouted, but my voice came out as a rasp. "You are wasting valuable time. *My* time. I will not tolerate another—"

The air pressure in the cavern suddenly increased. The river surged backward, its waters spilling over the banks and flooding treasures on the shore. The dog barked a frantic warning, but it came far too late.

In our panicked motions, our bodies occluded our lights. Fragmented shadows leaped upon the walls: a hand, a partial profile, a staff or handle, a writhing flag, a crooked arm and running leg. The drake cried in terror.

A dark mass rose out of the river. Water rushed down a wall of scales, each the size of a target shield. Along with the river spray, I felt a wave of terror radiating from the creature—the dragon. The magical compulsion chilled my veins and set my hands to trembling, but soon it washed over me and I stood fast. Among the screams of the weaker beings, I alone stood calm beneath the wyrm's eye.

In the shifting light, the dragon appeared black and dark blue, yet I saw a glimmer of bronze upon its scales. Holding the *Gluttonous Tome* under one arm, I retrieved the Shadowless Sword. Its magic revealed no illusion. A bronze dragon stood before us.

It turned its incandescent gaze upon me, and I knew only diplomacy would serve. Sheathing my sword, I said, "Forgive our necessary trespass, great wyrm."

"And shall I forgive your unnecessary theft?" The force of the dragon's voice bruised my eyes.

I raised the recombined *Gluttonous Tome* above my head. "I have simply retrieved the missing portion of my book."

"Your book?" said the dragon. "You fool! You have no idea what you've done."

"I know exactly what I have done," I said. "And I am no fool. My name is Count Varian Jeggare. You would do well to remember it."

"Boss," whispered Radovan. "Is that really the way you want—?"

"Be silent." Some vague absence distracted my attention. My fingers felt as if I had lost my rings, but the signet and my illuminating gem remained in place. Removing them and rubbing the tingling flesh beneath, I realized I had felt the sensation growing since the reunion of the *Tome*. I pocketed the rings.

The dragon spoke again, her voice like thunder. "I am Svannostel, guardian of the Sleeper, defender of the *Black Book*. If necessary, I will destroy you before you complete the transformation."

"What transformation?" said Radovan.

I found myself at a loss.

"So," said the dragon, "you do *not* know."

"I know the *Gluttonous Tome* contains all the wisdom of Runelord Zutha, his spells and insights into necromancy. It contains the secrets of reanimation and undeath."

"Those secrets are nothing but the teeth of a trap laid for necromancers craving false immortality."

"What do you mean?"

"You hold doom in your hands. The *Gluttonous Tome* is not only Zutha's grimoire. It is his phylactery."

"What's a phylactery?" said Radovan. Fear strained his voice, but he mastered it enough to stand beside me. The dog crept up to lie before me, tail between his legs.

"So, it is the vessel in which Zutha stored his mind and soul," I said. "The key to his undead immortality. Very well. I shall refuse to bring it to his corpse."

"You cannot refuse," said the dragon. "You are now in its thrall. Once rejoined, the phylactery requires only an appropriate body to restore the runelord to life. *Your* body."

The revelation chilled me. For a moment, I felt a fear that had nothing to do with the dragon's presence.

With an almost idle gesture, the dragon plucked the Varisian thief from the shadows where she had been creeping away. The thief dropped her flag and covered her face with her arms. The dragon set her, still cowering, at my feet.

Lowering its huge snout to my chest, the dragon sniffed. "There is something oddly familiar about you."

I tapped my chest. "My injured heart was healed by a dragon's."

"What dragon? No, do not speak. Open your thoughts to me. I will know the truth."

"No."

"What?" The dragon reared back, astonished at my defiance.

"I surrender my thoughts to no one." Even in my anger, I felt the gnawing presence of a thing—many things—that belonged to me within the dragon's treasure. With the *Tome* firmly under one arm, I stretched out my hand in the direction where I sensed they lay.

A handful of coins leaped from the pile, scattered by a ring that flew directly onto my finger. Another followed it, encircling my thumb.

"No," said the dragon. "It is not possible. Only Zutha—"

A gemstone escaped the treasure and flew toward my head. Rather than strike me, it orbited my brow like a planet around a star. An instant later, three more joined it.

"Look out!" Radovan ducked another ring that flew onto the hand with which I clutched the *Tome*. I dropped the book, but it did not fall. It levitated beside me, bound to me by some invisible bond.

By ones and twos, more Azlanti stones and enchanted rings returned—*returned*, I knew, for they were mine. They completed me, just as the *Black Book* had completed the *Gluttonous Tome*.

When the singing of displaced coins and treasures subsided, a ring adorned every finger and thumb. A halo of multicolored gemstones encircled my brow.

"Zutha's Crest and Crown," said Svannostel. If only for a moment, the dragon's voice sounded not fearsome but fearful.

"What are these things?" cried the necromancer. "What do they mean?"

"The weapons of Runelord Zutha," said the Pathfinder.

"But Zutha wielded a scythe," the necromancer insisted. "Didn't he?"

"As a staff of office, yes, and it too was a terrible weapon. But his true power lay within his rings and Azlanti stones."

"You were not only cursed to come here, Count Varian Jeggare," said the dragon. "You were fated."

"Fated? Explain."

"Unlike the *Gluttonous Tome*, which he inscribed with the blood of a thousand slaves, Zutha fueled those rings and stones with his own blood and a portion of his soul. Only he could wield them. He or his direct descendants."

The rings and stones whispered in my brain, presenting their powers before me in the manner that knights lay their swords before a king. With such weapons on my person and the secrets of the *Gluttonous Tome* at my disposal, I marveled to consider the changes I might work on the world—among the Pathfinder Society, in Cheliax, and beyond.

Radovan touched my arm. "Boss?"

I had been lost to reverie. The dragon was speaking.

". . . under my supervision. You may use the library in the upper chambers, and I will alert my brother at Vythded Monastery. Their library contains some relevant volumes. You may send someone back to reassure your guards, but I remind you how unwise it would be to invite further intruders into my lair . . . or to abscond with any of my treasures."

With the Crest and Crown of Zutha upon me and the final secrets of the *Gluttonous Tome* at hand, I had little to fear from a single hoard-greedy dragon. "Show me this library."

14
The Dragon's Lair
Radovan

Before letting us into the rest of her lair, the dragon called Svannostel gave us each a peek and a sniff.

I'd been close to a dragon once or twice before, but it's not the sort of thing you get used to. When she put her tarnished bronze snout up to me, I knew all it would take was a nudge to turn me into paste. When she inhaled, my hair rose up in the breeze.

After she had a good whiff, she said, "There is something wrong with you."

"I get that a lot." I tried not to make a face. Her breath smelled like fish and river water. "I used to have a condition. It's better now."

It wasn't a lie, exactly. It'd been a couple years since I last heard the devils that crawled through me to escape Hell. If Desna smiled on me, I'd never hear them again.

Svannostel sniffed the others. They did their best not to cringe, but I saw tears running down Zora's face.

The dragon didn't seem impressed with Eando, Zora, or Illyria. She gave Kazyah a little snort, like she recognized her smell. Kazyah didn't blink.

Svannostel bent down to sniff Arni, who whimpered like a big baby. Amaranthine flew to perch on his shoulders, spreading her wings to protect him. Svannostel's huge lips peeled back. For a second I was afraid she'd eat them both. Then I realized that was how the dragon looked when she smiled.

"So fierce." She raised her head. "Never touch the copper portal or the crystal in the scrying room. If you venture below this part of the river or up into the mountain, you are beyond my protection—but not my wrath."

She led us to the round gate and opened it with a wave of her claw. She spit lightning into the next room before inviting us to follow.

That next room was a huge, long cavern. Along the walls glowed copper pipes, howling as warm air poured into the room. Above them hung copper plates with reliefs of dragons in various situations, like a tapestry in a lord's mansion.

We sat on marble benches while the heated air dried our clothes. The boss took a seat before an image of a bronze dragon scratching runes into a clay tablet. He turned to Svannostel and said, "You are named for Svannost, the Father of History."

"You know the history of my people." The dragon sounded surprised. When he said something else in dragontongue, she arched her neck like she was impressed.

They talked a while in her language. The longer they went on, the more it seemed to irritate Lady Illyria, so I figured she couldn't understand any more than I could. I looked to Eando and Kazyah to see if they understood. He shrugged, but it was awkward and I could tell he was still scared. Kazyah closed her eyes like she was trying to commune with her ancestors. Either that, or that was what she did when she was scared.

When we were dry, Svannostel led us through a big gallery. "Here is some of what I have recovered of Xin-Gastash," she said. "There is so much more beneath us, but it would take all the dwarves of Janderhoff centuries to unearth the city."

Damned dwarves, I thought, but I kept it to myself.

Here and there, a bit of pillar or the corner of a roof stuck out of the cavern wall. Hunks of stone with frescoes or mosaics hung from chains in the ceiling. Statues stood around like party guests too shy to talk. One was a marble of a fat fellow gripping a reaper's scythe. One arm and half his head had crumbled away missing, but he had rings on all his fingers and half a crown of stones circling his head.

"Zutha," said the boss. "Last runelord of necromancy."

"Gluttony," said Eando. "That's what they called it."

The boss ignored him.

The other statues included knights, wizards, monks, dragons, some squid-cow thing, and gods.

One of them had its own shrine in a deep alcove. Standing on a stone over magic flames was the six-winged, star-headed goddess the oracle had called Lissala. From the ragged tab on her base I could see she'd been ripped from the smoking altar up in the Sleeper's head. The boss stared at her for a long time. Everybody else stared at the boss staring at her, but nobody said nothing. Nobody dared.

Past the huge gallery we walked up a wide curving ramp. I saw bones stuck in the floor or wall here and there, mostly people but sometimes a dog or a sheep. I guessed they were the ones who lived here when Earthfall shoved the mountain over their underground city.

We went through a few more caverns. Claw marks showed where the dragon had torn open larger passages for herself, but she'd also laid down steps and ramps, so I figured she'd had human-sized guests in the past. Or maybe, like one of the other dragons I knew, she could transform herself into an elf. I hoped she'd do that. The last one had been a real looker.

Despite the boss's grumbling about "subterranean conditions," the library turned out to be clean and dry. The ceiling was high as a cathedral's, with a spiral path winding up the wall for three levels above us. In five places, the path widened to form an open room with stone benches and tables, and then I was sure the dragon could make herself human-sized. How would she open books with those big claws of hers?

Svannostel lifted a claw, and a hundred floating lanterns lit up like stars. In the middle of the cavern glowed a yellow sun. Eleven worlds circled it on clockwork gears, some with moons. Their shadows prowled along the bookshelves.

"Nice orrery," I said.

The dragon didn't have eyebrows, but she looked like she wanted to raise one at my comment

"I'm smarter than I look."

Maps and charts hung on the walls above shelves packed with books and scrolls. The boss right away started browsing the library with Illyria and Eando while the dragon kept a storm-colored eye on them.

The rest of us poked around the big room. Svannostel had decorated the place with ivory dressing screens, metal grates, urns, sculptures, and other fancy bits and pieces scavenged from the buried city. It looked like a museum.

I kept an eye on Zora, in case her fingers got itchy. She saw me watching her and stuck out her tongue. That made me think of better uses for that tongue, but I could hear the boss saying, "Neither the time nor the place." Even when he's not sick from an evil book, he can be a spoilsport.

After the wizards had their tour of the library, the boss sat at a human-sized stone table to read his *Tome*. Eando and Illyria opened a few scrolls they'd found on the shelves. Svannostel ushered the rest of us to a hearth surrounding another tangle of copper tubes. She set it glowing with another breath of lightning and curled up around us like a giant dog. It made Arni nervous. He turned around eight or nine times before settling at my feet.

Which was weird, because he usually stuck to the boss.

"Count Jeggare says he will destroy the *Tome*," said the dragon from above our heads. She looked down at Zora, Janneke, and Kazyah, but her gaze settled on me. "But will he? The curse already lies heavy upon him. See how he ignores the rest of my library to read the *Black Book*?"

I patted Arni's head to reassure him. Well, maybe to reassure me. Then I leaned back and struck a confident pose. "The boss reads pretty much every book he finds. You can't hardly stop him. He wants to know everything. He needs to understand how it all fits. With this big library, I figure you know something about that."

The dragon stayed still for a moment, but then she gave a slow nod.

"Anyway, he's seen plenty of dangerous books before. Here's the thing: in the end, he closes them. He's the guy you *want* to read the book before the wrong guy gets hold of it."

The dragon nodded again. Zora and Kazyah did the same, like they felt better now that they'd heard me say it.

I wished I felt better, too.

Svannostel asked us about the crew we left outside, so we told her they were mercenaries we'd hired to escort us through the badlands in our search for the *Tome*. I got the feeling the dragon wasn't as worried about her hoard as she was about how we'd deal with the *Gluttonous Tome*. She told us it would take more than setting it on fire or tearing it to pieces to break the curse, which we already knew, and that she wanted us to be ready to act as soon as the wizards figured out the trick.

In a few hours it got obvious they weren't going to find the secret overnight. Kazyah and Janneke went back to camp for supplies, which meant Zora had to go with them.

That left me alone with the dragon. Svannostel went to her scrying room to talk with her brother, so I roamed. Following the sound of the river, I found two other caverns it passed through. On the way back through the gallery, I heard Illyria's voice. For a second, I thought maybe she was invisible, but when I took another step I couldn't hear her anymore. I stepped back and heard her again.

This one time the boss and I went to the Grand Temple of Asmodeus on a murder investigation. While waited for the Grand High Priestess, the boss showed me a "whisper corner." He had me stand there while he crossed the room. When he whispered, I could hear him like he was standing next to me.

I wondered whether the dragon even knew she had a whisper corner in her lair. If she did, I figured I'd better warn the others to watch what they said.

Back in the library, Lady Illyria and Amaranthine were sitting far away from the boss and Eando, who kept reading at their table. Illyria was trying to coax the drake into speaking, but Amaranthine only chirped and trilled.

"Is he in a nasty mood?"

"The nastiest," said Illyria. "Tell me that's just the book talking."

"It's the book," I said.

That was more or less true. I'd seen the boss in bad temper plenty of times, but less often since we left Egorian. When he was fighting a war, unraveling a mystery, or tracking down some lost artifact, he was at his best. Sometimes the drink got to him, but not too often these past few years. The worst I'd seen him was a couple times before when he'd been rubbing up against something wicked, and I was starting to think we'd never found anything wickeder than this *Gluttonous Tome*.

"Don't worry," I said. "Once we figure it out, he'll be his usual self again."

Illyria gave me a weak smile, but it didn't last long. She looked worried. I knew how she felt, but right there in plain sight of the boss, I figured I shouldn't ought to get too friendly with her.

I went back down to the hearth. I drank a little water, ate some dry rations, and laid down back to back with Arni for a nap.

When I woke up, Illyria was sleeping on a nearby bench, which surprised me after all the fuss about summoning her own cottage on the road. Eando was laying down his bedroll, yawning into his fist before going straight down into a hard sleep.

I went up to check on the boss. Arnisant followed me, head hanging low.

The boss didn't look up as I arrived. He just kept reading, jotting notes in his journal while his finger traced lines in the *Tome*. His face looked paler, and he was getting jowly. The Azlanti stones circled his head. Every once in a while, one would turn toward me like an eye that could see inside me.

The boss scratched away in his journal, rings clicking on his fingers.

I saw he had the *Tome*, the *Lacuna Codex*, and a copy of the *Lexicon of Paradox* in front of him. He'd marked the pages with little slips of paper. Arnisant lay down at the far end of the table, not at the boss's foot like usual.

"Read any bad books lately?"

My voice startled him. He reached out to cover the books, all protective until he realized it was just me. He gulped and winced like it hurt. His hands were shaking.

"What is it?" he said. He went back to writing a note.

"I just wanted to see how you're doing. Getting enough to eat?"

"No thanks to that woman. Between her hovering and that Pathfinder's incessant questions, I will never master the more powerful spells in the *Tome*."

"But you don't need to master them. You're going to destroy the book, right?"

He looked around, saw that no one else was nearby, and said, "There may be an alternative."

"But you promised—"

"These pages contain more than knowledge. Combined with these stones and rings, they represent more power than anything we have ever encountered. Think of it, Radovan: The one who wields Zutha's spells and weapons could transform the Empire." He lowered his voice to a whisper. "He could cast the infernal legions back to Hell."

The boss was careful not to talk treason, but I knew how he felt. More than anybody, he hated the House of Thrune. He was one of the few who remembered what Cheliax was like before they came to power. The Jeggare family had to swear loyalty. If there was one thing everybody in Cheliax learned, it was that if you talked treason, it was only a matter of time before the inquisitors paid you a visit. And then it was only a matter of time before the Hellknights took you, and you ended up on the tines.

"Maybe let's first break this curse," I said.

He set down his pen and looked at me. His eyes were bloodshot. "Removing the curse could be counterproductive."

"You remember how you asked me to tell you when you start to go peculiar?"

"Radovan!" He banged a fist on the table and right away looked like he regretted it. "If I seem passionate, it is because of the astonishing opportunity before me." Arnisant perked up as the boss raised his voice. I looked across the room to see that Eando and Illyria were still sleeping.

"It's just that Eando and Lady Illyria are worried about—"

"They do not bear the responsibility of a count of Cheliax. They are incapable of the risks and sacrifices demanded by great actions."

I could tell by his glistening eyes that there was no arguing with him. "Just let me know what you need me to do."

He crooked his finger. I moved close. He grabbed my neck with a clammy hand and whispered, "Find out what the others are saying. I can see them whispering about me."

His eerie voice made me almost as sick as what he was saying. "Me and Arni, boss. We got your back."

He nodded, turned away, and dipped his pen. "See that I am not disturbed."

Too late for that, I thought.

We spent days like that, the wizards reading and making notes, the rest of us trying not to bother any of them. Every day Eando and Illyria moved farther away from the boss. Sometimes one of them would go over to talk to him until he snapped. They started writing notes and leaving them on his table before making quick getaways.

I started taking turns with Janneke checking on the carriage. On my third or fourth turn, I found Kaid's Band burning orc bodies. The good news was the scouts spotted the marauders in time to set an ambush, and they didn't lose a single woman. The bad news was a couple orcs got away riding dire wolves. If they didn't move camp, the mercenaries could expect more company.

I told the boss, but he didn't want to hear it. All he said anymore was, "I must not be disturbed."

I resisted the urge to share my joke about that with the others. It might make them laugh, but I didn't want them thinking I'd lost my faith in the boss.

I told them about the orcs, though. Svannostel said, "I will deal with them. Will you come with me, Night Bear?"

Kazyah nodded. She put on her bear hat and cloak, and picked up her earth breaker. They started to leave.

"I want to go," said Janneke. She gave Zora a look. "Radovan, can you keep an eye on Zora?"

"Where's she going to go?" I said.

"Just don't let her escape."

"Do I look like a jail keeper?"

"All right, the manacles it is." She shrugged off her pack to find them.

"Dammit!" Zora let out a heavy sigh.

"Wait, wait," I said. "All right. I promise I'll keep an eye on her."
Janneke smiled, and I knew she'd played me. "Thanks," she said.
The big girls headed out.

"You're really going to watch over me?" said Zora.

"You prefer the manacles?"

She shot me a dirty look.

"I knew an elf girl who liked manacles."

"Why am I not surprised?"

I had an answer for that, but my heart wasn't in it. The fact
was, I didn't like keeping prisoners, not even for Janneke. I looked
at Zora pouting and asked, "Think you're wearing her down?"

"Not really," she said. "That hill giant wants her bounty."

The way the boss was paying her, Janneke didn't need the
money. I'd asked her about it before, and she said it was all a question of professional pride. If it got out that she'd let Zora escape
after capturing her, all the other bounty hunters would make fun
of her.

I didn't like to think about what would happen to Zora after
she got turned in. She'd made someone real mad—probably a
wizard. You don't want to make a wizard mad. And if you do, you
definitely don't want to get caught. I said, "You got a plan?"

"Back in Kaer Maga, I hoped the count would buy her off. He
seemed generous. Now I don't know what to think of him."

"He'll be all right after we break the curse."

"But will he make Janneke set me free?"

He could, if he wanted to. But I knew he wouldn't. I shook my
head. "The boss told Janneke she could take you in. In Cheliax, one
of the worst things you can do is break a bargain."

"Can't you talk him out of it?"

"Not after he gave his word."

She sighed and thought a while before talking again. "Listen,
I'm not asking you to do anything. But it might help me if, at the
right time, you did nothing. Just let me take my own chance."

I touched the lump on my jacket where my harrow cards were. "You gonna keep your hands off my stuff?"

"I only did that to get your attention." When I smiled, she added, "Not like that."

"I get it. You had a spell on you. This Master, Ygresta, he told you not to warn us about his plan, but he didn't tell you not to pick my pocket."

She nodded.

"I'll think about it," I said. "Meanwhile, until Janneke gets back, you stick to me like my shadow. Got it?"

"Got it. Say, there's something I've been wanting to ask you."

"Yeah?"

"What is it with you and dwarves?"

"What are you talking about?"

"I saw you jump out of your skin when you ran into some on Jeggare Street. Janneke made some remark, too. And when the dragon mentioned dwarves, you growled."

"I don't growl."

"You did."

"You were following me all the way from Jeggare Street to the Jug and got there before me?"

She shrank a little, like she expected me to be mad. "Yes."

"You must have spied on me in Beggar's Alley."

"Maybe a little."

"Huh. You're better than I thought."

She bloomed at the compliment. "So, dwarves?"

"It's a long story."

"It's a long way to camp and back. Janneke won't return for hours."

"All right, here's the short version: Janderhoff was the first bit of civilization we reached on the way back from Sarkoris. We'd had trouble with orcs all the way. The last band chased us right up to the gates of the city. Lucky for us, the boss had friends there. One of the guards actually started singing a song when he saw us. The boss sang back in dwarf talk. They did a little dance. It would have been comical if we weren't half-starved. The dwarves saw we were in bad shape, so after the greetings, they brought us in for a big feast.

"Now the boss warned me not to play patty-fingers with the fancy dwarf ladies. I think his exact words were, 'consign your attentions to the help.' You know, on account of I'm not a noble. And, you know, hellspawn."

"That doesn't bother everybody," said Zora.

"I know. I'm not exactly unlucky with the ladies."

"But the dwarf ladies . . . ?"

"So after we washed up and got a bite, I consigned my attentions to the help—or the ones I thought were the help. The boss was so tired, and he drank so much ale before I showed up from my bath, he left out one little detail. On special occasions, the dwarf nobles' daughters serve the guests."

"Oh no!"

"She was a pretty little thing, and friendly. You could say she was consigning her attentions to *me*, not the other way around."

"You like to brag about the women you've known. Elf girls. Dwarf girls."

"Don't forget Sczarni girls," I said with a wink. "It's not bragging if it's true. See, I can tell you like me."

"I like how easy it was to make you chase me. I like how easy it was for me to lead you to Kaer Maga."

"You like to think I'm going to let you go before Janneke gets back, but I won't."

"Not yet," she said. "I have yet to work my charms on you."

"Good luck with that. Anyway, we barely got out of Janderhoff alive. The girl's father was going to kill me or make me marry her—I'm not entirely sure which. He was so drunk, and so was the boss, I couldn't understand all the dwarf talk. Anyway, we didn't wait long enough to find out."

"It sounds like it was all an honest mistake."

"The boss explained that dwarves think all mistakes are dishonest."

"Goddamned dwarves," she said.

"Goddamned dwarves."

We went back to the library. Illyria and Eando were sitting farther away than ever. They'd been talking, but they changed the subject when they saw us coming.

Maybe the boss was right. They *had* been talking about him.

"Say, Radovan," said Eando. "Jeggare keeps comparing the *Gluttonous Tome* with other books from his satchel, but he won't let me see them. Do you know what they are?"

I knew, but I shrugged.

"Was one the *Lacuna Codex*?"

"The lagoon of what?"

He chuckled and shook his head, but Illyria gave me a hard look. She knew I was playing dumb.

As I walked away, Illyria and Eando started whispering again. They were in the same spot Illyria where had been when I'd heard her from the whispering corner. When we got far enough away, I nudged Zora. "Want to see something? Hear something, I mean."

"Is that your idea of making a pass at me?"

"Nah, my passes are smooth."

"Sure."

Thinking all the time whether that meant she *wanted* me to make a pass at her, I took Zora to the gallery and stood her in the place. "Hear anything?"

She turned her head to listen. "Maybe a little. It sounds like voices."

"Let me try." It was the same for me, just some indistinct whispering at first.

Then I heard Kazyah's voice: "I thought you would chase them all the way back to Urgir."

The dragon's voice said, "I'm grateful for your aid. Their sorcerers surprised me."

"I wish they'd come back," said Janneke. By her muffled voice, I figured she'd put on her helmet again. "I wanted to shoot the count's scorpion."

Someone else said something I couldn't make out, and they lowered their voices.

"Let's get back there," I said.

There was a surprise waiting for me. Everybody except for the boss stood around a table, leaning over books they'd left open.

At first I thought someone new had showed up, an elf standing a full head taller than Janneke. Her eyes were a lightning-scarred sky, her skin the battered bronze of storm light at dusk. Even though I knew she had to be the dragon, she looked soft enough to touch.

Svannostel turned as we approach. She raised an eyebrow and looked right at me. "I suppose there's something to be said for consistency of purpose."

"I didn't do anything."

"It's what you were thinking of doing."

I tried not to think about her soft blue lips and white hair, light as corn silk. Svannostel's eyes widened. I was only making it worse.

"Come on, I can't help it. Why don't you look like a dragon instead?"

"My claws are hard on books."

"What were you thinking?" Zora poked me in the arm.

"Never mind," Svannostel and I said together.

"Say, Radovan," said Eando. He pushed a few pages across the table at me. "Would you mind taking these notes to Jeggare?"

I looked at the parchment. He and Illyria had made some notes for the boss. "He might have questions for you."

"He's less likely to tear a strip off of you," said Illyria.

"Such fearful little creatures!" Svannostel snatched up the pages and walked across the library toward the boss.

Eando looked after her, but I caught him glancing at me before he pretended to go back to reading. Illyria soon did the same. Kazyah and Janneke just sat there trying not to look like they'd stopped talking when I showed up.

Svannostel came back a few minutes later, a blue blush on her cheeks. She was mad as hell. "No mere half-elf dares speak to me in that manner. To be so reckless, he is farther gone than we thought. The stones of the Crown activated as soon as I drew near. I could feel the rings humming with power. He has charged them with spells."

Kazyah stood. "Then it is time."

"Time for what?" I said.

"Radovan," said Illyria. She came to me and put her hand on my arm. "Come with me. Let's all retire to the gallery so as not to disturb the count."

I shrugged off her arm, but I followed her. We all did. I took a seat on one of the benches. Zora sat next to me, but the others formed a little half circle.

"We know how loyal you are to Count Jeggare," said Illyria. "We need you to help us help him."

"Forget it."

"You don't even know what we're suggesting."

"Whatever it is, you should tell it to him. I don't like this secret meeting stuff."

"He'll never find a way to break the curse in the *Tome*, or either of his other cursed books for that matter," said Eando. "He's not even searching anymore. He's spent all this time trying to learn the spells."

"Good!" I said. "Maybe one of them can destroy the book."

"You know he won't destroy the book," said Svannostel. Her face darkened. She grew taller, wings unfolding from her shoulders, what had looked like patterns on her gown spreading out to become her scales. In a moment, she towered over us. "He is giving in to its seduction. He will become the runelord!"

"Then get the book away from him."

"No one can do that," said the dragon. "You've seen how it hovers near him. The book is bound to its master."

"But the boss took Eando's book away."

"Not exactly," said Eando. "I could feel it back in Kaer Maga, when we each held one. It wasn't Jeggare taking it from me. It was the *Codex* calling to the *Grimoire*."

"Besides," said Illyria, "if it's true that Varian is descended from Runelord Zutha—"

"It is true," said Kazyah. "I asked my ancestors."

"—then even a more powerful wizard might not be able to take it from him."

"Besides," added Eando, "there's no fourth part of the book. It's complete."

"But we do know that Professor Ygresta escaped the curse through death," Illyria said.

"Sure, but he had someone ready to bring him back from the dead."

"So do we," said the dragon. She arched her neck over Kazyah, pretty much the one thing I could imagine making the shaman look small. "The Night Bear has scrolls."

"The oracle was entrusted with them in case a great hero of our people should fall," said Kazyah. "He passed them to me."

Once I'd seen a cleric use a magic scroll to bring a fallen general back to life on a battlefield. It was a rare and expensive spell, so I knew they'd never do one for me. The boss was rich and important back home, but we were a long way from there. I sensed a catch. "The boss isn't a great hero of your people."

"He shall be," said Kazyah. "If he can destroy the book and ensure that Runelord Zutha never returns to rule our lands, the Skoan-Quah will sing of his deeds."

The boss might like the singing-his-praises part, but I wasn't sold. "I don't like the idea. I'm his goddamned bodyguard! The whole point of my job is not to let him die."

"Only long enough to break the curse," said Illyria.

"Fine. Tell it to him."

"He won't hear it from us."

"You think I can talk him into letting you kill him?"

Suddenly, none of them could look me in the eye, and I realized what they were saying.

"You want *me* to kill him?"

"It would be quicker," said Eando. "Easier for him."

"I would do it myself," said Svannostel. "But it would be kinder and, frankly, less destructive to his corpse if you did it."

"You think you can take him now?" I snapped. "You said yourself, he's powered the rings and stones. I'm thinking maybe you're afraid of him."

"I am not afraid," said Svannostel. "I am only sorry that a man who seemed noble has fallen to such a dreadful curse. When I kill him, it will be with regret. It is a kindness to offer you the opportunity to do it yourself."

"You can all go straight to hell."

"Indeed," said an eerie voice even higher than the dragon's head. "And if you seek to harm me, I shall speed you on your way."

The boss came into view as he let go of his invisibility spell. He glided down from the gallery ceiling, clutching the *Gluttonous Tome* to his chest. Rings glowed on every finger. The Azlanti stones spun faster and wider around his head. Some threw rippling fields of energy around his body. Others twitched like war dogs eager to slip the leash.

Eando put a hand on his sword and stepped back. "Jeggare, be reasonable."

"You entreat me to reason while conspiring to assassinate me?"

"We only want to free you from the curse," said Illyria. "Kazyah was going to restore you to life."

"Is that what she is preparing to do?"

Kazyah spun on her heel, dragging her earth breaker in a circle around herself. Pebbles and dust jumped from the rock beneath her feet.

"Drop the book, Count," said Svannostel. "Remove the rings and stones. Then we can discuss our options."

"I will never bow my head for execution."

Arni came running from the library, hackles raised. He stopped beneath the boss, looking up at him and back at the rest of us, confused.

"There may be another way—" said Eando.

"I heard it all," the boss said. "I heard you implore my henchman to betray me."

"Now, boss . . ."

"Fear not, Radovan. I also heard your refusal. Let us deal with these betrayers so I can return to my preparations."

"Stay back, Radovan." Illyria pointed at the boss. "I'm sorry, Varian."

The next words out of her mouth were magic, but the boss was quicker. Before Illyria could finish the spell, a red tendril burst from her cheek and sewed her lips shut.

"I see now why you favor that spell," said the boss. His mouth twisted in a sneer.

Janneke raised her crossbow.

"Back off!" I put myself between her the boss. "We don't need a fight."

Eando feinted to one side before dashing in on the other side. He hissed, "Radovan, help us with—" before I put my heel in his breadbasket.

The boss started casting a spell of his own, one I'd never heard before. Before he was done, Kazyah finished casting hers.

A huge lump of bone-filled earth and stone rose up beneath Kazyah, bigger than any of the statues. Its eyes glowed like molten amber. Kazyah balanced on its shoulders, raised her earth breaker, and pointed at the boss. "Take him!"

Svannostel opened her mouth. Lightning blinded us all. When I could see again, a statue behind the boss was scorched black—except for a circle where he'd been hovering. One of his Azlanti stones skittered like a drop of water across a hot skillet, but it kept circling his head.

Svannostel roared. Inside the cavern, the sound was so loud I expected to feel blood trickling from my ears.

Amaranthine squawked in sympathy as Illyria used a sharp knife to cut the stitches that bound her mouth shut. She sputtered blood and gasped for breath.

Janneke's bow snapped. The cylinder flew toward the boss. A shimmering field deflected it. The cylinder broke open, spilling an empty net to the floor. Without missing a beat, Janneke fired two bolts. They bounced off the boss's magic shield.

The boss finished his spell. Even as the stone spirit marched toward him, a bony arm broke out of its body to clutch Kazyah's leg. The fleshless dead began climbing out. One after another, they fell like new-foaled calves or clambered up toward the shaman. Hunks of earth and stone fell away, but that didn't stop the elemental. It moved toward the boss.

"Radovan, look out!"

I dodged aside, but Zora had already tripped Eando with her flagstaff. He stumbled across the place where I'd just been. I hooked his ankle, and he went down again.

Arnisant barked and jumped against the earth spirit. "Don't hurt the dog," said Kazyah. "Grab his master."

I moved toward the boss, but my first step went right out from under me. I slid across a slick mess on the floor.

"Stay down, Radovan," said Eando. Still on the floor, he'd just finished some magic gesture creating the greasy stuff. "Stay out of this, if you won't help us."

Kazyah's earth spirit loomed over the boss, but it stopped about five feet short of grabbing him. The rocky thing had no face, but it still looked confused.

The boss clenched a fist, and a yellow gem flared on one of his rings. The spirit shuddered, clouds of dust pouring off of its limbs. The orange glow of its eyes turned bloody red.

The boss pointed at Kazyah, who was still standing on top of the elemental. "Crush her!"

Now obeying the boss, the elemental grabbed Kazyah by the leg. Surprised, she swung her earth breaker a moment too late. The spirit threw her across the room. She hit the wall. We all heard the sharp crack of her bear hat.

"Boss, don't!"

I stayed low to keep from slipping on Eando's grease, but I had the big knife in one hand and a couple darts in the other. Illyria was casting another spell. I threw the darts, but I held back at the last instant. None of them even went close to hitting her.

"Are you with me, Radovan? Or are you against me?"

"We don't need to kill anybody."

"With or against?!"

"Desna weeps!" I choked. "I'm with you."

Another blast of lightning hit the boss, and this time his shield didn't hold. He fell to the ground, and for a second his halo of stones sagged. He stood up from a crouch, his clothes singed and his hair smoking, his face scorched red and black. Still holding the *Tome*, he drew the Shadowless Sword and looked up at Svannostel. His purple eyes gleamed dark as hers blazed bright.

They both called out spells.

Out of the corner of my eye, I saw Janneke raise her double crossbow. I threw a few stars her way. They missed the bow string, but they sank into the wood. I pointed at her and said, "Don't!"

The dragon finished her spell. A magical weight settled on me. Arni wobbled as he felt it too. My limbs moved like I was floating in molasses. Svannostel had slowed me and the dog, but the boss didn't seem the least bit bothered.

He gestured with his sword, and a black ray shot into the dragon's breast. She trumpeted in pain and surprise. Her wings slumped, like the ray had ripped something out of her.

Thrusting his sword forward, he screamed a magic word. Everybody else screamed with him. Their bodies twitched and folded in pain.

Kazyah screamed too, but her voice sounded like a rockslide. I caught a glimpse of her bear cloak vanishing as she transformed herself into an earth spirit to fight the one the boss turned against her.

Illyria shook a wand at the boss. Blue-black bolts shot toward him. With a wave of his hand and a flash from one of his rings, he threw them back at her. She cried out as they sank into her chest. She stumbled back and fell over a stone bench.

Amaranthine flew at the boss. Arni jumped up and woofed, but he stopped short of biting the drake.

With a casual swipe, the boss slapped the drake out of the air.

"Don't hurt her!" choked Illyria, still doubled over in pain.

"Boss, let's get out of here," I said. "You've got the book. We don't need anything else here. You've won. It's over."

"Nothing is over until I am satisfied." He took a step toward Amaranthine and raised his blade.

Arnisant stood over the drake. He whimpered, but he didn't budge.

"Arnisant, move away!" The boss raised his sword.

"Boss, you don't want to do that." I let a riffle scroll slip from my sleeve into my hand. Thumbing the edge, I felt the cold magic run up one arm and down the other. On the way across, it left a chill in my heart. I stepped in front of Arni.

The boss pushed me aside.

"Boss." I put a hand on his shoulder, steady as a rock. My grip shifted on the big knife.

He turned, eyes wide in anger. "How dare you?"

Guided by the magic of the riffle scroll, my hand drove the big knife straight into his heart.

The boss opened his mouth, but only a dark red bubble came out. For a second his eyes locked onto mine. Then they shifted focus to something much farther away.

He dropped his sword. I held him up until he dropped the book. His blood poured over us both. I held him until the stones circling his head clattered on the stone floor. His head fell back. I lay him down on the floor, and then I lay myself down beside him.

15
The River of Souls
Varian

After sight left my eyes, I could still hear Arnisant barking and Radovan shouting useless apologies. After sound faded, I could still smell the sour odor of my body, soon to become the stench of corruption. Scent dwindled to nothing, but I could still taste the flatbread of my recent meal—my last meal—until all that remained was the tang of blood in my mouth. Taste dissipated, and all I could feel was the blood overflowing my lips. As that final sensation trailed away, some intangible miasma released me from its grip, and I knew I had escaped the gluttonous curse.

I had died.

Several times before I had lain close to death before medicine or magic revived me. Once I had even stood on death's threshold before a miracle repaired my cloven heart.

While I could not see, hear, smell, taste, or touch, my consciousness endured. I could think. I could wonder.

Perhaps, I prayed, I could dream.

In bleaker moments I had imagined death as a blank oblivion, despite my hope that the Tender of Dreams would clasp me to her bosom in the afterlife. I wondered whether Desna would preserve the fancies that had buoyed me through the darkest years of my long life. I prayed she could forgive my fealty to House Thrune and, by extension, Asmodeus, the Prince of Law. I feared damnation because I knew I deserved it.

Bereft of dimension and time, my thoughts drifted upon a void. Some indeterminate later, a sensation returned not to my body but to my soul. I experienced a buoyancy without temperature. Motion carried me, but by what vehicle or toward what destination I could not fathom. A thought of cold tickled at my consciousness. It collapsed into an abstraction of smell, of many absent bodies huddled against a formidable expanse. My soul passed among a host of others.

A silent panic disrupted the unseen herd. I felt a cacophonous terror. Soon after, countless gray vagaries appeared all around me. Sensing them without benefit of eyes, I "saw" that I was one of them, a speck among a vast throng.

The motion I had previously sensed became apparent. We spirits were like schools of fish swept up in a current. No mark indicated our trajectory, much less our destination, only a blank immensity in all directions. Gradually I perceived disturbances at the boundaries of our swarm.

Shapes, by turns black and blinding, moved to intercept predators diving into the stream. I yearned to see the intruders more clearly. By my yearning my perception honed in on the site.

A white-winged devil thrust a spear through the breast of an ashen-skinned hag. Her black claws snapped just short of a translucent blot before she flew away, screeching in frustration.

Intuition told me her prey was an untethered spirit, a dead soul—one such as I. We passed from the material world through the Astral Plane. Eventually, we would arrive at our deserved reward, but not before Pharasma judged us.

With that thought, my perception broadened further. Behind us I sensed innumerable tributaries feeding our stream, souls escaping a multitude of worlds. Before us, the channel of spirits terminated at the tip of a distant pinnacle. Slender as a needle, it rose from a distant city of golden walls surrounding streets and edifices of perfect arrangement. The tower could only be

Pharasma's Spire rising up from Axis. Upon its infinite height rested the Boneyard, where the goddess of death held court.

Another disturbance broke into the torrent of souls. Focusing on the intruder, I saw an attenuated figure, human in frame but with tendrils flowing from its shoulders like a cape, and a long tail waving behind its path. Its piscine jaws snapped at a brown-skinned angel wielding a sunlight sword. It snatched up a soul and flew away. The angel pursued, leaving its place unguarded for a moment.

Something else had been waiting for that moment.

A serpent-woman dove into the stream. Her many-colored feathers stirred souls as she passed. She made no move to steal them. Instead, she flew directly toward me, her glabrous hands reaching for my—not my face, for I remained bodiless. For *me*. She gathered me to her face and brushed me with her lips.

Her fleeting kiss felt as delightful as the brush of a butterfly's wings. Her reptilian eyes stared through me while her semi-human face remained a mask of indifference.

A thunderclap shook me. Like startled minnows, the nearest souls fled from me. Only the snake-woman remained. She twisted to either side, looking for the source of the disturbance.

"Return, Count Varian Jeggare," said an aching voice, like the yawn of a distant landslide. "Take up your bones, resume your mantle of flesh, and walk your mortal path again."

After a moment's hesitation, I recognized the distorted voice as that of the earth-shaman Kazyah, called the Night Bear. We had spoken seldom since the oracle's death. In matters arcane, I had been content to consult Kline and Lady Illyria, leaving Kazyah to act as guide and guardian on our journey to the Sleeper. Radovan knew her better, I suspected.

Radovan. Ironic that I should meet my demise by his hand. In the earliest days of our acquaintance, I remained ever on guard against treachery. In the end, his was the only soul I entrusted with my life.

Kazyah's voice echoed across the Astral Plane. She meant to guide me back to the material world, no doubt by casting a spell the oracle had inscribed for her. I paused to consider whether I wished to obey her summons. In the passage of souls I felt no suffering. My sensations were purely metaphysical. The uncertainty of my destination planted no vexation in my thoughts, only a mild and abstract curiosity.

"Varian." The snake-woman's lips did not move, but as her eyes gazed at me, I heard a voice far more familiar than the shaman's. Although I had not heard it in three-quarters of a century, there was no mistaking it.

The snake-woman flew away. I heard—or perhaps *felt*—the voice call again. "Varian, come to me."

The snake-woman vanished into the astral expanse. None but my fellow astral travelers remained near. I thought of closing eyes I no longer had. Then I saw:

Sunlight on a green meadow dappled in the shadows of summer leaves.

Fireflies dancing in the twilight above a blue meadow.

Midnight stars sifting silver through bare branches, a dead bird moldering in the snow.

Dawn dispelling the murk with rosy light glistening on the dew.

The meadow green again and filled with fluttering blue swallowtails.

"Varian."

Cool grass tickled my bare feet. Songbirds called from the boughs, and a scent of wildflowers dizzied my head. Pollen sweetened my lips. The morning sun blinded me as I turned, and then I saw my mother.

She appeared as I best remembered her, barefoot and grass-stained, the way we returned from our excursions at the summer house. She wore her ambling dress and the denim apron filled with pockets for our discoveries. A sprig of wild rosemary peeked out of one pocket. Another pouch bulged, overfilled with almonds.

Countess Pontia Jeggare appeared far younger than she had on the day of her death. With her black hair pinned loose behind her neck, she looked exactly as she had in my youth, when she was not only my mother but my teacher, my mentor, and my best friend.

"Begone, figment." My skepticism demanded proof, or at least evidence.

"Varian," she said. It was the voice I had known for the first few decades of my life. In life, magic can falsify such things. But after life? Only a god's power would suffice. All at once I abandoned skepticism for faith and believed: before me stood the true image of my departed mother, delivered to me by Desna, the Tender of Dreams.

I went to her. She stood still yet somehow remained just out of reach.

"We are in different places," she said. The morning light gave way to the vertical rays of noon. "This *here* exists only to let us speak."

"Is it a dream?"

She nodded. "Everywhere Desna's reach extends is at least part dream. You were full of dreams when I lived. I pray you remained so all of your life."

"Tell me you are somewhere . . ." I sought a word to describe what I wished for her. "You are happy?"

She nodded. Her violet eyes glistened, but not with sorrow. "Happier still to see you."

"How is it you can visit me?"

"You always had so many questions. In death I have found no answers, but everywhere there are many little wonders." She held out a hand. A butterfly alit upon her finger.

"Then why do you visit me?" I suspected the answer: I was not destined for the place where her spirit resided.

"In my last moments of life, I longed to speak with you one more time. Perhaps some emissary of the goddess has granted my wish." She made the sign of Desna over her breast, but not the simple sketch that had become my adult custom. She linked her thumbs and spread her hands across her collarbones, fingers curled and with a gap in the middle to suggest two pairs of wings. When I was a child, she would flap those wings to cast a shadow upon the wall. When the butterfly landed on me, it brought tickles. When I had grown too old for such childish signs of affection, she would make the gesture from across a crowded room whenever she thought I needed reminding that I was not alone among my predatory peers.

While my mother lived, I had never felt alone. After her death, it was all I ever felt for many years. The thought of her death reminded me of the unanswered questions at mine.

"Why did you never tell me that our family descends from a runelord?"

"Age did nothing to temper your curiosity," she said. "Nor did death." She looked at me, and I realized I once more had a body, or at least the illusion of one. Unadorned by Zutha's rings, my hands appeared as they had weeks before I discovered the *Kardosian Codex*. Not as old as they had looked a few years earlier, but neither as youthful as they had been when my mother was the age she appeared.

"Forgive me. In the weeks before I died, I had just begun to understand why you forbade me to practice necromancy. What I cannot understand is why you did not entrust me with the secret of our lineage."

"I meant only to protect you. In time I would have told you more. I always intended it. But then House Thrune usurped the throne, and I focused all my efforts on thwarting their machinations. And then they found me out. And then there was no more time."

The memory of that wicked day soured the pleasure of our reunion. In life, time had dulled the pain of her death, but it all came flooding back at the remembrance of her last words. "You made me swear again never to study necromancy," I said. "And not to oppose the House of Thrune. You feared for my life and for the continuation of our family. That I can accept. Yet could you not have told me I was a sorcerer?"

"A sorcerer?"

"The difference between a wizard and a sorcerer—"

"I know the difference." She smiled to see my surprise at her interruption. "One need not be a practitioner of the arcane arts to read a book. I read many on magic when you first expressed a desire to study at the Acadamae. But why did the masters not detect your talent? They never admit sorcerers."

"I assumed you had bribed someone to ease my entry."

"Well, in fact I did. The masters might not have been inclined to admit a boy who fell ill every time he tried to cast a spell, regardless of his intellect. What use is wealth and power if you do not use it to make those you love happy?"

"Why did you not simply tell me that we are descended of Runelord Zutha? You entrusted me with other family secrets. So did grandfather."

"Because of your insatiable desire to study everything, to know every reason, to master every talent you found within yourself. Can you honestly tell me you would not have studied necromancy if you knew your ancestor had ruled an empire with it?"

"A fraction of an empire," I said. "One-seventh of an empire."

"It is impertinent to correct your mother on a point of minutia."

My impulse was to argue that no aspect of the history of the runelords qualified as minutia, but her stern voice dispelled any thought of argument. "My apologies."

"You have not answered my question."

"I would have—" I meant to say I would have obeyed my promise, but before mother's ghost I could not dissemble. "I would have been careful. You could have trusted me."

"I trusted your curiosity. Do you remember when I forbade you to read your grandfather's diaries?"

Whatever mechanism of the afterlife gave senses to our spirits, they included the warmth of a blush. While I was ashamed to have been caught in the disobedient act, I did not regret it. "They were quite educational."

She gave me a wry smile. "Those of us who knew the family secret wished to leave it buried. House Thrune destroyed other houses with far less scandalous intelligence. But you would have searched for whatever lay beneath the darkest root of our family tree. I feared that what you might uncover, others might use against us."

Twilight lay a hand upon the day's shoulder. As we spoke, the sky—if it were a sky—grew dark. Stars smiled down at us.

"Considering my eventual fate, I suppose you were right to be concerned. Zutha's grimoire offered me great power. In the end, however briefly, I broke my vow and learned his dark magics. I intended to use them for noble purposes, but already their dark influence had begun corrupting me."

"If you are a sorcerer, how did you learn Zutha's spells? Were the runelords sorcerers?"

"No, they were indeed wizards. In some ways they were *the* wizards. Their specialties continue to define the schools of magic to this day."

"If they were wizards, why would their descendants become sorcerers?"

"No one truly understands how a sorcerous bloodline is established," I said. "Some sorcerers claim to be the descendants of dragons, angels, or other powerful creatures. It stands to reason that the runelords' descendants might have inherited some shadow of their innate magic."

"But if they were not sorcerers, what innate power did they have?"

As she had in life, my mother challenged me with the simplest questions—points so elementary that my colleagues never thought to pose them to me. "Well, they probably would not have had any in the beginning. It is conceivable that their wielding rune magic could imbue them—or their offspring, or their descendants several generations removed—with sorcerous abilities."

"If you say so," she said. "Such theory is beyond me. You always excelled in intellectual pursuits. Your passion for magical theory is what persuaded me to smooth your way at the Acadamae."

"Did it never occur to you that the reason I struggled to cast spells was that I was never meant to be a wizard? If I had known I inherited a sorcerous bloodline, I might have avoided decades of frustration and humiliation."

"Does it not occur to you that even in the afterlife one must not take an accusatory tone with one's mother?"

"My apologies."

She cupped her elbows and hugged herself as if feeling a chill. A breeze passed through the meadow. Clouds occluded the stars, but their edges began to bleed at the first gaze of dawn.

"It did occur to me. I am a Jeggare, after all, and while my interests do not include wizardry or sorcery, I bid you to remember who first instructed you in natural history, presented you with your first collection of the *Chronicle of the Inner Sea Kingdoms*, and sent you to the finest tutors in all of Cheliax."

"I remember, Mother. I beg your pardon."

"Also, I think I was the first to put a frog down your shirt. I hope I wasn't the last."

Her reminiscence dispelled the chill. The clouds parted, and the morning sun warmed us. "Sadly," I said, "you were not."

"I always thought you would benefit from a few more frogs down your shirt." She moved close and reached for my hands. I offered them but could not feel her touch as I felt the ground beneath us or the breeze in my hair. "I want to know about your life, Varian. There's no telling how long I can visit you here, before . . ."

"Before whatever judgment befalls me."

"Did you keep the Tender of Dreams in your heart, even as the queen demanded obedience to Asmodeus?"

"I did."

"Did you live a good life?" she said. "Did you strive to be a good man?"

"Sometimes." I wished I could have given her a more certain reply.

Her eyes glistened. "Do you forgive me for your not becoming a wizard?"

"But I did become a wizard," I said. "Granted, it took me decades to learn how to circumvent my, ah, impediment, but I discovered a forgotten form of scroll-making that allowed me to cast spells as a wizard."

"And yet you now think you are a sorcerer?"

"Yes."

"Who told you that?"

"Well, a sorcerer." I took her point. A blacksmith lays every problem on the anvil.

"Hm. What do you think you are?"

"I suppose I have been both a wizard and a sorcerer."

"And are others both wizards and sorcerers?"

"It is rare, but yes. I have read of such instances."

"Then how can you blame me for not telling you about our presumably sorcerous bloodline?"

"I—"

"All I wished was to prevent you from following our ancestor's path in necromancy. I never cared whether you were a wizard or a sorcerer, or both for that matter. I always encouraged you to pursue your interests."

"You did not trust me enough to tell the reason, even after I formally renounced the school of necromancy."

"Well, I confess that I enlisted help in guiding you away from that dark path."

"From the Acadamae masters?"

"No, from your servant, the bottle-washer who studied necromancy. Benno something."

"You told Benigno Ygresta that the Jeggare family descends from Runelord Zutha?"

"Of course not. I would never divulge such an odious secret, certainly not to a common fellow like him. Did you know his family picked grapes for House Drovenge? But when I heard you had struck up a camaraderie, I saw an opportunity to help you keep your promise."

"But Ygresta was an ardent proponent of necromancy."

"A little too ardent, perhaps?" She smiled. "Despite the limitations of his birth, he had the most natural guile I had ever encountered. It helped that he was sincere in his belief that necromancy is not inherently evil so that you would see him in a sympathetic light. It helped even more that he was never quite as clever as you. You would never have let an intellectual inferior win you over, even one with honest arguments. In these ways, he was the perfect agent of my will. It helped even more that this Ygresta could barely afford his first year's tuition."

"You paid him to manipulate me."

"I offered him the means to complete his education in order to help you keep your promise."

While my mother's interference rankled me even after all these years, my annoyance seemed trifling considering the circumstances of our conversation. Another question troubled me. "If you did not tell him, then how did Ygresta learn of my connection to Runelord Zutha?"

"First of all, I am dead, not omniscient," she said. "Second, what makes you think he did learn of our ancestry?"

"Well . . ." Her simple question forced me to reevaluate my theory. I had assumed Ygresta selected me as his cat's-paw because of my blood affinity for the *Gluttonous Tome*. What if instead he had chosen me for some other reason? Surely there were other capable Pathfinders—Eando Kline, for instance, who had already found the *Bone Grimoire*.

There had to be another reason. It had to have something to do with necromantic spells . . . which Ygresta believed I could not cast.

I had my answer.

As far as Benigno Ygresta knew, I graduated the Acadamae a failed wizard. For his purposes, I was the one Pathfinder capable of finding and understanding the missing volumes but *incapable* of casting its spells. Ignorant of my latent sorcerous ability or my discovery of riffle scrolls, he was mistaken on the latter point.

Armed with that knowledge, I could . . .

Well, I could do nothing. I was dead.

"Have I told you what you needed to know?"

"Yes, Mother. Thank you."

"Now, please, tell me about your life."

Not knowing where to begin, I thought of the fact that my human mother had lived less than half as long as I had. Part of the reason was my half-elven heritage. "I found my father."

As the meadow changed twenty times from day to night and then to dawn, I told her the story. In the beginning she wept for lost love. By the end, she was laughing and telling me stories of their time in the elven court.

She asked about my own loves, both those I concealed before her death and those that came after. She asked after our family, stopping me when the names of those born after her death became too numerous.

The days and nights flew across the meadow.

She asked which of my friends yet lived, and how the others had died. I told her I had died at the hand of a friend.

"The hellspawn?"

"You were the one who encouraged me always to *hire* halflings, never to buy them as slaves."

"I know, dear, but a hellspawn? And he stabbed you in the back."

"In the front, actually." I touched the place where my wound had been. "Right through the heart."

"How can you joke about such a thing?"

Perhaps I had left recriminations behind with my body. "In the tranquility of death, it is easier to see how I left him no choice. He always did prefer the dog to me."

"Is that another joke?"

I smiled. Jokes had been part of the private language Radovan and I developed over the years, even when—or perhaps especially when—I let him believe his vulgarity annoyed more than it amused. "Yes, Mother."

"Have you kept the other promises you made to me?"

"I have," I said. "In war and diplomacy and espionage, I have always served the ruling house. And I have hated myself for it with every passing year."

"Yet our house endures," she said. "You cannot anger the dragon and hope to live."

"Actually, I have found dragons to be considerably easier to treat with, compared with Queen Abrogail."

"Does Abrogail still rule?"

"I speak of the second of that name, great-granddaughter to the one you knew. Four others reigned between them, but she is by far the most dangerous. She re-bound the empire to Asmodeus."

"And you serve her."

"So that the Jeggare family may thrive, and so that I keep my promise to you, I do. And yet not long ago I held weapons of such power that I dared to imagine overthrowing House Thrune and casting the infernal legions back to the pit."

"And was it your promise to me that prevented you?"

"No," I said. "It was death." I mused on the irony of my situation. "The promises you demanded, they imprisoned me all my life. If I had studied necromancy, I might have been prepared to wield the weapons of our ancestor and avenge your death."

"Varian, I release you from your promises."

"To what end? That Pharasma might not judge me an oathbreaker among my other sins?"

"Are you blaming me for that?"

Perhaps I had blamed her, but no longer. "I might blame myself, but what is the point? My life is gone, and with it all the promises I made. Now I have only to face judgment for what I have done and what I have failed to do."

"Forgive," she said.

"You need no forgiveness."

"But you need to grant it." A swallowtail alit on her hair. Another fluttered onto her shoulder. I heard a distant rumble. The cycle of day and night came faster.

"Come back," said a distant voice. I no longer recognized it.

"No," I said. "I am dead."

"Forgive," said my mother. More swallowtails covered her. They flew away, leaving nothing but the empty meadow behind. The meadow dissolved, and I closed my eyes.

16
The Shadows of Xin-Gastash
Radovan

I didn't realize how hard Arni was biting me at first. Eando dragged me out from under while Kazyah and Janneke pulled Arni away by his hind legs. He snapped at them, and they let him go. He stopped barking and set up a mournful howl.

"Arni." My voice got all clotted up.

He ran out of the gallery. His howl carried through the passages of Svannostel's lair. Amaranthine flew after him.

"Wait!" called Lady Illyria. She had just dipped her finger into a jar of ointment to heal the drake. With her wrist, she wiped away a tear on her cheek.

Somebody touched my arm and almost got a spur before I checked myself. Zora backed away. She looked down at her bloody hand. I hadn't seen her get hurt in the fight, but I realized it wasn't her blood. I looked down at my sleeves, which Arni had shredded. He'd broken the skin in a few places, but not that bad. It wasn't my blood either. Then it hit me.

It was the boss's.

Kazyah knelt to pick up his body. Even with the weight he'd put on, he looked no heavier than a child in her arms. The rest of us followed as she carried him to the library and lay him down on a stone table. Seeing him like that reminded me of a mortuary slab, or maybe Ygresta's golem lab.

The tail of the big knife stuck out of his chest. Kazyah took the grip. I had to look away, but I couldn't stop hearing the sound it made coming out. I heard her set it on the table.

Eando put a hand on my shoulder. "I don't know what to say."

"Then maybe you should shut the hell up."

He took his hand off.

Janneke caught my eye from across the table. I stared back at her until she turned away.

"Bring me some water," Kazyah said.

Janneke ran toward the river passage.

Kazyah opened one of the bone cases hanging from her belt. She pulled out three scrolls with writing that glittered with diamond dust. She unfurled one and put away the others.

"Help me," she said to me. We pulled off the boss's jacket and shirt.

The wound was a dark red mess just left of his breastbone. I wanted to think it'd been quick. I just couldn't remember the moment I decided to do it. I told myself if I'd let him kill Arni, he wouldn't have been able to live with himself—but he wasn't really the boss at that point. I don't know who he was—a count of Cheliax, the Runelord Zutha, or something in between.

All I knew was one second I was his bodyguard and the next I was his killer.

Janneke came back with her helmet full of water. Kazyah had her tip it over the boss's chest. The water washed away the gore and left a dark purple line. The wound looked like a small thing to end a hundred-year life.

The thought of his age gave me a shiver. I counted back to the last day I knew the date. I did the arithmetic again. It was right, and I choked on it. That turned into a sob, or a laugh, or something. I sat down and held my arms, shaking like that jerk who can't stop laughing at his own mother's funeral.

"What is it?" said Svannostel. The dragon's voice still sounded big, but she stayed back to give us room around the table.

"Hell of a birthday present I gave him."

I felt everybody looking at me. After a few seconds, I felt them looking away.

Kazyah finished blotting the blood from the boss's body. She straightened his arms and legs and lay the scroll on his stomach. She gave us a look that told us to be quiet. She started to read.

The words were different from the ones she chanted to call her ancestors and the earth spirits. Reading them made the writing go soft on the page. Flecks of diamond finer than sand glittered in the ink. The magic words floated on the parchment like rotting leaves on a pond. As Kazyah finished her spell, the parchment crumbled away to nothing.

The boss's body lay still.

Kazyah looked down at him. She slapped her hand onto his chest. "Return, Count Varian Jeggare. Don your bones, resume your mantle of flesh, and walk your mortal path again."

"Come on, boss."

Eando went to the *Gluttonous Tome*. It lay on the cavern floor beside the Shadowless Sword. It looked the same as it had when the boss held it to his chest. Eando reached down but stopped himself before touching the book.

"What's wrong?" said Illyria. "Is the curse preventing his return?"

"I don't know," said Eando. "I thought the book would fall back into three pieces when he died. I just assumed."

"You didn't *know*?" I yelled. Illyria flinched when I turned to her. "What the hell have you been reading all this time? Your stupid little romance stories?"

She looked like I'd slapped her. "We thought it would work."

"You tricked me into killing the boss on a *hunch*?"

"It was more than that, Radovan," said Eando. When I showed him my teeth, he looked down. "It's all we had."

I turned to Kazyah. "There's something wrong with the scroll. Try another one."

"The scroll worked," she said. "I cannot force someone to return from death if he does not wish to come."

"That's crazy," I said. "Why wouldn't he want to come back?"

Everybody looked at me, their faces sad and guilty.

"He can't think we'd kill him again," I said. "The whole idea was to get him free from the book."

"He may not have understood that in his last moments," said Svannostel. "There was a madness upon him."

"Then ask, why don't you? You can talk to spirits, can't you?"

"Spirits of the earth," said Kazyah. "Spirits of my ancestors. The oracle might have reached him, but I cannot."

"You can't just give up," I said. "There's got to be a way."

"He has lived a long life," said Kazyah. "Longer than mine, I think. There comes a time to rest."

"Not for the boss," I said. "He wasn't done."

Illyria took out her monocle. She looked through it at the boss. She shook her head and turned toward the *Tome*. "I see no aura connecting them. He ought to be free from the curse."

"You said you couldn't see any aura on the book before."

"That's true."

"So what good will it do now?" I yelled. "Why are you messing with that lens? What use are you?"

"It's not her fault, Radovan," said Eando. "Take it easy."

"Don't you tell me to take it easy. You didn't just kill your best—"

That was more than I wanted to say to these jerks. Janneke put a hand on my shoulder. I shrugged it off, but she held on.

When I turned to yell at her, I saw the pain on her face. Maybe it wasn't like mine, but it was real.

"I'm sorry," she said. "We won't stop trying."

"He will not come," Kazyah said.

"Maybe not now," said Illyria. "Maybe the curse still affects him. It could be weaker now. Can you lift it with another spell?"

Kazyah frowned, thinking it over. "Possibly. I am not as powerful as my— as the oracle was."

"What if the *Tome* finds another master?" said Eando. "Would that free Jeggare's spirit?"

"Jeggare's oath was to destroy the tome," said Svannostel, "not to pass it along to another."

"Transferring the curse to someone else doesn't achieve our goal," said Illyria. "But now that it isn't linked to a person, can't we just destroy it?"

"Svannostel?" said Eando.

We went back to where the book had fallen in the gallery. We kept well away from it while the dragon opened her jaws and leaned forward. I shut my eyes. Out flashed the lightning, blinding even through my eyelids. The blast left a black scorch mark on the stone floor. Steam rose from the cover of the *Tome*, but it didn't look the least bit burned.

"Anyone know a pious king we could starve for a few weeks?" said Eando.

"This is no time for jokes," said Zora.

"It's not necessarily a joke, but I admit it sounds ridiculous."

"'Preposterous,'" I said. "That's the word the boss would have used."

Illyria nodded. A smile flickered on her lips before dying. "I was just getting to know him well enough to recognize his little idiosyncrasies."

We heard a sound from somewhere deeper in the dragon's lair. When it came again, I recognized Arni's bark.

"He's found something," I said.

"Intruders," said Svannostel. "Someone powerful enough to bypass my alarms."

Arni barked again. He sounded scared.

"I gotta find him," I said.

"The rest of you return to the library," said Svannostel. "Take the book."

"I will go with you." Kazyah began changing into an earth spirit. Svannostel didn't object.

"I'm not touching it," said Eando, eying the book.

"It's only harmful when read," said Illyria.

"Like I said, I thought it'd fall into three pieces when Jeggare died. I'm not taking the chance—"

"All talk, you two." I snatched up the book. I made sure not even to look at the cover, but if it turned me evil, it'd serve them right. Besides, what else was I good for now?

Illyria and Eando could cast spells without somebody else making riffle scrolls for them. Zora had a little magic of her own, and Janneke had her crazy crossbow. Arni wouldn't come near me. And after what I'd done with it, I never wanted to touch the big knife again. I didn't feel right using the scrolls the boss had made me, either.

Still, if something was coming for us, it was stupid to get all sentimental. Before heading back to the library, I picked up the knife, wiped it on my tattered sleeve, and made sure there was a riffle scroll in my side pocket. There were only a few left, but I was ready to burn them all. If whatever was coming for us wanted the *Tome*, it was going to find me and my big knife.

When we reached the library, I put the book down on the table nearest the boss.

Thunder echoed back from the lower passages.

"You think we ought to—?" Before I could finish the question, the cavern shook. Above us, the planets' gears squealed. A red world crashed to the floor.

Steam hissed in from the river caverns. Somewhere in the noise, I heard a familiar woof.

"Where's Arni?" I said. "I gotta go get him!"

"We should stay right here," said Zora.

"Agreed," said Eando. "Besides, he was attacking you before he ran off."

I moved toward the clouded passages. "Arni!"

The big dog came bounding out of the steam, drenched from nose to tail. Amaranthine clung to his shoulders, wings folded so tight she looked like a butterfly trying to get back into its cocoon. Arni ran past me to stand between Eando and Illyria.

The steam in the river passages thickened. Except for occasional flashes, I couldn't see anything farther than six or eight feet away.

"Don't go in there!" Janneke yelled. "You'll get scalded."

A little heat doesn't bother me. Still, Arni was back, and I couldn't see any better than a regular guy in steam. I backed up.

Illyria and Zora watched the way down to the gallery. Eando and Janneke watched the river passage. Between them, the boss's corpse lay on the stone table. It wasn't much of a bier for a count of Cheliax.

Lightning flashed again. It must have been closer—all my hairs rose up at the electricity pricking the air. The steam muted the sound of the thunder and landslides Svannostel and Kazyah must be throwing at the enemy. I couldn't hear their voices, only the crashing of air, earth, and water.

After a minute, we heard the sounds but didn't see any more lightning. The steam grew darker.

Illyria cast a spell and closed her eyes. The spell told her something, and she hissed, "They're coming."

She started to pour a circle of silver dust around us. Eando cast some protection on himself. Zora murmured a prayer to Desna and did the same. I snapped off a riffle scroll to make myself quicker.

The steam clouds turned the color of iron. Fingers of darkness wriggled out to touch the little stars floating beneath the library ceiling.

Illyria called out an arcane word and pointed. Where the darkness crept in, her light dispelled it. "Eando!"

"Got it." He cast another spot of light where the dark had killed a lamp.

Janneke shot a bolt into the steam. We heard it strike the cavern wall. She reached into her pack and loaded one of her special bolts.

Illyria's light vanished. As she cast another, Eando's dimmed as well. The darkness crept closer, surrounding us.

"Night Monarch, protect me." Zora unfurled her flag. As she swung the banner around her, its flapping edge left a faint blue glow that lingered around Zora. When its magic had set, she held the flag like a spear, ready to slash.

We kept our backs to the table. Soon we had only a little circle of light around us. The darkness kept pushing in.

Arnisant growled. Something growled back at him. In the dying light, I saw his hackles rise. "Easy, boy. Wait for them to—"

Arni charged into the dark. In a second, I heard him fighting something that sounded like another dog, or maybe a wolf.

"Arni!" I plunged after him. Janneke grabbed for me, but I slipped free.

I couldn't see a thing, which meant magic. The mist grew cold. I felt it beading like sweat on my arms. Cold fingers stroked along my neck.

"Radovan," whispered a woman's voice. I could tell by the thin chill of it that the woman wasn't alive.

"Leave him to me, sister," said another cold, flat voice.

"We leave him to the Master, Otto. See to your dog." The voice moved past me. I worried where it was going.

Keeping low, I moved quick back to the boss's table, expecting to find light. Instead, I bumped into Janneke. She almost cracked me with the butt of her crossbow before I called out her name. "It's me."

Somebody cast another light spell nearby. For a second I saw the shadow of a man throttling Zora as the shadow of a woman pulled at her flag and screamed at its touch. The shadow-woman let go, and the light vanished.

I dove to where I'd last seen Zora. I caught her by the waist and pulled her back over my hip. Without looking, I stabbed out behind us. The big knife ripped through something like a thin curtain. I thought I'd gotten tangled in Zora's flag, but the shadow-man cried out, "Kill him, Ada! His Hell-blade tears me!"

That's all the encouragement I needed. The second and third stabs earned me two more screams.

In the dark behind me, Eando howled. Letting go of Zora, I caught what felt like the Pathfinder's armor. Feeling around, I found a cold spot near his neck. Careful not to cut his throat, I ran the big knife through some filmy material around his face. Another creepy scream.

Another light came up, this time on the tip of a wand. Amaranthine balanced on Illyria's upper arm, her stinger lashing but hitting nothing.

Eando had one hand on his wounded shoulder. In the other, he snaked his short sword back and forth, like he was fanning away a bad smell. On the third or fourth swing, the dark cried out again. Our circle of light grew a couple of feet wider.

"This is no good," he said. "We can barely fight what we can barely see."

I caught a glimpse of gray Arni fighting a huge dog as black as shadows. I went for it, knife ready to open its guts.

Something grabbed the back of my jacket and pulled me off the floor. It was too strong and tall to be Janneke, so I kicked back and hit something thick and heavy. It didn't budge.

I lashed back with a spur. It hit with a meaty *thunk*, but it didn't loosen the grip on my jacket. I slashed the other way with the big knife. The blade sank deep.

And there it stayed while whatever I'd hit threw me across the dark room.

I tumbled ass over teakettle until I hit a stone wall. It hurt so bad I didn't even feel the impact when I fell to the floor.

For a while, it took all my concentration just to breathe. When I got good enough at that, I tried moving. That didn't work out so well, so I went to my backup plan and just lay there for a moment, listening.

Janneke's bow snapped off several shots, one big cylinder and three or four bolts. The springs on her crossbow squealed as she pulled the launcher back for another shot.

Zora's flag snapped. Once or twice I thought I saw a blue square of light in the direction where I heard it move. The darkness swallowed up the glow.

Illyria spoke and Eando sang a few more spells. Pale green missiles sizzled through a spot of darkness. I could have sworn I saw shreds of shadow floating down like swatches snipped from a cloak.

I managed a pitiful moan and rocked a little to the side. That hurt like hell, but I did it again. After a few tries, I got back on my knees.

That's when the fun began.

Whatever hit me broke ribs. One of them must have pierced a lung, because every breath made me want to bawl like a baby. My left shoulder was dead as a tree stump, but I could feel the pain of broken fingers. The big knife was gone, probably stuck in whatever had thrown me. The way I felt, it could keep the knife. I wasn't going back for it.

But then Arni yelped. With or without a knife, I had to go back for him.

Standing up, I wailed at all the pain beneath the pain I'd already felt. With my first step, I lost the breath to scream. Something gave under my left arm. I hoped that wasn't a lung collapsing. In the dark, with only Illyria's and Eando's brief lights to guide my way, there was nothing else I could do but hope.

I staggered toward the sound of Arni's fight, wondering whether I was going to be any use, fearing I was going to run into whatever had thrown me before I found the dogs.

The cavern floor rose up beneath me. It didn't throw me as far as the other thing had, but it dropped me onto Janneke. She would have cushioned my fall, except for all that steel armor. I almost wished I'd hit the stone floor instead. She cursed as her helm was knocked free and went clattering away into the darkness.

As I got to my feet, Eando added a light on his sword to the one on Illyria's wand, and I could see a few things nearby. A huge rock spirit had burst up through the floor. That wasn't all.

A patchwork giant stood over Janneke. It had one brown arm, another sickly green, its naked trunk in three shades of tan. Half a tattoo wound up one shin and disappeared into a shaggy thigh. The brute's head looked cobbled together from at least three different skulls, one of them from an ogre. Lightning crackled over the staples and pins that held it all together.

The monster had one foot on Janneke's crossbow. Her ammo spilled out across the floor. She rolled away, reaching for one of her clubs. The golem switched to her empty helm, pinning it beneath a club foot embedded with spikes. It leaned onto the helmet, crushing it flat.

Zora slammed her flag into the back of the monster's knee, but it didn't budge. The thing reached for her.

Illyria's light went out.

In her stone-spirit body, Kazyah rose up behind the golem, boulder fists swinging together to crush its mismatched skull.

Eando's light went out.

I reached out, not knowing what I'd touch or what I'd do with it. When I caught something, Eando called out, "It's me! It's me!"

"I lost my knife," I told him.

"Here." He pressed the grip of a dagger into my hand.

Figuring Kazyah's rock-body would protect her, I followed the smell of rotten meat and slashed. The knife scratched hard flesh. The stink got worse. "I got him!"

I heard Eando hacking away beside me. A second later came a sickening crunch, a brief yell, and the sound of him landing somewhere across the library. Not eager to take that trip again, I shifted right and ducked. The breeze of the monster's punch lifted my hair.

A clatter of stones fell all around us. Kazyah groaned, and I bet she felt what I did: exhaustion falling over me like a thick wet blanket. Just like the dragon did earlier, somebody had hit us with a spell to weigh us down, only this one was worse. I could barely lift my arms, much less escape the monster's reach. Tensing, I waited for the blow that would put me down for good.

But it didn't come. I heard a sucking sound and a clank of metal on the floor. There were some whispers I couldn't make out, and then heavy footsteps crossed the room, paused, and moved again. Slow at first, they picked up speed as they vanished in the direction of the gallery.

The cavern grew quiet except for Illyria's voice casting yet another light spell. That one failed, and so did the next. Finally, Zora's weak voice called out and a dim light appeared at the top of her flagstaff.

Zora stood panting beside the table with the boss's body. She reached down a hand to help Janneke to her feet. Illyria leaned against the opposite side, wand held high, waiting for the horror to jump out of the shadows again. Arni limped over, bleeding from bites and scratches. Back in her flesh, Kazyah pulled herself up by the table's edge. Her brown face looked pale under the black tattoos. I heard Eando groan somewhere in the dark. The dragon was nowhere to be seen.

One by one, the lights returned. At first we could see only the ceiling, but then the shattered walls and shelves came into view. A trail of blood led from where the golem had thrown me. Spatters here and there showed where it had smashed the others, but the monster itself was nowhere in sight.

"The *Tome!*" said Eando.

The table where we'd left it was empty. The Shadowless Sword lay nearby. I grabbed it. Nobody said a word. At first I heard the distant sound of dripping water and tumbling pebbles, but then I could make out a whisper.

"No, Otto," replied a wheezy voice. "You and your sister may go now."

"But Master—" said the flat voice I'd heard before.

"Obey me."

Amaranthine hissed as a pair of thin shadows slipped away through the cloud of dust and mist.

A third figure remained.

It looked like the shadow of a tall, fat man. It seemed to be wearing a fur collar around its hunched shoulders. Loose clothing spilled over its bulging waist, flowing like a gown. It leaned forward on a pair of canes studded with glowing purple and red stones.

"It's over," said the Master.

"You have what you want, Professor Ygresta," said Lady Illyria. "There's no need for any more bloodshed."

"I quite agree, my dear girl." A chuckle. "Oh, don't look so surprised. Violence was never my first choice, but my shadows warned me of your company's proclivity for mayhem. Despite what you might have imagined, I'm not some villain from your penny romances. I just want what everyone wants."

"What's that?" said Eando.

"To live."

"But you're the one who always told me necromancers needn't be evil," said Illyria.

"And I believe it still. But I also have no desire to perish from this world. There is so much I have yet to accomplish, so many pleasures I have yet to experience. It may be difficult for you to understand. Like Jeggare, you were born to wealth and privilege. Like most others, I toiled all my life for the slightest taste of what your kind take for granted. I cannot afford to bid on the famous sun orchid elixir to extend my life. I do not possess elven blood and the longevity it bestows. And so I bend the powers of necromancy to my will to extend my life."

"Unlife," said Illyria. "Not a life worth living."

"I beg to differ," he said. "No, actually, that's not so—I do not beg. Not anymore. Nor do I explain myself to dilettantes and bounty hunters, fortune-seekers and thieves. Speaking of thieves, I see you have adopted mine."

"Please, don't," said Zora. She cringed behind me. "I'll never—"

Ygresta let out a wheezy chuckle. "You've nothing to fear, Zora. As I said, I am not some playhouse fiend. I bound you with spells because it was necessary. I don't even begrudge your service to my old friend."

"'Old friend'?" I said. "You cursed him. You used him. You killed him."

"On the latter point, must I point out the obvious hypocrisy?" He pointed one of his canes to the sword in my hand. "While I enjoy a certain satisfaction in outwitting the famous Count Varian Jeggare, he did not need to die even after the curse took him. Having renounced necromancy, he could not use the spells in the *Gluttonous Tome* against me. I half-believed he would prove immune to its influence, but I trusted his curiosity to compel him to find the missing volumes. He deduced my plan sooner than expected, but that hardly mattered. Once he read the *Kardosian Codex*, his fate was sealed."

"That's a hell of a way to treat an 'old friend.'"

"Jeggare and I were never truly friends. He saw me as a servant, never as an equal. Something tells me you know something of that disparity. If I hated him at times, I also valued his friendship, however condescending it might have been. It brought me everything I wanted, in the end."

"It's not the end," I said. "You aren't the first jerk to think he's outsmarted the boss. He might be down, but he's not done with you. We'll make sure of that."

"You raise a troubling point. Ada overheard your efforts to revive the count. While I did not wish him dead, I would find his resuscitation before my plans are done quite inconvenient." Ygresta hooked a cane over his wrist and said a few magic words.

"No!" cried Illyria. I made to jump him, but the spell was too quick.

A thin green ray shrieked out from Ygresta's finger. At its touch, the boss's body crumbled. It left nothing but a fine gray dust with a jeweled ring where every finger and thumb had been.

"He will not follow me now," said Ygresta. "As for the rest of you, if I never see you again, may you live long lives and be grateful for them. If I do see you again . . ."

He swept his finger to point at each of us as his shadowy body faded.

17
The Shrine of Lissala
Varian

Hesitating at the threshold of flesh, my senses eased back into the world.

The scent of dust and ozone suggested another battle had occurred in my absence. The cold stone beneath me brought Ygresta's laboratory to mind. In returning to life, I had become a sort of reverse golem. Instead of a body composed of disparate pieces, it was my fractured soul the shaman's spell rejoined.

While voices spoke over my regenerated body, I considered my immaterial parts: nobleman, naturalist, investigator, soldier, archaeologist, diplomat, commander, explorer, spy, runelord descendant, wizard or sorcerer—I no longer knew nor cared which term applied. Servant of an infernal empire, loyal in oath and deed yet a rebel in my heart, I had lived a century's contradictions. Among my deeds and sins, there remained far too many variables to calculate what fate I deserved in the afterlife.

I heard Lady Illyria's voice. "Is he breathing?"

"It is difficult to tell," said Kazyah. I felt a warm hand upon my chest.

"The resurrection obviously worked," said Eando. "Otherwise his body would still be dust."

"I think he's breathing," said Zora. I smelled a hint of spice as she put her ear near my face.

"Come on, boss," Radovan said. "Give us something. Show us you're alive in there."

"You must fulfill your promise to my . . . to the oracle," said Kazyah. "Return and destroy the *Gluttonous Tome*."

"You're a lord of Cheliax," said Lady Illyria. "The Count Jeggare I know wouldn't let a trifling thing like disintegration prevent him from honoring his word."

"You're the only one who can beat Ygresta," said Zora. "That's why he let the rest of us live. We weren't worth his attention."

"Without you, I'm done here," said Janneke. "It'll be the same for Kaid. You'll be lucky if she doesn't commandeer your carriage."

"If we have to finish this thing without you, I swear I'm taking credit for the whole thing," said Kline. "With or without the *Pathfinder Chronicles*."

"Don't you want another glass of wine?" said Radovan. "Wouldn't you like to see the Fierani Forest again? How about a ride on those giant owls? We can fly back to Tian Xia, find another princess to break your heart."

"*Another* princess?" said Lady Illyria.

"I'm talking here," said Radovan. "Think about it, boss: the look on their faces when we ride back into Egorian in the Red Carriage. All the things you've done since we left, you'll be a hero."

The air pressure changed. I sensed the approach of an enormous creature.

"Desna smiles," said Radovan. "I figured we'd lost you."

"We nearly did." The dragon's voice sounded hoarse and weak. "If Ygresta is so mighty without the *Tome*, he will be unstoppable if he finds it."

"I got bad news about that."

As the others told Svannostel of their battle with the shadows and Ygresta's golem, I opened my eyes a sliver. Radovan had laid his tattered jacket over my lap to preserve my modesty. Otherwise, I was naked from head to toe.

Sitting up, I noted that all eyes had turned to Svannostel. The dragon's wings and flanks were bloody. One of her eyes had swollen shut, and she was missing scales along her snout. She held a crooked forelimb close to her chest.

Only Arnisant was undistracted. He rose up to put his paws on the edge of the table. Wagging his tail, he licked my hand.

The last act of my previous life of nearly one hundred years— no, I realized, of *exactly* one hundred years—had been to threaten him. Yet the hound forgave in an instant.

While the sickening presence of the *Gluttonous Tome* was gone, still I felt Zutha's rings nearby. The stones lay farther off, perhaps where I had fallen in the gallery. With a thought, I summoned them to me. Ten rings leaped to my fingers. A moment later, the Azlanti stones took up orbit around my brow.

By silent will, I called upon the ring with a platinum sihedron to conjure a garment black as shadow. As it wrapped its eldritch fabric around me, I realized my body was no longer bloated from the curse.

In fact, I felt—not different so much as renewed. My body felt fitter than it had in—well, better than it ever had. Gone were the lingering aches of age, hardship, and injury. Yet despite this physical rejuvenation, I also felt ineffably diminished. The spell that fetched me back from the River of Souls had also left something behind.

The others noticed my awakening. I stood up from the table. Each of them took a step or two away.

"Fear not. I am . . ." I had begun to say that I was once more myself, but a powerful intuition told me that I had become something quite different from my former self. "I pose no danger to you."

They continued to stare, still keeping their distance. They needed further assurance. They deserved more than that.

"My behavior . . ." To blame the curse would appear only a feeble evasion of my responsibility. After all, I had chosen to read the *Codex* and then the *Grimoire* and the *Black Book*. "Inexcusable. I cannot expect your forgiveness, but I offer my unequivocal apology."

Radovan offered me the Shadowless Sword. "Boss, I hope you understand—"

I took the sword and turned away, unable to look at him.

Awareness that his deed had been necessary did nothing to dull the shock that my friend had killed me. I wanted no revenge, but I could not shed an acute sense of betrayal.

I walked toward the gallery, desirous of solitude.

Illyria stepped in my way. The sight of her was almost as confusing as looking at Radovan. I had heard her plotting my death and trying to persuade Radovan to turn on me. No matter how much I understood the logic, I could only feel the sudden blow to my heart, the cut and the wound. "Varian," she said, "if there had been any other way—"

I withdrew from her, but the others moved to prevent my departure. Perhaps they feared I remained under the effects of the *Tome* and sought only to prepare myself to resume battle. In any event, I saw that I would not have the seclusion I craved until I assuaged their fears. Composing my face as best I could, I said, "Tell me what transpired during my . . . absence."

By turns they told me of their battles with Ygresta and his minions.

Svannostel and Kazyah first encountered the intruders in a chamber downriver. Ygresta had summoned a small army of restless dead, which the dragon and shaman proceeded to demolish. Because he cloaked his forces in darkness, they did not realize their enemies included a golem. Even if they had, they might not have realized the folly of attacking such a creature with lightning, which only made it stronger. Between the patchwork brute and Ygresta's spells, they had been forced to retreat.

The others told an equally confused story of a battle of light and shadow and confusion. The end result was as bad as I could have expected.

"Ygresta has the *Gluttonous Tome*," I summarized. "And you know his destination?"

"It must be the Cenotaph," said Svannostel.

"I've heard of the place," said Kline. "Wasn't it a fortress for the legions of Tar-Baphon?"

"It is the site where the Whispering Tyrant left his undead reserves before his defeat at Gallowspire," said Svannostel.

"What does that have to do with Runelord Zutha?" I asked.

"Zutha's crypt lies beneath the Cenotaph," said Svannostel. "I thought you knew that."

"Lady Illyria tells me that Tar-Baphon stole some measure of the runelord's power."

"It's true," said Illyria. "That is, it's true that I read it."

"That is also correct," the dragon said.

"Where is this Cenotaph?" I asked.

"At the southern edge of the Tusk Mountains, due north of Vigil."

"How far?"

"Perhaps half again one hundred miles."

"How long was I . . . gone?"

"Less than half an hour," said Kazyah.

I considered that fact along with the likelihood that Ygresta had projected a shadow of himself to infiltrate Svannostel's lair while his corporeal form lay many miles distant. Furthermore, the *Kardosian Codex* contained a spell allowing a wizard to walk through the realm of shadow, traversing hundreds of miles in a single night. For all my theoretical knowledge, casting the spell remained beyond my capabilities—but, based on his defeat of a dragon, not beyond Ygresta's.

"Boss?" said Radovan. "You want to sit down? Have a bite? You're looking a little thin."

"Death has freed me from the gluttonous curse." I patted my newly flattened belly and noticed how pale my hand had become. Something more than death and resurrection had happened to me. Was it connected to the curse? Had my previous healing by a celestial dragon's heart influenced the shaman's spell? The phenomenon bore further investigation, but later.

"This is exactly what we'd hoped would happen," said Kline. He offered a tentative smile. "We wanted to free you from the curse knowing Kazyah could restore your life."

"And losing the completed *Tome* to the Master of Shadows was an unexpected bonus?"

"You can't think any of us intended for that to happen," said Illyria.

"No, no, of course not. Your plan was logical, if rather punishing. I must apologize again. The experience of death—" I had no desire to share the details of my mother's visitation. "It has clarified my thoughts. Ever since reading the *Codex*, I have been afflicted by shadows of the mind. I underestimated Ygresta's manipulations. For whatever he may once have lacked in intellect, he has had years of planning to compensate. He learned powerful spells from the *Kardosian Codex*. The entire *Tome* is now in his hands, not by any treachery from you but by his own design. He has, in short, outsmarted me."

No one replied to that admission, perhaps because they realized how much it pained me. Radovan rubbed the back of his neck and suppressed a grin.

"It happens to the best of us," said Kline.

"But less often to you, we understand." Illyria placed a consoling hand on my arm to soften her mockery.

"Consult Svannostel's library for any further information you can find on the Cenotaph," I told her. "I shall retire to the gallery to meditate in solitude."

"What should the rest of us do?" said Radovan.

"See that I am not disturbed."

In Svannostel's gallery, I made a desk of one of the benches. While the dragon's library was comparatively comfortable, I associated it with my study of the *Tome*. No longer subject to its curse, I wanted a fresh start.

In my grimoire, I perused the spells I had collected over the past few years. As a sorcerer, I could command a relative few of them—but I did so at will and without preparation. As a wizard, I could inscribe any spell I understood onto a riffle scroll, so long as I was willing to endure the sickening side effect. That had been my relationship with magic these past several years. What my mother's shade told me made me wonder whether it was time to try something different—something I had not attempted since graduating from the Acadamae.

I reviewed the formula of a simple battle spell, setting each phrase in memory like a snare awaiting a trigger of words and gestures. I used none of the shortcuts I normally employed when creating riffle scrolls, inscribing fractions of arcane phrases on each page. I prepared the spell as any wizard might. Like any wizard, I felt its power nestle into my mind as easily as one of Janneke's bolts fit into her crossbow. When done, I braced myself for the nausea.

It did not come.

Emboldened, I chose a more complex spell. Yet while I had previously inscribed it on a riffle scroll, I found I could not fix it in memory. I understood it on an intellectual level, but somehow I could no longer master it.

Some power—whether death, the dragon's heart, or my subjugation to the *Tome*, I could not say—had removed my magical impediment, but like the victim of an injury to the head, I needed to rehabilitate my arcane skills.

While seeming closer to the truth, the analogy felt incomplete. My mind had not been injured but catalyzed, galvanized, impelled to become something else. I was not the victim of an accident but a pupa, no longer a caterpillar but not yet a butterfly.

Death had not changed me. It had allowed me to change. My transformation had been made possible, but it had yet to begin.

All of my former questions about whether I was a wizard or sorcerer washed away. I could not blame my mother's insistence that I renounce necromancy, thus causing my impediment, for she acted out of love. As her agent, Ygresta was equally guilty, but he was ignorant of my bloodline. I could not even blame the Acadamae masters, who accepted my mother's bribes out of greed, not malice.

Whether by misfortune or fate, I had come to a transformative moment.

I caused my own disability by rejecting necromancy. Now I could change that choice. Upon my fingers and brow rested the Crest and Crown of Zutha. And in my mind, as often as I cared to set them there, I could now hold any sort of spell.

I prepared all the spells I could manage, investing a few in riffle scrolls. By doing the same each day, I could expand my arsenal over time—although I feared I would not have much more time before I must face Ygresta or, if I were too slow, Zutha himself.

The thought of the runelord reborn reminded me of the goddess whose worship the runelords corrupted from an exaltation of virtues to an embrace of sins. I went to the shrine of Lissala that Svannostel had installed in her gallery. There I sat in lotus fashion and contemplated the icon of the goddess.

The snake-woman resembled my mother's astral messenger but for her six wings and the sihedron star where her head should be. I thought upon the conundrum of a deity whose teachings degenerated from seven virtues to seven sins. If Lissala could not sustain her own virtues, what hope was there for mortals? What hope was there for me?

Seven virtues. Seven sins.

Among the wealthiest families in an empire of wealth, House Jeggare funded artistic and charitable endeavors, from the grand opera to orphanages—but we hoarded more wealth for ourselves. Many pointed to House Jeggare as a bastion of greed.

Childless, I had long before arranged contingencies of succession. My cousins reveled in the knowledge that my holdings would one day fall to their offspring and sustain the lineage, yet they spied upon my every assignation for fear that I would beget an heir in a moment of lust.

Although some think me oblivious to my pride, it is but one side of a noble's sword; the other is honor. If sometimes I had turned the blade to the wrong side, one must consider on how many occasions the coarse or provocative tested a man of my station.

While I enjoyed great abundance, in no way could I be accused of common gluttony—not before falling into Ygresta's trap. One might, I suppose, tally the quantity of drink I had enjoyed as a related fault.

And if I often took my leisure abroad, such sojourns were often married to an embassy for the court or an excursion for the Pathfinder Society. Perhaps sometimes I lingered for too many weeks alone in my house. But was it sloth? I did not like to think so.

So many times I had been angry, usually with just cause. On the battlefield or in the face of violence or cruelty, I too had been violent and cruel. Surely it is not a sin to be so when circumstances require it.

My competitive spirit seldom manifested as envy. A few Pathfinders—Eando Kline among them—had reported discoveries I wished I had made. But could Pharasma judge me jealous?

She could, I feared. She could condemn me for every one of the seven sins.

Looking back over a century-old life, I could spy my sins like road markers. Much as I might strive toward virtue, like the later worshipers of Lissala I fell inevitably to sin. Perhaps that was the lesson of the goddess: there is no virtue without sin.

I thought of my mother's obscure martyr's death. Had she earned a place in Desna's realm only through sacrifice? I could never go back to a time in my first life when I was as innocent as she. What use then was a second life? Had I no path to redemption?

Unjust! The Shadowless Sword was in my hand. A wrathful impulse propelled my arm. I stabbed the statue of Lissala. The blade sank to the hilt, screaming in a shower of red and white sparks.

"Trickster goddess! Deceiver! Seducer!"

My fury evaporated as quickly as it had formed, replaced by shock at my profane act. Fearful that someone would witness my sacrilege, I pulled at the sword, but it would not budge.

What use were my apologies upon waking if I were only to sin again so soon?

Setting my foot on the statue's hip, I pulled with both hands. The sword budged, first with a squeal, and then with a blaze of forge-hot light. Blinded, I held the sword at arm's length.

"Sweet Tender of Dreams." My relief drained away as the light faded. The blade's once-fair surface had been stained and scarred by the heart of Lissala. Thassilonian runes glowed on either side of the blackened blade. On one side they spelled the Thassilonian word for FEAR. On the other, HOPE.

I stared at the blade, my horror that I had spoiled the gift from a princess gradually turning to awe that a goddess—or some servitor spirit invested in her likeness—had answered my profanation of her shrine.

But was it with a blessing or a curse? And did it come from Lissala? When one stands before the icon of one goddess and prays to another, the answer might come from either—or neither. I gazed at the runes on the blade, HOPE and FEAR, trying to remember whether those terms meant something slightly different to the Thassilonians.

"Which do you choose?"

I froze, for an instant fearing the statue had spoken. Yet the voice came not from a goddess but from the dragon Svannostel, who crouched behind me. Her gravest injuries had been healed, no doubt by the last of the shaman's spells.

"Does one choose?" I said. "Or are fear and hope inseparable?"

Svannostel nodded with an expression of approval. "So you do have some wisdom. Did you gain it in the afterlife? Or was it muted by the curse?"

"I will not guess your age," I began.

"More wisdom."

"Yet likely you have seen more years than I, and I have seen more than most of my countrymen. Benigno Ygresta is one of a scant few cohorts I have remaining." I knew only two other humans who had lived a century, both granddames of Chelish houses. I had not seen them in over four years, so I did not know whether they survived. "Perhaps Ygresta is the last."

"Are you building to a point or obscuring the fact that you have avoided my question?"

Her natural assumption of command reminded me of myself. I smiled, feeling a moment's kinship with the wyrm. "If I have learned nothing else in my hundred years, it is that things—and people—are never one thing or its opposite. Good and evil, civilized and savage, kind and cruel, dignified or arrogant . . . these are extremes, not naturally occurring conditions. Am I a human or an elf? Yes. Am I a wizard or a sorcerer? Yes. Do I hope to stop Ygresta from gaining the powers of Zutha, or do I fear that I will fail?"

Svannostel nodded. "Yes."

"Are the people in your library my servants or my friends?"

"They will do whatever it takes to help you. So will I."

"Ygresta's powers were already enough to defeat you and Kazyah, two of the most formidable beings I have met. The others cannot hope to survive another battle, even before he unlocks the powers of the *Tome*." I held up my hands and looked up to see my halo of Azlanti stones. "I have the only weapons capable of defeating Ygresta."

"I swore to prevent the return of the runelords," she said. "Even if it costs my life."

"I swear to do the same—but not at the cost of my friends' lives. You and I are bound by oath. Will you take me to the Cenotaph? And will you fight beside me there until we or Ygresta are dead?"

"Without telling the others?"

"Yes."

"They will loot my hoard."

"I fear we are likely to die at the Cenotaph. Will your hoard matter then?"

"You don't understand anything about dragons."

"You said you would know if even a coin was missing."

"I might have exaggerated to awe your friends."

"They believed you."

She nodded. "Very well. As you said, we'll probably die."

"Let us go now. Once we are well away, I will cast a spell to instruct Radovan to await us in Korvosa."

"So you still hope we might live?"

"So I hope," I said, saluting her with the Shadowless Sword. "And so I fear."

18
Seraph's Ladder
Radovan

Miles behind us, I saw the dust plume again. I couldn't tell which way it was moving, closer or farther off. I hoped it was Kaid coming back to say she'd changed her mind, but that wasn't likely. She'd had two days to catch up.

As soon as her mercs saw the boss flying off on the dragon, they started having second thoughts about the whole business. By the time the rest of us came out of the dragon's lair, they were ready to ride home.

"I signed a contract for an escort to the Sleeper," she said. "Not a full-scale invasion of the Hold of Belkzen."

When she put it that way, I couldn't hardly blame her.

Kaid invited Janneke to come with her. I was sure she was going to take her up on it, but Janneke said, "When I take a job, I finish it."

"Have it your way." Kaid put on her helmet.

"Wait a second," said Janneke. She gave Zora a hard look. "You can go with them if you like."

"What about your bounty?"

"The count's a rich man. If we get to him in time, I expect a handsome bonus."

"And if you don't get to him in time?"

"I caught you once," said Janneke. "I can find you again."

Zora glanced at Kaid. "How do I know your friend won't turn me in?"

"I'll never go back to Korvosa," said Kaid. "Besides, you said something about valuable magic to trade. I'll take that instead of your bounty."

Zora looked at me.

"Go on," I said. "Get back to Korvosa. And give your Sczarni buddies a message from me." I showed her the tines.

She hugged me around the neck and whispered, "Desna smile on you, hellspawn."

"You too, sweetheart."

Kaid's Band put Zora on one of their spare horses, and they rode west. We took the Red Carriage east, right toward the heart of Orcland.

For the whole next day, we kept our eyes open. The boss kept the spyglass in his satchel, so I couldn't get a good look at what was stirring up the dust. We didn't risk stopping during the day in case they were orc marauders, figuring we might outrun them.

On the first night, Kazyah communed with her earth spirits and told us the land was lousy with creatures for a hundred miles around. She couldn't tell us what was in any particular direction. Maybe it was orcs. It could just as soon have been some of those burrowers she'd sensed on the way from Kaer Maga.

I swung from the back ladder to the carriage running boards and let myself back inside.

Eando and Illyria sat on the front seat, comparing spellbooks or something. On the back seat, Kazyah snoozed beside Janneke. Arni put his head on the seat between them, hoping for scritches.

Rather than squeeze in, I lowered a side seat and put my back against the little wall between the front and back doors. I wished I'd had something to give Arni under the table. Since he'd seen me hurt the boss, he didn't come when I called.

Something about the crowded carriage bugged me. It took a second for me to realize Illyria must have summoned another driver to give Janneke a break. It made me nervous to think that a spell was holding the reins.

"You know, maybe the boss was right. We ought to have someone up top in case something happens."

"You were just out there," said Eando. "What did you see?"

I told him about the dust plume.

"I'd feel better if we could see what's causing that," he said.

"Varian has too much of a head start," said Illyria. "We can't stop to investigate every disturbance on the horizon."

"You're right, you're right," he said. "The most urgent thing is to reach the Cenotaph before Jeggare gets in over his head."

"If something's following us," I said, "we've got to be ready to put up a fight. Do we know a good place to stop tonight?"

"How about the stairs?" said Eando.

"What stairs?" I said.

"They're called Seraph's Ladder because they rise up toward Heaven. I've heard tales of spirits walking up or down the steps."

"Are they dangerous?"

Kazyah opened one eye. I guess she wasn't sleeping after all. "Only at midwinter," she said. "Or so the elders say."

"The orcs shun the site, don't they?"

Kazyah spread her hands. "I cannot say. Beyond their raids in our territories, I know little of their ways. You know more than I."

"My exploration of Belkzen occurred in less than ideal circumstances."

"You knew it was safe to camp in that landshark drift," I said.

When we found what looked like a crater in the grassy plain the day before, Eando looked around until he found some melon-sized dung pellets. He broke one open to see it was still wet inside. He said that meant the creature wasn't coming back soon, and other predators avoided the nests, making it a safe place to camp. Even Kazyah seemed impressed.

"We aren't likely to find another one tonight," he said. "Unless Kazyah has heard of some reason we should avoid the site, I suggest we stop at Seraph's Ladder."

"Good," said Illyria. "I've always wanted to see that monument."

"What is it?" I said.

"You'll see soon enough," said Eando. "If you climb back up top, you might see it soon. Look northeast."

I thought it ought to be somebody else's turn as lookout, but I knew they were all as tired as me. I stepped out and swung up top.

Once we got away from the mountains, the badlands eased down into plains. Grass hissed against the carriage's belly. The phony driver held the reins in the seat ahead of me, guiding the horses around rocks and gullies. Behind us, the sun was headed toward the red horizon. Ahead, the green sea of grass was turning blue with twilight.

Eando was right. I saw it right away.

From a distance, it looked a little like a giant tree stump. As we got closer, I could see its lines weren't natural but man-made. Or elf-made. Or giant-made. Something made it.

Closer still, I saw pillars supporting a rising stone curve. Then I saw it was a staircase. At the bottom was nothing but the grassy plain. The top rose a couple hundred feet above the ground, but it wasn't connected to anything. It just ended in open space.

I couldn't see any ruins where the rest had fallen. Maybe somebody had scavenged the stone for buildings. Or maybe whatever had been there got disintegrated, like the boss. I didn't know. It had to be something magic. If the boss were there, he'd have told us all about it.

He should have been with us.

As we drew close, Janneke swung up to the driver's seat and took the reins from the phantom.

"Got it!" she called down to Illyria, who dispelled her guy with a snap of her fingers. He actually tipped his hat at Janneke before vanishing, which was kind of a nice touch, I thought.

Janneke drove us once around the base of the steps before stopping underneath the stairs. The others got out, took a look around, and we all kind of nodded at each other. Since the boss ran off, nobody had taken charge. Sometimes Eando spoke up, and sometimes Illyria did, but nobody jumped to obey. We all just sort of thought it over and nodded, or else we put in our two coppers, and everybody else thought it over before nodding or speaking up.

I didn't like it. It didn't feel right.

Janneke and Kazyah saw to the horses. Eando and I put together supper. Arni prowled the area before chasing some little critter that ran from him. Illyria conjured her magic cottage, making sure to keep it behind the wide base of the stairs, where it wouldn't stand out against the moon or stars. We had shelter if it rained, and between the nearest column and the base of the stairs, we had plenty of cover.

Illyria said, "Shall we risk a campfire?"

The rest of us thought it over. Enough of us shook our heads that we ate a cold supper and sat in a circle between the carriage and the cottage. Arni sat near the rear of the carriage, out of arm's reach. Amaranthine perched on the top of the wheel above him, her reptile eyes moving from each of us to the next as we made our camp.

Once we got settled, I asked Kazyah, "What's so spooky about this place at midwinter?"

"I have never seen it," she said, "but it is said that on that night ancient spirits appear upon the stairs above us. Some are human beings. Others are unnamable things."

"Unnamable things?"

"Creatures from other worlds," said Eando.

Illyria nodded like what he'd said jibed with something she'd read.

Kazyah shrugged. "Whatever they are, these things walk among the human beings on the stairs, flickering in and out of sight. By dawn they have all vanished."

"That doesn't sound too bad," I said.

"One midwinter night, an old shaman and his granddaughter came to the stairs," she said. "The shaman told the girl to watch as he climbed Seraph's Ladder. He warned her not to follow him no matter what she saw.

"He began to climb the stairs. With each step, he grew younger. His white hair turned gray, and the pouches beneath his eyes vanished. His gray hair turned black, and his crooked back grew straight. He turned to look back at his granddaughter, smiling in his youth.

"As he looked down at the granddaughter, the young man saw the red stripe of a firepelt cougar stalking through the grass. He called out for the girl to run away. Frightened, she ran up the stairs toward him. He cried out for her to stop, but she was too afraid to hear his voice.

"With every step she climbed, she grew younger. The shaman ran down to stop her, but before they met she dwindled into a child, an infant, and then into nothing at all. He stood alone at the bottom of the stair, an old man once more."

"Desna weeps," I said.

"Is that a true story?" Illyria asked.

Kazyah didn't answer. When Illyria looked at Janneke, the bounty hunter shrugged. Eando stared at Kazyah, probably trying to figure it out for himself by the look on her face.

None of them could see as well in the dark as I could. None of them knew that Kazyah was the oracle's mother, not his daughter. But just by the way she told the story, they had to have heard the truth in it.

Illyria and Eando talked magic business for a little while. She'd used magic plenty on the journey, both in fights and in little ways like the conjured driver or fixing Janneke's crumpled helmet, but we hadn't seen much of her necromancer juju. Starting tomorrow, they decided, she could no longer hold back.

"It isn't something I've often done outside the Acadamae," she explained. "And after the way Varian reacted when I sowed those ghoul's teeth . . ."

"Jeggare hasn't exactly remained pure about renouncing necromancy," said Eando.

"Hey, cut him some slack," I said. "That was the book. He was under a curse. And don't forget he took on your curse, too."

"I know, I know," said Eando. "I'm not criticizing. It's just that sometimes, in the face of ruthless opponents, you can't be picky about your methods."

I caught Janneke glancing at me when he said that.

"What?"

"I think you know what," she said. "You said you were raised on the streets of Egorian, right? You talked to those Sczarni like you'd rubbed shoulders with their kind before. Tell me you haven't done a few bloody deeds."

"You mean like Kaid's Band making raids on the Bottoms?"

Janneke's back stiffened.

"They weren't liberating those slaves, were they? That much I figured out on my own. And when I mentioned Kaid's name back in Kaer Maga, I heard her band collected Shoanti scalps for Korvosans with a grudge."

Kazyah's head snapped around to face the bounty hunter.

Janneke looked away. "There were a lot of reasons I quit."

"Before or after a few bloody deeds of your own?"

Janneke scowled at me, but she got the point. I wasn't the only one with blood on my hands.

"Listen," said Eando. "We've all done things we wish we hadn't done. We can't change the past. What we can do is try to balance the scales. Stopping Ygresta from becoming a lich is a way to do that."

"Even if it means calling the dead to rise from the earth?" Illyria hefted a little bag. Ghoul teeth rattled inside. She looked to Kazyah like she was asking permission.

"It is a foul thing," said the shaman. "But if you summon these things to fight against another abomination . . ." She shrugged. "I guard my ancestors' graves. I do not care if you despoil the crypt of an azghat."

"Good," said Eando, who turned and lay down on his bedroll. "Now everybody get some sleep. We've got a long day of stupidly dangerous deeds ahead of us tomorrow."

By noon the next day we'd spotted two herds of aurochs.

The first was barely what you'd call a herd. A couple of bulls guarded five or six cows and three calves against something prowling the nearby grass. For a while we were too far away to see what it was, but we knew something was there by the way the aurochs moved all of a sudden. Then they'd stand still again while the bulls circled the others.

Just before we drove out of sight, I saw a giant wolf—a warg, easily twice as big as Arni—make a run for one of the calves. A bull charged it, and they fell together. The last thing I saw was the bull trotting back to his family and the wolf loping away with a big red wound in its flank.

Arni had his paws up on the open window. He whined, eager to chase down the warg.

"Settle down, pal," I called down from the roof.

He whined and sat.

The second herd was big as a storm cloud and so far away that I couldn't make out much detail. There had to be hundreds of the animals, maybe thousands. Lucky for us, they weren't anywhere near our path.

A couple times Janneke pointed to vultures circling in the distance. The grass had grown tall enough that there was no telling what lay dead or dying beneath them. I kept my eyes peeled for anything that moved. The way the wind blew waves across the grass made that harder than it sounds. Every breeze caught my eye. I could never tell whether I'd seen something stalking the carriage or whether it was just a wind furrow.

We stopped just long enough to water and rest the horses. Everybody except me helped rub them down. While they did that, I stretched my legs. I called Arni over a couple of times. The first time he pretended not to hear me. The second time he came halfway before changing his mind.

That was something.

The afternoon sun got hot enough that Janneke started pulling off the heavier pieces of her armor. I could tell she hated doing that by the way she started unbuckling a strap, only to stop with a curse. Ten minutes later, she'd tear off a pauldron or vambrace and slam it down behind her with the baggage.

I saw something to the north, five or six big dark figures lumbering in our general direction. I pointed them out.

Janneke stood up on the driver's perch. She kicked the carriage to get everybody else's attention. Kazyah and Illyria leaned out of the windows. Eando climbed up on the other side.

"Are those what I think they are?" he said.

"Mammoths," said Kazyah.

Squinting, I made out their shapes. They looked something like the elephants I'd seen in a nobleman's menagerie back in Egorian. They were covered in shaggy hair, and their tusks looked too heavy even for them. There was something weird about their backs, too.

"Oh, hell," I said. "Something's riding them."

"Orcs," said Kazyah. "They raid the Realms of the Mammoth Lords for mounts such as these."

"They've seen us," said Janneke.

Once she said it, I could tell they were changing direction. A distant sound echoed across the plains.

"War drums," said Eando. "If any other bands are in range, they'll hear the call."

"That's just great," I said.

Janneke cracked the reins over the team. The big horses were strong, but they weren't built for speed. Besides, the carriage was full.

"We need to lighten the load. Can you make us some phony ponies?" I asked Illyria.

"No," she said. "I prepared for battle, not riding."

Kazyah opened the carriage door and reached up for a hand. I pulled her up beside me. She looked out at the mammoths, frowning in thought. As they got closer, I saw one of the big shaggy beasts had drums hanging from either side. A pair of orcs on its back pounded away at them. On others, orcs squatted in wicker baskets bristling with spears and bows.

"They will drive us south unless we can go faster," said Kazyah.

"I'm driving as fast as I can!" said Janneke.

"Don't any of you know a spell to make them run faster?" I said.

Nobody answered me.

"Well, dammit, gimme those." I climbed up beside Janneke and took the reins. Surprised, she let me have them.

The moment I got close, the nearest horses began to whinny. One turned its head to see what it'd sensed creeping up behind him. When it saw me, its whinny became a scream. Its legs churned faster, kicking up clumps of grass and dirt.

"Sorry, boys." I cracked the reins and stood tall so they could all get a look at me as the panic spread to the lead horses.

Calling back to the others, I yelled, "Hold on! It's going to get bumpy."

The carriage jumped. I almost flew off the perch.

Behind me, Kazyah sat low on the carriage roof and began chanting in a loud voice. Janneke released the scorpion. As it rose up and snapped into place, she fit one of the big steel bolts onto the mechanism. The wind blew back her red-gold braids. Her eyes shone as much with excitement as with fear. She'd been dying for a chance to shoot that bow again.

Over the screams of the horses sounded the rumble of charging mammoths. I looked back to see a masked orc shaking a staff at us. I braced for whatever bad whammy he was sending our way.

Instead, the orc looked up to the sky. A gray blur flew down at him. Whatever it was, it scared the hell out of the orc. He howled so loud I heard him over the mammoth's thunder and the screams of our horses. He dropped his staff, covered his head with his arms, and tumbled back off his mount to disappear under the feet of the mammoths behind him.

"Nice one, Illyria," Eando shouted.

"That's Lady Illyria to you!" she called back. Probably she was joking to keep her courage up, but I couldn't tell. Holding onto the reins and not getting pulled down under the carriage were my main concern.

The roar of the charging mammoths got twice as loud all of a sudden. From out of nowhere, a herd of aurochs stampeded right into their path. I could have sworn they weren't anywhere in sight a second earlier. Then I realized Kazyah had finished her first chant. She didn't hesitate before taking up a different one.

The mammoths reared and trumpeted as the horned aurochs ran beneath them. Some of the orcs fell and disappeared under the stampede. Others held on for their lives, forgetting their bows and spears.

The stampede pulled down one mammoth and turned the rest away—all except for one. A gray-streaked bull plowed through the aurochs, his legs and belly bleeding from gores. Scars crisscrossed his trunk. He'd been in battle before, and he wasn't ready to quit. Standing in a palanquin on his back, two of the biggest, meanest orcs I'd ever seen had steel bows drawn back. One was pointing at me. I dropped low onto the driver's box. They released their arrows, and in the same instant I heard Janneke shoot the scorpion and shout a curse.

The orc's arrow creased my shoulder like a sword slash.

The reins jerked in my hands. I almost lost them. After a second of fumbling, I wrapped them around my wrists and got back up to my knees.

On the carriage roof, Janneke cranked back the scorpion for another shot. A long black arrow stuck out of her side.

"Janneke's hit!" I yelled.

"I'm all right," she said. Her weak voice told a different story.

The lone mammoth kept barreling after us, but only one blood-splashed orc remained on its back. The stampede had kept them from cutting us off, but they were gaining on us.

"Shoot the mammoth!" yelled Eando. As he climbed up to join her and Kazyah on the roof, I felt the carriage balance shift. I hunkered low, like that would help. Eando braced a hand against her side and pulled out the arrow.

"Gorum's guts and Cayden's cups!" she cried out in pain and irritation. "I was *aiming* for the mammoth!" While Eando pressed a hand to her wound and sang a healing phrase, she finished cranking the bow and fit another heavy bolt in place. "Why don't you shut up and help fight?"

"Dammit," he said, pulling a scroll from its case. "It's my last one. I was saving it for the Cenotaph."

"You can use it here, or you can use it in Hell," she said.

"Good point."

Kazyah gave Janneke a light slap. The bounty hunter turned gray—skin, hair, armor, everything. The shaman did the same to Eando, then reached forward to slap me on the shoulder. I felt my skin tighten, and I knew she'd made me hard as stone. I relaxed a little about the arrows.

"It's gaining on us!" cried Eando.

Sure enough, the mammoth closed in on our left flank. I pulled the reins hard to the right to get a little more space between us.

"Look out!" shouted Janneke. I ducked low again. When nothing came my way, I peeked back. The orc archer stood stock still, his bow half-drawn. A ghostly hand hovered a couple feet from his head, where it had left a hand-shaped mark on his cheek.

Janneke cranked the scorpion again.

"Finish him!" Illyria yelled from inside the carriage. "The paralysis won't last forever."

Grumbling, Eando unfurled his scroll and read the words. A fiery glow lit up the page, and a pea-sized flame shot toward the mammoth. A fireball exploded right between its tusks.

The big animal kept chasing us, its shaggy coat in flames. It left burning footprints and a greasy trail of smoke in its wake. Soon it was right behind us, its tusks bumping the back of the carriage.

"Now it's on fire," Eando said. "That's so much worse."

"Get down," said Janneke. She turned the scorpion, aimed straight back at the mammoth, and shot. The bolt disappeared.

She couldn't have missed, not at that range. Then I saw the dark wound where the bolt had sunk completely into the mammoth's skull. With a mournful sound, the beast turned to the side and fell.

Janneke let loose a cheer so vulgar it startled even me.

"That was a close one," said Eando. "But we did it."

"Do not celebrate too soon," said Kazyah. "Others heard the drums."

She pointed to another band of orcs approaching from the south. Most of them ran through the grass on foot, but several rode giant wargs. To the rear, a big orc with his tribe's banner behind his saddle rode on a giant black rhino. Beside him, a warg-rider blew a war horn.

Arni barked from inside the carriage.

"Drive on," said Kazyah. "They will not be the last to join the chase." She put her hands on my back and chanted a healing spell.

The horses were covered in lather, their eyes wide and frightened. I said, "I don't know how long I can keep running them."

"Until our skulls are gathered," said Kazyah.

Eando sighed. "I knew I should have saved that scroll."

19

The Cenotaph

Varian

Awaking with the dawn, I heard the steady drone of Svannostel snoring. Shattered weapons and crushed armor lay scattered along the bloody mountain path, but no bodies remained. Svannostel had devoured the orcs who tried preventing our approach to the Cenotaph. After glutting herself on their bodies, she declared it time for a nap, curled up, and dozed.

One of my Azlanti stones sustained me without food or drink, so I did not share her hunger. I could barely remember the voracity I had felt while in the throes of the gluttonous curse only days before. While free of Zutha's *Tome*, I remained trapped by our shared bloodline and my familial duty to ensure the runelord's tyrannical power did not return in the form of Benigno Ygresta.

After performing the calisthenics I had learned at Dragon Temple, I retrieved my grimoire and filled my mind with spells. On each night of our journey from the Sleeper, I inscribed more riffle scrolls from the spells I had not cast that day. Between those stored in my rings, stones, scrolls, and mind, an arcane arsenal lay at my command. I was prepared.

Squinting through my spyglass toward the sunrise, I could barely perceive the black line of the Shudderwood to the east. North of the forest, the Moutray River divided Ustalav from Sarkoris, where my journey from the crusade to Korvosa had begun. So far I had traveled, only to return near to my starting place.

Somewhere at the foot of the mountains lay the unmarked border dividing us from the counties of Ustalav. An old oath prevented me from setting foot in that misty principality, and I felt a small twinge of amusement at the idea that if only I had stipulated "until I die" or "as long as I live," I might now have crossed the border without breaking my word. Fortunately for my honor's sake, our destination lay within the Hold of Belkzen.

"Does something approach from the east?" While somewhat smaller than the other dragons I had encountered, Svannostel's massive body still made me feel insignificant beside her.

"Only memories," I said. Her gaze drifted south. I turned my spyglass but saw nothing. A dragon's eyes are keen, so I asked, "Does something approach from the south?"

"I had hoped my brother would come from Vigil," she said. "I told him of our task, but he has made oaths to those he protects. The young Watcher-Lord of Lastwall is bolder than his predecessors, but the Worldwound campaign diminished his forces."

Many cavaliers and templars from Lastwall had fought at my side in Sarkoris, but their first duty was to watch over Gallowspire, where the Whispering Tyrant remained imprisoned. Much as we might need their aid, I respected the Watcher-Lord's devotion to duty. While his forces kept vigil over Tar-Baphon, we prepared to prevent the resurrection of the runelord from whom the Whispering Tyrant stole his power.

Svannostel and I turned to gaze westward upon the Cenotaph.

The colossal pillar of black stone rose from the base of the mountain to tower hundreds of feet above us. Ahead, across a precarious bridge, stood a pair of doors composed of a pale green crystal. Far above us, another bridge led to a second set of doors.

"Zutha's crypt lies beneath the Cenotaph," said Svannostel. "Yet I wonder what lies behind those high doors."

They aroused my curiosity as well. I drew the Shadowless Sword and looked up at them. The sword's grip trembled in my hand. I sensed a wordless warning not to approach the higher doors. Whatever lay behind them was anathema to the sword, to me, or to everything.

"Ygresta will have gone to the crypt," I said. "Whatever he seeks must lay entombed with the runelord."

We crossed the bridge. Before us, the doors stood closed. While I lacked the skill of a trained tracker, even I could not help noticing the enormous footprints leading to the doors.

"Ygresta's golem?" said Svannostel.

"It seems likely."

We found no handle, knocker, or other device upon the doors. The Shadowless Sword revealed no obscuring illusions. I waved a hand before them, hoping they might react to my crest of rings or crown of Azlanti stones. "Open."

The doors did not react to my command, nor to my touch. I tried again in the tongues of ancient Thassilon and Azlant, then the guttural speech of orcs and several less likely languages.

"It was worth a try," said Svannostel. She tried to grip the door with a claw, but the seam between the doors was too narrow for her talons.

"How did Ygresta enter?" I mused aloud.

"The *Tome*?"

I nodded to acknowledge that was probably the case. "Yet Tar-Baphon found a way in."

"He was a mighty wizard."

"And I am not so mighty."

"I intended no offense."

"I have taken none. What I lack in power, however . . ." An impulse came to me, not from intuition's whim but—somehow, I knew—from my blackened sword. I drew a shallow cut along my palm and pressed my bloody hand to the doors. They opened.

"The blood of Zutha." Svannostel peered down at me in a troubling manner. I had not forgotten that she and her brother were guardians against the return of the runelord. If Desna smiled and we managed to dispatch Ygresta, would she feel the need to end Zutha's bloodline by slaying me?

We entered the Cenotaph.

The morning light seemed reluctant to join us. It oozed in acute shafts across a cluttered field of indistinguishable objects. Motes of dust glowed and dimmed by turns as they floated across the vast expanse.

As my eyes adjusted to the gloom, I saw that a grand hall lay before us. Around a vast circular pit stood ranks of countless undead soldiers.

They groaned and stirred at our approach.

Svannostel invoked a light at the tip of her wing. The undead shuffled toward her, heedless of the danger posed by a dragon.

I cast a light at the tip of the Shadowless Sword. The spell elicited a reaction from the blade's runes, which glowed a brilliant FEAR and HOPE on opposite sides. As the light touched them, the undead shrank away with a clatter of bones in rusted armor.

"Stand back," I said. "Before you stands the heir to Runelord Zutha."

A skull-faced commander called out, "With a bronze dragon at your side? You are no blood of Zutha."

"Who but the heir of Zutha is mighty enough to tame a bronze dragon as his slave?" The apology I would need to offer Svannostel for that remark diminished my fear of our likely deaths by comparison.

The dragon surprised me by adding, "I serve the master. He commands me to destroy those who defy him."

Her words cowed the rank-and-file soldiers, but another officer rose above them. He floated toward me and descended to hover a foot off the floor. By his bloody eyes and fangs, I knew him for a vampire. He hissed, "Prove your claim."

Hopeful that my resurrection had not removed the blessings of the celestial dragon's heart, I offered the vampire my empty hand. "Draw out my life, if you can."

The vampire's pale lips twisted in disbelief. He grasped my hand. I felt the beast's enervating touch gentled, muted, powerless to harm me.

The vampire realized my immunity. His eyes widened, then narrowed. He tensed to perform a more violent test. Before he could bite my wrist, I thrust the Shadowless Sword through his chest.

As the blade pierced his undead heart, a bolt of lightning blasted through him. His gelid gore showered the nearest soldiers. Removing the blade, I pushed his weightless body to the floor until the final death surrendered it to gravity.

"Forgive us, Master." An armored wight knelt before me. "An imposter came before you. He had your *Tome*."

"Find this imposter. Dispatch all of your troops. Bring him to me."

"It shall be done, Master. But it may take some time. He has gone below."

Svannostel lowered her head close to mine and whispered, "My brother might come."

"Leave the doors open. Do not interfere with anyone but the imposter. Leave anyone else to me."

"As you wish, Master," said the wight.

"Show me where he went."

The army parted. The wight pointed along the path to the yawning pit.

"Shall we?" The dragon lowered her shoulder. I climbed up between her wings. She beat them hard enough to flatten the nearest undead, then circled the hall twice before descending in a narrow spiral down the pit.

Along the pit walls we saw iron gates confining snarling ghouls. They wailed and strained their rotting arms toward us as we passed, aching for a taste of flesh. The stink of them made my skin crawl.

Landing at the bottom of the shaft, I felt the scabrous grasp of a ghoul upon my leg. With a swift stroke of my sword, I severed the limb and stepped away from the cell embedded in the floor. There were dozens all around us, and dozens more in the walls.

"Stay back," I commanded them. "Obey me, for I am the heir of Zutha."

The ghouls continued their savage attempts to devour us. Several more attempts to communicate with them went unheeded.

"They are mindless," said Svannostel.

"No," I said, recognizing the agony drawn in their faces. I had felt the same only recently. "They are mad with hunger."

"At least they're caged. Perhaps Zutha himself could not stop them from devouring his other minions."

Her suggestion sounded reasonable. "There may be a mechanism to release them all at once," I said. "If we had time, I would suggest we destroy them all."

"The 'imposter' is ahead of us. We have no time."

We found the golem's tracks and followed them past the Cenotaph's subterranean inhabitants. Some, recognizing the Crest and Crown of their master, slunk away. Others challenged us. The weak we destroyed with blade and claw. Whatever spell mastery I had surrendered at the shrine of Lissala, I had gained in empathy with the Shadowless Sword. Always incredibly swift, it now anticipated my thoughts and empowered my spells, directing them with flawless precision.

I incinerated a trio of mummified priests with a fiery spell. Svannostel tore a coven of ghostly hags to shreds of ectoplasm.

An honor guard of haunted armor barred our way, unleashing their armory of possessed blades. Channeling a spell through my black blade, I summoned my own battalion of flying swords. As the weapons clashed around us, I ruptured the guardians' armor with bolts of acid. Svannostel tore open the weakened hulls to spill the ruined souls upon the dungeon floor.

We paused to recoup our strength but dared not rest long enough to replenish our spells. Somewhere beneath us, Ygresta was delivering the *Gluttonous Tome* to the body of its creator. If he revived the runelord before we could stop him, all our hopes would become futile.

We came to a giant portcullis guarded by a pair of clock-work dragons. In design they resembled the great art of ancient Thassilon. In construction they exceeded the finest craft of gnomes or dwarves. Electrical arcs whirled within their glass eyes, and each motion of their joints crackled with blue sparks. Their mechanical heads swiveled toward us in an owlish gesture.

Raising a fist, I showed them the Crest of Zutha.

"You are too late," said one.

"The *Tome* has returned to the crypt," said the other.

"The blood of Zutha runs in my veins." Once more I cut my hand. "Taste my blood and open the gate."

"No," said the first guardian. "Zutha wakes."

"I wear the Crest and Crown."

"It does not matter. He who bore the *Tome* closed the way behind him," said the second guardian.

Running out of options and time, I resorted to the basest phrase of diplomacy. "I will destroy you if you do not obey me."

"Nothing in the Cenotaph can harm us," said the first guardian. It snaked its steel tail across the floor and scraped sparks from the stone. "Here we were born, and we have never left our station."

Admiring their construction, I frantically sought a flaw in their design: diamond-tipped claws, hammered bronze wings, copper conduits, ceramic ports, gemstone lenses . . . and electrical junctures. I recalled the paradoxical immunity of Ygresta's golem to lightning. Its mechanical parts should have been vulnerable to electricity, but its union with flesh channeled the energy into biological power.

These clockwork creations were purely mechanical. I doubted they enjoyed such immunity.

"Born here, never having left your station, you have never seen the sky," I said.

"What of it?" said the first guardian.

"Mechanical beings must fear the storm," I said.

"There is no sky here," said the second guardian. Even through its clockwork voice, I detected a note of uncertainty. "There is no storm."

"But there is," I said. "We bring it with us."

Once more anticipating my intent, Svannostel unleashed her lightning at the same moment as I hurled a bolt at the foot of the first clockwork dragon. The mechanical wyrm hopped back, shaking its mangled limb.

"It can hurt us!" Its cry was a shriek of gears.

"It can destroy you. Let me pass."

The guardians exchanged a glance through glass eyes. The second looked at me and said, "None but the creator could harm us." It bowed its long, articulated neck. "You may pass."

Once we were well beyond the gate, I said to Svannostel, "Remember that will *not* work on the golem."

"I remember." The dragon raised her leg in memory of her recent injury.

Beyond the gate, we found a ring of catacombs surrounding the central crypt. A stone seal inscribed with Zutha's personal rune lay broken in the passage. The crypt entrance was far too small for a dragon. Svannostel transformed into her elf form, and we fortified ourselves with wards. She held a finger to her lips and disappeared. Trusting that she followed, I entered the runelord's tomb, seemingly alone.

Twenty walls arched far upward to form a pointed dome of yellow marble veined in black. The ceiling reached so high I estimated it must come near the floor of the great pit, where the ghouls resided in their balcony prisons. Seven tiers of rusted sconces on each wall danced with continual flames. Their shadows writhed among the pillars below.

Ten alcoves ringed a central dais. Within their recesses gleamed precious gems and metals, racks of scrolls and rods, sculptures and time-ravaged tapestries, ancient armors and weapons forged of rare skymetal—a runelord's burial treasures.

Upon the dais, the *Gluttonous Tome* lay open on a marble sarcophagus. To either side, a seven-fingered candelabrum shed light across its pages.

At the head of the sarcophagus stood a monstrous golem, a patchwork of preserved flesh and bone with mechanical supports and joints. The monster held a huge scythe. I had seen the weapon's queer angles before, in drawings of Runelord Zutha and on a statue in Svannostel's gallery.

At the sarcophagus's foot stood a silent hound of utter black. Nearby, two human-shaped shadows crouched at the edge of the sarcophagus.

On the far side of the sarcophagus, Benigno Ygresta leaned upon his canes. Though it did not resemble the man I once knew, I recognized this corpulent figure from his shadow at the goblin attack. Now here he stood in the flesh.

His skin had taken on the gray-green sheen common to those who sup on the life-energy of their victims. White-headed red blisters dotted the fat folds of his eyelids and cheeks. Sweat pasted a few remaining strands of hair to his head. His blubbery lips glistened as he muttered over the book. He appeared oblivious to my arrival, so I introduced myself.

"After all these years, you still move your lips while reading."

Ygresta looked up, blinking. When his bloodshot eyes focused on me, he gave a wan smile. "I suppose it is poetic, if not actually inevitable, that you should be here. Ada suggested I return to scatter your dust to the winds. Perhaps I should have heeded that advice."

The two shadows shrank away from him, slipping across the floor like minnows in a dark current. Except for turning its gaze toward me, the golem remained motionless. The black hound moved slowly toward me, hackles rising as it growled.

"Surely you hated me enough to prevent my resurrection," I said.

"Hated you?" He scratched his chin, leaving a pair of purplish wounds where the skin sloughed off. "At times, I suppose I did. Your haughty manner, your condescension, and your trifling gifts—a single bottle of wine, when you sent cases to peers you barely knew. Hah! How could I not take it as an insult?"

"If you had wanted more, you had only to mention it."

"Mention it? Beg, you mean. Petition, crave, curry favor . . . the only interaction you welcomed from those born beneath you. You never knew what it was like to struggle. You were born high and wealthy. Pharasma's bones! Your illegitimate blood didn't even diminish you as it should. You kept the gift of your elven father's longevity even as your human grandfather absolved you of your bastardy."

Resentment toward the noble class was as common as the men who felt it. I was not entirely unsympathetic to their plight, but neither did I apologize for my blessings.

"So you pretended friendship because my mother paid your tuition."

"No, you insufferable snob! Don't you see that only made it worse? I accepted her money because I needed it. Without it, we might have been friends despite your imperious manner. I genuinely admired the way you grasped arcane theory so easily. I appreciated your help in my studies, despite the occasional snide remark about moving my lips or copying your work to help remember it. Even after you left the Acadamae, I looked forward to your letters. But you offered such redacted, cautious anecdotes that I could never forget, even for a moment, where it was I stood."

"And where was that?"

"In your shadow."

"So you decided to spend my life in the pursuit of your own immortality."

"Why not? You were the perfect tool—yes, *tool*! See how it feels to suffer offense from a careless word? But in this case you were no longer the master but the servant. And an unwitting servant, at that."

"How much of the *Tome* have you read?" I noticed that the book lay upon the sarcophagus, not hovering beside him as it had with me. His bond was imperfect, or perhaps he simply lacked the blood tie that gave me such a rapid connection to the book. "Or perhaps I should ask, how much have you understood?"

He grimaced at my barb. "Enough to know that I was right to bring it here, close to the remains of Zutha. The book feels his presence. Soon it will transfer his immortality to me."

I shook my head. "You always were an idealist first and a scholar second, Benigno. In your hope that the *Tome* contained the secret to lichdom, you saw only what you wished to see. The book does not grant you immortality. It is Zutha's phylactery. The key component of his soul resides within its pages. By bringing it here, you have only offered up yourself as his vessel. You are not becoming a lich. You are sacrificing your body to the runelord's soul."

Ygresta's lips trembled. Pink tears ran down his quivering cheeks. "I have been conducting this ritual for hours. Don't you think I understand that now?"

"That need not be your fate. I can spare you, Benigno." I drew the Shadowless Sword. "You must prefer a clean death to the doom that awaits you."

He stared in disbelief. He gasped or choked, and then the laughter came tumbling out of him. "Oh, Your Excellency, you have developed a sense of humor in your old age. No, I would rather endure as Zutha's vessel than bend my neck to your judgment."

"Very well, in that case—"

"Now, Durante!" Ygresta dropped his canes and snatched up the *Tome*.

The golem dropped the scythe and grabbed the sarcophagus lid. In the periphery of my vision, I saw a shadow and the black hound rush toward me. Anticipating their attack, I stepped to meet them, slashing.

The shadow cried out and withdrew the stumps of four thin fingers. The hound charged past me, vanishing once more into the darkness. A hellish baying filled the room, emanating from every shadow. The sound tickled at the back of my neck. It caused my palms to sweat and my hands to tremble. By force of will, I stifled the urge to flee.

Dust and bone particles rose from the open sarcophagus. For an instant it appeared as a swarm of buzzing insects. It soon coalesced into the figure of a man so corpulent as to make Ygresta appear merely chubby by comparison.

An ornate pike flew from one of the alcoves toward Ygresta. Despite his girth, the necromancer stepped back with great alacrity. Nevertheless, the spear's point impaled his foot. He howled in pain as Svannostel appeared, still in her strange elven form. Releasing the pike, she stepped back, already growing into her dragon shape.

"That one! Kill that one, Durante!" cried Ygresta. Still clutching the *Tome*, he snatched up one of his canes and wagged it at Svannostel.

With a mighty heave, the golem lifted the sarcophagus lid and hurled it at Svannostel. It struck her mid-transformation, crushing the elf-dragon beneath half a ton of marble.

Durante dropped the scythe and lurched toward me. The rotten amalgamation of murdered men creaked and squealed with every motion. I darted out of the way and slashed the ham of its half-mechanical leg. The sword cut deep, but the golem seemed oblivious to the wound.

Shoving off the sarcophagus lid, Svannostel rose to her full height. In an instant, six bronze dragons crowded the chamber. I knew five were illusions, and no doubt so did Ygresta, but the shadow minions threw themselves upon a figment. At their dead touch, the image vanished.

The miasma above Zutha's sarcophagus crackled like flameless embers. An aura of purple near to black surrounded the tiny motes of grave dust. They surged and flowed down onto Ygresta, pouring into his mouth and nostrils, under his clothes, forcing their way through every entrance.

"Svannostel," I cried. "The golem!"

Five dragon heads dipped down, one biting the golem by the shoulder and shaking him as a terrier breaks a rat.

With the golem out of the way, I raised a hand to blast Ygresta with a ring. The fiery ray spilled over him, burning his clothes and the last few wisps of his hair. Ygresta closed his eyes and screamed. The sound filled the crypt, changing tenor as it transformed from a scream of pain to one of apotheosis.

Ygresta opened his eyes. His irises, formerly brown, now gleamed Azlanti purple. As the crypt dust vanished, so did my old classmate. Only Zutha remained.

Sniffing and licking its bulging lips, the transformed body floated above the floor. Rolls of fat swelled and puckered with new sores as the spirit of the runelord began to claim his new fleshy vessel.

Zutha reached toward the *Gluttonous Tome*. After a moment's balk, it rose to levitate by his side. He reached for his scythe. It too shuddered with uncertainty before flying into his hand.

The hesitations must mean Zutha's new body had not yet come into his full power. So I hoped, and so I knew we had to act quickly.

"Varian Jeggare," he said, pronouncing my name strangely. "Varian Jeggare, Varian Jeggare," he repeated, as if growing accustomed to the words upon his tongue. He sniffed before speaking in ancient Thassilonian: "Blood of my blood. Child of my child."

I unleashed the power of my most destructive ring. The instant I willed it to fire, an invisible force struck my hand like a schoolmaster's rod across the knuckles of an insolent student. The stones orbiting my brow cracked against my skull as they fled from me to encircle the necromancer's head.

"Your friend restored me, great-grandchild, and you have delivered my most potent weapons," said Zutha. "Now bend your knee and serve your father."

"Never!" I spat out the word before considering a more guileful approach. I could not help but rebel at the notion of bowing before such a monster, no matter our blood relation.

While Zutha regarded me with disappointment, Svannostel fell upon him. The dragon's claws sheared hanks of flesh from Ygresta's carcass. Zutha grunted in irritation and swept his scythe around his massive body, the gesture as delicate as Zora's handling of her flag. The scythe came away bloody. One of Svannostel's talons fell to the floor.

She trumpeted her fury, rising up to blast Zutha with her stormy breath.

"Not the golem!" I shouted too late. There was no time to explain that I knew how the rings and stones defending Zutha could also redirect the lightning.

The white shower danced across an invisible barrier around Zutha. The runelord reeled, still weak as a newborn. Even so, his

Crest defended him. The power of the ring deflected Svannostel's breath to cascade over Durante's body. Electricity leaped from joint to staple, energizing the automaton.

"Otto, Otto," said Zutha, the shadow's name coming to him as mine had, through the dying brain of Benigno Ygresta. As Zutha spoke, his fluid flesh bubbled and filled its gaping wounds. "Otto, Ada, Durante." After a brief pause, he spoke again, this time in heavily accented Taldane. "Otto, Ada, Durante. Your former master created you. Now his body is mine, and you are my servants."

"We are, Master," said a fragile voice I assumed belonged to Ada.

"Kill the dragon as I gather my strength," he said. "And drag this boy of mine before me . . . on his knees prefer—"

Svannostel slammed the runelord to the ground.

As she raised her claw again, his body bobbed up to levitate above the floor. Where the blow had crushed his arm and face, the bones shifted, the flesh knitting back together, more pustulant than before. "I chose the location of my crypt for a purpose," he said. "Even in my weakness, you cannot destroy me here. The energies of the site sustain me, as they do all undead."

I had lost my only advantage with the rings and stones. What weapons remained to me and Svannostel now appeared insufficient. We had to flee or die.

I rushed toward Zutha. The shadow—presumably Otto—and his hound intercepted me. Once more, I evaded the hound and lashed out at Otto, my sword tearing a slice from his shadow arm. As I leaped to the lip of the sarcophagus, Durante pummeled me with a bucket-sized fist. I flew backward and crashed into an alcove full of dusty scrolls. Somehow I retained my grip on the Shadowless Sword, yet that small victory provided little consolation.

Svannostel buffeted our foes with her wings. I saw the battle through a veil of dust. She threw her massive body on Durante, biting and tearing. With a scream of metal, she pulled off one of his rotting arms and spat it to the side.

Gesturing with both hands, Zutha spoke a word of power. Svannostel reeled, her wounded claw clutching at her breast as the runelord's death magic wormed its way to her heart. The impact of her fall filled the room with dust and shadows.

Choking, I staggered back into the fray. The shadow hound rushed me. Its jaws clamped around my sword arm. With my free hand, I grabbed its throat and unleashed a shock of electricity. The stench of burning fur overpowered the smell of dust. The shadow hound's body shook until it released my arm and limped away, whining.

As the dust settled, I saw Zutha hovering above his own sarcophagus. In one hand he clutched his scythe. With the other he gestured toward the wall, where a great black hand gripped Svannostel by the throat.

Worse, the *Gluttonous Tome* rose up to hover by his side. His power grew.

Even so, hope surged in my breast as I saw the dragon still lived. Yet she could not survive for long. The giant hand pressed so hard the masonry behind her crumbled. Stones fell from far above as the hand crushed the supporting vaults. A mangled iron grate struck Svannostel's head and clanged on the crypt floor.

A desiccated body plunged after the grate. Another dropped onto Svannostel's neck and began gnawing at her scales. The dragon struggled to pull the ghoul away as the shadowy hand held her fast.

An intangible grip fell upon my shoulder, cold and enervating. I shrugged it away, but another gripped me from the other side. My strength spilled away.

"Bow," rasped Otto. As more stones and bodies fell around us, the shadows pushed me to my knees.

"Yes, Count Jeggare," said Ada. "Bow before the Master."

20
The Crypt of Zutha
Radovan

Hundreds of undead soldiers stood at the mouth of an open pit. We'd seen a few try to climb down, only to scramble back up again as some *things* down there snarled and tore at them. Even at a distance we could smell what they were. Nothing stinks like a ghoul.

Others jumped into the pit while their buddies watched. When they heard the clatter of bones from somewhere far below, they stepped back, shaking their naked skulls or the mummified lumps that used to be their faces.

"I don't think we ought to go in there," Zora said.

"Where else can we go?" I'd already made a circuit of the room after Illyria cast a spell to make me invisible and unsmellable to the undead. I hadn't found any other way down, but it was obvious that's where the action was happening.

"Varian has to be down there," said Illyria. "Zutha's army must be trying to follow him."

"Got any suggestions?" I looked around to see whether anybody else had an idea. Kazyah looked her solemn self. Zora looked like she'd rather be anywhere else.

"Let's ask for directions," said Illyria.

Before anybody could stop her, she walked straight toward the undead army. Even the drake thought that was a bad idea. She flapped back to perch on Arni's shoulders. She'd done that often enough that he was getting used to it. He barely even flinched. But when I started after Illyria, he whined to let me know he thought it was a bad idea, too.

The dead turned as we approached. I expected a fight, but they didn't go for their weapons. Most of them wore old armor covered in red rust and that green stuff whose name I forget. One wearing a few strands that used to be a plume on his helm stepped forward and opened his jaws. A scrap of leather that served as his tongue started to move, but Illyria held him still with a spell.

"Has the count passed this way?" she said before releasing him to speak. She was tougher than I'd given her credit for. Her voice barely wavered.

"You serve the master?" said the dead guy.

"Why else would we walk among you filthy things?" she said with a sniff. "Take us to him."

"We have tried," he said. "The hungerers devour those who seek to follow. We try to obey him, but less than half our number have made it down intact."

I peeked down into the pit. Ghouls snapped at us from a hundred little cells in the walls. Sometimes one shoved a scabby arm through the grate. Here and there, a ghoul gnawed on the bones of some undead soldier who'd tried to get past.

"Climbing down is a bad idea," I said.

"There may be an alternative," said Illyria. "While we cannot all fly, we can all fall."

I had an idea what she meant. "How we going to do it?"

"Together is best," she said. Every time she turned, the light spell on her brooch turned the shadows in a new direction. "That way I'm less likely to miss one of you."

"I would prefer to walk through the stone," said Kazyah. The way she looked into the pit, I realized she didn't like heights. The way I'd seen her fight, I'd been beginning to think nothing scared her.

"That's fine for you," said Illyria. "But we should stay together."

"It's all right," I said. "I've done this with the boss." I offered Kazyah my hand. She surprised me by taking it. We gave each other a squeeze.

"Go!" said Illyria.

We jumped into the pit, falling fast. Illyria said her spell, and we drifted soft as autumn leaves.

The ghouls wailed behind iron bars. I realized somebody had put them there on purpose, maybe to keep people like us from climbing down. Their stink got worse the lower we went.

We landed on mounds of shattered bodies. That they'd been dead long before they hit didn't make it any nicer. Arni clambered down from the heap, whining and skittish. You'd think a dog would love a pile of bones, but I couldn't blame him for wanting fresher. Kazyah took Illyria by the arm to help her down.

Four passages stretched away from the round room. Amaranthine hissed and beat her wings as a ghoul reached out from the nearest wall. Illyria moved away. So did the rest of us.

A claw scraped over my boot from a cell under our feet. "Watch your step!"

"Do you hear it?" said Kazyah.

It was hard to hear anything over the ghouls, but something was going on below us, below the ghouls in the floor. Crashing, thunder blasts, muffled voices. It was almost enough to bring the house down.

"It sounds like it's right underneath the floor," said Illyria. She looked to Kazyah. "Is there any way you could smash through this?"

"Can you make us float again?"

Illyria nodded. Kazyah waved us back. We gave her room to swing her earth breaker. She began the whirling transformation into a rock spirit. When the change was done, she raised a barrel-sized fist and punched the floor.

The first blow smashed open a cell pen and stunned the ghoul inside. The second crushed the ghoul to pulp and put a crater in the floor.

Kazyah kept at it until she broke through the floor, and the dead ghoul fell into another, much bigger room. Cool, dusty air blew up into our faces.

Kazyah widened the hole with a couple more smashes of her stony fist. I smelled lightning from down below and saw yellow lights all around the circular walls of a big room.

"Catch me!" I jumped in

"Not so—!" said Illyria, but it was too late.

As I fell, I had only a second to see what was going on: dragon, big floating hand, one-armed golem, black dog, fat reaper, and there—kneeling with a couple shadows squeezing his neck—was the boss.

"Illyriaaaa!"

Her spell caught me just in time. Floating felt a little like hitting the water. I tugged the big knife from its sheath and grabbed a shadow to pull its head back. My hand went right through it, feeling like I'd pulled it out of a bucket of ice water. I swept the blade across the shadow's neck anyway. A little tug and a hellish red glow told me the knife's magic did its trick. The shadow blew away like a burned sheet of paper.

"Ada!" screamed the other shadow. It lunged at me. That was good, because it had to let go of the boss, but I didn't want it touching me either.

I quick-stepped back, sweeping the blade to cover my retreat. I caught the shadow's hand before it showed sense enough to dodge. Reversing my grip, I got ready for a good stab to its heart—assuming it had one—and then something knocked me flat.

The shadow dog was on me, biting and scratching. Its weight held me down, so it had meat or something to it, unlike its pals. Rolling to the side, I lashed back with a spur and got a nice wet yelp.

The dog jumped again. This time I had the knife braced. The blade sank deep into the shadow hound's belly. I twisted and pulled the blade up, spilling its guts all over me.

"No!" screamed the shadow. He ran at me while I pushed at the dog carcass. He was going to get me before I freed myself.

Two quick strokes of light cut the shadow into three pieces. Like the first one, they shriveled and blew across the room.

The boss stood there with a weird black sword. I blinked when I realized it was the Shadowless Sword, only now it was black with runes on the sides.

The boss's face was a white mask. I thought maybe he was sick, or maybe he was still mad at me. I was afraid I might be next in line after that shadow. But he didn't stab me. Instead, he offered me a hand up.

"You should not have followed me," he said.

Behind him, Kazyah fought the golem, who'd already taken a pretty good beating. She lifted him off the ground and threw him across the room.

"Let's see how he likes it," I said. The boss didn't laugh. He didn't even look irritated at my dumb joke, so I changed the subject. "Did Ygresta get fatter?"

"Zutha has claimed his body," said the boss. "He has not recovered his full strength, but he already far more powerful than Ygresta."

"And Ygresta beat our asses."

The golem came crashing down on Zutha, but the big guy shoved him aside with a gesture. He pointed one of his rings at me and the boss. Its diamond head flared. Four crackling balls of lightning flew at us.

The boss shoved me down and made a fancy gesture with his sword. Whatever it was supposed to be, nothing happened before the lightning exploded all around him.

"Boss!"

He staggered back, flame flickering in his hair. He started a spell of his own, making the gestures with his free hand and the sword at the same time.

Svannostel roared, the sound shaking the room. She'd changed back into an elf to slip out of the giant hand, but now she was changing back. Next to her, Illyria had her hands ready for a spell, but she was waiting for something before she cast it.

Zutha began his own spell, looking at her. Illyria's eyes went wide, but she let her own spell go before cringing.

The boss didn't wait to see how that turned out. He ran forward and leaped over the tomb. On the downward arc, the Shadowless Sword cut through some magic barrier with a black-and-white flash. The blade met the runelord's wrist. The necromancer's fat hand fell away.

Zutha shouted. He sounded more surprised than hurt, but he was no less pissed. He swung his scythe around. The blade was big enough to cut a man in half, but it cut nothing but air. The boss had already rolled away, putting himself between Zutha and Illyria.

Always a gentleman.

Zutha yelled something I didn't understand and held up his stump. Black tendrils grew out of the wound, already forming a new palm and fingers. "You see?" he went on in Taldane. "You cannot destroy me. In my seat of power, I regenerate faster than you can harm me."

A shower of dust and stone fell on him from above. With it came a ghoul. The thing latched on and started gobbling at Zutha's fat shoulder.

"Off of me, you wretch!" He tried to shrug the thing off, but it held tight. "I am the master of this place. Obey me!"

"Hung—hung—hungry!" gibbered the ghoul. It tore chunks out of him, drool and blood running from its jaws. Next to Zutha, the *Tome* dipped, bobbing in the air like he'd lost concentration on keeping it there.

"Radovan!" the boss yelled. He showed me a hand sign that meant *distraction!*

There's a lot of ways to do that, but only one came to mind. I ran behind Zutha, who was too busy shaking off the ghoul to notice me. Maybe my knife wasn't as special as the Shadowless Sword, but it'd leave a mark. I stabbed the runelord in the spine.

Whatever whammy was in the big knife, it was enough to get through his magic shield. But then there was so much fat to cut through that I didn't see blood until the third or fourth stab. By then, my first cut had already sealed up. Zutha was right. He was healing faster than we could cut him down.

The boss and Illyria threw more spells at Zutha. Magic shields from his crown of stones absorbed them. Svannostel blasted him with lightning. Another floating stone sucked the bolt out of the air.

I kept stabbing until Zutha flicked a finger and threw me across the room. Between him and the golem, I was damned tired of getting tossed around.

The boss said something to the dragon. She snatched up a ghoul gnawing on her leg and threw it at Zutha. The ghoul latched onto him just like the first one. Slobbering in excitement, it dug in.

Zutha howled, this time in pain. "Obey me, scavengers!"

"More ghouls!" the boss shouted.

"Are you sure?" said Illyria. "You were very cross with me the last time."

"Confound it, I am certain that—!"

She was already spilling teeth from her pouch into her hand. She just wanted to get a dig in, maybe in case it was her last chance. Casting the boss's least favorite spell, she threw the teeth at Zutha.

"Kazyah, can you break the others out of their cells?" said the boss.

"I might bury us all."

"Can you escape on your own?"

She nodded.

"Then do it. We shall find another way."

Illyria threw handful after handful of ghoul teeth at the runelord. Some stuck like knives. Others disappeared into his rolls of fat. All of them sprouted ghouls. The things were born hungry, and they wasted no time feasting.

The boss ran over to Illyria and waved at me to join them. I limped over, avoiding falling stones and ghouls.

"You vexatious worms! Your punishment will last longer than my slumber!" Zutha's flesh grew back as fast as the ghouls devoured it. He threw off two of them. Three more scrambled up and savaged him.

Illyria rose from the floor, flying. Amaranthine flew after her.

"Stay close," said the boss. He snapped off a riffle scroll. "Cover me while I go in."

"He says we can't kill him here!"

"Perhaps not," said the boss. "But I can be vexatious." He ran toward Zutha, which looked like the worst possible idea. The runelord reached out a hand, aiming a ring. It began to flare, and the boss threw himself to the side to go for *Tome*—which had been his plan all along.

The Shadowless Sword licked out twice.

A scream filled the crypt, louder than Svannostel's roar or any of the explosion. I couldn't tell whether it came from Zutha or the open pages of the *Tome*. The sound stabbed deep into my ears and left puddles of blood in them.

Zutha reeled, flailing a regenerating hand toward the book. The ghouls chewed off his fingers and spat out the rings. They swarmed thick enough to knock the Azlanti stones out of their orbit. Without them, I wondered how long he could hold out before they ate every last bit of him.

The boss threw *Tome*'s front cover to Svannostel. The dragon caught it, said a spell, and disappeared.

He threw the back cover to Kazyah. She shifted back to human form to catch it.

"Now!" he yelled.

Kazyah chanted a spell and slammed her earth breaker into the floor. The impact sent deep cracks across the room and up the walls. Thunder rolled through the earth, shaking stone off the walls, spilling more and more ghouls out of their cells.

The boss slapped the *Tome's* middle pages onto my chest. "Take these."

I tucked them under my arm as the ground crumbled beneath us. "You keep it. I don't wanna get fat!"

"Then resist the temptation to read it." He hooked his arm around mine and pulled me into the air.

"I ain't tempted." I held tight to the book and to him.

Below us, Kazyah finished her spell and sank into the floor like it was a pool of water.

As ghouls rained down, Zutha bellowed more Thassilonian words. The bodies of ghouls muffled the sound, but I guessed more of it was curses than spells.

The boss shouted back in the same language. Whatever he said made Zutha curse louder, and then a ghoul grabbed both sides of his face and bit out the runelord's tongue.

As more falling stones and ghouls covered him, his squeals faded away. We flew up through the pit. Some kind of earthquake—and I had an idea what kind—had broken open all the cells to spill out the ghouls.

"Is that the end of that guy?" I said.

"Certainly not," said the boss. "Pray there are enough ghouls to keep him occupied for many years."

"They'll get full, won't they? Then he'll come for us."

The boss had nothing to say to that.

By the time we reached the main floor, the joint was jumping. Kazyah's earthquake had scattered Zutha's army. Some ran out of the Cenotaph. Svannostel hovered above them, beating her wings to knock them down, blowing lightning kisses to incinerate the ones that ran.

Illyria and Amaranthine were already flying out the open doors. The boss followed, slower on account of carrying me.

Outside, he paused long enough to let Svannostel join us. Then he closed the weird green doors with a touch. We flew down to the base of the mountain.

"Where is the carriage?" he asked. "Where are the others?"

"I'd say right about there." I pointed west.

His eyes widened as he saw the dust clouds. The sound of war drums rolled across the foothills. He dug the spyglass out of his satchel.

"They had to keep moving while we came inside after you. We tried to lose them, but this land is lousy with orcs, and we weren't flying."

"What is that cloud to the south?" he said.

Without a spyglass, I could only shrug. "Those guys are new."

As soon as I said it, I saw a third group coming from the southeast. The boss looked their way. More orcs. "They have warbeasts."

"Desna weeps," I said. "I thought the hard part was over."

Peering through the glass, he said. "Far too many."

"You need to learn how to make the carriage fly," I said.

His eyebrows rose, but he had to know I wasn't serious.

"Make for the carriage," he said.

"What about Kazyah?"

"She can escape on her own, and I cannot carry you with any speed." He took to the air. He and Illyria flew toward the carriage.

"Hey, what about me?" I knew I'd sort of killed him, but I didn't like being ditched. Before I could get sore, Svannostel swooped down and grabbed me by the arms.

"Hey, hey!" I yelled. "Shouldn't I be riding on top?"

"No."

She flew me to the Red Carriage. Eando was hanging onto the scorpion for his life while Janneke drove.

Behind them ran twenty or so wargs, wolves the size of ponies. Most had orcs riding on their backs. One had a bloody streak running down its side. Eando must have got off a good shot.

"Don't spook the horses!" I yelled.

Svannostel banked away as the horses screamed and veered the other way. I was bad enough for scaring horses, but there was no *not* spooking them with a great big dragon. At least they didn't turn back to the orcs.

On the second pass, Svannostel let go of me just before we reached the carriage. She was a good shot, too. I hit the roof, rolled, and hung onto the luggage rail. Down below, Arni woofed and stuck his head out the window.

"Stay put, Arni!"

I pushed Eando out of the way and started cranking the scorpion. "Reload! Janneke, we got two more groups coming in from the south."

"I can't turn toward the mountain!"

"Well, pick a group."

Ahead of us, the boss threw lightning at one war band while Illyria sent a blurry gray specter toward one of its shamans.

The orcs had scorpions of their own mounted on the backs of their war rhinos. One shot a bolt so close I thought it'd gone straight through the boss, but he didn't fall. Others fired arrows. Some fell past the wizards, but others ricocheted off their wards. That would only last so long, and the orcs were getting closer to them than we were.

"Svannostel!" I yelled, wanting her to go help the boss and Illyria, but she'd already circled behind us. She laid down a line of white lightning, frying the first rank of wargs. The ones behind leaped over them and kept coming. The horses screamed, but they couldn't run any faster.

Eando slapped a bolt into the scorpion. I turned it around to fire at the orcs closing in on the boss, but we were too far away.

"Go higher!" I yelled. That was pointless. The boss couldn't hear me from that distance, especially not over the battle screams of the orcs.

The orcs split into two groups. At first I thought they meant to surround the boss and Illyria. Then I saw that something else was cutting through them.

Two dozen armored mercenaries charged from behind. At their head, I saw Faceless Kaid's red plume.

"Yes!" Janneke punched the air.

I was happy about it too, but we were still outnumbered.

"Look!" Eando shouted. "Turn this thing around!"

I spun the scorpion back to point at the wargs. A big ugly one was close enough to nip at the back wheel. The angle was no good for me to shoot that one. Eando cast a spell, flinging a ball of acid down at it. The warg yelped and peeled away. I grinned to think we were routing them, but then I saw they weren't running. They were just letting their reinforcements through.

"Hell," said Janneke. "Dragons!"

I looked where she was pointing. Three blue-winged reptiles flew above the third group of orc marauders. I didn't like it any better than she did, but it could have been worse. "Don't be such a baby. It's only wyverns."

She didn't waste time shooting me a look.

Svannostel headed for the wyverns. They spread out, trying to come at her from all sides. She blasted one with a breath of storm. It went down, trailing a spiral of smoke.

The orcs threw everything they had at the dragon. Arrows glanced off her scales like fleas jumping off a dog, but a few stuck deep. A fireball blasted her hard enough to make her wobble in flight. Just as she was about to bank and snap up a wyvern in her jaws, another one swooped down and slung its tail around, stinging her with its tail-barb.

Svannostel veered away, slapping the wyvern with her own tail. It didn't have a barb, but it was heavy as an oak tree trunk. The wyvern went straight down, tried to catch itself, and crashed in front of a charging rhino. The driver tried to turn away, but the big beast trampled the fallen wyvern.

Suddenly I was in the air, tumbling end over end until I hit something hard enough to knock out all my wind. All I could see at first was a bunch of green and yellow explosions. I felt the heat of the fireball that flipped us. I heard the horses screaming. I couldn't figure out which way was up.

As soon as I stood, something knocked me back down again. There were feet running past me on all sides. Blinking and gasping for breath, I got to my hands and knees and crawled until I could see again.

The Red Carriage lay on its side, and so did the team, still caught in their harnesses. A little way past them, Janneke staggered to her feet. She'd lost her helm in the fall. That was becoming a habit.

Kaid's Band were jumping down from their horses and forming a shield wall around the carriage. They covered maybe half.

The boss stood on the side of the carriage facing the sky. He pulled Illyria up through one side window while Arnisant scrambled out of the other, followed by Zora and her flag. Eando staggered around from the other side. He had two black eyes and a bloody nose. The others didn't look much better.

"Get in formation!" Kaid yelled at Janneke.

All around us, the three orc bands regrouped. Two formed up together, while the third stood off to the side, too good for the others, or too bad. Their chief was big as an ogre—maybe he *was* an ogre—and he wore a cape of tattooed Shoanti skin.

It was too much to hope that they'd fight each other, but I prayed anyway. "Sweet Desna, I would appreciate a smile about now."

One of Kaid's girls—Stiletto—cut the horses loose from the carriage. The big fellows stood up and ran like hell in the direction of Ustalav. At least none of them had broken a leg, which was some kind of miracle. If Lady Luck was smiling on anybody just then, it was those horses. I hoped they ran all the way back to Elfland and got put out to stud.

The rest of us weren't going to be so lucky.

The bigger of the two orc bands started up their war music. I could feel the drums pounding on my teeth. Their shamans shouted blessings on the troops. The chief barked out a speech, working them up into a good lather.

The boss floated down from the sky and put a few riffle scrolls into my hand.

"Use them all," he said, before taking his own advice. We filled ourselves with strength and quickness and all the good magic we had left. Illyria busted out her own scrolls and kept a wand in one hand.

Eando had his sword in one hand and a dagger in the other. He gave me a nod and said, "I'm with you, all right?"

"All right," I said.

"I'm with you, too," said Zora. She'd already unfurled her flag. I saw she'd inserted a spearhead at the top. She knew this was going to be more than a Korvosan alley scuffle.

"The more the merrier."

When they came, the orcs deafened us with horns and drums. The way they smelled, they almost suffocated us, too.

They smashed into Kaid's mercenaries, punching holes through the line of shields. Those that broke past got arcane missiles in the face. A shaman made it through, turning his tusked head to pick a target. Before he could cast his spell, Illyria whipped a black lash of magic around his throat.

Seeing that, Eando and I got on either side of him, left our graffiti, and got away just as his guts spilled down to his ankles. Zora came in a moment too late, but that was just as well. Her face turned green at the sight of the eviscerated orc.

"Fill the gaps!" shouted Kaid. Her mercs obeyed, and the wall shrank a few feet shorter.

A berserker leaped the shield wall. He stood for a second on top of the carriage, deciding who to chop first. Like the shaman before him, he took too long. The boss put a lightning bolt through both him and the rhino charging into the wall. It fell on it side, sliding through Kaid's women and crushing the carriage boot and rear wheels.

Shadows fell across the field around us, growing smaller as they got close. Maybe more wyverns had come our way, I thought. But looking up I saw eight big rocks falling among the bad guys. Each one crushed an orc into a puddle. The screams came from the survivors as the boulders unfolded into orc-sized earth spirits and showed them the true meaning of berserk.

"Kazyah!" yelled Zora. She kept her flag moving, slapping arrows out of the air, snatching spells before they could hit us, and sometimes spearing an orc in the eye.

Once more in the form of an earth spirit, Kazyah waded into the orcs. She was bigger than all of the elementals she'd hurled at them combined. She snatched up orcs and crushed them in her stony fingers. The orcs sank spears in her. They hacked at her with axes and hammers. She started to chip away.

I yelled, "She needs help!"

"Stay within the shield wall," said the boss.

It didn't matter that he was right. I didn't like leaving Kazyah out there by herself.

Another orc made it over the shield wall. Somebody perforated him with arcane missiles. Eando cut him across the chest.

I put the big knife in his spleen. He went down, but killing him made me tired, especially after the fight in the Cenotaph. It was taking an awful lot of work to make one dead orc. If we had to do that much for every one of them, we were never going to make it.

Kazyah kept harrying the orcs outside our lines. Svannostel swept past now and then to drop lightning or bad magic on them. We killed dozens. It felt like hundreds.

More kept coming.

I was out of scrolls. Eando was down to blades. Illyria was down to her wands. Zora did what she could to support us, while another of Kaid's Band fell every time the orcs hit the shield wall. The boss used his sword more and more. He threw away a spent riffle scroll with a look like it was his last one.

Kazyah walked into the air above the orcs like she was climbing an invisible stair. Seeing her that way reminded me of her story at the Seraph's Stair: the old man and the granddaughter, the one growing old too fast. She let go of the elemental shape, becoming flesh and blood.

The orc spellcasters threw fire and frost at her. The archers covered her in arrows. Some flicked away as if they'd hit stone. Others sank deep into her. She threw back spells of her own, but when she looked our way she caught my eye.

For a second I saw her the way she looked before her son was born. Then I caught a glimpse of the old woman she ought to be. She looked at me and said something. I read the words off her lips:

Until our skulls are gathered.

I caught a glimpse of her skin turning to stone as she fell back into the sea of orcs. I like to think she sank into the earth and flowed through the ground somewhere far away. That's what I like to think.

Anyway, that was the last I saw of Kazyah the Night Bear.

"I can't believe we're going to die fighting orcs," said Illyria. "We survived the crypt of Zutha. This isn't the least bit romantic!"

"Goddamned orcs," said Eando.

"Goddamned orcs," I agreed.

A sound of thunder rose from the south. Lightning flashed across the sky.

"Go!" said the boss. He'd just finished casting the last of his flying spells on Illyria.

"Come with me!" She reached for him. Amaranthine curled around her upper arm.

"Go now," he said. I could tell by the way his body moved that his own spell was still working. He could have gone with her, but he stayed with us.

Illyria flew up to join Svannostel. They could fight from the sky. When the rest of us were dead, they could fly away.

The bronze dragon flew close overhead, blowing Illyria off course. Just as she righted herself, another bronze dragon followed the first.

"Am I seeing double?" said Zora.

The orcs' cheers changed to screams of panic. The thunder kept growing louder. The front lines fell back. Kaid's women lowered their shields, and we saw what distracted them.

An honest-to-Iomedaea cavalry charged through their rear lines. I recognized the sword and sun on their tabards. They were knights of Lastwall, dedicated to keeping the orcs bottled up in Belkzen and watching over Gallowspire, on the other side of their country. What they were doing here I couldn't figure. For a second I thought somebody had cast an illusion, but then I remembered that Svannostel had a brother.

Who lived in Vigil.

"We're saved!" shouted Eando.

"Don't get cocky," I said. "That's when you get killed."

He sobered up. We stuck near the boss and Zora, protecting each other's backs as a few desperate orcs ran our way instead of toward the ranks of knights. Bloody lances plowed furrows through the orc mob.

It was still hard work, fighting off the orcs until they ran. But soon it became short work.

When it started to look clear for us, the boss flew up to join Illyria. Their hair floated in the static left behind by the dragon's breath. They looked like the heroes in one of Illyria's romances, soaring above the field. Beneath them, covered in dust and blood, the rest of us bundled up the wounded and closed the eyes of the dead.

Epilogue
Vigil
Varian

In the great hall of Castle Overwatch, we paid our respects at
the Shattered Shield of Arnisant. Once known as the Shield of
Aroden, blessed by the now-dead god of humanity, its broken
remains offered mute testimony of the sacrifice demanded of
those who dared oppose the Whispering Tyrant.

"Your namesake bore that escutcheon, Arnisant." The hound
looked up at me when he heard his name. I scratched his curly
gray head. He had lost some of his plumpness during our recent
ordeals, but I restrained myself from offering him a treat before
suppertime. "He too was a very good boy."

Arnisant looked at the shield as if he understood my words.
The gesture seemed so human that even Svannostel turned her
head in a querulous gesture. Her comely elven form still seemed
strange to me after having fought her as a dragon in her lair. She
carried the *Black Book* in a leather pack slung across her shoulders.
She had assured me the book would remain secure even after she
transformed back into her draconic form.

Beside her stood her brother Xostromo, whose timely arrival
with the cavalry of Lastwall had spared us from making our own
version of Arnisant's sacrifice. Xostromo assumed a more natural
human form than his sister's metallic elf. He stood exactly my
height, a man of Chelish features with sun-bronzed skin and
silver-white hair. He wore the simple but fine garb of a monk of

Iomedae, complete with its linen satchel, in which he had secured the *Bone Grimoire*.

As we emerged from the castle into bright sunlight, Xostromo turned to me. "I am pleased to meet a lord of Cheliax who honors the great general."

"Despite the current regime, the people of Cheliax have never forgotten that Iomedae was one of us before her ascent to godhood. Nor shall we forget the sacrifice of Arnisant."

"May your travels bring you to Vythded Monastery one day." He offered me a martial bow. "But if they do, please do not bring the *Codex*."

I patted my own satchel. Until we could find a reliable manner in which to destroy them, we had agreed to hide the three parts of the *Gluttonous Tome*. "While the monastery may be defensible, please consider hiding the *Grimoire* elsewhere. No, do not tell me where. Do not tell your sister, either. It is better no one else can track them as easily as I did."

"We understand, Count," said Svannostel. "Remember, we have some experience in this matter."

"My apologies," I said. "I am perhaps too accustomed to giving commands both in war and afterward."

Xostromo said, "Will you accept Veena Heliu's offer to teach at the War College?"

"While flattering, the Precentor Marshal's offer was a mere courtesy."

"I think not," said Xostromo. "The tales of your actions in the Worldwound campaign have spread. It is only a matter of time before your part in thwarting the rise of Zutha is also known."

On the latter point, I feared he was correct. The best I could hope was to manage the narrative before it escaped Vigil. If I could trust Eando Kline, that effort was already underway.

One after the other, the dragons clasped my hand, transformed into their true forms, and took to the air. Svannostel flew west, along the River Esk toward her lair beneath the Sleeper. Xostromo went north, toward the Hungry Mountains and his brothers and sisters in Vythded Monastery.

After watching the bronze dragons depart, Arnisant and I went to the fabled stables of Castle Overwatch. Janneke emerged as we approached. Her new black-and-red armor stood out from the bronze-and-white uniforms of the castle guard. It would match the livery of my servants perfectly.

"Your Excellency," she said with a Chelish salute. She had been practicing the gesture ever since we agreed on her continuing service. "Your horses are fit and frisky. The hostler says there's been another offer to buy them."

"What did you reply?"

"Not at any price."

"And the carriage?"

"The wainwrights repaired the wheels, but they say the damage to the body appears to be repairing itself. Is that . . . normal?"

"No, but it is expected." The carriage's creator was a druid of great power—perhaps even more powerful than Kazyah the Night Bear. Even several years since its last repair, I had barely begun to discover all of its magical attributes. "Very good, Janneke. You may have the rest of the day to yourself."

"Have you spoken with Radovan?" she said. "That is, if I see him, should I tell him—?"

"Leave it to me."

"As you wish, Excellency." She made a perfect Chelish bow before withdrawing.

I left the castle and descended the hill. The sound of drums and flutes drifted from the northern markets as we strolled southeast. There, beside Southgate, I found The Lady's Shield-Hand, Vigil's most popular tavern.

Eando Kline awaited me at a window table. As he spied me, he signaled the barman to draw another draught. It arrived moments after I sat, along with a board of smoked meats, fruits, breads, and cheeses.

"Did you go to the lodge?" said Kline. Since our arrival in Vigil, he asked me the question every time we met.

"No," I said. "Did you?"

"You're the one the venture-captain keeps inviting for tea and 'a chat.'"

"What makes you think I would share our secrets with the Pathfinders? I have told you time and again that I trust the Decemvirate no more than you do."

He raised his hands in surrender. "I'm sorry, it's just you were with them for so much longer than I was, and you always seemed so pleased to publish your findings."

"I may indulge in pride—among other sins—but I am no fool."

"No more than any man, I suppose."

I disliked his insinuating tone. "What do you mean by that?"

"Nothing." He failed to suppress a sly smile.

"Do not toy with me, Kline."

"Oh, look, here comes Lady Illyria."

I stood at once, composing myself for a greeting before I saw that Lady Illyria was nowhere to be seen.

Kline drowned his chuckle with a long pull from his bitter ale.

"Very amusing." I sat and drank my own beer. It was cool and malty, its flavor improved rather than diminished by the tankard's wood.

"You sure you don't want to ride back with Kaid's Band?"

"I prefer a sea voyage to another trek across the Hold of Belkzen. I am weary of orcs."

"Eando!" called a man from across the bar. I turned to see a curly-haired Ustalav approaching. A scar formed a chevron across his nose and either cheek. When he saw me, his brow furrowed.

Kline shook his head, and the man veered off to walk straight out of the tavern.

"The bard?" I said.

Eando nodded. "He's a real piece of work. I first heard him telling the story of the Worldwound Gambit as if he'd been one of Gad's team. Later, he was telling the crowd he'd been in Whitethrone during the interregnum. I know for a fact he was nowhere near Irrisen."

"Then he's perfect. How much have you told him?"

"Pretty much everything, but with all of the critical details altered."

"My identity?"

"'A knight of Taldor,' not that it matters. By the time he tells the tale of Zutha's Crypt, he'll be the hero of the story, and no one will be able to identify you as his patron."

"Well done. The last thing I want is for word of my connection to the runelord to reach the court of Cheliax."

"Are you doing the same with the so-called 'Legend-Singer'?"

"Sharina is a legitimate playwright, although no less mercenary in her desire for material and, of course, funding," I said. "With her I have shared other tales, and for a different purpose."

Kline clacked his tankard against mine, and we drank. When I set mine back on the table, he reacted as if seeing something behind me. He snorted into his beer, then tipped it back to finish in a hurry.

"A valiant effort," I said. "But you cannot fool me twice."

"I should have known I'd find you boys in your cups," said Lady Illyria. "How many have you had?"

I stood in haste, careful not to spill my beer.

"Two," said Kline, slamming his tankard down and standing. "But I've got to go."

"Two, barkeep!" said Illyria. She took Kline's place and set a package on the table. She had her hair freshly coiffed in black roses frosted in a shade of purplish-red. She wore a white summer dress embroidered in a sash of the same hue—amaranthine, I realized—with one padded shoulder serving as a perch for the drake. Amaranthine hopped off her shoulder and claimed a piece of cheese from the board.

"Have fun, kids," said Kline. He paid the barkeep and left.

"What have you there?" I nodded at the parcel.

"A gift."

"Oh?" I reached for it.

She slapped my hand away. "It's not for you."

"Oh."

"Hm," said Illyria. "I can't decide whether that or 'Ah!' is more adorable."

"I assure you, I make no effort to appear adorable."

"That's what makes it adorable."

The barkeep placed a beer in front of each of us. Illyria took the one in front of me. "Kline said you'd had two. I need to catch up."

"I had only this one."

"Then you need to catch up with us." She nodded at the second tankard. Amaranthine arched her slender head over its mouth and licked at the foam. After a pleased trill, she lapped up more.

"Be careful," I said. "At her body weight, it will not take much to make her tipsy."

"You're a fine one to talk after all these daytime beers." She took a long draught that left a foamy mustache on her lip.

"I told you, this is the only beer I have drunk today."

"And how about the food?"

"Who appointed you the minder of my diet?"

"It's a voluntary position."

"I never asked—"

She put a finger on my lips. "You didn't have to, darling."

"Darling?"

"Would you prefer I not call you darling?"

I had to consider the question. "No. It is just—"

"I've seen you at your worst, haven't I?"

That was surely true. "And you still—?"

She put her hand on mine. "And I still."

"Well . . . Then . . . I, ah, I suppose . . ."

"You'll, ah, escort me home to Westcrown and let me introduce you to my, ah, mother."

"Now wait just a moment."

"Yes?"

"I never said anything about meeting your mother."

"Not yet you haven't."

Radovan

Zora pushed the boat off the shore and into the water. I looked back at the lighthouse. She was going to have to pass through the light at least once before getting out of range. If she was quick, she could make a clean getaway. I'd managed to break her out of the local jail, but if they caught her escaping it would be the castle dungeons for sure.

"You going to be all right?" I said.

"I'm still a little pissed Janneke had me put in jail. You could have said something sooner."

"I didn't want to tip her off that I planned to bust you out. Element of surprise. You know."

"You didn't actually have to break in, you know. Your boss could have bribed a guard."

"He sort of did," I said. "I'll let him know later. Anyway, be thankful it was only the city jail, not the dungeon. They say nobody ever escapes the castle dungeon here."

"There are worse things than being surrounded by drunks, I suppose. The worst thing was the food. Porridge morning, noon, and night. Nothing in it, either. It made me miss the trail rations." She put a hand on my arm but took it away again before I could do anything about it.

"What I meant was, you going to be all right in Ustalav?"

"I have cousins in Caliphas. Maybe there's something for me there. If not, I'll fish up enough coin for passage back to Korvosa. It's all the same to me, as long as I don't have to cross the orc lands."

"Goddamned orcs."

"Goddamned orcs," she agreed. She grabbed my collar and surprised me by pulling herself in for a kiss. There wasn't much to it, but it was a little something nice.

"See you around, 'spawn," she said.

"See you around, sweetheart."

She waited for the lighthouse beam to pass again before pushing off. I watched her go, holding my breath until I was sure she was out of range of the light. She made it.

I slipped around the wall and sauntered back up the hill. Kiss from a Sczarni girl makes me saunter.

The Watchknights and gate guards gave me the hairy eyeball, but nobody bothered me. Now and then I even got a nod from the ones that saw me coming in. When the crusaders escorted us back to town, everybody turned out to see us paraded up to the castle. We got a fancy reception, and the kid they'd made Watcher-Lord even made a speech. He was such a pretty fellow that parents held their daughters by the elbow to keep them from swooning. I didn't like him.

As I got close to the inn, Janneke yelled, "Hey, Radovan!"

I crossed the street to join her. The boss had bought her a fancy new suit of armor in Chelish colors. I never liked wearing the house livery, but seeing her in it made me jealous.

"How'd the jailbreak go?" she said.

"I don't know what you're talking about." I looked around but didn't see any city guards lying in wait or anything. "How the hell did you know?"

"I know you. I saw the way you and Zora were talking. I had a feeling you'd find a way to help her out. I'm glad you did."

"Then why'd you put her in the damned jail in the first place?"

"Because this way nobody can say I let her escape. The Vigil jailers lost her, not me. My professional reputation remains intact."

"You and your reputation should get a room."

She laughed a little too hard for one of my lamer jokes. She said, "Did you talk to the boss?"

I didn't like the way she called him that. I was the only one who called him that. "No, I'm supposed to catch up with him at the inn."

"He already left for the playhouse."

"Damn, I was supposed to go with him."

"Illyria's in her room. She has your ticket."

"Why didn't he take her with him?"

She shrugged. "Say, I've got the rest of the night off. Why don't you skip the play? We could go to that bar you like, the Drakkar. Maybe there'll be a fight."

"Nah, I'm not in the mood."

"Or we could skip the tavern and, you know, find someplace away from the boss's rooms."

That wasn't what I expected to hear, but for once, I wasn't in the mood for that, either. "Why do you keep calling him 'the boss'? We're taking a ship back home. We don't need a driver."

"He said he'd tell you himself." She grimaced. "Maybe you ought to hear it from me."

"What?"

"Count Jeggare hired me as his bodyguard."

My hands and feet turned cold.

"Maybe he's decided he needs two," she said.

I looked her in the eye. "He never has more than one. There was one guy before me. There was one guy before that. There's always one guy."

"Maybe he's got a different job for you," she said. "A better one."

There wasn't any other job, not for me with my knife, my spurs, and my big smile. Janneke knew it as well as I did.

I was fired.

There'd been times I wasn't the best at my job. When I stabbed him in the heart, I guess I became the opposite of a bodyguard. I couldn't blame the guy for wanting somebody else to watch his back.

"Come with me." Janneke tugged on my arm. "I'm buying. We'll get drunk and dance and step on so many feet they'll have to fight us."

"Thanks," I said. "I'm gonna turn in."

"If you change your mind . . ."

"You'll be at the Drakkar."

I turned away without looking back. I walked back to the inn and went up to my room. As I put the key in the lock, Illyria opened her door across the hall. She peered out, the drake on her shoulder. "You're late."

"For what?"

"Varian wanted you to accompany him to the play. He had something to discuss."

I waved her off. "I already heard it."

"He wanted you to see this particular play."

"I'll catch a puppet show in the market tomorrow."

"Come here." She crooked a finger to beckon me into her room.

Plenty of noble ladies had crooked that finger at me before, and usually I went into their rooms with them. It'd serve him right to tumble with his girl after he fired me.

I couldn't do that, though. Even in the worst of times, he'd been a friend. In the best of times, he'd be the closest thing I ever had to a brother. I stayed in the hall. "I don't think I oughtta."

"Don't be obstinate. I have something here for you."

Sweet Desna, I thought. Thanks for smiling on me with all the women tonight, but could you spread it out a little?

When she saw I wasn't budging, Illyria went inside to fetch something. I'd got the wrong idea. She wasn't trying to seduce me. She came out and gave me a package wrapped in fancy cloth. "Open it."

It was a new leather jacket, supple, with thick supports on the shoulders. It even had slots for my spurs, just the way I liked. I felt along the sleeves and found hidden pockets in all the right places. There was only one problem.

"It's purple."

"It's amaranthine," she said. "More red than purple. I thought it the perfect match between your color and mine."

I liked the red better, but gift horses and mouths. "Thanks," I said. "It's real nice."

"Now put it on, and go to the playhouse. Here! Here's your ticket. Hurry! You can still get there before the main show."

I didn't want to, but she watched as I changed my shirt and jacket, and pretty much shoved me down the steps and out onto the street. As I walked away, the drake flew over and perched on my shoulder. "Hey! Go back there, you."

"It's all right," said Illyria. "I could use a nap, and that curious girl would love to see a play."

It felt weird walking with a little lizard on my shoulder. She nibbled at my ear, and people looked at me funny. Funnier than usual.

The Legendary Playhouse was the actual name of the place, not like its reputation or something. The boss had been having secret meetings with its owner all week, but he never told me why. He must have made up his mind to give me the boot before we even got to Vigil. No reason to keep me in on things anymore.

The hell with him! I didn't need to go to his stupid play. I could just go to the Drakkar and find Janneke. But no, I didn't like that idea, either. It wouldn't feel right fraternizing with my replacement. Besides, I was stuck with the drake.

I'd go to his play. Maybe the boss—the count, I guessed I should call him now—didn't understand what it was like for me to put him down. Even though I knew we had a way to bring him back, it was the hardest thing I ever did. It was about time I gave him a piece of my mind for once.

The doorman used a lot of words to ask for my ticket. I put it in his mouth to shut him up. When he objected to that, I pushed him down and walked right up to the balcony. I was working up a good head of steam, ready to vent it all out.

The boss had reserved one of those boxes like at the opera only not as fancy. That was good for Arni, since they let him in to sit beside the boss's chair. As soon as he saw me, he sat up. He still didn't trust me since the thing. I showed him my empty hands. He poked me in the belly with that big snout of his before settling down.

Amaranthine flew off my shoulder. For a second I thought Illyria was right, and she'd come to see the play. Instead, she fluttered down to settle on Arni's side. She folded her wings, paced a circle on his side a few times, and settled down, purring like a cat.

Arni looked embarrassed for a second, but then he put his head down and relaxed.

"You missed a charming singer from Molthune," said the boss. "You would not have enjoyed the juggling. Second-rate at best."

"I was just talking to Janneke and Lady Illyria."

"I see Illyria gave you your gift. Do you mind the color? I had a feeling it might be purple."

"Listen, boss—Count—I got something to say."

"Wait, here comes Sharina. Sit down. You will enjoy this."

A dark-skinned beauty took the stage. By the applause, I figured everybody already loved her. She welcomed everyone to the playhouse and said, "Tonight we welcome a pair of special guests, Count Varian Jeggare and his comrade Radovan."

"What does she mean, 'comrade'?"

"Hush," said the boss. He stood to wave to the audience. When I didn't get up, he chucked me in the arm until I stood beside him. When the applause settled, we sat back down.

Sharina began to sing. Her voice was the kind that made you think there was a little magic behind it. A fancy gent in the front row tugged his pointy beard and dipped his finger in time with her music, so I got the impression he was helping her along with a spell. Anyway, by herself or with help, she sang a real pretty song.

It took a couple of verses before I realized what she was singing about. It was all stuff the boss and I had done since leaving Egorian.

"What's this about the prince's wolves?" I whispered. "How does she know about the celestial pearl and the green dragon?"

"Because I told her, of course. Now hush and listen."

Sharina sang about the Worldwound Crusade and how we'd had a part in the victories against the demons. She didn't exactly spell out everything that had happened to us, but she used our names. She sang about us like we were a big deal.

She made us sound like heroes.

She finished the song to another round of applause. She bowed and raised an arm to point at us again. The boss made me stand. I tried to smile without making it too scary as I whispered, "What the hell is going on?"

He smiled and made his fancy little aristocrat's wave to the crowd. They applauded for a long time, some of them calling out, "For Iomedae!" or "Free Sarkoris!" I didn't like it, all those people looking at us that way. Even after that song, they didn't know us. They didn't know what we'd really been through. I wanted to take them to a beggar's alley and show them the stumps and scars of the war veterans. All their clapping was making me tense. After they let us sit down, a couple of clowns came out to do pranks on each other, and we were off the hook.

"What is going on is that I am preparing our way to return to Cheliax."

"I thought you weren't ready to face Queen Abrogail."

"Perhaps I was not ready in Korvosa," he said. "But I am ready now. Yet I refuse to return with my head hung low. In our exile, we have accomplished great things, many of them to the benefit of the empire. It is the custom in Egorian to welcome those who return from battle as heroes."

"Yeah, I remember those pictures from your library." The boss didn't keep a lot of paintings of himself on the walls, but there were dozens in files. A lot of them showed him in a navy uniform. He said they'd sold them in the markets when the fleet returned from Sargava.

"Perhaps you will be shocked to learn that the celebrations of returning soldiers are not entirely spontaneous."

"I get it. You rich guys hire bards and heralds to send word back home. Warm up the crowd, like these clowns."

"Exactly so," said the boss. "The point is that you and I shall return to Egorian not as forgiven exiles but as celebrated heroes. While she may rankle that our efforts have also benefited her rivals, Queen Abrogail cannot deny that we have also served Cheliax."

"All right," I said. "If you come back a hero, she can't be too mad at you. The people wouldn't like it."

"That is my design," he said. "To make it as difficult as possible for Her Infernal Majestrix to deny my modest petition."

"What are you gonna ask her for?"

He turned to me. "I will set aside a portion of my northern estates for the creation of a new barony."

"All right."

I waited for the other shoe, but he only smiled and looked back down at the clowns.

"I don't get it," I said.

"Do not make me regret telling everyone you are smarter than you look." He poured wine into a pair of goblets and handed one to me.

"Are you saying I'll be the bodyguard for this new baron while Janneke looks after you?"

"No, Radovan." He raised his cup. "I am saying I will make you the new baron."

He sipped his wine while that sank in. When it did, I drained the cup and put it out for a refill. "When Janneke said you'd hired her, I figured it was because you couldn't trust me to watch your back anymore."

"On the contrary, there is no one I trust more with my life or—as was necessary this one and only time and never again—with my death. But your days of watching my back are over. I want you at my side, not as an employee but as a peer. An equal."

He raised another toast, and we drank. I thought about how he'd looked in Old Korvosa the day after he visited his old fencing master. I worried about the state of our heads tomorrow morning.

By the time the curtains opened on a new scene—another one I'd experienced in real life—I'd drained my fifth cup. I leaned close to the boss. "There's just one problem making me a baron."

He looked surprised. "What is that?"

"If I'm supposed to be your equal, shouldn't I be a count?"

About the Author

A reformed teacher and recovering editor, Dave Gross has written novels for the Forgotten Realms, Iron Kingdoms, and Pathfinder Tales settings, along with many shorter works. Read more about them at **bydavegross.com**.

Acknowledgments

For notes on the outline, manuscript, or both, thanks to Jesse Benner, Chris A. Jackson, Howard Andrew Jones, Jen Laface, Russ Taylor, Josh Vogt, Eddy Webb, and my editor, James Sutter. For continued advice on the behaviors and misbehaviors of horses, thanks to Jaym Gates. Special thanks to Lone Wolf Development for the excellent Hero Labs program that saves me so much paperwork.

Glossary

All Pathfinder Tales novels are set in the rich and vibrant world of the Pathfinder campaign setting. Below are explanations of several key terms used in this book. For more information on the world of Golarion and the strange monsters, people, and deities that make it their home, see *The Inner Sea World Guide*, or dive into the game and begin playing your own adventures with the *Pathfinder Roleplaying Game Core Rulebook* or the *Pathfinder Roleplaying Game Beginner Box*, all available at **paizo.com**. Readers particularly interested in the runelords may want to check out *Pathfinder Adventure Path: Rise of the Runelords Anniversary Edition*, and more information on Korvosa and Kaer Maga can be found in the Pathfinder Campaign Setting books *Guide to Korvosa* and *City of Strangers*, respectively.

Abadar: God of cities, wealth, merchants, and law.
Abyss: Plane of evil and chaos ruled by demons, where many evil souls go after they die.
Acadamae: Notorious school of magic in Korvosa.
Alaznist: Runelord of Wrath; one of the rulers of ancient Thassilon.
Ankar-Te: One of the Ring districts in Kaer Maga.
Arcanamirium: Prestigious school of magic in the city of Absalom.
Aroden: The god of humanity, who died mysteriously a hundred years ago.

Asmodeus: Devil-god of tyranny, slavery, pride, and contracts; lord of Hell and current patron deity of Cheliax.

Astral Plane: Plane through which the River of Souls flows.

Avistan: The continent north of the Inner Sea, on which Varisia, Cheliax, and many other nations lie.

Axis, the Eternal City: An urban plane of absolute order.

Azlant: The first human empire, which sank beneath the waves long ago in the cataclysm following the fall of the Starstone.

Azlanti: Of or pertaining to Azlant; someone from Azlant.

Azlanti Stones: Powerful magical items that float around the user's head, granting access to specific magical effects.

Belimarius: Runelord of Envy; one of the rulers of ancient Thassilon.

Belkzen: Short for Hold of Belkzen.

Bis: One of the Ring districts in Kaer Maga.

Blackjack: A legendary criminal in Korvosa who protects the poor and punishes the abusive rich. Often viewed as a folk hero.

Bloatmage: A spellcaster who increases the production of blood in order to fuel spellcasting, becoming grotesquely engorged.

Boneyard: Pharasma's realm, where souls are judged after death.

Bottoms: One of the Ring districts in Kaer Maga.

Calistria: Goddess of trickery, lust, and revenge.

Cantrip: A minor spell or magical trick cast by an arcane spell-caster (such as a wizard or sorcerer).

Castle Overwatch: Famous castle in Vigil.

Cavalcade: One of the Ring districts in Kaer Maga.

Cayden Cailean: God of freedom, ale, wine, and bravery. Was once mortal, but ascended to godhood.

Cenotaph: Massive obelisk-tower in Belkzen, with historical ties to several powerful necromancers.

Chel: Derogatory term for a citizen of Cheliax.

Chelaxian: Someone from Cheliax.

Cheliax: A powerful devil-worshiping nation.

Chelish: Of or relating to the nation of Cheliax.

Cinderlands: Badlands in eastern Varisia.

Cleric: A religious spellcaster whose magical powers are granted by his or her god.

Decemvirate: Masked and anonymous ruling council of the Pathfinder Society.

Demons: Evil denizens of the plane of the afterlife called the Abyss, who seek only to maim, ruin, and feed on mortal souls.

Desna: Good-natured goddess of dreams, stars, travelers, and luck.

Devil: Fiendish occupants of Hell who seek to corrupt mortals in order to claim their souls.

Diabolist: A spellcaster who specializes in binding devils and making infernal pacts.

Dis: A layer of Hell.

Divination: School of magic allowing spellcasters to predict the future, find hidden things, and foil deceptive magic.

Downmarket: One of the Core districts in Kaer Maga.

Drake: Smaller and less intelligent cousins of true dragons. Sometimes short for "house drake," meaning one of the smallest and best-natured breeds of drakes.

Druid: Someone who reveres nature and draws magical power from the boundless energy of the natural world.

Duskwarden: Subterranean rangers devoted to protecting Kaer Maga from the creatures that dwell beneath it.

Dwarves: Short, stocky humanoids who excel at physical labor, mining, and craftsmanship.

Earthfall: Event thousands of years ago, in which a meteorite called the Starstone fell to earth sending up a dust cloud which blocked out the sun and ushered in an age of darkness.

Egorian: Capital of the devil-worshiping nation of Cheliax.

Elven: Of or pertaining to elves; the language of elves.

Elves: Long-lived, beautiful humanoids identifiable by their pointed ears, lithe bodies, and pupils so large their eyes appear to be one color.

Familiars: Small creatures that assist certain types of spellcasters, often developing greater powers and intelligence than normal members of their kind.

Fiends: Creatures native to the evil planes of the multiverse, such as demons, devils, and daemons, among others.

Gallowspire: The former stronghold of the Whispering Tyrant, now turned into his prison.

Garund: Continent south of the Inner Sea, renowned for its deserts and jungles.

Ghouls: Undead creatures that eat corpses.

Gnomes: Small humanoids with strange mind-sets, big eyes, and often wildly colored hair.

Goblin Dog: Disgusting doglike rodents used as mounts by goblins.

Goblins: Race of small and maniacal humanoids who live to burn, pillage, and sift through the refuse of more civilized races.

Golarion: The planet on which the Pathfinder campaign setting focuses.

Golem: A type of humanoid construct given life by a spellcaster.

Gorum: God of battle, strength, and weapons.

Gray Maidens: Former elite guard of the queen of Cheliax. Fell into disrepute after recent civil unrest. For more information, see the Curse of the Crimson Throne Adventure Path.

Half-Elves: The children of unions between elves and humans. Taller, longer-lived, and generally more graceful and attractive than the average human, yet not nearly so much so as their full elven kin.

Half-Orcs: Born from unions between humans and orcs, members of this race have green or gray skin, brutish appearances, and short tempers, and are mistrusted by many societies.

Halflings: Race of humanoids known for their tiny stature, deft hands, and mischievous personalities.

Hall of Whispers: College of necromancy at the Acadamae.

Harrow Deck: Deck of illustrated cards sometimes used to divine the future. Favored by Varisians.

Harrower: Fortune-teller who uses a harrow deck to tell the future—or pretends to.

Hell: Plane of evil and tyrannical order ruled by devils, where many evil souls go after they die.

Hellknights: Organization of hardened law enforcers whose tactics are often seen as harsh and intimidating, and who bind devils to their will. Based in Cheliax.

Hellspawn: Someone with fiendish blood, such as from ancestral interbreeding with devils or demons. Often recognizable by their horns, hooves, or other devilish features. Rarely popular in civilized society.

Hemotheurgy: The magical practices of bloatmages.

Highside Stacks: One of the Ring districts in Kaer Maga.

Hold of Belkzen: A region populated primarily by savage orc tribes. For more information, see *Pathfinder Campaign Setting: Belkzen, Hold of the Orc Hordes.*

Horser: Derogatory Korvosan term for Shoanti.

Hospice: One of the Core districts in Kaer Maga.

House Drakes: Slang term for the tiny, intelligent cousins of true dragons commonly found in the rooftops of Korvosa, where they feed on lesser vermin and combat the imps that infest the city.

House of Thrune: Current ruling house of Cheliax, which took power following Aroden's death by making compacts with the devils of Hell. Often called the Thrice-Damned House of Thrune.

Imp: Weakest of the true devils, resembling a tiny, winged humanoid with fiendish features. The most commonly found devil on the Material Plane. Often used as a familiar.

Inner Sea: The vast inland sea whose northern continent, Avistan, and southern continent, Garund, as well as the seas and nearby lands, are the primary focus of the Pathfinder campaign setting. Formed by the impact of the Starstone during Earthfall.

Iomedae: Goddess of valor, rulership, justice, and honor, who in life helped lead the Shining Crusade against the Whispering Tyrant before attaining godhood.

Janderhoff: Dwarven city in southeastern Varisia.

Kaer Maga: Legendary city of refugees, outcasts, and criminals situated inside the walls of a giant stone monument. For more information, see *Pathfinder Campaign Setting: City of Strangers*.

Karzoug: Runelord of Greed; one of the rulers of ancient Thassilon.

Keleshite: Of or relating to the Empire of Kelesh, far to the east of the Inner Sea region.

Kellids: Human ethnicity from the northern reaches of the Inner Sea region, traditionally characterized as violent and uncivilized by southerners.

King Xin: The founder of the Thassilonian Empire and creator of the runelords.

Korvosa: Largest city in Varisia and outpost of former Chelish loyalists, now self-governed. For more information, see *Pathfinder Campaign Setting: Guide to Korvosa*.

Krune: Runelord of Sloth; one of the rulers of ancient Thassilon.

Kyonin: Elven forest-kingdom largely forbidden to non-elven travelers.

Lady Luck: Desna.

Lady of Graves: Pharasma.

Lastwall: Nation dedicated to keeping the Whispering Tyrant locked away beneath Gallowspire, as well as keeping the orcs of Belkzen and the monsters of Ustalav in check.

Liches: Spellcasters who manage to extend their existence by magically transforming themselves into powerful undead creatures.

Lissala: Mostly forgotten goddess of rune magic; popular in ancient Thassilon.

Magnimar: Port city in southwestern Varisia, best known for its many monuments, including the enormous bridge called the Irespan.

Mendev: Cold, northern crusader nation that provides the primary force defending the rest of the Inner Sea region from the demonic infestation of the Worldwound.

Mendevian: Of or pertaining to Mendev.

Necromancy: School of magic devoted to manipulating the power of life and death, as well as the creation of undead creatures.

Orc: Bestial, warlike race of savage humanoids from deep underground who now roam the surface in barbaric bands. Possess green or gray skin and protruding tusks. Almost universally hated by more civilized races.

Oriat: One of the Ring districts in Kaer Maga.

Paladin: A good and lawful holy warrior. Ruled by a strict code of conduct and granted special magical powers by his or her deity.

Pathfinder: A member of the Pathfinder Society.

Pathfinder Chronicles: Books published by the Pathfinder Society detailing the most interesting and educational discoveries of their members.

Pathfinder Lodge: Meeting house where members of the Pathfinder Society can buy provisions and swap stories.

Pathfinder Society: Organization of traveling scholars and adventurers who seek to document the world's wonders. Based out of Absalom and run by a mysterious and masked group called the Decemvirate.

Pharasma: The goddess of birth, death, and prophecy, who judges mortal souls after their deaths and sends them on to the appropriate afterlife; also known as the Lady of Graves.

Pharasma's Spire: The plane on which Pharasma's realm is found.

Pharasmin: Of or relating to Pharasma or her worshipers.

Phylactery: Magical item that holds a lich's life force, keeping him or her from being killed until the object is destroyed.

Plane: Realm of existence, such as Heaven, Hell, or the mortal world of the Material Plane.

Quain: Nation far to the east of the Inner Sea region, in Tian Xia.

Realm of the Mammoth Lords: Cold and relatively uncivilized land at the far northern end of the Inner Sea region, inhabited by loosely confederated tribes of Kellids.

Riddleport: Notorious Varisian port city full of mercenaries, thieves, bandits, and pirates.

Riffle Scroll: Magical scroll shaped like a flipbook, which is activated by flipping the pages rapidly.

River of Souls: Procession of recently deceased souls traveling from the mortal world to Pharasma's Boneyard for judgment.

Runelord: One of seven evil wizards who ruled ancient Thassilon.

Sable Company: Elite Korvosan military unit.

Sargava: Former Chelish colony, now independent.

Sarkoris: Northern nation destroyed by the Worldwound.

Scroll: Magical document in which a spell is recorded so that it can be released when read, even if the reader doesn't know how to cast that spell. Destroyed as part of the casting process.

Sczarni: A subgroup of the Varisian ethnicity known for being wandering thieves and criminals, and contributing greatly to prejudice against Varisians as a whole by other cultures. Often pass themselves off as non-Sczarni Varisians while attempting to avoid detection.

Shadow: Insubstantial undead spirits that take the form of shadowy silhouettes, and can't be injured by normal weapons

Shelyn: The goddess of beauty, art, love, and music.

Shingles: Slang term for the network of rooftop pathways and dwellings in the Korvosa's older and poorer section.

Shining Crusade: The organization responsible for defeating the Whispering Tyrant and his minions a thousand years ago.

Shoanti: Indigenous peoples of the Storval Plateau in Varisia.

Sihedron: Seven-pointed star representing the seven runelords of ancient Thassilon as well as the seven sins or schools of magic.

Skentok: Derogatory Shoanti term for someone who is damaged but still useful.

Skymetal: Metal that falls to Golarion as meteorites and has exceptional (and sometimes magical) qualities.

Sleeper: Monument in central Belkzen in which an enormous stone dragon statue coils around a crag.

Slip: Racial slur referring to a halfling, used primarily in Cheliax.

Sorcerer: Someone who casts spells through natural ability rather than faith or study.

Sorshen: Runelord of Lust; one of the rulers of ancient Thassilon.

Spellbook: Tome in which a wizard transcribes the arcane formulae necessary to cast spells. Without a spellbook, wizards can cast only those few spells held in their mind at any given time.

Starstone: Stone that fell from the sky ten thousand years ago, creating an enormous dust cloud that blotted out the sun and began the Age of Darkness, wiping out most preexisting civilizations. Eventually raised up from the ocean floor by Aroden and housed in the Cathedral of the Starstone in Absalom, where those who can pass its mysterious and deadly tests can ascend to godhood.

Storval Plateau: High, rocky badlands making up the eastern portion of Varisia.

Sun Orchid Elixir: Extremely rare potion produced only in Thuvia, capable of temporarily reversing the effects of aging and prolonging one's life.

Taldane: The common trade language of the Inner Sea region.

Taldor: A formerly glorious nation that has lost many of its holdings in recent years to neglect and decadence.

Tar-Baphon: The Whispering Tyrant's mortal name.

Tarheel Promenade: One of the Ring districts in Kaer Maga.

Ten: Slang term for the Decemvirate.

Tender of Dreams: Desna.

Thassilon: Ancient empire located in northwestern Avistan and ruled by seven runelords. Destroyed by the fall of the Starstone.

Thassilonian: Of or relating to ancient Thassilon, as well as the name of its language.

Thrune: Relating to the House of Thrune, Cheliax's ruling family.

Thuvia: Desert nation on the Inner Sea, famous for the production of a magical elixir which grants immortality.

Tian: Someone or something from Tian Xia.

Tian Xia: Continent on the opposite side of the world from the Inner Sea region.

Tines: Raised fork on which Chelish criminals are sometimes impaled. Also the name of a rude hand gesture from Cheliax.

Torag: Stoic and serious dwarven god of the forge, protection, and strategy. Viewed by dwarves as the Father of Creation.

Towers (game): Gambling game using a harrow deck.

Transmutation: School of magic devoted to changing the properties of a creature, condition, or thing, such as changing its shape or transforming one thing into another.

Tshamek: Derogatory Shoanti term for outsiders.

Ulfen: A race of warlike humans from the cold nations of the north, particularly the Lands of the Linnorm Kings.

Ulfen Guard: Famous all-Ulfen military unit maintained as bodyguards by Taldor's grand prince.

Undead: Unnatural creatures made or spawned magically via necromancy, often by animating the corpses of living things.

Undeath: Magical life granted through necromancy, breaking the usual cycle of souls.

Undercity: The dangerous and unexplored passages and caverns beneath Kaer Maga.

Ustalav: Fog-shrouded gothic nation of the Inner Sea region.

Ustalavic: Of or relating to the nation of Ustalav.

Varisia: Frontier region at the northwestern edge of the Inner Sea lands, of which Korvosa is the largest city.

Varisian: Of or relating to the region of the frontier region of Varisia, or a resident of that region. Ethnic Varisians tend to organize in clans and wander in caravans, acting as tinkers, musicians, dancers, and performers. Often have strong family ties and are maligned as thieves and swindlers.

Venture-Captain: A rank in the Pathfinder Society above that of a standard field agent but below the Decemvirate. In charge of directing and assisting lesser agents.

Vigil: Capital city of Lastwall.

Vudra: Exotic continent far to the east of the Inner Sea.

Vudrani: Someone or something from the exotic continent of Vudra, far to the east of the Inner Sea.

Wargs: Monstrous and oversized intelligent wolves.

Warren: One of the Ring districts in Kaer Maga.

Watchknights: Knights devoted to keeping order in Vigil.

Westcrown: Former capital of Cheliax.

Whispering Tyrant: Incredibly powerful lich who terrorized Avistan for hundreds of years before being sealed beneath his fortress of Gallowspire a millennium ago.

Widdershins: One of the Core districts in Kaer Maga.

Wizard: Someone who casts spells through careful study and rigorous scientific methods rather than faith or innate talent, recording the necessary incantations in a spellbook.

Worldwound: Expanding region overrun by demons a century ago. Held at bay by the efforts of the Mendevian crusaders.

Wyvern: A brutish draconic creature not as intelligent or cunning as a true dragon.

Xanderghul: Runelord of Pride; one of the rulers of ancient Thassilon.

Zutha: Runelord of Gluttony; one of the rulers of ancient Thassilon and an infamously powerful necromancer.

For half-elven Pathfinder Varian Jeggare and his devil-blooded bodyguard Radovan, things are rarely as they seem. Yet not even the notorious crime-solving duo is prepared for what they find when a search for a missing Pathfinder takes them into the gothic and mist-shrouded mountains of Ustalav. Beset on all sides by noble intrigue, mysterious locals, and the deadly creatures of the night, Varian and Radovan must use both sword and spell to track the strange rumors to their source and uncover a secret of unimaginable proportions, aided in their quest by a pack of sinister werewolves and a mysterious mute priestess. But it'll take more than merely solving the mystery to finish this job. For shadowy figures have taken note of the pair's investigations, and the forces of darkness are set on making sure neither man gets out of Ustalav alive . . .

From best-selling author Dave Gross comes the first novel featuring Varian and Radovan's adventures, set in the award-winning world of the Pathfinder Roleplaying Game.

Prince of Wolves print edition: $9.99
ISBN: 978-1-60125-287-6

Prince of Wolves ebook edition:
ISBN: 978-1-60125-331-6

PRINCE OF WOLVES

DAVE GROSS

In the deep forests of Kyonin, elves live among their own kind,
far from the prying eyes of other races. Few of impure blood
are allowed beyond the nation's borders, and thus it's a great
honor for the half-elven Count Varian Jeggare and his hellspawn
bodyguard Radovan to be allowed inside. Yet all is not well in the
elven kingdom: demons stir in its depths, and an intricate web of
politics seems destined to catch the two travelers in its snares. In
the course of tracking down a missing druid, Varian and a team
of eccentric elven adventurers will be forced to delve into dark
secrets lost for generations—including the mystery of Varian's
own past.

From Dave Gross, author of *Prince of Wolves* and *Master of
Devils*, comes a fantastical new adventure set in the award-winning world of the Pathfinder Roleplaying Game.

Queen of Thorns print edition: $9.99
ISBN: 978-1-60125-463-4

Queen of Thorns ebook edition:
ISBN: 978-1-60125-464-1

PATHFINDER

TALES

QUEEN of THORNS

DAVE GROSS

After a century of imprisonment, demons have broken free of the wardstones surrounding the Worldwound. As fiends flood south into civilized lands, Count Varian Jeggare and his hellspawn bodyguard Radovan must search through the ruins of a fallen nation for the blasphemous text that opened the gate to the Abyss in the first place—and that might hold the key to closing it. In order to succeed, however, the heroes will need to join forces with pious crusaders, barbaric local warriors, and even one of the legendary god callers. It's a race against time as the companions fight their way across a broken land, facing off against fiends, monsters, and a vampire intent on becoming the god of blood—but will unearthing the dangerous book save the world, or destroy it completely?

From best-selling author Dave Gross comes a new adventure set against the backdrop of the Wrath of the Righteous Adventure Path in the award-winning world of the Pathfinder Roleplaying Game.

King of Chaos print edition: $9.99
ISBN: 978-1-60125-558-7

King of Chaos ebook edition:
ISBN: 978-1-60125-559-4

PATHFINDER TALES

KING OF CHAOS

DAVE GROSS

PATHFINDER®
CAMPAIGN SETTING™

THE INNER SEA WORLD GUIDE

You've delved into the Pathfinder campaign setting with Pathfinder Tales novels—now take your adventures even further! *The Inner Sea World Guide* is a full-color, 320-page hardcover guide featuring everything you need to know about the exciting world of Pathfinder: overviews of every major nation, religion, race, and adventure location around the Inner Sea, plus a giant poster map! Read it as a travelogue, or use it to flesh out your roleplaying game—it's your world now!

EXPLORE YOUR WORLD!

paizo.com